These Regency
lovers never expe...
especially not like...

Candlelit
Christmas
Kisses

ANNE HERRIES

ELIZABETH BEACON

2 BRAND-NEW
Regency Christmas Romances

Candlelit
Christmas
Kisses

ANNE HERRIES

ELIZABETH BEACON

First published in Great Britain 2012
Mills & Boon, an imprint of Harlequin (UK) Limited,
Eton House, 18-24 Paradise Road, Richmond, Surrey TW9 1SR

CANDLELIT CHRISTMAS KISSES
© Harlequin Enterprises II B.V./S.à.r.l. 2012

Captain Moorcroft's Christmas Bride © Anne Herries 2012
Governess Under the Mistletoe © Elizabeth Beacon 2012

ISBN: 978 0 263 90237 2

25-1112

Captain Moorcroft's Christmas Bride

ANNE HERRIES

Anne Herries, winner of the Romantic Novelists' Association ROMANCE PRIZE 2004, lives in Cambridgeshire. She is fond of watching wildlife and spoils the birds and squirrels that are frequent visitors to her garden. Anne loves to write about the beauty of nature and sometimes puts a little into her books, although they are mostly about love and romance. She writes for her own enjoyment and to give pleasure to her readers.

Previous novels by the same author:

MARRYING CAPTAIN JACK
THE UNKNOWN HEIR
THE HOMELESS HEIRESS
THE RAKE'S REBELLIOUS LADY
A COUNTRY MISS IN HANOVER SQUARE*
AN INNOCENT DEBUTANTE IN HANOVER SQUARE*
THE MISTRESS OF HANOVER SQUARE*
FORBIDDEN LADY~
THE LORD'S FORCED BRIDE~
THE PIRATE'S WILLING CAPTIVE~
HER DARK AND DANGEROUS LORD~

*A Season in Town trilogy
~ The Melford Dynasty

and in the Regency series The Steepwood Scandal:

LORD RAVENSDEN'S MARRIAGE
COUNTERFEIT EARL

and in The Hellfire Mysteries:

AN IMPROPER COMPANION
A WEALTHY WIDOW
A WORTHY GENTLEMAN

Dear Reader,

This year I've had the pleasure of writing a Christmas story for you. I very much enjoyed doing this and hope you will enjoy the story of Selina and her sisters, who have been forced to leave their home because of the inheritance laws that existed at the period. Selina has a secret memory she keeps enshrined in her heart; the memory of a dashing young captain who kissed her and then went off to war. When the new earl comes to claim his estate, where Selina has become a temporary tenant, she and he are in for a shock.

Will the Captain Moorcroft of her dreams and the new earl prove to be the same man—or will she discover that her idol was but a dream? Christmas is the time when wishes ought to come true, so perhaps Selina's dream will be granted.

Happy Christmas to all my readers and thank you for continuing to buy my books. I hope you have as much fun with this one as I did writing it.

Anne Herries

PROLOGUE

Summer 1810, Bath

SELINA Searles, aged sixteen, innocent and on the verge of womanhood, looked around the crowded Assembly Rooms and felt a tingle of excitement. She was a pretty girl, full of life, happy and thrilled to be at her first ball. Her mama had told her that she was too young to be brought out in London society until the following year. However, since they were in Bath, because dear Mama had been laid low with a chill and Selina had volunteered to care for her, she was being allowed a special treat.

'I shall expect you to behave properly, dearest,' her mama had told her. 'This is your first dance, and you must remember the rules of polite society. If a gentleman asks you to dance, you may do so, but before you waltz I must approve your choice. On no account are you to flirt, nor will you leave the ballroom in the company of a gentleman, and you must never, never allow a man to kiss you unless you have accepted a proposal of marriage. You will do no such thing, for you are too young and it is unlikely to happen, but remember the rules, my love, and you will not go far wrong.'

'Yes, Mama,' Selina had said and smiled. 'You've told me all this before, and I should not dream of disobeying you.'

Her feet tapping to the music, Selina waited patiently to be asked to dance. She was an exceptionally lovely girl, some might say beautiful, with melting brown eyes and dark hair that curled about her face before being swept up into ringlets that fell on one shoulder, but it was her vivacity, her joy in life that shone out of her, lighting up the room. A girl like that could not go unnoticed for long, and indeed it was not much more than five minutes before she was asked to dance by a gentleman who presented himself as Lord March.

He was a very correct gentleman and held her at precisely the right distance, so that when he asked for a second dance, which was a waltz, her mama immediately granted her permission. Selina hardly had time to catch her breath at the end of the dance before she was besieged with gentlemen asking for dances and every space on her card was filled. Her mama looked on indulgently, as if she had expected this to happen, nodding her permission each time Selina looked at her. Every waltz had been taken, and Selina was soon lost in the excitement and delight of being a raging success.

It was not until about halfway through the evening that she noticed a gentleman dressed in a magnificent scarlet-and-black uniform. Suddenly it was as if a hundred candles had been lit, for his presence seemed to light up the room. Selina noticed that he was immediately the centre of a large group of young men and women, and she could hear their laughter from across the room. The newcomer was the most handsome man in the room—and popular, for it seemed everyone wanted to be near him. After a moment he seemed to become aware of her interest, and their eyes met briefly. She felt a tingle of excitement run through her and could not turn her eyes away, though she knew she ought.

It was as though an invisible bond stretched between them, and her pulses raced as he excused himself to his friends and began to walk towards her. Selina's mouth was suddenly dry, her heart beating like a drum in her breast. He was coming. He would ask her to dance, but her card was full. What should she do? Her breath caught in her throat as she gazed up into his eyes and felt as though she were drowning.

'Captain Moorcroft at your service, Princess,' he said, his dark eyes bold and filled with confidence as he swept her a bow and seized her card, striking out Lord March's name, which appeared next on her list. 'March will not deny me, or I'll challenge him to a duel.'

'I am not a princess—and you ought not to have done that,' Selina reproved, but she was laughing because her heart had leaped at the sight of him, and the touch of his hand made her breathless with a strange excitement she had never known. All at once she felt reckless and wildly happy. 'My name is Selina Searles.'

'Robert Moorcroft, sweet Miss Selina,' he said, and

the seductive note in his voice wiped all caution from her mind. 'You are mine, and if any here dispute it, they may call me out for it. My angel…'

With that he took her hand and swept her out on to the dance floor, whirling her round and round until she was breathless and laughing, her mama's warnings all but forgotten. For the whole of the dance, her feet scarcely seemed to touch the floor, and she wished it could go on for ever, but then the music was ending, and as he led her to the side of the floor, her next partner was there to claim her.

Selina felt a sharp stab of disappointment. Robert Moorcroft stood watching her for a moment and then turned away. She wished with all her heart that she had an empty card and might dance with him all night, but convention would have allowed him no more than three dances at most.

As her dance ended and her partner thanked her, Selina realised that she'd hardly noticed him, lost in a dream. Her eyes had been searching the room for the young captain. Turning away, with the intent of seeking her mama while she waited for her next partner, she felt a touch on her arm and found herself gazing up at Robert Moorcroft once more.

'I have settled it with Hendricks that this dance is mine,' he said, and drew her into his arms as the next waltz began.

Selina was too shaken by her storm of feelings to deny him. Waltzing in his arms was a dream, like floating in a blue sky on a summer's day. She felt herself drifting away on a cloud of pleasure as he whirled her round and round, and she wanted the dance to last for the rest of her life. To feel like this was something that even in her most romantic dreams she had not imagined. She longed for the moment to go on and on endlessly.

When their dance ended, he kept hold of her hand and strode towards the open doors that led onto the terraces, taking her with him.

'I have made you hot,' he told her, with a smile that sent her heart fluttering. 'We shall take a little stroll in the garden until you feel able to dance again.'

Selina knew that she ought to refuse, but she could not find the words. Besides, it was what she wanted above anything. She had never felt like this in her life, and something told her that she must seize the moment or it might not come again.

Outside, he led her away from the lights of the ballroom to a secluded spot by some rose bushes, the deep, intoxicating smell of which she knew would remain with her for the rest of her life.

'You are so beautiful that you make me want to weep,' he whispered softly against her ear. 'I have never seen a woman as lovely as you, my angel—my Selina. I adore you. You have captured my heart.'

'Oh...' Selina was lost. This was flirting, and her mama had told her she must not flirt with gentlemen—but he was the one flirting. She had done nothing but give herself up to the delight of dancing with him. 'You...you should not...'

Before she could say more, he lowered his head, one

hand about her waist as he pulled her in close. She could feel the pressure of his hand in the small of her back and the hardness of his strong body. His mouth was cool and soft on hers, the pressure light at first but increasing as her own lips opened in response. His tongue entered, touching hers lightly in a way that sent little spirals of pleasure skittering down her spine.

'What should I not?' he whispered as his kiss ended, and he pressed his lips against her throat.

Selina trembled. Such sensation coursed through her entire being. The response of her body to his was sweeping away all thought, all sense of what was right or wrong. How could this feeling be wrong when it was so glorious?

It was the best thing that had ever happened to her—and the worst. For she sensed that if she were not careful. her reputation might be lost, and yet she was caught by the moonlight and the moment, incapable of repulsing him.

'Should I not kiss you, or…?' His hand was at her breast, fondling her through the thin silk, and then he had pushed down the neck of her gown. His lips closed over her breast, sucking delicately at her nipple.

It was so shocking that she was stunned, and yet a ripple of desire shot through her and she moaned. For a moment she was delirious with pleasure, but then she remembered her mother's warning and broke away, tugging her gown into place. What had she done? To allow such a liberty was to forget that she was a lady—but in his arms she could happily forget the world.

'You forget yourself, sir. I am but sixteen and…and we should not be here.' As she turned away, he caught her wrist, turning her back to face him. 'Please, let me go,' she begged. 'You will ruin me, sir.' All of a sudden she was shivering and afraid of what she'd done.

'I shall return for you,' he vowed, and for a moment his eyes burned with a silver light in the darkness. 'Never forget me, Selina Searles. I have put my brand on you. I adore you and one day I shall claim you. You will be mine. Wait for me…'

'You must not say such things, for you do not mean them!' she cried and, tearing herself from his grasp, fled back to the lights of the ballroom, not stopping until she was in the ladies' restroom, where she splashed her cheeks with cold water and tidied her gown.

He had not meant the things he'd said to her. Of course he had not—because she'd tasted the brandy on his tongue. He was undoubtedly drunk, and in the morning he would have forgotten the things he'd said and done—but she would not forget.

Selina knew that in one respect he had spoken the truth. Captain Robert Moorcroft had put his mark on her, and she would never, ever be the same again.

CHAPTER ONE

Late autumn 1817, Bedfordshire

'WHAT are we going to do, Selina?' Amy Searles looked at her elder sister fearfully. 'How shall we manage now that Mama…' She choked back her tears as her sister shook her head. 'It was hard enough when we had Mama's jointure, but now…'

'Please do not remind me,' Selina begged. Her face was tight with grief. Their mama's rapid decline and sudden death had happened no more than six months after their father had shot himself, having gambled away his fortune at the tables. 'Something needed to be done even if Mama…' She swallowed hard because the tears were so very close.

Only two days had passed since they'd buried their beloved mother, and the girls had been left to care for their younger sister, Millicent, who was just twelve years of age. 'We have her jewels. We could sell those, I suppose, or some of the silver—but that will not solve the problem of where we shall live. Cousin Joshua owns the house now. It only remained Mama's home while she lived.'

'We both have a little money that Grandmama Robinson left us,' Amy said. 'Is it enough to purchase a house, do you think?'

'One hundred pounds might buy us a small cottage, but if we spent that we should have nothing left to live on.' Selina bit her lower lip. 'We might be able to rent a cottage somewhere.'

'What about your season? You were to find a rich husband so that we did not need to worry about money.'

'Had Mama not been taken ill, we should have all gone to London next spring, and you would have been sure to find a husband, but...' Selina sighed. 'You know what happened. There is no point in weeping over it, Amy. All thought of a season must be forgotten now. We shall just have to look for somewhere else to live. One of us must care for Millie, and the other...should look for work as a companion or something of the sort.'

'Oh, Selina...no,' Amy protested. 'Look at us. Who would employ either of us as a governess?'

'I said as a companion. There must be plenty of ladies who need a pretty, intelligent girl as a companion—I would employ you had I the money, dearest.'

'You mean some crotchety old dear who wants me to run after her all day?' Amy looked mutinous. 'I couldn't bear it, Selina. No, you must marry a rich man and rescue our fortunes. You are so beautiful it must be easy for you.'

'Do you feel it fair to marry someone entirely for the

sake of money? Should one not at least feel some sort of affection for one's husband?'

'Well, yes, if one could choose,' Amy said practically. 'But what else can we do—short of selling ourselves off as slaves?' She hesitated, then, 'You wouldn't consider marrying Cousin Joshua, I suppose?'

Selina shuddered. 'I would rather hire myself out as a scullery maid,' she said. 'I would marry if I could find someone I could live with—but Cousin Joshua? Would *you* wish to live with him, Amy?'

'No!' Amy made a wry face. 'He might let us stop here for a while if you were nice to him, Selina. He likes you.'

'He is angry with me at the moment because I refused his offer of marriage. It is unfortunate that he is our only relative on Father's side. The elder of Papa's brothers, Sebastian, and his son, Simon, were drowned ten years ago. I believe they might have allowed us to stay here, for Uncle Sebastian was always kind to us, but Cousin Joshua is different. Mama had only her aunt Mabel, who died two years ago, as you know. She left Mama what she had but it was very little—just that pearl necklace and a thousand pounds, which is what has paid for our clothes this past two years—yours, mine, Mama's, Millie's and the servants'. I daresay there isn't above two hundred pounds left in Mama's account.'

'Well, we shall soon know.' Amy glanced at the beautiful mantel clock. 'Mr Breck will be here in an hour, and he will tell us how much we have to live on now that Mama…'

Once again Amy almost dissolved into tears.

'If we have to sell some things, that mantel clock should be worth several guineas—enough to keep us for six months, I daresay,' Selina said thoughtfully.

'You cannot sell that, Selina.' Amy was shocked. 'It was one of Mama's favourite things. Her father gave it to her for her last birthday before he died.'

'I know that.' Selina sighed. 'I want to keep all Mama's things when we move, but if we do not have enough to live on…' Her words died away as she heard the sounds of a carriage drawing up outside.

Amy went to the window of their small parlour, then turned to look at her. 'It's Cousin Joshua.'

'Oh, no, why did he have to come today? Surely he cannot be so impatient to move in? He has a perfectly good house of his own.'

'Which is why he may sell this one.'

'Yes, I know. He did speak of it.' Selina drew her shoulders back as the parlour door opened and the housekeeper announced the arrival of their visitor. 'Good morning, cousin. How pleasant to see you. Will you not come to the fire? I am sure it is cold out.'

'Thank you, Selina.' Her cousin nodded and moved to the fire to warm his hands. 'I knew you were expecting your father's lawyer this morning. I have some news for you myself, but I shall wait until the lawyer has had his say.' He paused to clear his throat. 'You must not expect good news, cousin. Sir Richard had little left but this house and a few fields, which I understand bear a mortgage. Since the house and what remains of the estate are entailed, I fear they come to me, which means I must provide for you in some way.'

'You are very kind, cousin,' Selina said stiffly. 'But Mama had a little money of her own, and I hope it will not be necessary for us to become a burden on your purse.'

He had the grace to look awkward as he said, 'I know you girls are of an independent mind, but I'm not short of a bob or two—neither am I insensitive to your grief. I should certainly not ask you to move out of this house for at least a month—and even then you know you may all have a home with me.'

'But that means we must leave before Christmas!' Selina exclaimed, and then turned away before she could lose her temper.

'You are so very kind,' Amy said, because Selina was still turned away, her hands clenching at her sides as she struggled against her emotions. 'But truly Selina speaks for us all—we shall be independent if we can.'

'If you can, of course,' he agreed, much mollified by Amy's sweet smile. 'I am not made of stone, Miss Amy. I could not see my cousins starve or be deprived of all their precious things. I know some of the furnishings belonged to your mama, and I've already told him he will have to furnish part of the house himself.'

Selina turned, her eyes wide and startled. 'Whom do you mean? Have you already let the house to a tenant? It is only a few weeks until Christmas. I did not think you would expect us to move so soon, cousin.'

'Well, I shouldn't, of course—except that I think you would all do better staying with me for the festivities.

This house is expensive to keep up, you know. Your mama could scarcely afford it these past few months, and some of the necessary repairs have not been done.' There was a hint of reproach in his voice. 'I did offer to do them for her, but she said she would not trouble me and intended to see to them herself—though we both knew she could not afford the iniquitous prices these builders charge. Ladies will have their way, but now that the house has passed to me, I shall, of course, be sending someone to do the repairs quite soon.'

Selina looked at her sister. Neither said anything, but they both knew that this was their cousin's way of making it impossible for them to stay in the house, despite his earlier claim that they could remain for at least another month. Selina was about to reply when the housekeeper announced the arrival of their family lawyer. He was early, but being a punctilious man had no doubt set out early lest the roads were bad.

'Well, at least we shall know the truth now,' Selina said, but her heart sank as the lawyer was announced, and she saw from his face that the news was far from good.

'Good morning, Mr Breck,' she said, and went forward to meet him with outstretched hands. No matter how heavy her heart, she would not forget her good manners. 'It was so very kind of you to come out on such a cold day, sir.'

'It is cold for the time of year, though we have less than two months until Christmas, Miss Searles. I must tell you at once that I have been looking into your dear mama's affairs, and the outlook is not good—but I think I may have solved one of your problems at least temporarily.'

'Oh…I think you must tell us what you mean,' Selina said. 'Please, come and sit by the fire, sir. You have been a good friend to Mama, and we shall not stand on ceremony, even if you are the bearer of bad news.'

Mr Breck flicked out his coattails and sat on a substantial chair close to the hearth. He had chosen their late father's chair, and the sight of a man sitting there brought a lump to the girls' throats, but neither of them said a word. They were breathless, their eyes betraying their fear as they waited.

'As you know, your father had secured the house to your mother for her lifetime, but he was never able to break the entail, which would have cost him too much of his slender capital. That part of the estate which was entailed bears a mortgage, and all the land your father owned personally was sold before his death to pay his debts.'

'Yes, sir. You told Mama when Papa died,' Selina said. 'But Mama's jointure was safe, and we think she had a little money of her own—is that not so?'

'Yes, she did have a little of her own, and she was left a thousand pounds by her aunt, but most of that has been spent. The dear lady honoured me with the care of her slender funds, as you know, and I did manage to invest a small amount, which will bring you in two hundred pounds a year, but besides that you have only seventy-five pounds in capital…'

Selina gave a little gasp. 'So little…' She swallowed

hard as she saw her sister's stricken expression. 'We had hoped it might be two hundred pounds or so.'

'Your dear mama spent quite a bit on clothes and the things she wanted to give you and your sisters. Of course all her furniture and jewels belong to you, and I daresay they may fetch a thousand or two—if you care to sell them.'

'We may have to if we are to find ourselves a new home,' Selina said, and glanced at her cousin, who had the grace to look ashamed. 'We are determined to be independent of Cousin Joshua, even though he has kindly offered us a home in his house.'

'Well, I thought you would say that, Miss Searles,' the lawyer said, and looked pleased with himself. 'Which is why I have taken the liberty of arranging something—if you could bring yourself to accept?'

'Anything,' Selina said fervently, and then realised how rude she sounded. 'Within reason, of course. I feel we must not be a burden on others.'

'I've told you—' her cousin began but swiftly closed his mouth as the lawyer began to speak again.

'Well, this might suit you. I have an elderly client who owns an estate. He recently became ill and has gone abroad for his health. He is hoping that his nephew will take over the estate, for it is entailed on him. However, the nephew currently lives in Italy, and though I have told him his duty is to return to the estate, he has informed me that he is content for now to leave it entirely in my hands. I am to manage the estate—and to install a housekeeper in the house, with a few servants to keep it in reasonable condition. However, the nephew does not wish it to be let to a tenant because he may one day choose to live there—though he thinks not for some years yet.'

'Are you offering me the position of housekeeper?' Selina stared at him in surprise.

'Well, yes, in a way,' her lawyer said. 'What I thought was that you and your family could live there—and take with you the servants you intend to keep. I shall pay their wages and make you some small remuneration—say three hundred pounds a year.'

'Nonsense!' Cousin Joshua was outraged. 'How dare you suggest that my cousin become a paid servant? She and her sisters will live with me, as I told them right from the start.'

'No, cousin, we shall not.' Selina's voice was cold and proud, and all eyes turned on her. 'I am three and twenty, and you are not my guardian. Mama left the care of my sisters to me, because she trusted me to care for them—and I shall.'

'You will not consider becoming a housekeeper?' He looked shocked.

'I think it may be the perfect solution,' Selina said, and turned with considerable relief to the lawyer. 'However, I could not accept the wage, Mr Breck. What I can accept is that you allow us to live there as your client's tenants in return for keeping the house in good order. I shall undertake to help you with the estate, for I was used to helping Papa, as you know. I am well able to do bookwork, and to supervise the maintenance of property—and if you have good bailiffs and farm managers, I can liase with them and report to you.'

'Well…it is not exactly what I intended…but I see no reason why it should not work. However, I must insist that you allow me to pay the wages of the resident servants at least. It is a big house, and you could not afford to keep enough staff unless I contribute—as my client's agent, of course.'

'How many servants are there?'

'Just two outside men and an elderly butler, Trent, who was too old to travel with my client. He wishes to remain at the house until he can no longer work. You will need at least two maids and a cook if you are to live there comfortably.'

'Yes, I think we shall,' Selina said. 'Mama's maid, Jane, Betty, our maid of all work, and Cook all wish to come with us and have declared they will work for nothing but their board. Also Papa's groom, Jeremiah. He says nothing shall make him leave us but death, and I cannot kill him, so I must keep him. I shall, of course, pay them something—but you must leave that to me, Mr Breck. I shall contrive somehow—even if I have to sell Aunt Mabel's pearls. Mama gave them to me, and if need be I shall sell them.'

'Oh, Selina, you love those pearls,' Amy protested tearfully.

'Yes, I do, but this is a solution for us, dearest. Do you not see how perfect it is? We shall live quietly but we shall still be ladies, even if we have very little money. We may entertain occasionally—and we shall meet people living nearby. It is possible that one of us might—'

'You cannot possibly live on two hundred pounds a year,' Cousin Joshua cut in rudely, looking annoyed. 'If you refuse my offer of a home, I shall wash my hands of you. You will get nothing from me—not a penny.'

'Sir, that is not necessary,' Mr Breck remonstrated. 'I am more than willing to pay Miss Searles a retainer for looking after the house if she wishes.'

'I shall remember that, and if I become desperate, I may reconsider,' Selina said with a smile. 'You have been very kind, Cousin Joshua—however, I must decline your offer of a home. We shall be packed and ready to leave within three days. I should appreciate it if you will not send your builders in until after we have left,' she added dryly.

'You will regret this,' he said, giving her a furious look. 'Just remember that this arrangement is only temporary. The nephew could return at any time. Just don't come crying to me when you're homeless and destitute.'

'Now, that is not called for, sir.' Mr Breck looked outraged. 'If such a thing should happen, Miss Searles must apply to me, and I shall find her a cottage she can afford to rent until such time as she is married.'

'And who will want to marry a woman with no fortune and two sisters in tow?' Cousin Joshua said harshly. 'Only a fool would consider it.'

With that he strode from the parlour, leaving silence behind him.

Selina recovered first. 'I fear I have upset our cousin,' she said calmly. 'Do not judge him too harshly, Mr Breck.

He has little from his inheritance but the house, and you cannot blame him for wanting it to be free of occupants who pay nothing.'

'Mr Searles is a warm man. It would not have hurt him to allow you to live here free of charge as his tenants.'

'No, it would not,' Selina agreed. 'However, he has long held a ridiculous notion that we shall marry, and I think he hoped to force my hand—but nothing would make me consider it.'

'It was not what your mama hoped for,' the lawyer said. 'She believed you would marry well once you had your chance at a proper come-out.' He hesitated, then, 'I suppose you would not allow me to advance you the money for a season?'

'How good you are!' Selina exclaimed warmly, shaking her head. 'Really kind—but I could not allow it. I might never be able to repay you. No, do not say it doesn't matter, because it does. We may be poor, but we are honest, and we have our pride, sir.'

'Yes. I was afraid you might not accept—but your own idea is better than mine. Though I wish you would allow me to pay you for looking after the estate. An extra three hundred pounds might have provided enough for Miss Amy to have a come-out in a year or so…'

'No, Selina must not be made to feel guilty on my account,' Amy said instantly. 'She is the beauty of the family. I am confident that something wonderful will happen. Before you arrived we had nowhere to go—now we have a new home. What is the name of the house, sir?'

'Banford Hall,' he replied, and smiled at her. 'It is an

old property, Miss Amy—gothic, some might call it, and rather beautiful in my opinion. The family has lived there for centuries, and parts of it are medieval.'

'How exciting!' Amy exclaimed. 'Does it have a ghost?'

'Any number of them, I should imagine,' Mr Breck replied with an indulgent smile. 'I doubt they will bother three intelligent young ladies like yourselves.'

'I am becoming more excited by the minute,' Amy said, and gave him a sparkling smile. 'Mama always said she did not know how she would have managed without your help, sir—and you have gone to so much trouble for us.'

'Not at all, m'dear.'

The lawyer looked ridiculously pleased, and Selina smiled inwardly. Amy always said that she, Selina, was the beauty of the family, but her younger sister was herself a very charming, not to say fascinating, young woman. Given her chance she would no doubt marry well.

'As a matter of fact, it will suit me admirably to have you installed as a family rather than leaving it to a housekeeper—for sometimes, you know, they tend to neglect a house if the owner is abroad.'

'You can rely on us to keep it in good order. If I should discover some necessary repair, may I apply to you for the cost?' asked Selina.

'Certainly, certainly. His lordship—my client's nephew, that is—was explicit. He wants everything as it ought to be, especially for his tenants on the estate—but for the moment he is content in Italy and does not wish to live there. I believe he thinks his uncle, the old earl, may recover and wish to return home, though for myself I think there is no prospect of it happening. He has gone to a warmer climate to spend his last days in comfort and will not think of returning.'

'Well, if he does he shall find his house in good order. Should he be pleased with what we have done, he might offer us a home—if I continued as his housekeeper.'

'Would you consider it?'

'Only if it is a choice of that or going to my cousin for help.' Selina shuddered delicately. 'I would prefer to be independent—unless I find someone I would care to marry, of course. We are not quite destitute, sir. As well as our two hundred a year, our aunt left each of us fifty pounds and a small token of jewellery. The jewellery is not worth selling, except for the pearls Mama passed to me, of course. Mama's jewels may be worth as much as five thousand—' She broke off as she saw the lawyer's frown. 'You think I overvalue them?'

'Most of your dear mama's jewels were sold to pay your father's debts, Miss Searles. Your father had cop- ies made. I believe there is one pair of genuine diamond drops that remain, and the pearls you mentioned which were left to her by her aunt.'

The two girls looked at each other aghast. Selina was the first to recover.

'We have even less than we thought,' she said grimly. 'At least we need not part with what we have of Mama's. You have the diamond earbobs, Amy. Millie has a gold bracelet and I have the pearls. Even if the rest of what we thought heirlooms are just fakes, they look well enough to pass for being genuine if we have to wear them to a ball. Still, we are not destitute. We shall manage, but we must be very careful.'

'I am sorry to be the bearer of more bad news.' Mr Breck looked upset. 'I had thought you knew.'

'We had no idea things were so bad. I wondered why Mama did not sell something when she needed to repair the roof in the west wing. Now I understand. At least we have her furniture and her clothes…' She paused. 'Unless they are earmarked for a bill?'

'No such thing,' Mr Breck assured her heartily. 'You may take everything that was particularly your mama's when you leave.'

'You can be assured that we shall take nothing Cousin Joshua is entitled to think his own.'

'I should like Papa's duelling pistols,' Amy said. 'He taught me to use them and I have a fondness for them.'

'Well, since they are personal property and not part of the estate, I see no reason why you should not take them—his clothes belong to you, and any other small personal items.'

'So we can take his hip flask and his signet ring?' Amy asked. 'That would mean each of us had a small keepsake.'

'I can see no reason why you should not take every-thing that was personal to your father. The estate con-sists of land, houses, furniture, important silver, books and pictures.'

'Then we shall take as much as we can,' Selina said. 'I shall hire a cart to move our belongings, for I should not wish to use anything that rightly belongs to my cousin.'

'Our riding horses are our own,' Amy said, 'but the carriages and the carriage horses belong to Cousin Joshua. I think we must hire a carriage to take us to our new home, Selina—and Jeremiah must bring the horses.'

'I have thought about that,' Mr Breck said. 'I think it may be possible to buy a chaise and a pair of horses cheaply for you—but I shall enquire into the matter. It may be best to hire something for now. I will visit you at Banford Hall soon to see how you are settling in.'

'At least we shall have time to settle before Christmas,' Selina said. 'I am feeling much better for your visit, sir. Please, will you dine with us—and stay the night?'

'I should be delighted to dine,' Mr Breck said. 'However, I think a room at the inn might be advisable—now that the three of you are alone. It was different when your dear mama was alive.'

'Yes, very different,' Selina said, and the tears caught at her throat.

She blinked hard, because weeping would not help them. Her sisters were relying on her to make a life for them. It would be hard for them all, moving to a new house and leaving their friends behind. Her youngest sister was upset enough as it was.

'But Mama is at peace now, sir. She would not want us to break our hearts for her. Mama loved us dearly. She would want us to be happy—and that is what I intend. I shall do my best to make it a good Christmas. I know I speak for my sisters when I say you and your family would be welcome to visit with us this year. We may have a few guests—for I am sure we shall make friends with some of our neighbours—but I should be honoured if you would come to stay for a few days, sir.'

'Well, if that isn't handsome of you, Miss Searles.' The lawyer beamed his pleasure. 'I shall ask Mrs Breck her pleasure and be sure to let you know what plans she has—but I am truly honoured to be asked.'

'Mr Breck is very kind,' Amy said after their guest had left that evening. 'I should not have dared to take Papa's pistols had he not said I might. There are several things that Papa thought of as his own, and if we take all of them, we might sell one or two if need be.'

'Do not take anything of real value, Amy, or anything that Cousin Joshua might think is his by right. It would only bring him down on us, and although he might not actually demand we return it, he would certainly make us aware that we had something of his,' Selina warned.

'He is such a beast,' Amy said, and set her mouth in a mutinous line. 'There is a picture in Papa's study that I should love…'

'Please do not be tempted, dearest. I know the one you mean and it is quite valuable. Father inherited it himself, so it was not his personal property. Cousin Joshua would be sure to notice that—and I really do not care to have him preaching at me again.'

'Oh…' Amy sighed. 'It is so hard to leave things we've known all our lives.'

'Be grateful we have as much as we have,' Selina replied. 'It has been a long day. I am for my bed. Tomorrow we begin packing. I am determined to leave nothing behind that is ours—and I want to be ready within the three days.'

'Supposing the earl's nephew decides to come home to Banford Hall from Italy sooner rather than later?'

Selina frowned. 'We must pray that he does not,' she said. 'Should he return we must take Mr Breck up on his offer to find us somewhere to rent, as we cannot afford to purchase even a small cottage. Or there is the possibility that I may be offered the position of housekeeper at Banford Hall for real.'

'You wouldn't truly take it?'

'Only if we were desperate—and we are not that yet.' Selina smiled at her. 'Go up now, dearest. If you are not tired, you may begin your packing.'

'What about the books?' Amy asked. 'I suppose all the books belong to the library and are therefore part of the entail?'

'Mama's own books are ours—but, yes, I suppose the others do belong here.'

'I cannot leave my favourite poets!' Amy wailed. 'There are three books that never leave my bedside.'

'I daresay Cousin Joshua will not notice those,' Selina said with a smile. 'Take them, but do not pack a trunk with books, Amy. I assure you he would notice if you cleared an entire shelf.'

'No, just those three. After all, Mama did buy them for Papa—so in a way they are hers, or at least his personal possessions and therefore not part of the estate.'

Selina did not argue with her sister further. She was quite sure that Millie would also claim two or three books, as she might herself, but she could not truly deny any of them. Only an insensitive brute like Cousin Joshua would insist that they must leave their home so soon after Mama's death. A kinder man would have allowed them to remain until Selina married and made other arrangements for her sisters.

She was thoughtful as she went to her own bedchamber and closed the door. Tears had been hovering all day, but she'd kept them at bay for the sake of her sisters. The prospect of leaving her home was tearing her apart inside, though she'd tried not to show it to her cousin or the lawyer. She knew that she was taking a huge risk by accepting Mr Breck's offer. Here in her home, with all her familiar things about her and the servants who had known her all her life, she had managed very well, taking over the reins when her father died and her mama went into a slow decline. Being the mistress of an old house with just a handful of servants—some of whom she did not know—was a very different affair.

Selina's head came up, and her expression was one of pride and determination, even though her eyes sparkled with the tears she still refused to shed. She would manage. Even if the nephew returned and they had to move to a tiny cottage, she would manage somehow.

She would contrive to give Amy a season next year, and with any luck, her vivacious sister would marry well and solve all their problems. With judicious economy, and by asking a favour of one of Mama's friends, she might manage something for Amy, but it would be too much to expect the same for herself.

No, she must give up her hopes and dreams of a man she could love and respect—though if a presentable widower were to ask for her, she might just take him. All she asked was that he should be good-natured, and not a pompous prig like her cousin.

The thought of her cousin's face when she'd accepted Mr Breck's offer made her smile. Joshua had been so sure she would cave in and marry him that his indignation had been almost amusing—except that she knew he would find some way of paying her back if he could.

CHAPTER TWO

'MY UNCLE is dead?' Robert Moorcroft looked up from the glass of wine he had been staring into and glared at his secretary. 'No, damn it! I understood he expected to live at least a year or more. It was the reason he left England to find a warmer climate.'

'He had a nasty chill,' Henry Norton explained. 'I daresay it was the stress of the journey from England or being caught in a sudden rainstorm. You knew he was a sick man, Robert. It was always on the cards that he might go suddenly.'

'Poor devil. He expected to have a few months of peace and quiet—away from that barn of a place. It must have been hell for him these past few years. First his wife dead of a fever and then two of his sons—both succumbed to the same sickness.'

'I daresay it was an inherited weakness. You told me Eliza Benton was always sickly.'

'Yes, I imagine so.' Robert nodded morosely. 'It didn't help living in that draughty old house, I daresay.'

'Why do you dislike it so?'

'I spent the worst two years of my life there. Uncle William was in mourning for his wife and then his sons—and my father was recently dead from that carriage accident. My mother died when I was born, of course, and my uncle's family was closer than my own because my father went into himself and forgot he even had a son. That same year I'd been sent down from college. The atmosphere at Banford was positively oppressive. I wanted to escape as quickly as I could, and I did. After the freedom of the army, I vowed I would never return.'

'Well, you're the earl now,' Henry said, and smiled affectionately at his friend. After being invalided from the army, he'd taken the position of Robert's secretary, though he was a gentleman's son and had his own small estate in Devon. Perhaps he, too, was hiding—in his own case because of physical scars. Robert's scars were mental; they might not show, but they were just as crippling. 'You owe the old man a duty—even if you only stay long enough to sell the place and see the old retainers right. At least you have no entail to worry about. You are the last of your line.'

Robert groaned. 'Don't remind me, Nor.' He used the nickname from their army days. 'I suppose you're right, as always. I told that lawyer fellow to get a housekeeper, so if we leave in a couple of weeks, she should have the place in good heart—wouldn't you think?'

'I doubt she'll have changed it much in that time. You should give her a month—besides, you've business here. That's if you intend to ask the comtesse to marry you?'

Robert wrinkled his brow. 'The fair Adelaide. She is a beauty, Nor. I could do a lot worse. I suppose I ought to think about an heir—but not for that damned house. If I do settle back in England, I shall pull the house down and build something modern—or simply sell the place.'

'Don't you think that would be rather a shame? It does have a certain charm. You could use the money to put in some decent plumbing and refurbish it…repair the roof where necessary.'

'Why should I throw good money after bad?' Robert asked, and yawned. 'That house drained my uncle of the will to live…or at the very least, it contributed to his decline. I inherited a fortune from my mother's family. Why should I waste it on that place?'

Henry shrugged. 'It's entirely up to you, my friend. In your place I would want to make it into a home again. But if you have bad memories associated with it…'

'What of you?' Robert asked. 'You came here with me because neither of us could face the thought of going home after that last show in France. Too many friends lost…too much death and pain. The weather suits you here, Nor. Will you be able to stand the cold at home?'

'My leg still pains me,' Henry admitted, then touched the puckered scar on his left cheek. 'This doesn't hurt at all; it's just ugly, though better than it was at first. I have no hope of finding a woman to marry me, for I shan't be married for pity—and who could love me looking like this?'

'You are an ugly devil,' Robert said cheerfully. 'But I

love you for yourself, Nor—and any girl with half a mind would see your worth if you gave her the chance.'

Henry smiled wryly. 'I thank you for your kind words, milord. However, I should not want to inflict this on some poor girl who needed to marry for the sake of a place to live. No, I'll rub along nicely as your secretary—until you're bored with me. Then I'll go home.'

'In that case you'll be with me for life.' Robert grinned. 'You can see your scars, Nor—but mine are too horrible to bear. Only you could have got me through these past few years. I think I should have gone mad without you.'

'We need each other,' Nor agreed, and smiled. 'Well, are we going or not?'

'We'll go—but not for a few weeks. I'm not sure about the lovely Adelaide. She fancies herself as my wife—but could she stand me when I'm having a nightmare? I'll think about it for a couple of weeks or so, and then, depending on her answer, we'll go back to England.'

'All right,' Nor said, and nodded. 'Now, what about this other business?'

'You mean was my uncle right to suspect that he was being cheated?' Robert frowned. 'If I'm going to make enquiries, I might as well start now. You can write to my lawyer in England and set an agent on it. I cannot see why anyone would wish to harm my uncle, for he was a generous employer and a decent landlord.'

'Some twisted revenge for past hurts? A man sacked or a poacher arrested?'

'I suppose revenge might be the reason.' Robert lifted his wineglass and drained it. 'Remind me to have a few cases of this shipped back when we go, Nor. I doubt my uncle has anything drinkable in his cellars.' He rose to his feet and ran long, sensitive fingers through his dark hair. He was a handsome devil, strong and lean, with a face that reflected his emotions all too often. 'I'll ride over and visit Adelaide. I suppose you don't want to come? Miss Bartlet is very pretty, too, you know. I am certain she doesn't want to be a poor relation all her life.'

'That may be the case, but Miss Bartlet shudders every time she sees me. No, thank you, Robert. I'll stay here and write your letters—and I'll see about shipping some wine. We might sell a few dozen cases. It would be worth looking into the idea of shipping wine home, especially if we're going to live there for a while.'

'Leave it all to you, Nor,' Robert drawled, and laughed huskily. 'I'm a lazy devil. What would I do without you?'

'Go to the devil a little faster than you are already?' his friend suggested, giving a snort of laughter.

Shaking his head, Robert Moorcroft, lately become Earl Banford, left the villa that had been his home for the past two years or so, since Napoleon's surrender. Obviously he couldn't hide away here for ever. Despite his reluctance, he was the heir to an old line, and he would have to provide an heir for the future one day. The only thing in doubt was whether he did it in that draughty old barn or built himself a new house...

'Oh, my goodness,' Amy said as the coach drew to a halt in the courtyard of the house they'd caught glimpses of for the past ten minutes or more. 'Those towers and the tiny windows. It's like something out of Udolpho…so romantic…'

'It's big,' her more practical sister said, and felt her stomach catch with nerves.

She really hadn't expected the house to be this large. It was impressive, with its towers and the soft, faded grey stone of its old walls, but daunting, a little forbidding. A myriad of tiny windows sparkled in the late-autumn sunshine, their leaded panes like so many diamonds twinkling as they caught the dying rays of the sun on a day that had been unseasonably warm.

'A place like this needs an army of servants to keep it as it ought to be.'

'Mr Breck told you that only one wing is in use for the family. The other two were closed up years ago—and the folly is actually unsafe.'

'How do you know that, Millie?' Selina looked at her. 'Were you listening at the door?'

'No, I read the letter he left for you—the one that tells you where all the keys are kept and all the other things he thinks you ought to know.'

'Indeed?' Her sister gave her a quelling look. 'Since I did not give you permission to read my letter, you were prying, miss.'

'If you don't pry, you never know anything,' Millie said, and looked pleased with herself. 'I may only be twelve—thirteen next birthday—but I'm old enough to understand. You shouldn't treat me as if I were a child, Selina.'

'No, I shouldn't. You *are* old enough to understand,

miss—which is why I was cross when I caught you trying to pack that *Book of Hours*. It is medieval and far too valuable to hope that Cousin Joshua would not notice if it went missing.'

'He's a mean pig,' Millie said, forgetting that she was a young lady. 'Why should he have it? Papa said it was to be mine when I was sixteen. He promised me I should have it.'

'Well, he ought not to have made a promise like that,' Amy said. 'Anyone knows that book is entailed, Millie. We were allowed to bring only personal things—that book must be worth near a thousand guineas. Cousin Joshua would certainly come after us if we took something so valuable. I had to leave that painting I liked, too.'

'It just isn't fair...' Millie bit her lip as she looked at the house. 'It looks a bit creepy. I bet there will be ghosts.'

'Papa told us all there was no such thing as a ghost—not the kind who rattle chains, anyway—only unhappy spirits tied to a place or house,' Selina reassured her calmly.

'I hope there *are* ghosts,' Amy said, and opened the door to jump down before the postilion could do it for her. 'I can't wait to see inside.'

As she began to walk towards it, the front door opened, and an elderly man dressed in black came down the steps to greet them. At his back was a woman of a similar age and two male servants who appeared to be outside workers.

Selina's servants had travelled in a second small coach behind them, with the baggage on a wagon at the rear.

They had arrived now, and by the time all three girls had got out, the servants were grouped behind them. When Selina moved forward, they followed, rather like guards of honour, as if prepared to defend her.

'Miss Searles?' The butler came forward, his eyes flicking to the women behind her, his expression wary. 'I expected you earlier.'

'We suffered a small delay at the last posting house,' Selina told him with a smile. 'You are Trent, of course. I am so relieved that you have remained at your post. I am sure your help will be invaluable.'

'Well, ma'am,' Trent said, visibly melting under the warmth of her smile, 'I am sure I felt it my duty to the new earl. If traditions are not to be lost, he will need someone who recalls the old days when he decides to come home.'

'Yes, of course,' Selina replied easily. 'And so shall we, for this is to be our home in the meantime, and we wish to do everything as it ought to be—and I know you will be able to tell me how things used to be, Trent. Although we may need to change certain things. I have only a few servants, as you see. My groom is bringing the horses, but I shall have to acquire a chaise for our use.'

'I daresay there is one you may use in the coach house, ma'am—and the carriage horses are still here. The earl did not wish to dispose of them, you see. My brother's grandson has been helping out in the stable while we waited to see what happened.'

'Well, that would be useful—though I'm not sure I ought to take advantage.'

'A tenant is entitled to use all the facilities, ma'am.'

'Well, we shall see,' Selina said. 'Our goods are not far behind us. I see you have two strong men. Do you think they could unload the wagon for us?'

'Certainly, ma'am, it's what they're here for. They will take your trunks up first, and then you may wish to direct them where to put your furniture.'

'It will mostly go in our bedrooms. There are only a dozen pieces or so—also some china, glass, silver and linen. I have a beautiful spinet and a sewing table, also a pretty desk which may go in the parlour...'

'We have several parlours. You must allow me to give you a tour, ma'am. You will want to decide which is for your personal use.'

'How kind you are, Trent. I was afraid you might resent us because we're not family,' Selina said gently.

The old man looked sad. 'We've lost our family, ma'am. All but the new earl. Until he decides to take a bride and bring the house back to life, we shall be glad to have a family like your own staying here.'

'Thank you. Perhaps I may introduce you to Miss Amy Searles and Miss Millicent, known to us all as Millie.'

'Pleased to meet the young ladies, I'm sure,' Trent said, and turned towards the elderly lady standing behind him. 'This is Nanny Barnes. Nanny had nowhere else to go, so like me she decided to stay while she was of use. Nanny is very good at preparing tisanes and the like—and she's more than capable of helping to keep the rooms tidy, Miss Searles. She won't ask for more than her keep.'

'Oh, I think Mr Breck intends to pay you all a wage,' Selina told him. 'I shall certainly see that you receive remuneration of some kind. For the moment we shall manage with a small staff, but in time Mr Breck may consider it necessary to bring in others—particularly for the outside work.'

'The old earl only used a few rooms, ma'am,' Trent said, clearly feeling he needed to give her the status of an older woman, as she was the head of the household. 'Should you wish to entertain on a large scale, you would need more than you have presently—if you do not mind my saying so.'

'As you know, we are in mourning for our mother,' Selina replied, a catch in her throat. 'We shall not entertain much for a while.' She frowned as a phrase he'd used more than once registered warning bells in her mind. 'You spoke of the new earl—has the old earl died? We understood he was expected to live some months—even a few years if he removed to a better climate?'

'Yes, that is so, Miss Searles. Unfortunately it seems he was caught in a sudden thunderstorm while out walking. The soaking he received gave him a nasty chill, which turned to pneumonia and led to his sudden demise.'

'How very unfortunate,' Selina said, and her heart caught. 'You have not heard when the new earl intends to return?'

'We suppose he will not think of it yet, since he has leased the house to you, ma'am,' Trent said, and led the way inside. 'Would you like Nanny to bring you some tea to the back parlour? It gets the evening sun and we had a fire lit there earlier. Your servants will need to find their way about before they start work, I imagine.'

'Would it be too much trouble for you, Nanny?' Selina glanced at the elderly lady, who had merely inclined her head when she was introduced yet watched them anxiously.

'No trouble at all, ma'am,' Nanny replied, taking her cue from Trent. 'If the young ladies would join you in the parlour, Trent, I will bring some refreshments—and then we'll take you up once your things have been carried up.'

'I should love to explore,' Amy said. 'Tell me, Mr Trent—is there a minstrels' gallery here, and do you have any priest holes?' Her excitement showed in her pretty face. 'I am hoping one of the towers is haunted!'

'We have a minstrels' gallery in the great hall, miss,' Trent told her, an indulgent look in his eyes. 'We have two priest holes, but I fear there is no haunted tower. We don't have any skeletons in the cupboard—though the family *has* been unfortunate these past years.'

'Will you show me the house?' Amy asked. 'I can't wait to see simply everything.'

'The folly is out of bounds, miss,' Trent told her. 'It's dangerous because some of the stonework is crumbling. But there's no reason you shouldn't explore the rest of the house and estate whenever you wish.'

'Not yet, Amy,' Selina said. 'We must give Jane and Betty time to get our things settled, and for the moment no one has time to show us the house. I do not want you getting lost on your first evening.'

'Oh, nonsense,' Amy said. 'I shall not lose my way— but if you want me with you until things are ready, I suppose I must wait.'

'I'm hungry,' Millie said. 'I don't suppose there's any cake?'

'I'm sure Nanny baked something this morning,' Trent told her. 'She has been cooking for all of us since the earl left and most of the servants decided to move to a better place. Not that you could blame them for leaving in the circumstances. This house has been like a morgue for the past three years or more.' He looked embarrassed. 'I'm sorry, ma'am. I forgot for a moment that you're in mourning, too.'

'Yes, we are,' Selina agreed. 'But you mustn't think we intend to dwell on our sorrow, for we don't. Mama would hate it if we all went around with long faces. She always wanted us to be happy, and she will want us to make the best of our situation. We shall wear black or grey until Christmas, when I intend to hold a little party. However, we shall be at home to our neighbours, should any call— and we shall attend small dinners soon. We may also ask one or two people to dine here on occasion, but nothing resembling a party until Christmas.'

'That sounds very much better than we've been used to,' Trent said, patently relieved. 'I daresay we could send to the village for extra help should you need it, ma'am.'

'We are accustomed to keeping our own rooms tidy— at least Amy and I do our best.' Selina arched one delicate eyebrow at her youngest sister. 'I am trying to teach Millie to be a little more careful of her things, but sometimes I despair of her.'

Sensing the teasing note underlying Selina's words, Trent smiled and nodded. Having delivered his new family to a charming parlour that overlooked the back lawns and rose gardens, he left them to go in search of Nanny and their refreshments.

'What shall we do if the new earl comes home?' Amy asked in a low voice as the butler left them. 'He instructed Mr Breck to employ a housekeeper, not let the house to a non-paying tenant.'

'We shall pay our way,' Selina said firmly. 'I do not wish for any remuneration, but I intend to keep the house in good order. We shall all clean our own bedrooms. Amy, you will do the flowers for the rooms we use, and Millie can help by picking up books, scarves and any other personal items we leave about. It is my intention to make an inventory of the linen and household goods. I shall beeswax the furniture in the rooms we use, for it has not been done in an age. Cook will rule in the kitchen as always, Jane will organise our clothes, and Betty will see to the other housework and help Cook. We may need help from the village for the laundry, but if we all do our share, I see no reason why we should not bring the house to life again.'

'Amy is always leaving things about,' Millie said, looking put out. 'I do not see why I should pick her things up.'

'You leave far more about than I do. Besides, I'm doing the flowers—and that takes ages,' Amy replied.

'You can change jobs if you wish,' Selina said, 'But I cannot do it all myself, and so you must help. I shall help with the estate, as well as organising the house, keeping our accounts and ordering what we can afford from the local suppliers. Please do not argue, Millie. I am finding the prospect quite daunting enough as it is.'

Millie looked self-conscious. 'I'm sorry,' she said. 'It's just all so new and...so horrid without Mama. I shouldn't have minded where we were if she was with us.'

'Please don't cry, my love,' Selina begged, her throat closing. 'I do know how you feel but...we are lucky to have this chance. Even if it only lasts for a few months, it will give us the opportunity to decide where we want to live when the earl does come home.'

'I wasn't going to cry.' Millie sniffed hard, holding back her tears. 'But why did Cousin Joshua have to be so mean?'

'He is entitled to instruct the builders to make repairs. Mama ought to have done it sooner—indeed, it was truly Papa who was at fault. Instead of gambling his money away in London, he should have stayed at home and looked after his estate.'

'I shall never understand how it happened,' Amy said, her eyes glittering with suppressed anger. 'Papa never gambled to excess. I think he must have been cheated.'

'Why did he gamble at all?' Millie asked.

'Because he knew that the estate was suffering,' Selina explained, as she had several times previously. 'We had two bad harvests, and there was that nasty sickness that killed off most of our prime herd of cattle—and then Father made a bad investment with some merchant or other. He hoped he might win a few thousand pounds to tide him over until the harvest came in.'

'Instead, he lost what money he had and—' Amy

choked. 'I shall never forgive him for doing that to Mama. She loved him so much, and his death in that manner broke her heart.'

'It broke all our hearts,' Selina said, and held out her arms to her sisters. 'Come here, my dear ones. We have each other and in that we are lucky. We may be poor, but we still have our pride and our love for each other—as long as we have that, we shall manage.'

'You shame us,' Amy said, and brushed her tears away. 'You've had most of the burden to bear—and then Lord Markham stopped calling when he learned Papa had—' She broke off and shook her head. 'No, we shall not think of it again. Millie, we must help Selina all we can. The work will only take an hour or so in the mornings and then we may do as we like. I cannot wait to explore and discover the history of the house. Do you suppose there is a library and records of the family?'

Selina nodded and hugged both of her sisters in turn. 'That's right, Amy. We must all find ways to enjoy ourselves. It will seem more like home when we have our own things about us—and it will not be long until Christmas. We shall have a little party then, and presents, all the decorations we brought from home—and we'll make new ones.'

They heard a little cough from the hallway and then the door opened. Nanny entered, followed by Trent, who carried a large tray. He set it down on a table next to Selina's chair. Nanny had brought a stand on which she had placed plates of cakes, dainty pastries and some little sweet treats. Clearly it was not the work of a few minutes, which meant she must have spent some hours earlier that afternoon in preparing for their arrival.

'How lovely,' Selina said. 'Nanny, you must have worked very hard. I cannot thank you enough for making us feel so welcome.'

'I had some help, ma'am,' Nanny said, and looked self-conscious. 'Sadie is not quite as she ought to be. No one in the village will employ her, but she comes here to be with me because I helped her when she needed me, and the old cook here showed her how to cook. Makes wonderful cakes, she does—never asks more than a few pence and her dinner.'

Selina sighed inwardly as she saw her slender funds diminishing rapidly. At this rate she would have to apply to Mr Breck for more help with the servants' wages, but Nanny's words left her little option.

'I can see someone has worked extremely hard,' she said. 'You must thank Sadie for me. Does she live in the house?'

'Oh, no, miss, Sadie is a wild creature, a law unto herself. She can be an angel one day and the next she's off roaming the woods, getting up to who knows what. I think she has a hut in the woods somewhere.'

'I see. Well, at least she is no trouble to you, then.'

'Good as gold, she is, with me—but not always with others, if you see what I mean.'

Selina feared she did. This wild girl Sadie sounded more of a liability than a help, but she would not turn her away unless she caused trouble in the house. She tasted the cake cautiously, half expecting to find salt had been used instead of sugar, but it was in fact delicious.

'This is very nice,' she said. 'I do not think my cook could do better.'

'I'll tell my girl you were pleased,' Nanny said, and smiled. 'Like a daughter to me, she is, ma'am—for all her faults.'

'Well, I shall expect you to look out for her,' Selina said. 'In the meantime, I can pay her a shilling a week and her meals—if that is sufficient? If you think she needs more, I will apply to Mr Breck.'

'No, please don't do that, ma'am. The old earl told me to send her away—thought she was a troublemaker, he did, and Mr Breck would say the same. A shilling and her dinner will do very well for Sadie.'

'Then I shall allow her to come here, providing she causes no trouble in the house,' Selina said. 'Clearly you are fond of her, and I have no wish to cause anyone unhappiness. There is sufficient of that in life without creating more.'

She'd had her share of it—not least the disappointment she'd suffered when she was sixteen and her first love affair had come to naught, leaving her with sweet but empty memories.

'That's what I always say.'

Nanny nodded approvingly, and Selina knew she had passed the first test with flying colours. How many more there would be before she was fully accepted here she did not know, but she had a feeling she would soon find out.

* * *

'The library is wonderful,' Millie said the next morning, when Selina found her two sisters sitting in the parlour they had used the previous evening.

It smelled of lavender, and she realised they had been polishing and cleaning with a will. The beautiful old furniture was gleaming and nothing was out of place. They had positioned their mother's sewing box beside a comfortable chair they had brought with them, and the men had carried in the delicate spinet to stand before the window. On the mantelpiece were the silver candlesticks that had belonged to their mama, and a French silver-gilt clock with painted enamel sides. She might almost have been in her own home, and a lump came to her throat.

'Oh, you have been busy. Everything looks...like Mama's parlour.'

'Except it is too tidy,' Millie said. 'We always left our books and our sewing about, but otherwise it is very like home.'

'Yes.' Selina smiled, because they had worked hard to please her. 'Is there a good selection of books—books you can read and enjoy?' So often people filled their libraries with boring books covered in leather to look smart, which they never read.

'Oh, yes.' Millie sighed with pleasure, for reading was a particular favourite with her. 'There are novels, plays, books of poems, as well as history—and a wonderful Bestiary with marvellous drawings that have been coloured in.'

'Then you will not miss Papa's books so much. I hated

telling you that you must leave your favourite books, dearest.'

Millie looked away with a little shake of her head, a rather odd expression on her face. Selina wondered, but then forgot as Amy went into raptures about the family journals and the portraits she'd discovered in the gallery.

'Trent showed me the priest holes and the minstrels' gallery. They are in the west wing, which is not used now—though it could be, for there is nothing wrong with any of the rooms. All the furniture is under dustcovers, which makes it look sad, but it could be brought to life again with a little industry.'

'We might open it up for Christmas,' Selina said. 'I have been so busy with sorting out cupboards and the household accounts that I haven't seen as much as I would like of the house. However, I promised Mr Breck I would see to the business of the house and what I can of the estate accounts. Mr Breck has employed a bailiff to overlook the tenant farmers, and a couple of keepers for the park, but from what I've seen, two gardeners are hardly enough. I mean to pry into everything so that I can send Mr Breck my report by the end of the week.'

'After luncheon you *must* at least explore this wing,' Amy said, just as the gong sounded. 'Ah, that sounds as if it is ready. You know we are to have a simple buffet now and serve ourselves? Mr Trent offered to serve us himself, but I said we shouldn't need him until this evening.'

'Quite right. I believe he has enough to do with cleaning the silver and making sure everything is as it ought to be downstairs.'

'It's quite an adventure looking after ourselves, isn't it?' Millie said, surprising them both as they all trooped into the little dining parlour. 'I thought I should hate it but I've had fun.'

'Yes, of course you have,' Selina said. 'We can make what we want of our lives. We do not need a house filled with servants and lots of money to be happy.'

'I should like a new dress for Christmas, though,' Millie said. 'Mama said I would have my gowns made in a different way when I was thirteen—and my birthday is the week before Christmas.'

'We haven't forgotten,' Amy said, and raised her eyebrows at her elder sister. 'When do you ever let us?'

'Please do not quarrel now,' Selina said. 'We can still have new gowns sometimes, Millie. It's just that they may not always be the best silk—and we may have to make them ourselves.'

'I can't sew!' Millie exclaimed with horror. 'Please don't say I have to make my dress myself, Selina.'

'Amy and I will make it for you,' Selina promised. 'Besides, you must learn to set simple stitches. I wish we had some way of earning money that was acceptable in society, but I fear that if Amy became a companion she would lose her chance of a good marriage. Perhaps you should have a little season in Bath next spring, Amy. It is not so expensive as London, and we might contrive a wardrobe for you—but I am not sure we could all go. Besides, I shall be busy here.'

'What about Great-Aunt Hilda?' Millie asked. 'I know

she and Mama did not like each other—but she sent us all a present for our christenings.'

'And nothing since,' Amy reminded her. 'She and Mama fell out over something, and Aunt Hilda has never visited or sent even a card since. She would not consider taking me to Bath with her. I am not sure I should wish to go if I were beholden to *her*.'

'It all depends how much my pearls bring when I sell them,' Selina said. 'I am certain one of Mama's friends would take you, providing we did not expect her to pay for your clothes or expenses. If you found a rich husband, he might give Millie a home with you. I should then be able to find work as a companion, or perhaps a governess…'

'No, you would not,' Amy contradicted. 'If he wanted to marry me, he would have you to stay often. Given your chance, I am sure you would find a rich husband.'

'I suppose I might.'

Selina held her peace. She was not at all sure she wanted to marry for the sake of a fortune and a home. She was finding her present position more than satisfactory. Indeed, had it not been that she feared to spoil her sisters' chances, she would, she thought, be content to find a position as housekeeper in a house much like this one.

Selina had refused the three hundred pounds a year Mr Breck had offered to pay her, which would have solved all her financial problems, because it would not do for the sister of two young ladies who had yet to establish themselves in life to be known as a paid housekeeper. If they were taken care of, she could be quite independent without worrying how it might affect their lives. No one would even have to know that she existed.

The more she thought about it, the more she thought that she would be content to work for her living. It might be preferable to marrying a man she did not love just to gain a home. Or was she just being foolish because of a long-held dream?

The picture of a young soldier's face entered her mind, and she smiled at the memory. He'd swept her off her feet that night, giving her a taste of feelings and sensations so intense that she knew no one else would ever measure up. Indeed, she'd been so carried away that she had allowed him liberties no decent young woman should. Did that make her a wanton?

He'd said he would return to claim her one day—what did that mean? Had he meant marriage or...? Her cheeks flamed. Had he thought her wanton because she'd been carried away by her feelings? Sometimes Selina was shocked when she recalled what he'd done, but then she remembered how sweet had been the touch of his lips, and she could not be ashamed of what had been so pleasurable.

No, she would not let her thoughts dwell in the past. Time enough to think of her own future. First she had to make sure that Amy and Millie were safe, and until then she must struggle on as best she could.

CHAPTER THREE

'YOU are jesting?' Henry Norton stared at his friend in genuine surprise. 'She turned you down? Have her wits gone begging or did you offend her?'

Robert smiled wryly. 'You know me too well, Nor. I was too direct, of course. Told her it would not be a love match while assuring her that I was fond of her and found her desirable as a companion and a mother for my children.'

'I am not surprised she turned you down. Indeed, I wonder that you escaped unscathed to tell the tale. Knowing her temper, I would have expected you to bear some injury. What possessed you to say such a thing to the lady? You might have known she would be angry. The fair Adelaide has a score of gentlemen languishing at her feet.'

'Well, they may take their chances with her and good luck. She is beautiful but a spoiled brat,' Robert said, and touched his cheek with feeling. 'Not quite unscathed, Nor. The lady packs quite a punch, believe me.'

'No less than you deserved.' Henry was unsympathetic. 'If you wanted her to accept, you should have… But of course you didn't.' He nodded knowingly as he saw Robert's expression. 'You felt it your duty to offer for her, after flirting with her so outrageously for months, but you never truly wished to marry her, did you?'

'I confess it was done out of duty, for I had unwittingly led the lady to believe an offer was forthcoming.' Robert sighed heavily. 'I have behaved very badly. I know she is all that most men require in a wife, but she is not for me.'

'Good grief, what are you looking for—a saint?'

'No…' Robert laughed in an oddly defensive way. 'Would it be too much to ask that the lady should love me—or at least hold me in warm affection? I know I'm not the easiest of men. My nightmares would scare a young woman. I thought since Adelaide had been married once before she might be looking for a marriage of convenience, but it seems she demands utter devotion, and that I cannot promise. I'm not sure I shall ever be able to give my whole self to a woman. I've seen too much, Nor—cried too many tears. My heart broke on the Spanish Peninsula campaign, and I'm not sure I can feel love again.'

Henry nodded. He felt much as Robert did. The death of so many friends had left deep wounds that might never heal. But Robert had suffered more. Henry had watched him as he held Juanita in his arms, nursing her through a night during which she had been racked with terrible pain—pain inflicted by a renegade band of English soldiers. To see a young and beautiful woman destroyed so utterly as Juanita had been was something any man might find hard to forget. Raped, beaten and left for dead, she'd lived long enough to tell her tale, name her torturers, and die in her lover's arms.

Sometimes Henry wished she'd died sooner, before he and Robert had found her. Perhaps then his friend would have recovered. But the experience had scarred him deeply, leaving him with terrible nightmares that haunted him still, even after two years spent recuperating in the peace and warmth of the hills of Tuscany.

'Well, since there is no longer a reason for you to stay here, perhaps we should return to England.'

'Yes, I believe we should,' Robert agreed. 'You wrote to Mr Breck and told him I would return before Christmas?'

'I told him it was your intention. But you do not intend to visit the Banford Hall estate at once, I think?'

'It will keep for a while. We shall go to London. Breck may arrange for the townhouse to be opened up, and we'll go there for a week or two. My own estate was small and disposed of when I decided to stay here, but the money was invested. I shall want to investigate the state of my finances, which I believe to be more than adequate. As I told you, Nor—I do not think I can bear to live in that mausoleum of a house. It will have to come down if I'm to live there, but it may be better just to sell.'

'I'll write to Breck again before we leave, warning him of your intentions. When shall we go—next month?'

'Why not sooner?' Robert smiled. 'We'll pay a brief visit to Paris, and get home in time to prepare for Christmas.'

* * *

Selina looked around her with satisfaction. She and her sisters, and Jane and Betty, had spent the past three weeks cleaning and sorting out the neglect of years. The parlours, drawing room, dining room and breakfast parlour were all now in good order. Furniture had been polished, carpets beaten and silver burnished. The main staircase—a magnificent relic from medieval times, intricately carved—when they arrived had been ingrained with dust. Now the dark oak gleamed with polish, its faded beauty restored.

'It looks much better now, Miss Selina,' Betty said with a nod of satisfaction. 'I've never sneezed so much in my life without having a chill—everywhere was so dusty. I think the drawing room had not been used in years.'

'Well, we have made big changes.' Selina was pleased because she had discovered some beautiful pieces of walnut furniture that had been languishing under dustcovers in the unused wings. By bringing in useful items like desks and small tables, pretty chairs with spindly legs and a comfortable sofa, she had transformed the rooms they were to use. The heavier, ugly pieces had been transferred to one of the unused rooms. 'Everything in here was so heavy and dull—and all those lovely things going to waste...'

'I hope the new earl won't mind.' Betty looked doubtful. 'Some folk hate things to be changed, you know, miss.'

'Well, he isn't here, is he?' Selina replied. 'If he cared about his uncle's home, he would have come back at once to see what needed to be done to set it to rights. Besides, all I've done is make the rooms we use comfortable and pretty.'

'You've certainly made them your own,' Betty said. 'I'd best away to the kitchen, miss. Cook is making puddings and cakes for Christmas, and she needs a hand.'

'I thought Sadie was helping her?'

'Her?' Betty sniffed. 'Comes and goes as she thinks fit. That one is more trouble than she's worth, mark my words. You'll rue the day you allowed her to stay.'

'What has she done?'

'I'm not one to tell tales, miss, you know me—but she's been hanging around with James the gardener. A girl like that... Well, stands to reason he's only after one—' Betty broke off and blushed. 'I shouldn't have said that, Miss Selina.'

'No, you shouldn't,' Selina said. 'Unless she causes trouble, I shan't send her away, Betty. Nanny cares for her, and she keeps her in line. I'll give Nanny a hint about James and she can warn Sadie to be careful.'

Selina had caught only glimpses of Sadie, for the girl seemed to avoid the family. Once or twice she'd caught her peering in at the window when she'd been talking to Cook in the kitchens, and she'd seen her running across the lawns at the back of the house on two occasions, but otherwise Selina would hardly have known she was there had Nanny not told her.

Selina frowned as she thought of the beautiful wild girl who was not quite a part of their household. She was a law unto herself, dreamy, and apt to walk off in the middle of a task, so Cook said, and then come back a day later expecting to start again where she'd left it. Selina wasn't sure whether she was a little simple or just wild and contrary, but she had caused no trouble thus far.

Indeed, everything had been going very well. They had begun to receive one or two callers—just the vicar and some of their nearest neighbours—and she was thinking of having an afternoon when she would invite ladies to call for refreshments. They had met others when they attended church on Sundays, and everyone seemed friendly and a little curious about the family at Banford Hall. So far two gentlemen had ridden over to ask if they could be of any help. Both were gentlemen farmers, men of independent means, but they had country manners and lacked the town polish that she and her sisters had been used to in their friends. Neither was quite what Selina hoped for as a suitor for her sister.

'Miss Searles...'

'Yes, Trent...' Selina was brought back from her reverie by the elderly butler's arrival. 'Is there something I can do for you?'

'A letter has arrived marked as urgent. I thought I should bring it to you at once.'

'An urgent letter?' Selina looked at him in surprise and some consternation. She took the small envelope from the salver and glanced at the writing. 'It is from Mr Breck...' Opening it swiftly, she gave a little gasp of shock and turned pale. 'Yes, it is important, Trent. Thank you for drawing it to my attention. Do you know where Miss Amy is, by any chance?'

'She is in the small parlour, miss. Shall I tell her you wish to see her?'

'No, I shall go to her,' Selina said. 'Please excuse me.'

Leaving the butler staring after her in a puzzled manner, Selina walked swiftly to the parlour they had made their own. She was fortunate to find Amy at her sewing. Their younger sister was, of course, in the library, which was her favourite place at any time of day.

'I am not sure what to make of this,' she said, and handed Amy the letter. 'Mr Breck says we are to remain here for the moment, but I am not sure how we can.'

Amy read the letter and looked at her in consternation. 'He says the earl is expected in England any day now. Oh, Selina, after all our hard work—and just when we were beginning to make friends.'

'Apparently the earl does not intend to live here for the moment. It seems he will make his home in London— and he is thinking of pulling down the house and building a new place.'

'Oh, how could he?' Amy stared at her in genuine distress. 'This house is so beautiful and has so much history.'

'It is also draughty, and if all the rooms were opened up would require a small army of servants. We have worked hard ourselves, Amy. Betty could never have managed it alone.' Selina looked ruefully at her hands. 'I shall have to wear lace gloves when we have visitors, for my hands are a disgrace.'

'And now he will come and take it all away from us and destroy everything we've done.' Amy's eyes glittered angrily. 'It is so unfair, Selina.'

'Life is often unfair,' Selina said, and sighed. 'Do you remember when Mama took me to Bath seven years ago? I was just sixteen then, and she needed to take the waters for her health.'

'Yes. I remember you seemed very quiet when you returned.' Amy frowned. 'I don't see what... Sorry, please continue, Selina.'

'There was a man—a captain in the army. He was so handsome, and he was about to depart for Spain. He and his friends were at an assembly that Mama and I attended. My card was filled before he arrived, but he...he cut in and started to flirt with me. I felt as if I were in a dream, Amy. He said such things to me—told me I was an angel straight from heaven...so beautiful that I made his heart weep. He took me out into the garden and kissed me, told me that he adored me and that one day he would come back for me. I'm not certain what he meant, but I think he was a little squiffy, because the next day he passed Mama and I as we walked to the pump room and did not even glance my way. I suppose that he was merely flirting with me...'

'How perfectly horrid of him,' Amy said, outraged for her sister. 'What happened after that? Did you tell him he was not a gentleman?'

'I did not have a chance. I learned from a lady whose house we visited that Robert Moorcroft and his friends had departed for Spain, where they were to join Wellington— or Wellesley, as he was then known—on campaign.'

'So he was merely flirting with you and drunk on the

eve of leaving for war?' Amy frowned. 'I should have been angry with him for taking advantage.'

'No, I wasn't angry.' Selina smiled. 'I was young and foolish. I should not have gone into the garden with him that night. Mama had warned me about allowing gentlemen to take advantage… But I liked him so much, and it all seemed so romantic. I was carried away on a tide of pleasure and I forgot Mama's warnings. Of course I know now he was just flirting with me—but somehow I have never been able to forget him.'

'Is that why you do not wish to marry for money?'

'I suppose it may be,' Selina replied. 'I shall not say he broke my heart, for he did not—but he spoiled me for others. I have not been able to see any other man in the same light.'

'Yes, I understand that,' Amy said. 'Is he the reason why you took this position?'

'In a way. Since I have no real desire to marry, I thought this would be a way out of our difficulties. But if the earl returns and no longer requires my services…'

Amy frowned. 'What are we to do? You were thinking of inviting our neighbours to a Christmas Eve party. Shall we still be here, or must we look for another home?'

'Mr Breck insists that we must stay as we are for the moment. He will speak to the earl when he sees him and ask if we may stay on until he is ready to demolish the house.'

'Who is going to demolish the house?' Millie asked, coming in at that moment. She had a book in hand, and had obviously been immersed in it until that moment.

'What are you whispering about? Why does no one ever tell me anything?'

'The earl is returning to England. He intends to live in London for the moment, but apparently he wishes to pull this house down and build a new one in its place.'

'He can't,' Millie wailed. 'Oh, I hate him. I've just got to like being here. Men are horrid. I wish they would all go to war and get killed so we could live as we please.'

'Millie! That isn't nice,' Selina admonished. 'The earl is not concerned with us for the time being, so we may carry on as we wish. Mr Breck is coming down next week to have a look at what we've done and make a check on a few things I pointed out to him. He may know more of the earl's intentions then. If he gives us a few months, we shall be able to find a nice cottage somewhere.'

'It won't be like living here, in this wonderful old house,' Millie said and her eyes filled with tears. 'We shan't have many books, and there are so many I want to read.'

'Well, perhaps the earl won't want to be bothered with this place for a while,' Selina said hopefully. 'I should not have come here had I thought this would happen—but it seemed ideal for us. Had we been granted a few months of peace, Amy might have found a husband, and I…well, I might have found something, too.'

'Don't worry, dearest,' Amy said, a gleam in her eyes. 'I'll find a husband by Christmas—you see if I don't. All we have to do is give a few dinner parties and invite all the eligible men and their mothers and sisters.' She smiled confidently. 'I might not catch an earl or a lord, but I don't mind a sir—or even a plain mister if he is rich enough.'

'No, you must not rush into marriage for our sakes,' Selina said hastily. 'Please promise me you will not, dearest. I want you to be happy. Millie and I will manage in a cottage for the time being if we have to—but you must marry well. You were born to shine in society, my love, and I refuse to let you sacrifice yourself for us.'

'It would not be a sacrifice if he could give me the things I want—and provide a decent home for you.'

'But you like to mix in good society, and you long for a season. No, Amy, whatever happens I will not have you sacrificing yourself for us. Remember you are not yet twenty and I am your guardian. I shall not allow it.'

'You would not refuse me if I really wished to marry?'

'Not if you were in love and the gentleman was suitable,' Selina said firmly. 'Do not give up yet, my dears. We owe this placing to Mr Breck, and should we need to move on, I think we can rely on him to help us. We shall simply carry on as before.'

'My instructions were that you should employ a *housekeeper*, sir,' Robert said, glaring down at the lawyer from his superior height. 'My uncle did not wish for a tenant and neither do I.'

'You said you would not be returning for some years, my lord. I thought there could be no harm in it since the young ladies were in such desperate straits. They had to leave their home before the builders moved in—and they have taken good care of your property, I assure you. Miss

Searles is an excellent manager, and had been helping to care for her father's estate for the past three years.'

'I take it she is a spinster of advancing years?'

'I would not say that, sir—though she is not a *very* young lady. In her early twenties, I believe. Miss Amy is nearly twenty, and the youngest girl will be thirteen shortly.' Mr Breck threw him an anxious look. 'It was my intention to visit them tomorrow and discuss the matter. I have heard of a house that might be suitable, but it will not be vacant until the second week in January. If you could see your way clear to allowing them to stay until then...'

Robert's expression hardened. 'You say she is acting as an unpaid housekeeper?'

'It was an arrangement that I thought suitable, my lord, though I offered remuneration. Miss Searles felt unable to accept a monetary reward. She needed a home quickly and the house was empty. She and her sisters and her servants have moved in—and I've had good reports of her. She has already found some things that she thought needed to be brought to my attention regarding the tenants of one of your two farms.'

'Indeed? What may that be? I should hardly have thought a young, single woman capable of finding something my uncle or his bailiff had missed.'

'It was to do with a tithe that was payable to the church but had been mistakenly paid to the estate, but it does not, however, show up in the accounts. Also, there was a matter of a lease on some land that had lapsed, and the tenants had been allowed to stay on—if no rent is paid, they could claim the land in another few years. I have already set the matter of a new lease in hand, so you may thank her for it.'

'Remarkable. One wonders how my uncle's man of business could have overlooked something of that sort—unless he had good reason?' Robert said thoughtfully.

'Precisely. Miss Searles thinks there might be some kind of relationship between the agent and the tenant. Your uncle's agent left rather abruptly when the earl told him you would be taking over the charge of the estate. I think what Miss Searles uncovered may be the tip of the iceberg, my lord. I daresay your uncle had been cheated for some years.'

'In that case I cannot put off my visit for as long as I planned. I must go down and poke about—discover just what has been going on.'

'Will you wish Miss Searles and her family to leave?'

'No, of course not. I am not a barbarian and nor do I have a heart of stone. I think there are enough rooms for us to share a house for a while. Pay your visit as you planned, Mr Breck—and tell Miss Searles I shall come down in eight days from tomorrow. She may hire some more servants from the village and open up the west wing. I shall move in there with Henry Norton and Jobis. Jobis was my batman in the army, and he looks after me as well as most valets—though I admit he does not understand how to black my boots. I have hired a man to help for my stay in town, but I shall not be taking him with me to the country. Henry, Jobis and my grooms are all I need for the moment.'

'As you wish, my lord.'

Robert stared out of the office window at the busy London streets. Rather to his surprise, he had found them dirty and less than welcoming after the warmth and beauty of Italy.

'Before I can think of pulling the house down, I must have plans drawn. If you could furnish me with the name of a good architect, I shall ask him to come down—perhaps stay over Christmas and give me an idea of the cost of a complete rebuild.'

'Very well, my lord. It is generous of you to agree to my clients staying on in the house for the moment. I shall tell the ladies they can stay until the new house is vacant—which means they can have Christmas where they are. I believe it was Miss Searles's intention to give a little party for your neighbours.'

'As I am in official mourning for my uncle, it must not be a large gathering, but I see no reason why she should not have a small one if she wishes—though you did say she is also in mourning?'

'Yes, my lord. However, she wanted to get to know her neighbours.'

'Who will not be hers for much longer...'

'She will not be moving too far. The house I have found is a large farmhouse no more than ten miles from your estate. The owner is settled abroad and the tenancy is for five years—should she wish to take it.'

'Then she must do as she thinks fit,' Robert said, and frowned again. 'The name seems to ring a bell, but I do not recall having met the family.'

'Her father was Lord Richard Searles, and her mother

was a Seymour of the Devon branch—but they were country gentry. I believe they rarely visited London. Lady Searles was often an invalid. Some years ago she paid a few visits to Bath to take the waters, but then her health deteriorated and she stayed at home. Her husband visited London alone sometimes—and that was when he was…unfortunate enough to lose most of his money at the tables.'

'You say the house was entailed?'

'It was free of a mortgage, but some of the land was pledged to the bank. Their cousin inherited it, as he is the last of the male line, and he intends to let or sell what is left of the estate.'

'And he could not be persuaded to allow the ladies to live there?'

'He claimed they would be better with him—but Miss Searles declined. She feared his intentions towards herself and did not wish to marry him.'

'She would rather become an unpaid housekeeper than marry respectably?' Robert's frown cleared. 'She sounds an interesting and determined young woman, Mr Breck. Pray tell her she may stay on in the house until next year. I shall not bother her—but she may leave the management of the estate to me. She will continue in the role of unofficial housekeeper. I have no interest in such things.'

'I am certain she will be grateful, sir,' Mr Breck said. 'I cannot tell you how you have relieved my mind.'

'You exceeded your brief,' Robert said. 'It might have been awkward had I returned with a bride.'

'Your lordship is thinking of marrying?'

'Perhaps...' Robert was disinclined to reveal more of his personal plans. 'For the moment Miss Searles and her family may remain in residence. If she will kindly have the west wing prepared for my arrival, I shall be obliged to her.'

'Of course, my lord. I am certain she can have no objection to sharing the house with you. It is, of course, your house.'

'I am glad you have remembered that fact,' Robert replied with a hint of sarcasm. 'Might I advise you to follow my instructions to the letter in future?'

'Yes, my lord. I was wrong, but...' Mr Breck quailed before his look, feeling chastened. 'Of course. Just as you say.'

'No need to look so crushed,' Robert said, and laughed. 'Just a friendly word of advice. Had you asked beforehand, I might well have granted your request. I had no thought of visiting the estate while my uncle lived—but it is clearly my duty, and I now understand why he wished me to take charge of it. If there is one thing I cannot tolerate, it is that an elderly man grieving for his lost loved ones should be cheated. If I discover there was more than the customary practice going on, heads will roll...'

'You must not blame yourself, Mr Breck,' Selina said, concerned to see how distressed the lawyer looked as he told her the news. 'You have given us a breathing space—and if the new house is not too far away, any friends we make here will be near enough for us to visit.'

'I fear the property is nothing like this, Miss Searles.

I was so sure you would have this for at least a year or more, which might have given you time—' He broke off, looking self-conscious. 'Forgive me, I presume too much.'

'Not at all, sir. It was my hope that I might see my sister make a good marriage. If she should be fortunate enough to do so, I could leave Millie to her care and take a position in the house of a lady for myself.'

'You must not think of it, my dear Miss Searles. As a temporary arrangement, it is allowable, but you should be living as a lady—not serving one as a housekeeper or a companion.'

'I think I may not have much choice. I am past the first flush of my youth, sir. I should have had my season three years ago, or sooner, but circumstances would not allow. Papa still had a little money then, and Mama, too. Now I have no prospects and very little as a dowry. Indeed, what I have may need to be spent to ensure Amy has her chance.'

'Well, you must not act precipitately,' he advised. 'Now, you understand the situation? I am sure you can manage to live under the same roof as the earl for a few weeks.'

'Yes, that should not prove too difficult,' Selina said, managing to smile. 'My offer stands, Mr Breck. If you would care to bring your wife to stay for the Christmas period, we should be glad to have you.'

'Alas, Mrs Breck has made arrangements for her family to visit us. She is most disappointed, for she is of a romantic turn of mind and would have loved to see this place before…the earl may decide to pull it all down and build a new home for himself and his wife.'

'He is newly married?' Selina enquired.

'Oh, no. I believe he may have it in mind, but I have heard nothing definite. Please do not tell him I mentioned the possibility, for it was merely a chance remark.'

'I should not dream of it,' Selina replied. 'Were I to have continued here as the tenant, I should have asked your wife to visit later in the year, but I fear we must leave as soon as this other house becomes vacant.'

'Then you will take it?' Mr Breck looked relieved. 'I promised your dear mama to do what I could for you, and if I have found a solution to your problems, I am happy.'

Selina refrained from telling him that Lady Searles would be less than pleased with the way things had gone for her beloved daughters. Mr Breck had done his best and they must just make the most of it. At least they would still be here for Christmas. Even if they did have to share the house with its rightful owner.

'He is here,' Millie said dramatically as she threw open the parlour door eight days later and entered, carrying a basket of eggs she had fetched from the farm nearest to the estate. 'I saw his chaise arrive. He has brought a baggage coach weighed down with trunks, boxes and crates. Trent says he has collected some art treasures in Italy, but they are to be stored for the moment—until he builds his new house. So we shall not see what is inside them all.'

'You must not *think* of intruding on the earl's privacy,' Selina told her sister. 'Just because you can walk into the west wing unheeded, you must not take advantage. The earl is entitled to expect common courtesy from us—all of us. If we wish to speak with him, we shall either send a message by Trent, asking for the favour of an interview, or we shall go to the side door and ring the bell, just as if we were paying a visit to one of our neighbours.'

Millie's mouth set in a mutinous line. 'The library is between the two wings. I do hope he will not ban us from using it. I shall simply die if I cannot read more of those wonderful books.'

'When he has had time to settle in, he may—' Selina had been going to say he might pay a courtesy call, but at that moment Trent entered the parlour, looking a little flustered.

'Forgive me, ma'am,' he said. 'The earl has just arrived, and he asks that you attend him in the library.'

'There you are,' Millie wailed. 'I *knew* he would say it was his. It will be just like Cousin Joshua all over again.'

'It is not the same at all,' Selina replied, sounding calmer than she felt. She smoothed her skirts, then patted her hair, tucking a wisp behind her ear. She had dragged it back into a tight knot at her nape, hoping it made her look older. 'I shall come at once, Trent.'

She left her sisters whispering together and walked in a measured pace toward the library. Because Millie loved it so much, she had allowed her sister to have some comfortable chairs installed, rather than the hard sofas which had been there previously, and a fire would have been lit that morning, as it was every day. Reaching the door, she knocked and then entered.

Two men were standing before the fire. As they turned to face her, her heart caught with sudden pain. She knew one of them immediately, and the shock held her as if she had turned to stone. He had changed, but she recognised him for the dashing captain who'd kissed her on the eve of his departure for Spain. How could it be? She had thought never to see him again, but here he was— yet who was he, exactly? Could he be the Earl Banford?

'Good morning, gentlemen,' she said, and dipped in a slight curtsey. Her heart was racing wildly, and she felt as if she might faint, but she held her raging emotions on a tight rein. 'I am Miss Searles—Miss Selina Searles. My sisters are Miss Amy and Miss Millicent.'

'Miss Searles.' The man with a scarred cheek inclined his head. 'Henry Norton at your service. I am secretary to Earl Banford—or, as he prefers to be called, Captain Moorcroft.'

'And also my friend,' the slightly taller of the two said, with a wry look at his companion. 'Nor and I saw service together. He takes care of all the tedious business for me and I tolerate his company. I have not yet seen much of the house, but I must congratulate you on the difference you've made to this room, Miss Searles.'

Selina caught her breath. As soon as he spoke, all the memories came rushing back, threatening to overcome her. His smile was just the same, but the years had aged him, taking that bright youth and enthusiasm from his face. His eyes were different, shadowed, as if he had seen too much sorrow and pain—as of course he must have, for she'd heard tales of the harshness of war, though she could have no idea of what these two men had suffered. Mr Norton's face bore a terrible scar from his left eye to his chin, and she noticed that he walked with a limp, and his left hand was covered with a glove. She guessed that it had sustained an injury that he did not wish to reveal to the world.

'I am glad you have no objection to my changes, my lord,' Selina said, keeping her cool smile in place. 'My youngest sister is a great reader and loves to spend much of her time here. I realise that you may wish to make the library your own, but perhaps she may continue to borrow the books?'

The earl hesitated, then inclined his head stiffly. 'I, too, enjoy reading. I daresay we may come to some arrangement—providing she is quiet when I'm working on estate matters.'

'I assure you she will be as quiet as a mouse. Once she has her nose in a book, it takes a Herculean effort to get her out of it.'

'A true reader,' Henry Norton said with a smile. 'I shall look forward to meeting the young lady. Now I shall leave you, Robert. I daresay you wish to be private with Miss Searles. I know you have things to discuss.'

'You do not have to leave,' the earl said, but his friend merely smiled at Selina and went out.

The earl stared at her in brooding silence for a moment or two, then, 'I am sorry if my arrival has made things awkward for you, Miss Searles. I had no intention of coming down yet, but Mr Breck seems to think you have uncovered evidence of my uncle being cheated?'

'Yes, that is so,' Selina agreed. 'I am sure it was the case. The agent who was almost certainly behind most of it has left, but I think there may be more serious offences than I have yet had time to uncover. I have not delved too far, because I was not certain how you would feel about a woman prying into your affairs.'

'I would normally resent anyone prying,' he said, with a mocking lift of his eyebrow. 'However, in this case I can only thank you for the service you have rendered me. I shall ask you to show me the evidence another day—perhaps tomorrow morning if you are not too busy? After that you may leave the estate accounts to me.'

'Certainly, my lord,' Selina said, her head up as she met his hard gaze. 'I was merely trying to save Mr Breck too many trips down here—and to pay for my accommodation.'

'I think you may consider your rent paid,' the earl replied, still with that faintly sardonic smile on his lips. 'As I said, I may not have seen much of the house yet, but what I have seen is a credit to you. Trent told me that you and your own servants are responsible for most of it?'

'I have hired two maids to clean and serve in your wing, my lord. Also a former footman asked to return when he heard you were intending to take up residence. I told him he must come to you, and I believe he intends to wait on you tomorrow. I did not wish to presume too much, my lord.'

'For goodness' sake, call me Moorcroft—or sir,' the earl said a trifle impatiently. 'Until recently I was Captain Moorcroft of the Fifth Cavalry, and to be honest, I preferred it that way.'

'As you wish, my...sir.' Selina felt the heat in her

cheeks. Just for a moment she'd glimpsed the man who had stolen her young heart, but he had disappeared again almost at once. 'I daresay you did not wish for the bother of an estate like this. My father always said that large houses like this were more trouble than they were worth—but of course his estate was nothing like this must once have been.'

'My uncle was in mourning for a long time. He let everything slide, and some of the land was lost to bad debt—and perhaps malpractice, as you have already seen.'

'Yes, I imagine it must have been that way.' Selina lifted her eyes to his. 'If you would care to inspect our wing later this evening, I shall be delighted to show you.'

'I shall visit if you invite me, but it isn't a case of inspecting. Your wing is your home until you are ready to move, Miss Searles.'

'You are very generous.' Selina blinked back the stupid tears that hovered behind her eyes. She might have known he would not remember her. Just as he had changed, so had she. They had both been young and eager that night, but life had taken its toll, and they were now very different people. 'I have warned Millie she must not intrude on you. I fear she has been in the habit of going wherever she pleases. My sisters are both delighted with the house, sir. They adore the minstrels' gallery and the priest holes.'

'Yes, I remember seeing them for the first time as a young boy—before things changed.' His mouth drew into a thin line. 'I believe my uncle suffered more tragedy than any man should in losing his wife and sons to the same malady. At the time I did not understand why his house was like a mausoleum, but I have since learned what it is to lose those you love.'

'Yes, I believe it must have been terrible at times out there during the war. We heard tales, of course, but it is difficult to imagine what went on.'

'You should not try, Miss Searles. Believe me, you do not wish to know.'

For a moment there was such horror and grief in his eyes that she was shocked. She felt cold all over and her spine prickled. What could have happened to him to make him look like that?

'I believe I have nothing more to say for the moment,' he said. 'I should like to rest. Trent has offered me refreshment—but I understand the cook is employed by you?'

'Yes, she came with me—together with my mother's maids and my groom. The other servants are, of course, in your employ. However, since they all work together, I believe we may share their services. You do not have a dining parlour in your wing, so perhaps you will dine with us this evening?'

'Yes, that may be for the best. I shall have to make other arrangements after you leave or perhaps before. Excuse me now, Miss Searles. I have work to do.'

Selina felt herself dismissed. He had treated her politely, but she knew that he considered her to be just one step above a paid housekeeper—perhaps equal to a poor relation he had given a temporary home.

Fighting her chagrin, and a stupid feeling of disappointment that he had not immediately remembered her as the girl he had kissed on that magical summer evening, she left him to brood alone in the library or whatever he chose to do. She had warned her sisters they were to stay away from his wing of the house, and she must do the same—unless requested to present herself, as she had been today.

She was so stupid to care! It had been but a fleeting moment—something she ought to have forgotten long ago, as he clearly had. They had both learned to feel pain and to live with the loss of loved ones, but he had moved on with his life while she... No, she was not that foolish girl. She was Miss Searles, and if requested to walk in moonlit gardens with an officer she did not know, she would have more sense than to agree.

At least she'd been saved the embarrassment of his thinking she was presuming on their encounter that night. He'd had her story from Mr Breck and been generous enough to allow her to stay—and that was the end of it.

She must concentrate on making this a better Christmas for her sisters than the previous one, when they'd been grieving for their father and their mama had been lying prone on her bed.

This year they would have goose with all the trimmings, presents and greenery throughout their part of the house. Since the great hall was in Lord Moorcroft's wing, they would not be able to bring in the Yule log, but she would make their wing as festive as she could.

What Lord Moorcroft chose to do was entirely his affair. Cook would provide sufficient food for all of them—he could join in or brood alone with his kind but terribly scarred friend...

CHAPTER FOUR

'I THINK he looks like a pirate,' Millie said, though since she'd never seen one, other than in drawings in her book of tales of the sea, she could hardly be called an expert. 'He is very bold and handsome—and his eyes laugh at one.'

'And where did you see Mr Norton?' Amy challenged as she looked up from her embroidery the morning after the earl's arrival. 'I hope you didn't go marching into the earl's wing?'

'Selina said I might continue to use the library, but I was to leave if the earl asked me to. I knocked at the door and Mr Norton was there. He invited me in and he was nice.'

'Yes, he *is* nice,' Amy agreed. 'I think he must have been as handsome as the earl before he was so horribly wounded.'

'I like him as he is now,' Millie avowed. 'He told me he intends to catalogue the library and set it to rights. I asked if I could help, because I know where a lot of the books are, and he said if I was very careful and used gloves to handle the older, more valuable books, I could. He made me promise not to take a book away without noting it in his ledger, and I promised.'

'It sounds as if he likes you, Millie. If you'd been four years older, he might have married you. You could have lived here as his wife then.'

'He has an estate of his own in Devon. When the earl marries, he will go home and marry himself.'

'How do you know that?' Amy gasped.

'Because I heard them talking last night.'

'What do you mean?' Amy stared at her. 'You didn't go into their wing— Oh, Millie. Selina warned you not to. The earl might have been so angry.'

'Well, I left something in the minstrels' gallery. I had to fetch it or—or they might have thought it belonged to them, and it doesn't.'

'Millie…' Amy looked at her in sudden suspicion. 'What have you done? If you've stolen something of the earl's, you must give it back at once and apologise.'

'I haven't stolen anything…not from the earl.' Millie glanced guiltily over her shoulder. 'Please do not tell Selina, but I brought the *Book of Hours* with me in my trunk. I know she said I shouldn't, but Papa gave it to *me*—truly he did, Amy. I'm not lying.'

'I know he told you you could have it,' Amy said. 'But in truth he had no right, Millie. Selina is correct when she says it belongs to the estate. If Cousin Joshua discovers it is missing, he will come here and ask Selina where it went. He is within his rights to demand that you return it. It is medieval and so precious, my love.'

'It would be precious to me if it wasn't worth any money,' Millie said, but hung her head. 'I know I shouldn't have done it, Amy—but I did, and there's nothing we can do now, is there?'

'We shall have to see what happens,' Amy said. 'Hush, now, Selina is coming. I think she has been going over the accounts with the earl.'

'I do hope she isn't upset. She looked as if she might cry when she came back from seeing him last night.'

'Well, here you are,' Selina said as she entered the parlour. 'I was thinking we might take a walk to the village this afternoon. I wanted to call on the vicar and ask if he and his wife would like to dine with us tomorrow. I am planning a party the week after next, and he will know who we should ask to our first dinner.'

'A dinner party?' Millie said. 'It's my birthday that week. Is it for my birthday, Selina? If so, I should like to invite Mr Norton.'

'I expect we shall invite both the earl and Mr Norton. Lord Moorcroft intends to bring a chef from London in time for Christmas, and he is bringing down one of the large oak trestle tables from the attics. I think he will use the great hall as a dining parlour when he entertains, and his smaller parlour when he and Mr Norton wish to dine alone.'

'Why can they not take all their meals with us?' Millie asked. 'I like Mr Norton and—and the earl doesn't seem too bad if you ignore his scowls. He doesn't always know he is scowling, you know. Mr Norton says his bark is worse than his bite.'

'Millie!' Selina shook her head but smiled at her sister. 'You shouldn't say such things, even if Mr Norton does. He has the privilege of friendship. I have offered the earl the service of Cook, should he wish to accept, but he says it is to be a temporary arrangement. However, since there is only one kitchen, the arrival of a London chef may cause some friction.'

'I thought he meant to stay only a short time,' Amy said with a frown. 'That his intention was to bring an architect from London, make plans to pull the house down and have drawings made for a new one.'

'I have not been informed of any changes in the earl's plans,' Selina said. 'He did compliment me on how pleasant his wing is since I had the furniture rearranged, and he sent his regards to you, Amy. He thanks you for the flowers but says he will not trouble you in future.'

'Oh…' Amy sighed with disappointment. 'I enjoyed doing them, but if he does not wish for flowers…I have plenty to do here.'

'Exactly.' Selina's eyes glittered with pride. 'The west wing is the earl's home and this is ours. As long as we remember that, there will be no conflict of interest.'

'Mr Norton says I can help him in the library, but I am to go away if the earl wants to work there,' Millie said. 'I wish *he* was the earl. We could all be together then, like a family.'

'Just remember you are a guest in the earl's house, Millie. We may think of entertaining a few friends at

Christmas, but then we shall have to start packing our things ready to move again.'

'Do we really have to?' Millie made a face. 'I should like to stay here for ever and ever.'

'Well, you can't,' Amy told her. 'I hate the idea of this house being pulled down, but we can't stop it.' She stood up. 'I've decided I'm going to draw the outside of the house from various angles. I want a memory I can keep. And if you behave, I shall colour one for your birthday, Millie.'

'Will you draw the minstrels' gallery and the priest holes for me?'

'I should have to do them from memory.'

'Mr Norton would let you draw them if you asked.'

'Yes, he might—but he would have to ask the earl for his permission,' Selina said. 'I think there can be no objection to your drawing the house, Amy. Even if the earl does not appreciate it, he might like to have one of your drawings to remind him of what it looked like one day.'

'I think I shall make a start now—before nuncheon,' Amy said. 'Will the gentlemen be joining us in the breakfast parlour?'

'I think the earl has asked to be served in his own parlour or the library. He has tea tables, which will do for such a meal, but no dining table—except the huge one that almost fills one end of the great hall.'

'How silly of him to bother with all that when he could dine with us,' Amy said. 'Please excuse me, Selina. I must fetch my painting things.'

'And I must...' Selina looked about herself and felt suddenly at a loss. She had hardly had a moment to spare since they'd arrived, but the house was now in good order, and the earl had lifted the burden of the estate from her shoulders. 'I think I shall do some embroidery until nuncheon. This afternoon I shall walk to the vicarage.'

Amy departed in search of her sketching things. Millie followed her, saying she had mislaid a book she wanted, and Selina was left to amuse herself. She picked up a piece of embroidery, put it down again, and wandered over to the window. It was too nice a day to stay indoors, and she was restless now that so much of her work had been taken over by the earl.

Her interview with the earl had gone well enough. He'd seemed impressed with her accounting and had agreed that his uncle had been systematically cheated by his agent, and perhaps by other servants who had since left his employ.

'There is little I can do now,' he'd said with a rueful look. 'But I shall send a new lease to the tenant who has not paid his rent for some years, together with a bill for money owed. If he has receipts from my uncle's agents, he must present them. I shall then have proof of theft and can prosecute.'

'I agree you should pursue this matter,' Selina had replied. 'It was wicked of them to do such a thing—and unfair to the tenant if he believed he was paying rent to the earl.'

'Unless he was in on the scam?'

'Yes, I suppose he might have been, since he would soon have been able to claim the land.'

'My uncle was at fault, but his grief made him ill. I think he knew he was being cheated—which was why, at the last, he asked me to help. After his last surviving son died, he had no one else to turn to.'

'You did not expect to inherit?'

'How could I? When I was young, he had three sons. I enjoyed staying here then, but later, after my aunt and her two younger sons died, it became a house of sorrow. My cousin John left home as soon as he could escape— only to die in an accident—and I was glad to purchase my colours and go to war. I thought it would be glorious...'

'I fear you found it otherwise,' Selina said, faltering as she saw the frost in his eyes. 'You must have been reluctant to come back to a house you remembered as being dark and empty.'

'I was extremely reluctant,' the earl said, and frowned. 'I did not expect so many changes, Miss Searles.'

'Oh...forgive me. I merely wanted to make it comfortable for you, sir.'

'As you have. I was pleasantly surprised. And the wing you are using has never looked so well. I don't know what you've done. I'm sure it did not look so comfortable before.'

'I changed the furniture, took some pretty pieces to the wing—and of course the spinet and some of the things in my parlour are Mama's.'

'Ah, that explains it,' he said. 'My own wing needs a little more of what you have, I think.'

'You wish me to return the furniture I have borrowed?'

'No, not at all. I have some things of my own which will make the changes I require.'

'Oh… I thought… Someone said they were to remain in store until you rebuild…' Selina blushed. 'Forgive me. I am presuming too much.'

'It was my intention to leave the crates as they are, but now I see no reason to do so. The house has a certain appeal it formerly lacked, Miss Searles. Henry tells me it would be sacrilege if I were to tear it down—though he concedes the east wing needs some modernisation.'

'Yes, it is not in as good a condition as the rest of the house,' Selina said. 'However, there is nothing that someone after the style of Mr Adam or Mr Sheraton could not put right—a designer with a delicate, modern touch, but simple rather than ornate. This house does not need all the French gilding that is becoming so popular—' Once again she broke off as the earl's brows rose. 'Forgive me. It is your house, not mine.'

'Yes, I rather fancy it is,' he replied, giving her a brooding look that made her stomach clench. 'However, I think I agree with you. Henry forbids me to give it the Italianate touch I first thought of…'

Seeing the glint in his eye and guessing that he was provoking her, Selina refused to rise to the bait. 'I daresay your architect will be disappointed if you change your mind about pulling the house down.'

'I have not yet completely decided,' he replied, the brooding look returning to his eyes.

'No? Well, you have plenty of time. After Christmas

we shall make plans to leave as soon as we can, and you will have the house to yourself.'

'There is no particular hurry,' he said, surprising her. 'I understand you mean to give a small party? I may invite a few friends myself—but it cannot be a large party, for I am still in mourning for my uncle.'

'As we are for Mama,' Selina assured him. 'However, she would want us to have a small dinner party, and we shall trim the house—our wing, of course—and shall give each other presents. My sisters have been grieving for too long, sir. I wish to make this as good a Christmas for them as I can; though I cannot give them expensive gifts, they shall have something nice.'

'It is an age since Christmas was celebrated in that way in this house.' The earl narrowed his eyes. 'Do you think I should bring the Yule log into the great hall? You could entertain your guests there, if you wished.'

'I think my sisters would like to see the Yule log brought in, if you will permit? However, I shall only invite six or eight guests at most. We should get lost in your great hall, my lord.'

'Yes, I suppose so. Unless my guests were here, too.'

'Would it not become a large party, then?'

'Perhaps.' He shook his head. 'We shall discuss this again another day, Miss Searles. If you will excuse me? There is much to do.'

'Yes, I know.'

Selina had bitten back the words she'd longed to say. She could easily have helped him cast his accounts, for she had a talent for figures that amazed most people who were unable to see how she could simply look at a column of figures and come up with the correct answer without making notes or scribbling. Several people had challenged her totals in the past, particularly when she'd corrected their mistakes, but when they checked, they had invariably been forced to concede that she was right.

'I shall not disturb you again, sir—but you are welcome to dine with us every night until you make your own arrangements; and I know Cook will be happy to send a light lunch to you here.'

He had thanked her, and she had left him to a task she was sure he did not wish to tackle—a task which would have been a pleasure to her. More than once she had been tempted to offer her services, but he would have thought her presumptuous, and she did not wish to try his patience, for he had been generous—almost too generous.

Had Selina not been aware that he was gaining as much from the arrangement as she, her sense of pride must have made her leave at once. It was an unusual arrangement, and one that some might think not quite proper. Yet she could see no reason why they should not live in harmony, providing both respected the invisible lines between them. They were under the same roof, and yet there were two separate households—which was quite respectable. If it were not for the library, which could be entered from either wing, they might lock their doors and be entirely shut off one from the other. She wondered if the earl had considered locking the door into his wing—or whether she ought to. However, that would mean Millie would be restricted.

Surely there was no harm in them all meeting on mutual ground?

It was no good. She must find something to fill her time—and put the earl and his affairs out of her mind. She would be here for only a few more weeks, and then she would probably never see him again.

Feeling the tightness in her chest as she realised how much pain that would cause her, Selina scolded herself for being foolish. He was not the man she had kissed in those moonlit gardens. He had been young, carefree, and on the verge of a great adventure. For some reason his life had turned sour, and he had forgotten the girl he'd promised to return to and wed one day—as she ought to have forgotten him long ago.

He had never intended to keep his promise. It had been just the foolish flirting of a young man who had drunk too much, perhaps because he was a little afraid of his future despite being on a high of excitement. Selina smiled at the memory and told herself to let it go. The Earl was a very different man. He could have no interest in a girl of her age, who had little fortune and was at the moment acting as his unpaid housekeeper.

She would take a turn in the gardens. The sun was shining, and with her fur-lined cloak about her shoulders, she would not feel the cold.

'What are you looking at?' Henry asked as he entered the library and saw his friend standing by the long French windows. He joined him, looked out, and saw the two young women. One had set up an easel and was sketching; the other was watching her and smiling as she encouraged her efforts. 'Yes, they do make a pretty picture, Robert. Which do you have your eye on—Miss Searles or her charming sister?'

'Neither,' Robert replied, and moved away from the window. 'I leave such things to you, Nor. Either of them would make you a comfortable wife, for they are both charming in their different ways.'

'Miss Searles seems very capable of running a house like this. You should take advantage while you have the chance, Robert. You spoke of needing a wife, and I daresay she might be grateful for the chance to be mistress here.'

There was a teasing look in Henry's eyes, but Robert did not reply in kind. His brow furrowed as he glanced at the accounts and wondered why he had found them so unappealing once Miss Searles had left the room.

What *was* it about her? He felt it was important, but the pain had crowded out all his happier memories. The men who had suffered and died—the women who had been raped, beaten and murdered by rampaging soldiers, some of them English—had filled his mind. Especially Juanita, the lovely young woman he'd tried but failed to save.

'I keep thinking I should remember Miss Searles,' he said. 'There is something at the back of my mind…an elusive memory. It's stupid, I know, but I feel it's important.'

'You could hardly have known her before you joined the army, Robert. It is more than seven years…she would still have been in the schoolroom.'

'How old is she, do you think?'

'I believe she will be four and twenty next spring.'

'No more than three and twenty?' Robert was surprised. 'She seems older. I would have said six and twenty at least.'

'It is her black gowns and the way she pulls her hair back,' Henry said. 'Miss Millie told me that she is thirteen next week, Amy is nearly twenty, and Selina is three and twenty. I see no reason why she should lie. I find her sometimes tactless, but always truthful. She told me my face is a bit ugly, but she thinks I was handsome once and she likes me. If I like she will marry me when she is seventeen—especially if I bring her here to live.'

'Good grief!' Robert shouted with laughter. 'The chit is certainly not lost for words.'

Henry smiled. 'I find her honesty refreshing. She has no idea of causing offence or hurt, and none is taken, I assure you.'

'You wouldn't think of it—of marrying her in a few years' time?'

'Miss Millie…no,' Henry said, but he looked self-conscious.

'You've fallen for one of them. Is it Miss Searles?' Robert narrowed his gaze. 'No, it's Miss Amy, isn't it? Good Lord! You've only known her a day, Nor. You can't be serious. You must be ten years her senior.'

'Eleven, actually,' Henry said, and smiled ruefully. 'Ridiculous, isn't it? One smile and that was it. I can't believe it happened like that…out of the blue. I thought that kind of love was a myth, but it isn't. I'm too old and too ugly for her. She was kind and made a point of looking at me without flinching, but I know she could never feel anything for me. However, I'm afraid that I've lost my heart. She's the woman I want, Robert. Not that I shall allow her to see it. She is too far above me.'

'Ridiculous! You are the best man I know—the staunchest friend, the kindest person I've ever met.'

'For God's sake,' Henry said, revolted. 'I can do without that rubbish, Robert. No, it is a lost cause. I know it. But I shall do all I can for her without making myself a nuisance.'

'She might welcome an offer. You may not be the richest man in England, but you have no need to be my secretary.'

'You would be lost without me—and I without you,' Henry said simply. 'Please forget I spoke. I should not have told you.'

'Well, you must do as you think best, of course.' Robert looked thoughtful. 'It does happen, you know—love that strikes out of the blue. I remember once at a dance in Bath… No! It can't be…' He stopped and a look of pleasure came to his eyes. 'Her name…yes, I'm certain it was Selina…but she looks so different…'

'What are you saying?' Henry asked, intrigued. 'Have you remembered where you know Miss Searles from?'

'Yes, I think I have.' Robert grinned at him. 'How could I have forgotten? It seems so long ago…like another lifetime. But of course I was a different man then.'

'You actually knew her?'

'Not exactly knew.' Robert laughed and shook his head. 'Do not ask, Nor, for I shall not tell you. I am only just beginning to remember—some of the details escape me. It was just before I left to join my regiment—and I was a little drunk that night. Actually, I was *very* drunk, but I remember this girl…she was so beautiful, like an angel…'

'You are talking of Miss Searles? She is beautiful, of course, or she might be if she dressed differently—but an angel? That implies innocence?'

'She must have been all of sixteen at the time. Too young to have been out, of course. I cannot imagine what her mama was about, taking her to a ball at that age.'

'No doubt she kept a watchful eye on her?'

'Perhaps. I cannot recall much of what happened, but…' Robert smiled oddly. 'No, do not question me with your eyes. I shall not reveal a lady's indiscretion or my own. Good grief! Do you think *she* remembers?'

'Perhaps. It depends on what you did or said that night, Robert—does she have cause to remember?'

'To be honest, I can't remember what I said to her, but I think I danced with her and then…' He shook his head. 'She must have forgotten. We only met once. Besides, I have changed so much—as has she.' He frowned. 'I wonder why she hasn't married.'

'I daresay she did not have the chance. Millie has told me their sad history. Her papa gambled their money away, and there was none for Selina or Amy to have a season, and then, when he was desperate, he killed himself. That sent their mother—who was always delicate—into a decline. The will allowed them to live in the house until she died, but then… Well, you know the rest.'

'You've certainly been busy!'

'Millie is very forthcoming—particularly when one talks to her as an equal. I think her sisters tend to treat her as a child, which she assures me she isn't. I think I agree with her. Like Miss Searles, she has had grief and responsibility thrust upon her, and she has grown up faster than her years—which is sad, in a way.'

'Yes, for all of them.'

'Miss Amy seems the least affected. She does not show it in her manner—she has a joy in life that is hard to resist.'

'You *are* smitten,' Robert said dryly. 'You should definitely propose, my dear Nor.'

'We shall see how things progress. I would marry her rather than see harm come to any of them.'

'How gallant,' Robert drawled. 'You were ever the gentleman. I fear I am a careless devil and shall not lose my heart so easily.'

'What of the angel you met so briefly?' Henry raised his brows.

'She no longer exists. Somewhere along the way, she died, as did the dashing captain of her dreams. If she ever dreamed of me. I daresay she thought me an uncouth drunk who made free with her person…and breathe a word of that to another person and I'll wring your neck.'

'As if I would,' Henry said, and smiled. 'You know, Robert, I had wondered if you were lost to us for good—but I think there may just be a chance for you yet.'

'Forget any foolish idea of romance, Nor. You may have fallen in love with Amy, but my heart is untouched. It died

one hot Spanish night, and I do not think I can feel love—
or any other decent emotion except guilt and regret.'

Robert stared at himself in the mirror as he dressed for
dinner that evening. He had decided to take Miss Searles
up on her invitation, for it seemed foolish to make the
staff serve two separate meals when they might all dine
together. And if he was a little curious to discover whether
or not anything remained of the young woman he seemed
to remember kissing in a moonlit garden, he would not
admit it—to Nor or to himself.

No, it was simply a matter of practicality. Until his
chef arrived, it would just make more work for her cook.
Besides, he did not fancy dining alone with Henry in the
great hall. They could, of course, eat in the library, but it
would still make extra work.

Tying his cravat in a style that had taken him some
years to perfect, he brushed an imaginary speck of dust
from his coat and prepared to leave. His memory of that
night in Bath was distinctly hazy. He thought he'd kissed
her, but he could not recall what he'd said or what she'd
replied. He had a feeling he'd gone a little too far and
she'd broken away from him, but his memory would not
function properly, and he did not know what had happened after the kiss.

Did Miss Searles remember him? Had she even known
his name? He must surely have introduced himself. But
she would have forgotten the small incident long ago,
wouldn't she? It could not have meant anything to her—

the clumsy attentions of a drunken officer. If she did remember, she could feel nothing but animosity towards
him.

Was that why she dragged her hair back and made herself look older? Was she afraid that he might try to take
advantage of her again?

Robert felt the heat spread over his entire body. It
was embarrassing. He had been a foolish youth, carried
away on a tide of excitement and fear. Even while he'd
longed for adventure, he'd known full well that he might
be killed.

Yet he'd come through the wars almost unscathed, apart
from a few small wounds that had healed easily. No, his
scars were mental. He would never forget Juanita's broken body, or the way she had wept in his arms before she
died as the result of the cruelty of a pack of drunken dogs.
They had thought her one of the enemy and had raped her
brutally, inflicting wounds on her body and her mind—
wounds that she could never have recovered from.

His own men. Men he'd nurtured, cherished and wept
for had behaved like animals. He'd been forced to punish
them—to hang the ringleader, a man he'd truly liked until
that moment. It had been unlike Harris to behave so ill,
for he had been generally a good man and caring of his
soldiers, but in the heat of bloodlust, he'd gone berserk
and committed the foulest of crimes. The look in his eyes
as Robert had condemned him to hang had been like a
dagger thrust in his heart.

It was not that he'd loved Juanita, but she'd helped him

to nurse Henry through his sickness and had not deserved such a cruel death.

How could he ever forget the things he'd seen and done out there? It was impossible. He was dead inside.

If he married it must be for the getting of an heir—to a sensible older woman who understood what such a marriage would be about. Was Miss Searles such a woman? Robert wasn't sure. The girl he'd kissed on a moonlit night was someone different—a dream of love that had vanished under the punishing heat of Spanish skies. Robert hardly knew her. Henry seemed to have broken all barriers and was already treated as one of their family, but he...he was the earl, and they were guests in his house.

He sighed as the elusive memory disappeared like mist. Perhaps if he found it hard to remember then she did, too. He hoped so, for otherwise... Good grief! Had he made her any promises that night? His thoughts whirled in confusion, then he dismissed them. She'd surely known he was drunk. She was far too sensible to have believed anything he'd said that night.

No, he doubted she even recalled the incident. She would have given some sign. Besides, she must have had other suitors. He could not imagine why she had not married. Even if she had little dowry, there must have been someone... Mr Breck had told him her cousin wished to marry her, but she'd taken this house on rather than accept. Clearly she was not desperate to marry or she would have accepted the offer.

Frowning, he left his bedchamber and walked slowly down the stairs, through the library. Even before he reached the dining room, he could hear laughter. Henry sounded so relaxed and happy. He hadn't heard him talking so animatedly for years.

Smiling, he walked into the room—and then caught his breath as the woman in yellow silk, trimmed with an overskirt of black lace and similar frills to her neckline, turned to look at him and memory came rushing back into his mind. She had been wearing yellow that night, too, and her hair had been dressed in becoming ringlets. The colour suited her, and if she were to soften her hairstyle a little, she would still be beautiful.

Robert felt the ice round his heart crack a little. Surely he had called her an angel…and he'd done other things, too—things that made the heat rush through his body once more.

How could he have forgotten? For one glorious hour, he had fallen madly in love. He'd always intended to contact her, to tell her that he'd meant every word, but caught up in the excitement of his first campaign, he had forgotten—and then it had all turned sour…

CHAPTER FIVE

Why was the earl frowning at her in such disapproval? Selina's heart caught. Did he think she had put off her blacks too soon? Was he shocked that she and her sisters were all wearing colours this evening? Amy had chosen lilac trimmed with grey lace, Millie a dark blue trimmed with satin ribbons of a matching shade.

'Miss Searles. You look remarkably well this evening.'

'Mama told us before she died that we were not to wear black for her longer than a month,' Selina said a trifle defensively. 'We shall continue to wear grey during the day until Christmas, but we promised that a month after her death we would wear colours in the evenings.'

'You have no need to explain yourself to me, Miss Searles,' he replied a trifle stiffly. 'I confess I was a little surprised to see the change, but I find it pleasant.'

'We talked it over and decided that we would follow Mama's wishes,' Selina said. 'However, when we drive out we shall continue to wear mourning so that we do not shock our neighbours. I was intending to ask you this evening if we might have the use of your uncle's carriage and horses tomorrow, should you have no use for them. My groom will take us, as we should like to drive into the nearest town to purchase some materials and things we need to ensure that Christmas is a success.'

'Of course you may have the carriage whenever you please. The horses are in need of some exercise, and I should take my own curricle if I wished to go visiting—which I have no intention of doing for the moment.'

'Thank you. You are very kind. I do not wish to presume on your good nature more than necessary, sir. I am sure there must be moments when you have wished us all to the devil.'

'There you would be wrong,' he replied, and smiled. 'You and your sisters have brought this house to life, Miss Searles. It will be a pleasure having you all here until after Christmas. I have not yet decided whether I shall take up residence here, but there is plenty of time for me to make up my mind next spring.'

'Your gardens will be so beautiful in the spring, sir,' Millie chimed in, without being asked. 'It would be a shame to destroy something as beautiful as this house. Do you not think of all the history that has gone on here—of the people who have lived and laughed here?'

'Millie!' Selina and Amy spoke together in unison.

'You really must not speak your mind so freely,' Selina continued, her cheeks hot as she threw a look of apology at the earl. 'You have no idea of what you are saying.'

'Miss Millie meant no offence,' Henry said. 'Robert knows that, Miss Searles.'

'Of course.' The Earl inclined his head to them, though the look in his eyes was distinctly chilly. 'It is precisely because I think of the people who lived and died here and their unhappiness that I have thought of pulling the house down and building again.'

'But surely dying is part of life?' Millie said impulsively. 'I did not mean just your uncle, sir—and I beg your pardon if I have distressed you. There must have been many generations of your family, and they cannot all have been unhappy. Your uncle must have been happy here once? Mama was unhappy towards the end, but she told us to remember the good times—and that is what we do.'

'That is enough,' Selina said sternly. 'If you cannot behave you may go to your room, Millie. I shall not tell you to curb your tongue again. We are guests here, and you will remember that, if you please.'

Millie's cheeks went bright red, and she looked as if she might burst into tears in the ensuing silence.

'No, do not scold her,' the earl said after a moment. 'She is quite right, and I have been a fool to dwell on my uncle's unhappiness. What happened to him was unfortunate, but there was a time when this *was* a happy house.'

'And shall be again,' Henry said. 'Ah, I think that is the dinner gong. Shall we take our places at table? Miss Millie, will you honour me by sitting beside me, please? I should like to talk to you about our self-appointed task in the library.'

'And what is that, pray?' the earl asked as Millie went silently to her allotted place. 'If Nor has embroiled you in one of his schemes, Miss Millie, you must not let him become a slave driver—for I promise you he will if given a free hand.'

'Some chance I have of keeping *you* to your desk if you choose to go riding or visiting instead,' Henry said, and gave him an approving nod. He smiled at Selina, as if reassuring her. 'Millie discovered that I was embarking on the reorganisation of the library, and she nobly offered to assist me.'

'She will be in her heaven,' Amy said, and smiled at him. 'It was kind of you to let her help, sir, because she lives for books. Papa indulged her, but Mama was afraid she might ruin her eyes.'

'Oh, I do not think a love of books ever hurt anyone,' Henry said. 'If you need an escort into Long Melford, I should be glad to accompany you tomorrow. I think you will find it is the nearest town, and it has several shops that you will find of interest—though if you cannot find what you need, I should be glad to send to London for you.'

'How kind you are,' Selina said, recovering her tongue. 'I think our needs are fairly simple, and most haberdashers will be able to supply us with silks and ribbons and some lace. We already have the cloth we require. A good general merchant should supply the other goods we need—almonds, essence and sugar to make marchpane, dates, nuts and preserves, of course. Cook has already started on her cake, and her puddings were made before we left home. We have been using preserves we brought with us, but must now replace them.'

'You must send your accounts to me,' the earl said.

'If we are to share our Christmas celebrations and other meals, I insist on paying for the supplies we need.'

'I should not dream…' Selina met his gaze and blushed. 'We shall provide the things I have named, sir—perhaps you would care to see to the beef, capons, ham—even a goose or even two?'

'Our farms will supply everything of that nature, of course. If that is your wish. And you must leave the wines to me. I imagine our guests would enjoy my uncle's champagne and brandy. And I have some very good Italian wine on its way, which I think we shall all enjoy.'

'That sounds perfectly acceptable,' Selina said, and smiled, her feeling of embarrassment fading. 'The vicar is dining with us soon, and we are to have a small family party the week after next. I hope you will join us for each occasion, both of you. It is Millie's birthday. She will be thirteen, going on thirty-five, and I have not yet decided what she deserves as a gift.'

'I should like a book,' Millie said promptly. 'If you really want to know. There was a Bestiary I liked in Papa's library, but that would be too expensive, Selina, so I do not mind what you give me.'

'Well, you will just have to wait and see, miss,' Selina said, and sent her sister a forgiving smile.

Looking round at the group about the table, she breathed a sigh of relief. Millie's outspokenness had caused some embarrassment, but the earl seemed to have recovered his equilibrium and had actually gone out of his way to make her sister feel less uncomfortable. As for Mr Norton, he was kindness itself—and if the way he looked at Amy was an indication of his feelings, he already cared for her.

Selina noticed that the two of them were talking animatedly. Millie was butting in now and then, but not as often as she normally did. She glanced at the earl and saw that he was looking at her in an oddly thoughtful way. A little tingle started at the nape of her neck as she saw his expression. What was he thinking? Was it possible that he had remembered her? Surely not! That kiss must have been just a small, unimportant incident to him—as indeed it ought to have been to her.

Had she been given the season her mama had intended, she would almost certainly have married. Had there been no loss of Papa's fortune and no suicide, she would not have spent so much time at home, caring for her delicate mama and her sisters. The romantic image she'd had of that moonlit garden should have faded. She should have fallen in love again...

She gave herself a mental shake. *Had* she fallen in love with Robert Moorcroft that night? Yes, of course she had. Selina had never truly understood what her feelings were—it was just an enchanted moment in her young life. That was it, of course. She had been so young—sixteen, innocent and impressionable—and Captain Moorcroft had been so handsome and bold, several years older. His kiss had inflamed her passions and captured her heart.

He was still a handsome man, but that boldness—that devil-may-care manner that had caused her to lose her senses in a madcap moment of sensual pleasure—had disappeared. Earl Banford was a different man—just as she was a different woman.

Selina was not sure whether or not she truly liked the man he had become. Surely there could be nothing left of anything either of them had felt that night? He had been drunk, and she'd been swept away on a magic carpet of enchantment. Selina was no longer that young girl. She had been foolish to allow herself even to think of that ridiculous incident—for that was all it had been, of course. Just a girl's dream of romance, and it should be shut away like her other dreams.

When Papa had died and left them almost penniless, and Mama had become so ill, requiring Selina's constant attention, she had put away her dreams of love and marriage. She knew now that even if she stretched her slender funds to the limit, they could barely afford for Amy to have a season, even if one of Mama's old friends would act as her chaperone. Selina must keep her thoughts firmly fixed on the future and the position she must seek once her younger sister had found someone she could love. Amy must be given every chance. She would not be allowed to throw herself away on the first man who offered, because with her vivacity and her looks, she might aim higher than a mere baronet. Perhaps even a marquis... or an earl?

Glancing at the earl, she found his eyes disconcertingly still on her, even though her sister was laughing and making Millie and Mr Norton laugh too. No, she could not convince herself that Moorcroft, as he would have her call him, was showing any interest in Amy. Rather he was staring down the table at *her*, an almost pensive expression in his eyes. She could not tell if he were annoyed, bored, or merely lost in his own thoughts.

He had eaten his soup and his meat, but as the puddings were carried in, he pushed back his chair, rising to his feet and saying, 'No, Henry, stay and finish your meal with the ladies. I have something I wish to attend to—if you will excuse me?'

With that he was gone. His leaving caused silence to fall once more—a silence that made Henry feel it necessary to apologise for.

'It happens sometimes,' he said. 'You must forgive Robert, Miss Searles. At times he feels that he cannot bear to see others happy. I daresay he was remembering…something that happened when we were in Spain. It haunts him still. You must not be distressed, for he did not mean to be rude.'

'There is no need to apologise, sir,' Selina said, and smiled. 'I daresay we can be rather noisy at times.'

'Would you consider calling me Henry when we are together like this?' he asked. 'I feel myself family already, and I wish to be of service to you in whatever way I can.'

'Thank you, Henry,' Selina said, and smiled again. 'I think I should like some pudding. After all, we should not let all Cook's work go to waste, should we?'

Alone in a garden sadly without the benefit of a summer moon and distinctly chilly, Robert wondered what had made him leave the company so abruptly. He had been in the habit of taking solitary walks at night in Italy, where it was very much warmer, and had come out without his greatcoat. If he were not much mistaken, winter had taken a turn for the worse and they would soon have snow.

Watching Miss Searles with her family, he'd suddenly felt like an outsider, shut out from the warmth and the intimacy of the group. Henry was obviously accepted by them as family, and he had taken on the role with evident pleasure. Always honest, he'd already admitted to Robert that his feelings were engaged, and that should Miss Amy show any preference for his company, he would offer for her, even if his chance of her accepting was slim.

She would be a fool to turn him down; although, given her chance to shine in society, the beautiful Amy Searles would undoubtedly become the rage—just as her sister had that night in Bath. The pity of it was that because of their straitened circumstances, she would probably never get her moment of glory—which was a shame for her and her family. However, should Nor propose and be refused, Robert's sympathy might be transferred to his friend. Henry's scars were not something that could be hidden away or forgotten; he must live with them for the rest of his life. Robert could sometimes forget his pain— at least for a while.

He had forgotten for a short time at dinner. Watching, rather than participating in the lively banter, he had felt happy for a while—and then something had brought the memory to mind, and he'd felt guilty that he was alive and enjoying himself. How could he be happy when Juanita lay in her grave—murdered by his men? Men he ought to have taught to behave in a civilised manner even under the heat of battle. All that beauty and passion gone for ever, only her pain a living memory that haunted him day and night. And *he* was to blame, because he had not controlled his men.

After so many years the pain should have dulled. Indeed, he hadn't been aware of it for most of the day, with his thoughts preoccupied with the house, the estate— and the intriguing family who had settled in his home. They were like cuckoos in a blackbird's nest, and if he'd had any sense, he would have found an empty house on the estate or in the village and moved them there before he arrived.

It was too late now to make them move before Christmas. Henry was enjoying life for the first time in years, and he—he had no need to be sucked into their enchanted circle. Good grief, the house was large enough. If he chose he could shut himself away in his wing and never see them...

The trouble was that he was like a moth being drawn to the flame. He wanted the warmth of their charm and beauty. His lonely soul was craving something he had lost so long ago. But his instinct told him that if he drew near, he would singe his wings.

He could never put himself at risk of such pain again. For a moment he could hear Juanita's screams, and he put his hands to his ears, trying to block out the sound. But it was inside his head and could never be shut out.

When he was restless like this, he needed exercise. It was bitterly cold, and he was not dressed for it, but he needed to run and run hard. The only way to shut out this tearing agony was to exhaust himself physically, so that when he returned to the house he would fall asleep and achieve that peace he longed for so desperately.

Selina stood at the window at the top of the hall and looked out. Trent had told her that the earl had gone into the garden without his greatcoat and had still not returned by the time the others parted and sought their beds.

'It's bitter out, miss,' the elderly butler had said. 'I fear for him on a night like this—his family had weak chests. If he were to take a chill...'

Selina understood his fear of losing the last of the line. If the earl died, the estate must pass to the Crown, and it would probably stand empty for years until every effort had been made to discover a distant relative. If none were found, it would eventually be sold, and by then it would have decayed to the stage where it would almost certainly be pulled down.

'I should not worry too much, Trent,' she'd said kindly. 'The Earl survived the war and must, I think, be stronger than his cousins were.'

'I hope so, miss—but it isn't wise. It isn't wise at all.'

Selina could not disagree. She had gone to her room but, finding it impossible to rest, had donned a warm wool robe and taken up a position at this window, which looked out over the front of the house, watching for Moorcroft's return.

It was almost one o'clock in the morning when he finally returned. She saw him walking towards the house. He paused for a moment and looked up, almost as if he sensed he was being watched. Then she saw someone go out to him. It was Henry Norton. He took hold of the earl's arm and half pushed him inside. She could hear nothing, but she sensed that Nor was using the privilege of old friends to scold Moorcroft.

A feeling of relief crept over her as she realised that Henry must have done this many times before. He would know how to care for his friend—because they *were* friends, rather than employer and secretary. Henry Norton did not work because he needed to, or to amuse himself, but because he could not leave his friend. They had both been terribly scarred but in different ways.

Selina's throat caught, and for some nonsensical reason, she found that her cheeks were wet with tears. She brushed them away. How foolish! She had hardly cried when Papa died, though she'd sobbed for Mama—to cry for a man she scarcely knew was beyond foolish. He would not want her tears.

Turning away, she went back to her room and threw her robe over a chair. She was glad to snuggle down into her bed, and after a few minutes of rather serious reflection settled down to sleep.

'You damned fool,' Henry said in a severe tone. 'This isn't Italy, and it's cold enough for snow. What the hell did you think you were doing?'

'To be honest, I didn't think,' Robert replied, and gave him a rueful smile. 'I am sorry to keep you from your bed, Nor. You really must stop watching over me as if I was your child.'

'When you start behaving like an adult, I'll go to bed

and leave you to yourself,' Henry said. 'Now, drink this hot toddy and no arguments. I don't want you going down with a chill.'

'I never have chills,' Robert said. 'I'm as strong as an ox. Give it here and I'll drink it—but you must go to bed. And, Nor...'

Henry turned as he reached the door.

'Thank you. I'm a fool and I'd be dead without you.'

'Rubbish,' Henry said. 'You are a fool, but you would survive.' He hesitated, then, 'Let it all go, Robert. I know what happened, I know you feel responsible, but you were not to blame. Those men lost their heads in the heat of their bloodlust; they weren't the first and they will not be the last. It is a beast that lives in some men, and you could not have known.'

'Yes, you are right.' Robert shivered. He was still cold all the way through, even though he was sitting by a roaring fire wrapped in blankets. 'I'm trying. Believe me, I don't want this nightmare to continue.'

'I was hiding in Italy just as you were, Robert. I've decided it's time I started to live again—and so should you.'

'I'm glad for you. I really am. You deserve to be happy.'

'I'm not sure I shall be happy. I have no right to ask her, Robert, and unless I can be sure I could make her happy, I shan't—but whatever happens I'm not going to hide away. I am who I am—scars and all. People may love me or hate me, but I'm not going to apologise for how I look.'

'No need, Nor,' Robert said, and sneezed. 'Miss Millie told you she thought you were quite ugly but she still likes you.' He laughed mockingly. 'If one sister won't have you, you may wait for the other to grow up.'

'Go to bed, Robert,' Henry said with a sigh. 'Or I may very well strangle you.'

'Aye, aye, Captain,' Robert said, and sneezed again. 'Get out of here before I infect you.'

Henry went. His expression was thoughtful as he sought his own room. Coming here might be the best thing that had happened to them both—or the worst.

'Miss Searles…' Henry Norton looked at her apologetically as he entered the breakfast parlour the next morning. 'Forgive me. I promised to escort you and your sisters into Long Melford this morning, but I fear I must cry off.'

'Oh…' Selina's heart caught as she looked at his face. 'Is something the matter, Henry?'

'I fear Robert took a chill last night,' he said. 'I waited up for him and he was frozen to the bone. As you must have seen this morning, the ground was hard with frost, even though there was no actual snow.'

'A chill?' Selina clasped her hands at her sides because she feared they might tremble and betray her. 'Is he very ill?'

'He is sneezing and he has a cough. I have forbidden him to get up, and I made him drink a hot toddy last night, but I think he is feeling rather unwell.'

'Yes, I should imagine he might.' Selina hesitated. 'I could make him a tisane to ease him before we go?'

'If your cook or your maid would do that, it would

surely suffice,' Henry said. 'I see no reason why you should put off your day of pleasure, Miss Searles.'

'If I am to call you Henry, you must call me Selina,' she said. 'I know Millie is looking forward to the trip, and I wish to buy her birthday gift, so I think we shall go. I am sure Moorcroft will do well enough in your hands. You have nursed him through worse, perhaps?'

'Actually, it was the other way around,' Henry said, and smiled oddly. 'I almost died on the field of battle, Miss Selina—and should have done so afterwards had it not been for Robert's devotion. He pulled me through by sheer force of will and because he would not leave my side. Juanita nursed me some of the time, but it was Robert's determination that I should not die that made me cling to life when it seemed there was no point.' His smile disappeared. 'It was later that Robert…when she died in terrible pain and he held her to the last…'

'Juanita? What happened to her? Is that why he looks so tortured at times?'

Was she the woman Robert Moorcroft had loved? The thought stabbed Selina to the heart.

'He cannot forget her. He feels responsible for her death. She was very beautiful, and a creature of fire and passion.' He shook his head. 'We are a sorry pair, Selina—but there is a bond between us. I should hate to lose him to a chill.'

'Yes, I am sure you would. I will ask my maid to make a tisane. She made them for all of us when we were ill— but if he is no better soon, you should send for the doctor.'

'He refuses to have one—calls them quacks. They

killed as many as they saved out there, you see. So many of our comrades died of fever and gangrene. Most prayed they would die on the field rather than suffer the ministrations of the butchers—as we called the surgeons.'

'Please watch over him, and if need be, ignore his wishes for once,' Selina said. 'I shall speak to my maid—and I will speak to you again when we return.'

Selina did her best to put her concerns for the earl out of her mind as they set out for town a short time later. It was such a treat for her sisters to visit the shops, and she had put by some guineas for the occasion, giving them both a share to spend as they pleased, while keeping the larger part to purchase the things they needed for Christmas.

The shops in Long Melford were more than adequate for their needs, and by the time they had partaken of light refreshments at the Bull Inn, which was said to be haunted, they had already completed most of their shopping and were laden with parcels. Betty and their groom then took charge of their parcels to allow them to complete their shopping, and it was past three in the afternoon when they started back for Moorcroft Hall. The light was fading. By the time they arrived, it was dark.

Lights had been lit in several of the front windows and the lanterns outside the porch were blazing. A trap drawn by one restless horse stood outside the house, and was being walked up and down by a groom Selina had not previously seen.

She went up to him, her heart racing as the pleasure

of the day was forgotten in her anxiety. 'Has the doctor been sent for?' she asked.

'Yes, ma'am,' the groom replied. 'I'm the doctor's man—he's with the earl now.'

Even as he spoke, the door opened and she saw Trent standing there in the porch. The doctor was taking his leave as Millie and Amy gathered their parcels and walked towards the butler.

'Is something wrong?' Amy asked. 'Is the earl worse?'

'He is sick with a fever, miss,' the doctor replied. 'I have given him some of a mixture that may help but he was very hot. I fear the worst—this is a family prone to succumbing to such illnesses. I should have been called earlier.'

'Is it true, Trent?' Selina asked, following her sisters in, her arms filled with parcels. 'Is the earl very ill?'

'He is in a fever, miss.' The butler could not hide his anxiety. 'Two of his cousins were took this way… I never thought it could happen again.'

Selina caught her breath. 'No, it must not be allowed to happen. Moorcroft is a strong man. He cannot be allowed to die of a fever.'

She hurried inside and dumped her parcels on a nearby sofa, then walked down the hall, through the library and into the earl's wing. She was uncertain of where the earl's bedchamber was situated, but as she started to climb the stairs, she saw Henry leave one of the rooms. He walked towards her, carrying a tray on which was a bowl of soup, cold and congealed, and a glass containing what had probably been a hot toddy.

'Miss Selina,' he said, sounding grateful to see her. 'I am glad you're home. He's burning up and he won't be sensible. He refuses everything I try to give him and says he wants to be left alone.'

'I remember Papa was the same when he was very ill of a fever once,' Selina said. 'Has he had any of the mixture the doctor left?'

'A few drops, but he spat most of it out. He hardly seems to know me… I think he is out of his mind with this fever. I've never known him this bad.'

'He was so foolish last night,' Selina said. 'Let me see him, please, Henry. I nursed my mother for many months, through fevers and chills and other sickness. I have some little skill, and I shall be pleased to do what I can for him. I refuse to allow him to die just because his cousins had weak constitutions.'

'Robert has borne so much. I fear he has given up and wants to die.'

'Well, he shall not do so,' Selina declared, setting her mouth in a hard line. 'My sisters have seen enough sorrow these past months and years. I refuse to let Moorcroft spoil their Christmas. He is going to get better if I have to—' She laughed as she saw the surprise in Henry's face. 'Well, I do not know what I shall do, but I am determined that he is not going to die.'

'Thank you…' Henry looked overcome. 'I must confess that with all the gloomy faces from the staff and the doctor, I had almost lost hope.'

'Well, I shall not,' Selina said. 'You care for him, and I

will not have him ruin Christmas. Together we shall pull him through this fever. Now, take me to him so I can see for myself how ill he is.'

'Are you sure it is quite proper, Miss Selina?'

'I do not give a penny piece whether it is proper or not,' Selina replied, with such fervour that Henry laughed.

'Good for you,' he said. 'I feel much better already.'

Selina moved towards the room he had just vacated. She hesitated one second, then opened the door and went in, her heart jumping. A huge fire was burning in the grate and the bed was piled with blankets, which the earl had tossed back. He was moaning, and as she approached the bed, he screamed out and sat up in bed, staring at her with wild eyes.

'It's a bloodbath!' he cried. 'We'll all be killed. Save the wounded...take them back through the lines...'

'Now, you can just stop all that nonsense,' Selina said firmly, and placed a hand on his brow. He was burning up and it was no wonder. She tossed back all of the blankets save for one light one, saying over her shoulder to Henry, 'It's too hot in here. See if you can pull one of the logs from the fire, please—and open the window for a few minutes to let in some fresh air.'

'The doctor said we must keep him warm.'

'There is a difference between warm and boiling hot,' Selina said in a calm, practical tone. 'I have found with fevers that it is best to keep the patient cool. However, someone must sit with him at all times, because he must not be allowed to turn icy cold. It may mean taking blankets off and sponging him with cool water—and then, later, he may need to be covered over again. I shall do what I can for him now. I suggest you leave us. Take time to eat and rest, Henry. We shall share the nursing between us—and Jane will make us a jug of her tisane, which is nicer on the tongue and of as much help as the doctor's medicine, I think.'

'Your mama's maid's tisane? Yes, he swallowed that earlier and seemed better for at least half an hour. Then the fever returned and seemed more intense.'

'I daresay the fever will wane and then return several times,' Selina replied, while fetching cool water from the washstand. 'They always seem to be so much worse at night, I find. Please go and take some rest for yourself. I have eaten, and I will have a cold supper later.'

'Thank you. I am most grateful for your help—and Robert will be too when he recovers…if…'

Selina turned and saw that Henry was in great distress. 'Oh, you poor man. You care for him so much, do you not?'

'He is my brother and my saviour and my friend.'

'As you are his, I imagine,' Selina said, and nodded. 'I cannot tell you that he is not very ill, for he is—but I have seen fevers like this before, and they are not always fatal. If one is devoted in one's nursing, the outcome can be a complete recovery.'

'What should we have done had you not been here?' Henry smiled at her and went out, leaving her to continue her work alone.

When the door had closed behind him, Selina pulled

the bedcovers right back. The Earl was completely naked, and for a moment she felt heat suffuse her cheeks, but she placed a cloth over his private parts and began her task. Another cloth was dipped in cool water and wrung out. She began to bathe his chest, arms, shoulders and his long legs, not forgetting his rather beautiful feet. Her papa's feet had not been so perfectly shaped, but then every part of this man's body was glorious—and she should not be thinking such naughty things when the poor darling was so ill.

Selina had been the one to nurse her father when he was ill, just before that last fatal trip to London. She'd sometimes thought that if she had not nursed him so devotedly, he might not have gone off to the card tables and ruined them, but that was a wicked thought and she banished it firmly. Her mother had mentioned the possibility more than once.

'If he'd died of his fever, Selina, you and the girls would have been so much better off. I have so little to leave you.'

'Hush, Mama, you do not mean it,' Selina had soothed her. Of course Mama had not meant it, but the fact remained that Papa's reckless last fling had ruined their lives.

'Juanita…'

A sobbing cry from Moorcroft's lips brought Selina's thoughts back to the moment. She had finished her bathing and drying and covered him with a sheet and a thin blanket. She placed a hand on his forehead. He was thankfully a little cooler.

'Please…do not die… I cannot bear it… I don't want to punish you but I have to… Forgive me…'

'Hush, dearest one,' Selina said, and bent over him. She hesitated, then bent to brush her lips over his cheek. 'I am here. I do not know what troubles you, but you must rest. You are safe now. I shall not let you die. I promise you will be better soon.'

She felt him relax under her soothing hand. His hands unclenched and he lay back with a sigh.

'That's it, my brave hero,' she said, and kissed his lips lightly. 'You've suffered so much, but I shan't let you die. You must live—think of my poor sisters. If you were selfish enough to die, they would be so miserable—and poor Henry would be heartbroken. Surely you cannot be so selfish as to inflict such pain on us at Christmas?'

'Mama…' Robert murmured, and a smile touched his mouth. 'Do not scold me, Mama. I did not mean to let the boar in with the sows…'

Selina smiled as she realised that her scolding tone had taken him back to his childhood. That was good, for it meant he dwelt in a time before he had known so much suffering and pain.

'Well, I *shall* scold you, you foolish man,' she said. 'If you do not take your medicine and get better soon, you will find me a hard taskmaster.'

'I'll be good, Mama,' he said, and she saw that he had drifted into a peaceful sleep.

'You must not worry too much, Henry,' Amy said as they ate a rather solemn supper in the smaller dining parlour.

'Selina is the best nurse you could find. The doctor said that Mama would have died years before she did had my sister not cared for her so lovingly.'

'Yes, I could see she was quite capable,' Henry said, and a slightly wicked smile lit his eyes. 'Robert has been ill many times, Miss Amy. He is actually very strong—but difficult as a patient. I've sometimes had to use force to get him to swallow his medicine.'

'I thought you told Selina…' Amy stopped and stared at him, understanding dawning in her eyes. 'You pretended he was worse than he is—didn't you?'

'No such thing. When I spoke to her, I was truly concerned, but she has already worked her magic,' Henry said.

'I think she enjoys looking after him. It might be the very thing for them both.'

'*Now* what are you thinking, Miss Amy?'

'Only that they are both lonely people—would you not say so?'

'Robert needs to be loved and brought back from the shadows,' Henry said, and looked thoughtful. 'They have haunted him for too long. I do not have the right to tell you the whole story, Amy—but he has suffered as no man should.'

'Yes, you can see it in his eyes sometimes,' Amy agreed. She paused, then, 'I think you have also suffered, sir.'

'I almost died on the field of battle, and after in the surgeon's tent. Robert saved my life, and my scars have ceased to cause me pain. I have accepted that I am ugly, and I can live with it. I have discovered that it means little to true friends.'

'No—how could it?' Amy said, and smiled at him in a most beguiling manner. 'All it means is that you are a very brave man, sir. I think I should not like to go to war and see the things you and the earl have seen.'

'I thank God for it that you have not,' Henry replied, looking grim. 'War is no place for ladies, Amy. Even those who have the courage to follow the drum run terrible risks—and if they die, their deaths are more terrible to bear than all the rest. The cruelty of some men shames us all—and Robert more than most, since he was their captain.'

'Is that what happened to the earl?' Amy shook her head. 'No, do not tell me. I am not a complete innocent, Henry. I can imagine the things that might happen to a woman who finds herself caught up in war. I think people do terrible things when they are seized by bloodlust.'

'And what do you know of such things?' His eyes had begun to sparkle again. 'Don't tell me—Millie read a book about the Vikings and their berserker madness, did she not?'

'Yes, of course. My sister and I are both very interested in history, which is why we were excited to come here to live. The books Millie reads are far beyond her years, and not at all suitable for a very young lady. You would think she would have nightmares, but not a bit of it. She adores reading about the most awful things, and she is wonderful at telling ghost stories at Christmas. If the earl is better, we may be in for a treat, because I'm certain she will be inspired by the Yule log.'

'Your sister is wise beyond her years—indeed, you are a remarkable family. Each one of you is unique and quite outstanding.'

'Selina could have devoted her life to the sick in another life,' Amy said. 'And Millie should be a professor of history at a university if she were a man—and what should I be? I lack my sisters' talents, I think…'

'In my opinion you lack nothing,' Henry said. 'But I shall not tell you what I think, for you will blush and tell me I am flattering you.'

Amy laughed. 'You are the one blushing, Henry, and I am a wretch to tease you when your friend is so very ill.'

'No, no—do not apologise. Your laughter has eased me, and despite a little exaggeration to your sister, the fact remains. Robert does have a nasty fever—and such fevers have been known to kill even strong men.'

'Not when my sister is in charge,' Amy said confidently. 'She has such plans for Christmas, because she is determined to make up to us for all the sadness we have endured these past months. I am certain she will bully the poor man into getting well. Selina can be a very dragon when she likes, you know.'

'And there was me thinking she was an angel,' Henry said, and laughed softly.

'Oh, she is that too,' Amy said, with the affection that never lay far from the surface. 'But do not make the mistake of thinking she is as mild and gentle as she appears.

The earl will discover that when she says "swallow your medicine", he will swallow if he knows what is good for him.'

Henry laughed. 'I almost pity him,' he said. 'Yet again I think it may be exactly what he needs to bring him back from the shadows.'

CHAPTER SIX

'SHE is worse than Major Barton,' Robert grumbled when Henry brought water to shave him some days later. 'I tell you, Nor, you have no idea what she's put me through this past week. I have been forced to swallow the vilest stuff imaginable, made to wake up and eat gruel when I wanted to sleep—and refused decent food. If I don't get out of this bed soon, I shall murder her.'

'That's better,' Henry said, and grinned at him. 'You are feeling stronger at last. Shall I tell her I can manage alone now? I know she can be a dragon at times. I have it on the highest authority.'

'Who told you that? Miss Millie or Amy?' Robert scowled at him. 'Do you know that she has been bathing me with cool water—stripping me off and washing my body while I was in that fever. Damn it, I wasn't wearing a stitch. What does that say for her modesty?'

'Did she not cover your…er…private parts?'

'Well, yes, she said so when I told her she was behaving in a most improper way for a spinster lady.'

'So you came to your senses at an awkward moment, did you?' Henry's eyes sparkled with humour. 'What did she answer you?'

'She said that I need not fear for my modesty and implied that she was indifferent to my person, for a patient has no sex and they are all the same to her. Apparently she has nursed her father, her mother, her sisters—and one occasion one of the male servants.'

'I trust you will not repeat that in company?' Henry said. 'What Selina may have said to you in confidence she would not wish known to others.'

'Selina, is it?' Robert glared at him. 'Just what has been going on while I've been out of it?'

'Nothing untoward,' Henry said with serene indifference. 'As for Selina—she is a perfect angel. I daresay you might have died if she had not been so devoted in her nursing.'

'Nonsense! You would have pulled me through. You've done it in the past.'

'You've never been quite as ill as you were that first night. I was truly worried until Selina took charge, but you soon rallied once she had cooled you down. Your fever came back three times, but between us we sat with you every moment of the day and night.'

'Well, it was generous of her to give up so much time,' Robert conceded grumpily. 'I daresay she would have rather been preparing for Christmas.'

'Yes, I imagine she might—especially since you started to get better and complained nonstop every time she gave you medicine.'

'Well, it stops today,' Robert said, a grim expression in his eyes. 'I refuse to be treated like a naughty boy. Do you know what she said to me this morning?'

'Pray enlighten me. I know you will...' Henry turned away to hide his smile.

'She said that I was a selfish man to be ill, and she was not going to let me spoil Christmas for her sisters by dying on her.'

'Yes, I've heard her tell you that a few times,' Henry said, and nearly choked as he tried to hide his amusement. 'Sorry, I've got a tickle in my throat, I think.'

'Well, don't be ill,' Robert warned. 'She will make you pay for it, Nor. I'm telling you...'

'You cannot mean it,' Henry said. 'At one time you were calling her your mama.'

'I was off my head—and she scolded me just the way Mama did when I was ill as a child, after I went swimming in the river and caught a chill.'

'I thought you didn't catch chills?'

'I don't—haven't for years.' Robert glared at him. 'You can take that grin off your face and help me get up. I'll shave myself. It seems she's got you all under her thumb.'

'If you feel able to...' Henry invited, and stood back.

Robert pushed the covers off, swung his legs over the edge and put his feet to the floor. When he stood up, he felt a most unpleasant sensation, as if the floor were rushing up to him, and sat down abruptly, cursing.

'I'm as weak as a kitten.'

'The doctor said you should stay in bed for two weeks.'

'Damned if I will. It's only just over two weeks to Christmas, and I've things to do, Nor.'

'Miss Selina said that was rubbish. She thinks you should try sitting in a chair by the window today and see how you are tomorrow,' Henry said gleefully.

'Oh, she does, does she?' Robert threw him a look calculated to kill at ten paces. 'Well, as it happens, I don't feel like getting up today. I shall stay in bed—and you may shave me this time.'

'Whatever you say,' Henry said, and hid his smile. 'Shall I bring you something to read? Or would you prefer to work on your accounts?'

'Trying to give me a headache? You can bring me a book—poetry or history or something of the kind. It's ages since I bothered to read anything other than the news sheets.'

'I'll see what I can find,' Henry promised. 'And when I've shaved you, I'll get you a plate of good beef and some pickles, if you fancy it.'

'Thank you,' Robert said, and laughed. 'How do you put up with me, Nor?'

'When you're ill, with great difficulty,' his friend said. 'I'll bring you some food, but you must eat it at once so I can take the tray away, or Selina will have me put on a court martial…'

'He wanted to get up but decided to stay in bed for at least today,' Henry said when he took the empty tray back to the kitchen and found Selina there, in the middle of stirring a rich cake mixture. 'He has cleared his tray, as you see.'

'How did you manage that?' Selina looked up and smiled. 'I am relieved to hear he is being sensible at last. When he banned me from his bedchamber, I thought he meant to get up to spite me.'

'Oh, it was easy enough,' Henry said, but refrained from telling her how Robert had grumbled about her. 'I think he will begin to get stronger now, and I daresay he will be down soon enough.'

'We've had several visitors asking after him,' Selina said. 'I was obliged to say I wasn't sure how he went on and to tell them that *you* were his nurse, as you have been much of the time.'

'Very sensible of you,' Henry said. 'I think the reason he was so annoyed was because he thought he might have compromised you. Should it become common knowledge, you might suffer some loss of reputation, Selina.'

'It hardly matters for my sake. Since I shall be seeking a position as housekeeper, my ability as a nurse will not be held against me. I care only for my sisters' sake. If Amy or Millie were to be harmed…' She shook her head. 'How can anyone outside the house ever know? No one calls in the evenings, and I have been downstairs during the day. Besides, Jobis cared for him much of the time once he began to recover. I made it clear to our visitors that the two households are separate.'

'Yes, so Amy told me. The arrangement may be unconventional, but it is not unknown for two households to live separately in one large house. If the door was locked at our side of the library, no one would ever know how easy it is to go from one to the other.'

'We must remember that when we have guests,' Selina said. 'Tomorrow is Millie's birthday. She told me she hoped the earl would be well enough to dine with us but I wasn't sure. I shall, of course, leave his nursing to you now that he is through the crisis, but we shall hope that you at least will come. Millie would be disappointed if you did not.'

'I shall certainly be there, even if Robert cannot manage it,' Henry assured her. 'Jobis can take his meal up if I am otherwise occupied. I am not certain Robert will make it downstairs by then, but I think he has a gift for Millie—as do I.'

'You really shouldn't,' Selina said, looking and feeling delighted. 'How very kind. She does set great store by her birthday, though I've told her she ought not.'

'Your sister is refreshingly honest,' Henry said. 'How much easier life would be if everyone were as open and natural as Millie.'

'Well, yes, I suppose so,' Selina said, and laughed. 'We never have a dull day with her. She was subdued when Mama was ill, and she cried as much as any of us when she died—but she recovered quickly and bounced back to her normal self. She says that Mama told her not to be unhappy, because she would be with Papa and the babies she lost. Millie firmly believes that heaven is a beautiful place, where the sun shines and birds sing.'

'It will be a shame when she loses that innocence.'

'Yes. I remember I was much the same until I was sixteen.'

Henry's gaze narrowed, intent on her face. 'Did something happen when you were sixteen?'

'I fell in love,' Selina said, and smiled. 'For one night I was gloriously happy, because I thought he loved me too—but the next day he passed me without seeing me. He went away and I never saw him again.'

'And did that break your heart?'

Selina considered. 'I felt hurt when he ignored me, but then decided he had not seen me. It was such a foolish incident, and yet for some time I believed my bold hero would come galloping back, sweep me up on his horse and ride off with me into the sunset. Then Mama took a turn for the worse, Papa started to gamble recklessly—perhaps because he could not bear to sit at home and see her fading—and I finally grew up.'

'Yes, very understandable,' Henry said, managing to look mildly interested instead of hanging on her every word, as he actually was. 'Do you ever think of him now?'

'The memory still makes me smile,' Selina replied. 'Should we ever meet again, we should be different people, of course—older and wiser. I am not suffering from a broken heart, sir. That would be nonsensical. No, no—I remember it as a young girl's dream. My dreams today are very different.'

'Would I intrude if I asked what they were?'

'Not at all,' Selina said with a smile. 'Now I think of my sisters. I hope that Amy will make a good marriage. She would shine in society given the chance. And as for

Millie—well, I hope to find a good home for her, and to be able to send her to a school where her thirst for knowledge would be answered. She had a governess until Papa died. Since then I've given her lessons in drawing, dancing and the pianoforte, but she needs no urging to learn.'

'Your wishes for her are creditable,' Henry said. 'You know that there is no pianoforte here, of course? I realise you have a spinet, but you must wish for more musical instruments. The late earl had them all removed when his wife died.'

'Yes, Trent told me something of the sort. I believe he actually had his wife's pianoforte smashed to pieces when in the first flush of his grief.'

'He could not bear anyone else to touch it. If Robert were to take up residence here, I think he would need to purchase an instrument.'

'Yes, for it is pleasant to play to one's guests in the evening, or have them play to you.'

'I must speak to him. It would be good to have one in time for Christmas, and one could be delivered from Long Melford in two days. We brought several fine things with us from Italy and from France, but mostly art, statues and furniture. Robert had some idea of hiring a house while this was pulled down and rebuilt. Now I am not quite sure what decision he has made concerning his future.'

'Moorcroft has been too ill to think of it. He was unfortunate to succumb to a fever so soon after coming here. We must pray that his illness has not given him a dislike of the place.'

'I think he is merely frustrated—for, as he says,

Christmas is creeping up on us, and there are things he wishes to do before then.'

'Of course. His architect will be here any day now. I know my sisters hope that the earl will decide not to have the house knocked down.'

'Yes,' Henry agreed. He did not enlighten her, but he rather thought Robert's plans were heading in an entirely different direction.

Hearing the knock at her parlour door the next morning, Selina quickly hid her needlework in her sewing box and called out that whoever it was might enter. She was surprised that anyone should knock, since her sisters and Henry never bothered, but wandered in and out at will, and the servants knocked and entered immediately rather than waiting.

Her heart raced when Robert walked in. He was properly dressed in skin-tight buckskins, white shirt, dark blue waistcoat and a coat that fit his shoulders superbly, his cravat exquisitely tied.

'Good morning, Moorcroft,' she said, and rose from her chair. 'Are you going visiting?'

'I *am* visiting,' he said, and smiled a little uncertainly. 'I came through the front door and was admitted by Trent, who told me I should find you here.'

'I see…' She felt a flutter about her heart. 'So this is a formal visit? Is something wrong, my lord?'

'No—not unless you are so angry with me that you forbid me your side of the house. I have come to thank you for all you've done for me—and to apologise for my abominable behaviour. Henry assures me that I was extremely ill and might have died had you not done…all you did.'

Selina smiled in relief. For a moment she'd feared he was about to ask her to leave his house. 'Please sit down, Moorcroft. There is nothing to forgive. After your generosity to us, it was the least I could do.'

'I fear I am a bad patient. I sometimes wonder why Nor puts up with me—and you had no reason to help me or to care.'

Selina glanced down at her hands. 'You were ill and deserved my help, sir. I would do the same for anyone who needed nursing.'

'Perhaps you have missed your vocation? We needed women like you out there in Spain—and later in France.'

'Yes, I am certain the men suffered greatly at the hands of the surgeons,' Selina said. 'Henry has told me something of what he and his comrades endured.'

'Henry has become a favourite with you all, I think?'

'Yes.' Selina smiled. 'It seems as if we have known him all our lives. Millie adores him. She follows him around like a puppy and he tolerates it—indeed, he encourages her to talk to him.'

'Millie selected some books for me to read yesterday. She gave them to Nor and sent me a message—she would very much like to visit me, but feared it might be thought improper, and since she did not wish to embarrass me, she had refrained, but she hoped I would enjoy the books. I thought it most kind in her—and her choice was surprisingly good.'

'Do not tell me that Millie is learning discretion?' Selina laughed softly. 'I am surprised she did not march into your bedchamber and perch on your bed.'

'As you did?' He quirked an eyebrow.

'Oh!' Selina gasped. 'Now, that is not fair, Moorcroft. In my case it was very different. You know it was.'

'As I recall, you took liberties with my person that would normally be taken only by my wife—or a trusted man.'

'I…' Her cheeks burned like fire and she clasped her hands in her lap. 'I beg your pardon if I offended, but I preserved your modesty—and the bathing helped you. If I was wrong…' She stumbled over her words and could not go on.

'I am teasing you, Selina.'

Looking up, she saw the humour in his eyes and her stomach clenched. There was such warmth, such admiration in his look, that she felt heat spread through her and a tingling sensation that she hardly dared to name.

'You are not angry? I know that I took a liberty, but all I cared for was that we should not lose you to the fever. Trent, the doctor, even Henry all seemed to think you might succumb to the weakness that your uncle's family had—and I was determined it should not happen.'

'Yes, I know.' His tone was almost caressing, and his mouth curved in a playful smile. 'I remember being scolded and told I was a thoughtless, selfish man, and if I thought you were going to allow me to spoil Christmas by dying, I was much mistaken.'

Selina laughed. 'I talk almost as much nonsense as

Millie—especially when I am worried. Everyone seemed to have given up on you.'

'But you had not,' he said. 'At one time I thought you were my mama, but I do not think she was as strict as you, Miss Searles.'

'I have a wicked tongue,' she said, but she knew he was merely teasing her and found she enjoyed it. 'As you have, Moorcroft. In you I think I have met my match.'

'Yes, perhaps,' he agreed. 'In the circumstances I think we have gone beyond the stage of Moorcroft and Miss Searles. Would you consider using my name, as Nor does, at least when we are all together here? I should like to be accepted as a friend, Selina. I wanted to tell you that there is no hurry for you and your family to leave this house. If you would prefer to find your own home, then I should not dream of standing in your way, but if you wish to stay here for a time, you are welcome.'

'That is most generous…' Selina dropped her eyes. The look in his was confusing her. She might almost think— But that was ridiculous. His heart was in Juanita's grave. He was not in love with *her*. He was showing his gratitude for what she'd done while he was ill. 'I should be glad to stay a little longer than was agreed. If I could get to know some of your neighbours and establish Amy as a respectable young lady, then if I send her to one of Mama's friends for a season in London, she may have a chance of a good marriage.'

'You do not intend to go with her?'

'In all honesty I could not afford to do so,' Selina said. 'If I sell some pearls—which I intend to ask Henry to do for me—I can give my sister her chance to shine in society. Who knows what may happen then? Should she marry well, I shall be assured of a good home for Millie—and I may then look for a respectable position with a lady of consequence.'

'Is that really what you want?' Robert's gaze narrowed. 'You are not beyond hope of a marriage yourself.'

'Oh…perhaps. But I shall have very little in the way of a portion,' Selina said. 'Amy is the one to shine for us all. I think Millie would do well at a good school for young ladies, and it is my hope that it may happen, should my sister marry a considerate gentleman.'

'I am sure her husband would think it his duty to provide a home for both her sisters if that were the case.'

'I think I should prefer my independence. But I shall do nothing until Amy is secure.'

'Supposing she were to fall in love with one of my neighbours or friends? Would you still insist that she had a season?'

'I should ask Amy what would make her happy,' Selina said. 'We have spoken of her come-out so often that I believe it is what she wants above all else—but if she changed her mind, I should not impose my will on her.'

'Are you truly the angel you seem?'

Selina looked at him, her eyes opening wider as she caught a note of irritation and disbelief. 'I would not think myself anything of the sort,' she retorted, rising to the bait instantly. 'I daresay I am often unreasonable and demanding…'

'Yes, indeed you are,' Robert said, and his eyes sparkled with a devilry she had thought lost in him, making her heart stop and then race wildly. 'When we first met I thought you an ice maiden—then I discovered that the calm front was merely that. You have a temper, Selina, and passion.'

'Moorcroft!' She rose to her feet and went to the window to stare out. A thick fog was creeping across the lawns towards the house. Just for a moment she saw a man staring at the windows of her parlour, but then he was lost in the mist and she thought she must have imagined it.

'Robert. I thought we had agreed?'

He was close behind her. His nearness made her as nervous as a kitten, and her stomach spiralled with something she thought might be desire—which she quickly suppressed. This was ridiculous...

His hand was on her arm. He turned her to face him. She made the mistake of looking up into his eyes and caught her breath. For a moment she thought he was going to kiss her and trembled inwardly, but then suddenly something came crashing through the window, making them jump back and look at each other in shock.

'Damn it!' Robert looked through the broken glass. 'There's someone out there.'

'I thought just now...but the mist closed in...' She glanced at his face. 'Who could want to frighten us?'

Robert had bent down to retrieve the missile—a large stone—which she now saw had a piece of paper tied round it. He removed the paper and read the words written there, a scowl on his face.

'The scoundrel. What the hell did he think he was doing?'

'What does it say?'

Robert handed her the scrap of paper, on which the words *'You're next. The line of the Moorcroft devils will be no more'* were scrawled in an uncultured hand. She gasped, for the implication was clear.

'It's a warning to you, Robert.'

'Apparently.' He frowned, and then looked at the shattered glass. 'You were not hurt? He might have injured you. Forgive me. I had not thought there was any danger here.'

'I do not think it was intended to harm me.' She frowned. 'Can it mean what it seems to mean? Is someone actually threatening your life?'

'It would seem so. I have thought—but, no, this does not concern you. I shall have someone clear up this mess and repair the glass. Also it seems I must employ more keepers. I have been remiss. If there is an assassin hanging around, I must make sure that you and your family are protected.'

As he turned away, Selina caught his arm. 'Why do you not leave this to Henry? You are just up from your bed.'

'And completely better. I assure you there is no need to worry—either for my health or for any other reason. I'm very hard to kill—as the French discovered.' He smiled at her. 'Please say nothing to your sisters. I would not spoil their Christmas on any account.'

'Do not...' she said faintly. 'I shall keep your secret because you ask it—but they would all be more concerned for you than their celebrations.'

'You have my word nothing shall mar our festivities,' he said, and then walked to the door and left.

Selina stood staring after him, and then left the room and went to the library, where she knew her sisters were both ensconced before the fire with their books and sewing.

Henry was working on something, but when she beckoned to him, he came to her and a few quiet words later left in search of his friend.

'Where has Henry gone?' Millie asked. She picked up a leather journal with a brass clasp and showed it to her sister. 'He bought me this for my birthday. I opened it at once, though I knew you would say I should wait until dinner, when you and Amy will give me your gifts.'

'I thought it would be more fun to open them this evening,' Selina said, 'but you will find my present on your bed, and I think Amy may have placed hers there too. You may open them now if you wish.'

'Thank you, dearest Selina.' Millie threw her arms about her, hugged her and ran off.

Amy looked at her, arching her brow. 'What was that about?'

Selina told her about the stone through the window, but omitted the threatening message. 'I daresay it is a disgruntled labourer—perhaps someone who was dismissed when the late earl decided to close the house.'

'How unpleasant,' Amy said. 'You were right not to

tell Millie. She would never stop talking about it. Do you suppose there is any danger to us?'

'Very little—if any at all,' Selina said. 'However, Moorcroft will increase the number of keepers patrolling the grounds, and that should deter any foolishness in future.'

'I remember something happened when Papa dismissed one of the footmen at home,' Amy said. 'He threw mud at the front door, and there were other small incidents until Papa had him arrested.'

'Yes, well, I expect the earl will see to it—and Henry will help him,' Selina said. 'Please say nothing. Moorcroft does not want any fuss over the incident.'

'Of course not. It is something for the gentlemen to see to, is it not?' Amy stood up and gathered her sewing. She walked to the window and looked out. 'The fog is getting thicker. It's freezing too, which is always horrid. I would prefer snow to this. It is as well we visited Long Melford while the weather held.'

'Yes, it is,' Selina agreed. 'What did you buy for Millie for her birthday? I gave her a book of poems and a lace handkerchief I'd made.'

'I made her a pencil case and bought her a pretty comb for her hair.'

'She will be pleased, I daresay.'

'She was pleased with Henry's journal. I wonder what Robert has for her...'

'Robert?' Selina arched her right eyebrow. 'Does he have a gift for her?'

'I believe he intends to give her a present this evening. Henry hinted as much when I saw him earlier.'

'Well, she has been spoiled this year,' Selina said. 'I am embroidering handkerchiefs for both Henry and the earl for Christmas. I made a study of Moorcroft's family crest and it looks very well.'

'How clever of you,' Amy said. 'I have made a silk scarf for Henry, and I thought of something similar for Moorcroft, but your handkerchiefs are a much better idea.'

'I expect he has loads of them.'

'Not with the Banford crest—besides, yours will be exquisite because they always are. My plain sewing cannot compare with your embroidery, dearest—and you know it to be true.'

'I would not say that…' Selina murmured, because her mind was elsewhere.

'Are you worried about something?' Amy looked at her sister oddly. 'Is there something you haven't told me?'

'If I have not then I may not,' Selina said, and smiled, bringing her mind back to the subject of Christmas. 'Now, have we thought of everyone? I should not wish to miss any of the servants. They must all have their gifts.'

'Yes, of course. Millie has been helping me prepare. I think we shall have presents for everyone ready in time. We have made lace nightdress cases for Jane, Cook and Betty from one of Mama's old gowns—and I know you will give them money, for you told me so.'

'Yes, just a little gift—though not what Mama would have given before…' Selina hesitated. Should she tell her sister that they might not have to leave as soon as they had expected, or should she wait and see?

For a time in the parlour that morning, anything had seemed possible, but the brick through the window had left a shadow hanging over them once more. She'd seen the teasing light die from Robert's eyes and knew that he'd been driven back to that dark place he'd seemed to have thrown off for a little while.

Who could want to kill him—and why?

She remembered the chilling message. Someone hated the Moorcroft family. Was it possible that the late Earl's son had been murdered rather than meeting with a fatal accident?

Selina felt cold all over. If anything were to happen to Robert now...

She had sensed the barriers crumble as she nursed him, her feelings overcoming her natural caution. While he'd been ill she had been able to admit that she was in love with him—that he meant more than she could ever allow him to see.

Had she always loved him? Was she still the foolish child who had dreamed a dream of romance under the moonlight?

Selina knew that she had grown up. Therefore, if she loved Robert Moorcroft, it was the man she had met again so recently who had touched her heart. Was it possible to fall in love so swiftly twice? She would have dismissed it as nonsense had it not happened to her once at that ball and then a second time—when she'd seen him lying helpless in his bed.

Her feelings had swept over her in a great rush, and she'd known that she could not let him die because he meant too much to her. It was ridiculous, of course. She could not expect that he would feel the same towards her—though his gratitude *had* driven him to offer her friendship and the chance to stay on here in this house for a while.

Was she foolish to have dreams? If Robert cared for her—if he liked her enough to offer more…

No! The practical Selina reasserted herself. To ask for more would be greedy and stupid. Love was something that happened, and it had happened to her—but that did not mean it was mutual.

Yet his concern when that stone had broken the window had been for her and her sisters. Was it just the natural concern of a gentleman for the ladies living under the protection of his roof—or could it possibly mean more?

Selina shook her head as the gong for nuncheon sounded in the hall. She would not embarrass him or herself by presuming that the look in his eyes just before the unpleasant incident with the stone meant anything other than a gentleman's natural exuberance on having recovered from a nasty illness—and gratitude to his nurse.

'It points to what we feared—that someone wants revenge on your family,' Henry said, and read the scribbled note again. 'Have you any idea what your uncle or his son may have done to incur such hatred?'

'None whatsoever,' Robert said, and frowned. 'I had

considered the idea that my uncle had an enemy, but thought it a figment of my imagination.'

'You think that the late earl's death may not have been from his illness?'

'It was sudden. His doctors thought he had a year or two left if he resided in a country where the climate was more temperate. Had he not been caught in a sudden storm…who knows what might have happened to him? The accounts show he had been cheated of money over some years.'

'This is serious, Robert. If he means business, you must be always on your guard.'

'Yes, it appears so. I am well able to take care of myself—but I am concerned for the ladies. I had told Selina that she was welcome to stay for as long as she wished, but if I thought she was in danger in my house…'

'Yes, that is a concern,' Henry agreed, smiling inwardly as he noted the unconscious use of Selina's first name. 'However, the note seems clear enough. It is you he wants out of the way—the question is, why? You cannot have harmed him. We have hardly seen anyone since we arrived here, and in Italy we had friends but no enemies.'

'I was not the earl then,' Robert reminded him. 'His hatred seems directed against the family. I wonder…' Henry's brow rose as he hesitated. 'I thought I was the last of the line, but…'

'You think there may be a forgotten cousin who might inherit if you were dead? Surely the lawyers would know if that were the case?'

'I asked my uncle if there was anyone else. I was reluctant to come here, as you know. He said I was the last legitimate heir.'

'So there might be a bastard?'

'I suppose he might have meant that.' Robert frowned. 'I ought to have enquired further—but I do not see how my death would benefit a bastard. As things stand, the entail ends with my death. If I leave no will, the estate will then pass to the Crown, as well as the title. A bastard cannot inherit the title or the money.'

'Yes, that is true. So why would he wish to kill you? Unless…'

'You have thought of something?'

'There is one possibility that occurs to me—but if you are the last of the line…'

'Perhaps it is not actually about money or inheriting but merely revenge.' Robert was thoughtful. 'I shall write to Mr Breck about various things, ask him to make enquiries—I shall also enquire locally, to discover if someone had a grudge against my uncle or my cousin.'

'It might well be as simple as an unfair dismissal in the mind of a former employee.'

'Revenge for past slights?' Robert nodded. 'That makes sense—but why me? What can I have done? I do not even know who is behind this.'

'You might know more than you think.' Henry hesitated, then, 'I was going over the accounts you did not finish earlier this morning. Selina saw me and pointed out several discrepancies that were difficult to spot—she's a marvel with figures. Quite puts me to shame.'

'She seems capable in many ways,' Robert said, his

frown deepening. 'Are you suggesting that this person—
or persons unknown—was attempting to completely ruin
my uncle?'

'It is possible that the estate was being systematically
robbed. Perhaps your uncle suspected it but did not know
how to stop it. He was too old and ill to pursue the rogue.'

'I think you may have hit upon the answer,' Robert
said. 'I am now a target because whoever it was fears that
I have discovered his wrongdoing and believes I *shall*
pursue him.'

'As you will, once you have all the proof you need.'

'It seems most likely to be the agent my uncle dismissed just before he left for Italy—wouldn't you say so?'

'A man by the name of Harvey Simpson.'

'If that is his real name—which is in doubt. If he believes he has been slighted by…his father?' Robert looked
struck. 'Good grief, do you think that was it? Could this
man be my uncle's bastard?'

'It would explain why he hates the family—especially
if the late Earl cast off his mother. If he subsequently refused to acknowledge his illegitimate child…'

'But to murder people?'

'I have known men to murder for less,' Henry pointed
out. 'We must make further enquiries, Robert. Trent has
been here for years. He might have heard rumours of a
bastard child.'

'I wonder what his real name is—the name of the
woman who was my uncle's mistress, I suppose.' Robert
frowned. 'I cannot imagine him taking a mistress while
his wife lived. He adored her. And yet he must have done

so if his bastard is old enough to have obtained a position as agent here.'

'Do you suppose your uncle knew he was employing his bastard?'

'I doubt it. Had he wished to acknowledge him, he could surely have done so—especially after his sons died. I can understand why he might wish to keep it a secret before that—but why not do something for him at the last? He might have tried to overturn the entail or adopt this man outright.'

'Surely that is what this man feels?' Henry said. 'He must believe the late Earl's refusal to acknowledge him to be a slight that deserves punishment.'

'If this bastard even exists at all. You realise we are simply speculating at this stage, Nor? Inventing a case to fit the situation. We could be completely wrong. We do not even know for certain that murder was done. It could all be down to a series of tragic accidents.'

'Yes, that is true,' Henry agreed. 'But why else should someone try to ruin your family—and quite possibly kill one or two of them? Why should he threaten *you*?'

'The threat to me may be intended to deter me from pursuing him,' Robert said. 'But I have no answers, Henry. Only more questions.'

'What do you intend to do next?'

'I shall write to Mr Breck. I shall also speak to the vicar and employ agents to look into the possibilities. We need more keepers to patrol the grounds, but nothing further until the New Year. Selina would never forgive me if I spoiled Christmas for her sisters.'

Henry nodded. 'Have it your own way. I know you, Robert. You will not rest until you find and punish the culprit—especially if he murdered your cousin and your uncle.'

Robert's eyes were flinty. 'If he did, he deserves to hang for his crimes. Yet we must tread carefully, Nor. No harm must come to our guests. If the rogue becomes more dangerous, I may have to ask our friends to leave us for a while—but not until after Christmas.'

'Are you happy, dearest?' Amy asked as she tucked the bedcovers around her younger sister. 'Did you have a good birthday?'

'Yes,' Millie said, and kissed her. 'I've never had so many lovely gifts—and I cannot believe that the earl gave me such a book.'

'It is lovely—and valuable, I think,' Amy said. 'You said you wanted a Bestiary and now you have one. You are very lucky.'

'Did I thank him enough?' Millie said seriously. 'It came from his own personal collection, you know. I wanted to hug him but I thought he might not wish it.'

'You thanked him ten times. I think that was quite enough,' Amy said, and smiled. 'Go to sleep now, my love. Tomorrow you must work on your Christmas gifts for the earl and Henry.'

'Yes, I think the earl will like the drawing I made of his folly,' Millie said. 'I went there again early this morning before the mist closed in, just to make sure I had all the details right. It was very odd. Each time I've been before the door was locked, but this time it was wide open. I looked in and called but no one answered.'

'You did not go in, I hope? You know Henry told you it might not be safe? There is some question of the tower being in poor repair.'

'I remembered, and I was very sensible,' Millie said. 'I'm thirteen now and no longer a child. Do you think I should tell Henry what I saw?'

'Yes, I think you should tell him. If you explain about the drawing, I'm certain he will not spoil your surprise by telling the earl.'

Millie nodded. 'He's a good sport, isn't he? You like him a lot, don't you, Amy? I think he wants to marry you. I offered to marry him when I grow up—but I think he wants you.'

'Now, that is foolish,' Amy said, her cheeks pink. 'Go to sleep and tomorrow you can tell Henry what you saw at the folly…'

CHAPTER SEVEN

'I KNOW it isn't important,' Millie said the next day as she joined Henry in the library, where he had begun to list some of the books he'd arranged by category. 'But Amy thought I should tell you just in case someone does not realise the tower is unsafe.'

Henry looked at her thoughtfully. 'I shall speak to Robert about this when he returns from his appointment with the vicar this morning. Do not worry, Millie. I shall not spoil your surprise, but this may be more important than you realise—and we do not wish anyone to be hurt, do we?'

'Oh, no. It was dreadful when the earl was ill. Selina was so upset. I hate to see her cry. She only cried once when Mama died, and not at all when Papa… Well, we don't talk about that. It would be awful if someone was fatally injured and Christmas had to be cancelled.'

'Yes, it would,' Henry agreed, and smiled at her. 'I have not looked forward to celebrating it so much since I was a lad in short clothes. Do you suppose there are decorations in the attics here?'

'We brought all ours with us,' Millie said. 'And you are going to bring the Yule log into the great hall, so we could decorate that with greenery, holly and mistletoe. I saw some beautiful holly near the earl's folly. We could all go to gather it and divide what we find between our two wings. If we're going to have the Christmas Eve party in the hall, we must make kissing boughs.'

'Yes, indeed we must,' Henry agreed. 'I shall look in the attics and see if I can find anything that we might use to make our wing more festive—and I'll take a look at that holly. Thank you for telling me about the unlocked door.' He hesitated, then, 'Have you finished your sketching at the folly?'

'Oh, yes. I shan't need to go there again—except when we all go to gather the greenery. If you are trying to warn me to be careful, Henry, there is no need. I am very sensible now I'm thirteen.'

'Yes, I know you are,' he agreed, and hid his smile.

What she had told him was interesting. Very interesting indeed.

Robert left the vicarage feeling pleased with himself. It had been a good move to ask the Reverend Hadder for his advice about Christmas and the old traditions, for the vicar had been full of ideas for a children's party at the vicarage hall.

'If you would finance the party this year we could give

all the children from the farms and the village extra gifts as well as food for their families.'

'I shall be delighted to do so,' Robert had told him. 'I am not ready to give a party for all the villagers this year, sir. My uncle is too recently dead. But we shall hold a small private reception on Christmas Eve, and I should be pleased if you and your family would attend.'

'We should be delighted, sir. It will be wonderful to have a family at Banford Hall again—and if you make the customary gift to the villagers, they will be eager to help you in any way they can.'

'Of course all the traditions shall be upheld,' Robert assured him. 'You remember the old days well—before my aunt and my parents died, I imagine.'

'Oh, yes, my lord. I remember the first time you attended church with your dear mama—such a lovely lady. Your aunt was always sickly, of course, as were two of your cousins—though we thought John stronger.'

'I wonder…did you ever hear of any scandal attached to my uncle's name, sir? Any mention of a secret bastard?'

The Reverend Hadder looked shocked. 'No, indeed, I have not, my lord. The late earl was a pillar of society and he worshipped his wife. I am certain there was no clandestine affair. Even after she died he would not have… No, no, you have that wrong.'

'I am glad to hear it. There was some tale of it, but I thought it could not be right. However, it seems that someone may have held a grudge against the family.'

'A grudge, you say?' The vicar looked thoughtful. 'I do recall something—some unpleasantness—a few years back. It was before your aunt died, if my memory serves me right, but I fear I cannot quite recall what it was. I think threats were made against the late earl and some of the estate property was damaged. I think the dower house was burned down and they said it was deliberate—but it is too long ago for me to remember what started it all. I was just the curate here then, you see.'

'The dower house…' Robert mused, nodding. 'Yes, I do recall that happening. I was perhaps fifteen or so and away at boarding school. I spent Christmas with some friends that year, and my father told me there had been a fire when I saw him in the New Year.'

His expression became grave, because it was not long after that incident that one tragedy had piled on another and the earl's family—and his own—had been plunged into a deep, dark place from which he had been desperate to escape. His own father's death had been a bitter blow for a young man.

Robert felt ice at the back of his neck. He had never questioned the accident which had led to his father's death. These things happened, and his had been an unfortunate family. Neither parent had died as a direct result of the accident, but he had been seriously injured, and the resulting fevers and infections had been fatal.

Could that accident have been part of a chain of vicious revenge against the family? He felt sick at the idea, and could hardly keep from spewing up his guts in front of the vicar.

'I'm sorry not to be able to help you more, my lord.'

'You may already have helped more than you think,'

Robert told him. 'However, should you think of anything—what caused the unpleasantness with whoever it
was—I should be grateful to hear from you.'

'Certainly, certainly. I shall get out my old diaries. It
has always been my habit to write of what is happening
around me, my lord. I daresay I shall find what you need.'

Robert had taken his leave and begun the ride back to
what he had begun to think of as home, despite his initial
determination to pull the old house down. He had discovered the house had a certain charm, and his plans to
improve the east wing, add more modern kitchens and
refurbish his own would possibly be all that was required.
Yet in his heart he knew the changes were more to do with
the people living in his house than the house itself. If the
Searles family were to depart, it might soon become the
empty mausoleum it had once seemed.

He was aware of one or two people tipping their hats
to him as he rode through the village. He acknowledged
their salute and smiled. Whatever resentment had existed,
it did not seem to have spread to the villagers. He could
not imagine what might have caused someone to feel such
deep resentment against the family that they would attempt to ruin them all—and perhaps worse.

Yet he could be making a mountain out of a molehill.
The stone and the cryptic message might be a trick, and
all the deaths in his family simply natural illnesses. Even
the fire at the dower house might have been due to care-
lessness, or a spark caused by a freak bolt of lightning
during a storm.

Henry had written to London, seeking agents who

could work in secret to discover what lay behind the systematic fleecing of the estate and the recent threat to his own life, but perhaps Robert was making too much of it. His uncle might have dismissed an employee who had somehow found a way of cheating him; it could be as simple as that and if so would be easily settled once he found the culprit.

Riding by the folly, which he'd enjoyed playing in as a young lad, Robert decided to take a look at the structure. Trent had told him that his uncle had declared it unsafe some years earlier, and as a result it had been locked and neglected ever since. However, as he approached, he saw that the door was hanging wide open on its hinges, blowing back and forth in the wind. He felt again a touch of ice at his nape, because the key was supposed to be kept in the estate office and was available only to him or trusted servants. Who could be in there?

Dismounting, Robert looped his horse's reins over a bush and approached cautiously. He had a pistol in his coat pocket. Reaching for the weapon, he drew it and put his finger on the hammer, cocking it ready in case the intruder set upon him. He reached the door and looked at the flight of stone steps that led to the top. According to Trent, it was unsafe in places.

'Is anyone there?' Robert called. He waited a moment, then heard a sound coming from the top of the tower. 'You'd better come down, whoever you are. This place isn't safe…'

There was no reply, but he hadn't expected one. He put his foot on the first step cautiously, mounting it slowly and carefully. As far as he could see, the stonework was in perfectly good order and not dangerous. It was mere moments before he reached the top and the little room that provided a viewing tower over the estate. He heard the noise again, and then something came straight at him. His finger jerked on the hammer, but he was in control and he did not fire—which was just as well for the unfortunate pigeon, which was desperate to escape and flew past him and down the stairs.

Reaching the empty room at the top, Robert laughed as he realised that the only occupant of the tower was a bird. He had no idea why his uncle had forbidden anyone to use the folly, because it was clearly in excellent repair. However, he had a feeling that someone had been here recently. The floor looked less dusty than it ought, and there were the remains of what appeared to be a half-eaten loaf of bread in a corner of the room: perhaps what had drawn the pigeon to seek a place to roost when the door was left open. As he was about to leave, he heard a sound down below and realised someone was shutting the door.

'Wait a moment!' he called. 'I'm up here. I'm coming down now.'

He went quickly down the steps but the door had been shut, and when he tried the latch, he discovered that it was locked. Robert hammered on the door and called out for whoever it was to return and let him out but there was no answer.

Damn it! He had not been prepared for a trick like that. Robert frowned. The door was stout and would resist his attempts to break it down; all that would result in would be a sore shoulder.

He ran back up the stairs and looked out. A horse was riding away—his horse, if he were not mistaken—its rider bent over its neck, as if he were in a hurry to get away. From this distance it was impossible to see who it might be, but the man was slight and wore a hood over his head.

'Damn you.'

Robert was furious with himself for being taken in by such a foolish trick. He should have ignored the open door and returned with Henry to watch his back. It just had not occurred to him that someone would seize the opportunity to lock him in the tower.

What possible outcome could the culprit hope for by playing such a trick? Robert frowned as he made his way back down to the door. Had he not been carrying his pistol, he would undoubtedly have been trapped for hours, perhaps days, before someone thought to look here.

A slither of ice trickled down his spine. Could the culprit have been hoping that he would never be found? The spectre of a slow death by starvation made him feel icy cold.

Ridiculous! Henry would have raised the alarm by nightfall and men would have scoured the estate. He would only have had to break the glass at the top of the tower and shout loudly enough—but it was bitterly cold, and it would not have been a pleasant experience to be trapped here, even for a few hours.

Robert thanked providence for his habit of always carrying a loaded pistol. He retreated to a safe distance and fired at the lock. The wood shattered, and it was then the work of a few minutes to force it open. He was frowning as he left the Folly and began the long walk back to the house.

He could no longer doubt that he had an enemy. Yet if the fellow had wanted him dead, why had he not just entered the folly and killed him? It would have been easy enough to make it look like an accident—a blow to the head and then a fall from the window or down the steps should have been sufficient.

Perhaps his enemy knew that Robert would not be as easy to dispose of as a sick old man.

His brow furrowed as he wondered if his cousin's accident had been murder—and what of the earl's sudden death? Had it been the natural end to a sick man's life, or had his been death hastened by some vicious act of spite?

Robert was feeling angry by the time he arrived at the house. If his horse had gone for good, he would feel guilty, for the beast had served him well and did not deserve the fate that might await it.

As he entered the house by a side door, Henry was talking with his groom in the hall. They both turned to stare at him and he saw relief in their faces.

'We were just about to start a search for you,' Henry said. 'Your horse came home by itself. Did you have an accident?'

'Something of that nature,' Robert said, and glanced at the groom. 'Is Marlin hurt, Jed?'

'No, my lord. He just came cantering into the stable yard on his own. We thought you must have taken a tumble.'

'No, I left Marlin tied to a bush and someone made off with him. I thought that was the last we should see of him. I am glad the thief thought better of it.'

'It wouldn't have been easy to sell a horse as distinctive as yours, my lord,' Jed replied. 'He's a fine beast—and the saddle has your crest on it. People would have been suspicious—especially once it became known your horse had been stolen.'

'Well, I am glad to have him back. Give him a good rubdown and a bucket of hot bran mash to make sure he takes no harm.'

Henry looked at Robert through narrowed eyes as the groom left them, clearly much relieved. 'Now tell me what really happened.'

He nodded when Robert repeated his tale but showed no surprise.

'You do not seem surprised, Nor?'

'Millie had seen the folly door left open. I was going to speak to you when you returned from the village. It didn't occur to me that you would see it for yourself and go to investigate.'

'Who would play such a trick?' Robert asked. 'Why just lock me in the tower? Why not try to finish me off—and why steal the horse and then let it go knowing it would probably find its way home? Once the horse was found, it was inevitable that a search would be made—much sooner than if the horse hadn't come home.'

'It doesn't add up,' Henry agreed. 'If this person wants to kill you, it was his perfect opportunity. You were armed, but he couldn't have known that. He could have shot you—or tried to knock you down the stairs—but instead he locks you in the folly and steals your horse, which he then abandons.'

'Perhaps he doesn't truly wish to murder me—just frighten me.' Robert was puzzled. 'I don't understand, Nor. A true villain would not have played such a trick. It is almost like a child's trick. You don't think... Millie wouldn't have done it, would she?'

'Millie has been here helping me all morning. She wouldn't have done such a thing, Robert. How could you even think it?'

'No, I beg her pardon. It's just that I have a feeling something is hiding right under our noses and I don't know what it is.'

'Well, be careful when you go out alone,' Henry said. 'If the culprit was unarmed and shocked to see that you had discovered he'd been using the folly, he might have acted on impulse—more as a warning than anything else.'

'Yes, it could have been a warning,' Robert said. 'I think our theory about the bastard may have been wrong, Nor. The vicar seems to recall some unpleasantness a few years back but cannot be more precise. I must keep an open mind here. It would be a mistake to think someone wanted to murder me in hope of the title and the estate— no, I believe there is a deeper mystery here, but for the moment I have no idea what it might be.'

'Well, we must hope the agents we've sent for can discover it,' Henry said. 'I think we must carry on as usual for the sake of the ladies—but keep a sharp eye out from now on, Robert.'

'I shall have new locks put on the folly. If someone has been using it to hide in, they will not find it so easy to get in again.'

'How did they get the key in the first place? We keep all the keys in the estate office, and I have the key to that. I've already checked and our key to the folly is still there.'

'Whoever it is must have had access to the estate office at one time, and perhaps a copy once existed,' Robert said, and frowned. 'It all seems to point to the agent my uncle dismissed when he let several of the servants go and came out to see me in Italy—Harvey Simpson.'

'It may all be much simpler than we thought—just a case of a rogue agent in fear of being brought to book for his crimes,' Henry said.

'Yes, possibly,' Robert said. 'And he is right to fear, because fraud and theft may be the least of his crimes.'

'Your uncle's death?'

'Once again this is conjecture. I return to it merely because I have no other theory to replace it.'

'But since your uncle took no further action against him, Simpson had no real reason to murder him,' Henry pointed out.

'My uncle was old and sick; his death might have been natural—just as my cousin's accident might have been—but someone is trying to frighten or harm me. If not because of the fraudulent accounts, then why?'

'I wish I could tell you,' Henry said. 'I hope your Bow Street Runner will be able to solve the mystery.'

'There is a visitor to see you, ma'am,' Trent said, hovering in the door of the little parlour where the ladies were busy with their various tasks. 'I showed her into the blue parlour, for I did not think you would wish to be disturbed here.'

'No, indeed. I prefer this room to be private so that we may leave our things where we choose.' Selina stood up and brushed at the skirt of her gown. Tiny pieces of silk clung to the grey wool, and she picked them off before following Trent from the room and through to the front of the house.

He threw open the door of the blue parlour with a flourish. 'Miss Selina Searles. The Comtesse Adelaide de Saracosa, Miss Searles.'

Selina entered the parlour, seeing a young woman poised by the window overlooking the imposing drive. Long blonde locks curled down from beneath her bonnet, and when she turned, they framed her lovely face with the green satin.

'Miss Searles,' she said, and smiled and offered her gloved hand. 'Forgive me for intruding. You must be wondering who on earth I am.'

'I do not believe we have met, ma'am,' Selina replied easily. 'Are you perhaps a friend of my mama? She had many friends I was not acquainted with, I believe.'

The comtesse seemed to frown, to hesitate, before inclining her head. 'Yes, of course. I knew her briefly when

I was just a child in petticoats. My mama was her friend but they lost touch some years ago. I returned from Italy recently to learn that your dear mother had died and that you had been cast out of your home.'

'We were not exactly cast out,' Selina replied, wondering why she had a tingling sensation at her nape. 'Our cousin inherited the estate, because it was entailed. He offered us a home with him but we preferred to be independent.'

'Yes, so I've heard,' the comtesse said. 'You were fortunate that the earl allowed you to become his tenants—though I believe it is for a short time only?'

'Yes, perhaps. I am not yet certain of the future. We are settled here until sometime next year.'

'How convenient. Sharing the house is an unusual arrangement—but if you are brave enough not to care what the gossips say…' The comtesse shook her head. 'No, I shall not repeat such scandalous lies, my dear. I am perfectly certain everything is respectable and that the two residences are separate.'

'Yes, quite separate,' Selina replied, feeling her hackles rise. 'I am not sure why you are here, ma'am.'

'You do not wonder why I know that everything is respectable?' The comtesse smiled. 'Dear Robert asked me to be his wife quite recently. I told him I would consider the matter. I have done so, and here I am. My mind is made up and I shall give him my answer soon. However, it would not do for me to stay with him and Mr Norton—and I do not have friends in the district. I am certain you could not refuse me a bed for a few days. It would surely be some recompense for Moorcroft's generosity in allowing you to stay here.'

Selina's mind whirled with shock. Moorcroft had asked this beautiful woman to marry him and she'd told him she would consider her answer—now she was here and it was obvious what her answer must be. She had come here prepared to be married, and she had clearly heard gossip concerning the nature of the relationship between the earl and his tenants. Her pointed disclosures were intended to make certain Selina understood the situation.

'You wish to stay here, in my part of the house?'

'Would that be so impossible for you? You must surely have a guest bedroom? You cannot expect me to stay with Moorcroft without a chaperone?'

'No...' Selina swallowed hard. She could hardly tell this woman that she did not wish for a guest. 'I do not know if you realise, but I have few servants. We are still in mourning and live very quietly here—though Moorcroft plans a party for Christmas, I believe.'

'I shall not be much trouble to you,' the comtesse said. 'I have my own maid, who will naturally wait on me and take care of my clothes and my room. My grooms may assist yours and carry out any duties you wish.' She smiled in a way calculated to charm. 'I knew you could not refuse me. Moorcroft would not ask, for he would never impose, but I am sure he would expect you to give me a room in your wing.'

'I see no harm in it,' Selina said, though she did—she did. How foolish she'd been to allow herself to dream, or to see more in a man's eyes than was truly there.

Of course Earl Banford would not be interested in a woman like Selina Searles, who had neither great fortune nor family to recommend her. He had been kind and generous—but she ought to have known that he was too far above her. The Comtesse de Saracosa was clearly both rich and well connected. She was also a widow, and by the look of her mouth could be sulky and sharp-tempered.

But now Selina was being spiteful, because the comtesse's arrival had thrown her plans into confusion and spoiled her dreams of a Christmas miracle. Ever since the moment when Moorcroft had recovered enough to come downstairs and speak to her in the parlour, Selina had begun to cherish a dream that he was falling in love with her—as she had with him. Now that dream had splintered into a thousand pieces and must be forgotten.

Lifting her head, Selina fixed her smile in place. 'Forgive me, ma'am, my manners are appalling this morning. I was surprised by your unexpected arrival—and by your news. Naturally there must be a room here for the earl's…intended bride. I shall ring and have the servants prepare the yellow guest room. It is, I believe, the best room we have and it should be yours. I have been using it but my things can be moved to another room in an hour or so. I shall have some refreshments brought to you.'

'Any room will do for me, Miss Searles. Please do not put yourself to any trouble.'

'Oh, no, it will not be any trouble,' Selina replied. It would be a wrench, for she loved the room she'd made her own, but it *was* the best room, and in the circumstances she would have to make arrangements to move as soon as possible after Christmas. 'Would you wish me to ask Moorcroft to come and speak to you?'

'Not until I've had a chance to settle into my room and change my gown. One feels so untidy after a journey—do you not agree?'

'Yes, I expect so,' Selina said. 'I'll have biscuits and wine brought for you here, and some hot water taken to your room. If you would like to wait, I shall supervise the moving of my possessions.'

She left abruptly, because her throat was tight, and had she remained in the room, she might have given herself away. It was ridiculous to feel like weeping, of course. She had always known that Moorcroft had forgotten her—but to see the woman he loved here in this house was more painful than she could bear.

She ran quickly up the stairs. There was a smaller room at the other end of the hall, as far away from the one the beautiful comtesse would be using as she could get. It would not be as comfortable, but it hardly mattered since she would leave this house as soon as she could in the New Year.

'My lord, you have a visitor,' Trent said from the doorway of the library. 'Shall I show her in here—or to the parlour in your wing?'

'A visitor? Female?' Robert frowned. 'Could you not say I am not at home? I am rather busy.'

'Miss Selina said I ought to tell you the lady had arrived, and she insists on seeing you immediately.'

'And the name of this lady?'

'Comtesse Adelaide de Saracosa, my lord. Miss Selina
has given her the yellow room. It was her own, sir—but
she has moved for her.'

'Has she? Good grief, why?'

Robert frowned as he brought his mind back from his
ledgers. He could imagine what tale the comtesse had
told Selina. Had she come here to tell him she'd changed
her mind about marrying him? Lord, he hoped not! His
offer had been made out of a sense of duty, because he'd
led her to expect an offer in Italy, but he'd been relieved
when she'd turned him down. It was deuced awkward.
He wondered why Selina had asked her to stay, and then
groaned inwardly as he realised what Adelaide would
have told her—and what Selina must think.

'Show her into the best parlour, Trent. Tell her I shall
be half an hour or so and ask her to wait.'

'Yes, my lord.'

Robert was on his feet as Trent left the library. Adelaide's
arrival was a nuisance, but he could hardly request her to
leave at once. He wasn't sure whether she would be entitled to sue for breach of promise if he told her that he no
longer wished to marry her. She'd turned him down! For
goodness' sake, she had no right to walk back into his life
this way! He cursed himself. What a fool he'd been even
to flirt with her, to give her cause to expect an offer. In the
end he'd had no choice but to ask, only it hadn't seemed
to matter then.

It mattered now. He had no wish to marry Adelaide.
It was the last thing he wanted, and her presence here
was an added problem to a growing list. She would be in

the way, for he owed her the duty of protection if nothing more.

Robert took a turn about the room as his mind twisted and turned. He was caught like a bird in a trap and there was no easy way out. If he followed his inclination, he would make things clear to Adelaide at once and ask her to leave—but he knew what a spiteful tongue she had. If she guessed the reason behind his change of heart, she would tattle to all the gossips about his unusual living arrangements and people would assume the worst. Selina's reputation would be in shreds before the week was out.

What the hell was he going to do? He could only hope that whatever had made Adelaide change her mind reversed itself and that once she sensed his coolness towards her she would take herself off.

He was about to go in search of her when the door opened and Selina entered. She stopped, the colour surging and then leaving her face as she saw him.

'Forgive me—I thought you should know that Comtesse Adelaide de Saracosa has arrived. She asked if she might stay and I agreed, naturally. As she pointed out, she could hardly stay in your wing without a chaperone.'

'No, I suppose not,' Robert replied. He hesitated, then, 'I am sorry she has imposed herself on you, Selina. Had she written I should have asked her to delay her visit until I was ready for company. As one of several guests, it would have been acceptable for her to stay with me.'

'Yes, I see.'

Selina was avoiding looking at him. She believed he was going to marry Adelaide—perhaps that he was in love with her. She must think that he had been playing fast and loose with her.

'Selina…Miss Searles…' Robert faltered. 'I did make the comtesse an offer, but it was not…' He shook his head as Selina lifted her eyes to his, and he saw the air of indifference she was attempting to maintain.

What could he say to her? He was in a difficult situation—not just because of Adelaide's arrival but because of the mystery hanging over him. If someone was trying to murder him, he did not wish to endanger Selina or her family. To tell her what had been in his mind was pointless until he could extricate himself from his entanglements.

'My offer was not accepted at the time…'

'She was considering her answer and has no doubt come to give you her decision,' Selina said in a cool tone. 'Naturally this changes things, Moorcroft. I think you need to employ more servants—and we shall keep a quiet Christmas in our wing. You may wish to entertain on a larger scale now that your…friend has arrived. My cook will be unable to cater for your needs in that case, and you should send for your chef without delay.'

'Selina, I was looking forward to sharing Christmas with your family.'

'Were you?' For a moment her eyes searched his face. 'You and Henry will, of course, be welcome to pop in, but I think you should lock the door to the library so that your wing is closed off from ours.'

'Then I shall. Millie may still have the run of the library, naturally. I can work elsewhere.'

'That is ridiculous. This is your house. My sister must take a few books and return them when…before we leave.' Selina turned away.

'I told you that you might stay as long as you wish, Selina.'

'Yes, but that was before…' Selina caught her breath. 'I think I shall write to Mr Breck. We must move as soon as we are able after Christmas. Your wife will not wish for another family living in her house.'

'Selina…'

Robert swore softly as he spoke to a closed door. Damn it! Adelaide had no right to come here with her tales of his promise of marriage. She'd turned him down and that should be the end of it.

'But, Robert, darling, how can you be so cruel?' Adelaide said, fluttering her long lashes at him. 'When I have come all this way to give you my answer?'

'You gave me your answer in Italy.'

'Did you think it was final?' Adelaide pouted at him. 'Darling, don't you know that a gentleman is expected to *win* his lady? If at first you don't succeed, try and try again. It would have been polite to ask me again.'

'I have no idea why you're here,' Robert said, and glared at her. 'I don't beg, Adelaide. If you'd wanted a lap poodle, you should have looked elsewhere. I do not ask twice.'

'You are breaking my heart, Robert. You know I adore you. I was a little put out that day. You must admit you were a complete bear. You might at least have *pretended* to be in love with me.'

'Why? I thought it best that there should be no false pretences between us. I offered you marriage then because I needed an heir—and you are beautiful. I found you desirable and thought we might achieve a respectable relationship.'

'And now?' Adelaide's eyes narrowed, green and sharp like a cat's. 'What has changed?' She walked to the window and glanced out. 'You cannot prefer that drab creature to me? I heard gossip but I did not credit it—and when I saw her I knew it was all nonsense. She is a nobody—nothing.'

'Miss Searles is a respectable young woman. She cares for her sisters, and that is why she took the position here… as a kind of housekeeper-tenant. I do not pay her a wage, but she and her sisters have a home in return for helping me to set up my establishment.'

'You do not need her now that you have me. Send her away, Robert. Invite some of our friends down and give a party. We can announce our engagement—they all expect it. If you send me away there will be a terrible scandal.'

'What *is* going on in that mind of yours?' Robert said sternly. 'I assure you that there has been nothing of an intimate nature between Miss Searles and I—or any member of her household with any member of mine,' he added.

'Has Henry found love at last?' Adelaide tittered. 'My poor companion, Miss Bartlet, was terrified he meant to ask her to marry him. She would simply have died if he had, of course. She could not bear him near her.'

'Then she is an insensitive idiot,' Robert said harshly. 'What Henry feels or does is none of my affair—or yours, Adelaide.'

'But I might make it mine,' Adelaide replied, and smiled spitefully. 'I do not imagine your friend would enjoy hearing Selina Searles's name banded about by the gossipmongers.'

It was on the tip of Robert's tongue to correct her misapprehension that Henry was in love with Selina, but decided to keep his silence. Henry's feelings were engaged, but he had no way of knowing how Miss Amy felt, and it would not do to make her the butt of Adelaide's spiteful tongue.

'Well, since Miss Searles has been good enough to give you a room, I suppose you may stay for a while,' he said, giving her a cold, hard look. 'But if you expect me to make you another offer, you will be disappointed. I think you will be bored here, Adelaide, since I intend to invite just a few neighbours for Christmas Eve. You would do better to return to London and wait for me to visit when I am out of mourning.'

'And leave the field to the enemy? I think I know better than that, darling.' Adelaide smiled. 'I daresay you are angry because I turned you down and you wish to punish me a little. Well, I shall humour you, dearest Robert. I do not think it will take you long to realise that I am more suited to your needs than the drab Miss Searles. Besides, unless you wish to find yourself being sued for breach of promise, you *will* keep your word to me.'

'I fear you will not find me easy to blackmail,' Robert replied. 'If you know what is good for you, Adelaide, you will leave now.'

'Force me to leave and you will be sorry—or it might be more accurate to say that Miss Selina Searles will be sorry. Once the gossips learn that she and her family have been running in and out of your rooms at will…'

'That is a lie,' Robert said, and glared at her. 'Our wings are separate and we do not intrude upon each other.'

Adelaide laughed mirthlessly. 'Who will believe *that*, Robert? I assure you the gossips are already watching eagerly for some proof that their suspicions are correct. One word from me, and Miss Searles will be ostracised from all decent society.'

'Would you really stoop that low?' Robert stared at her and saw the colour come and go in her cheeks. 'Why? What has changed? You told me you did not wish to marry a cold fish like me. I do not think I have changed in a few short weeks.'

'I told you—I was merely playing a waiting game. It is customary for gentlemen in love to ask more than once.'

'You may wait a lifetime and I shall not ask.'

Adelaide had been sitting in an elegant elbow chair, protected from the heat of the fire by a fine embroidered screen. She got up without answering and went to stand by the window to look out at the park, her back to him.

'Circumstances have changed.' Suddenly she turned to look at him, accusation in her green eyes. 'You will not deny having seduced me—having taken me to bed on more than one occasion?'

'No, I do not deny it.' He had slept with her twice—at her invitation—which was the reason he'd felt himself honour bound to offer marriage when he'd realised she expected it. 'What…' his gaze narrowed, becoming intense '…are you telling me?'

'I am carrying your child,' Adelaide said. 'What have you to say now, Robert? Will you reject your own child—make that child a bastard born out of wedlock and ruin me? Or will you behave as a gentleman and honour your promise to me?'

The pain slashed through Robert like a knife. How could he ever have found this woman amusing? Yes, he'd had two passionate nights with her, but he was almost certain he had not been her only lover since her husband had died three years previously. Had there been anyone else after he'd left Italy? Could he be certain the child was his?

'You are wondering if there was anyone after you,' Adelaide said. 'The answer is that I was on the verge of an affair, and I had hopes of an advantageous match, but then I realised that I was *enceinte* and I knew it could only be yours.' She moved towards him, looking up into his face with cat-like eyes. 'You wanted an heir, Robert. I might already be carrying your child. Will you send me away knowing that—knowing that I could be desperate, ready to take my own life…?'

'Do not be ridiculous! You could quite easily hide the birth and—'

The words stuck in his throat. How cold and callous that sounded. If she was truly carrying his child, then the situation was impossible. It had been difficult enough when he'd thought it merely a matter of scandal, of being sued for breach of promise—and perhaps the loss of reputation for Selina.

His child… His own flesh and blood. He turned his back on her, staring out at the park, his expression as black as thunder. Caught in a trap of his own making! He had been careless because nothing had mattered to him. In the sunshine of Italy, he had lived for the moment, and if this had happened before he saw Selina again, he would have accepted it—might even have been pleased to think he would have a child.

The thoughts in his mind were harsh and bitter. For several minutes he could not speak, for he was being forced into a place he did not wish to go, but it seemed he had no choice. At last he turned to face her, his expression cold, angry.

'I shall make enquiries into your behaviour after I left Italy. If I discover you have lied to me, you will be sorry, Adelaide.'

Sensing her victory, she laughed softly and moved towards him. 'I have told you the truth, Robert. Much as you might wish me to the devil, I *am* bearing your child. I am willing to submit to an examination by a doctor of your choice, who will, I am certain, confirm what I say. Stop glaring at me, dearest Robert, and accept your fate as I have mine. I did not force you to my bed, as you will admit.'

Robert sighed heavily. Much as he wished things otherwise, he had to admit that he *had* been willing, even eager to lie with her. At the time he'd thought her exactly what he needed—a woman who would give him an heir and turn her head away if he strayed; a woman who might take lovers of her own once the succession was assured.

He was trapped and it was his own fault. For years he'd shut out any real feelings he'd had, living for pleasure and amusement, haunted by memories that tore him apart and made him turn away from a true relationship.

Selina had broken down the barriers when she'd nursed him. He had remembered the angel of his youthful dreams and he'd dared to dream again. Now his dream was ended. Selina was already hurt, and would be more so when she discovered the truth. Any feeling she'd had for him would be driven out by a natural disgust. She would think him a heartless rake, a man who had careless affairs. It would seem to her that he had given her cause to expect an offer when he was promised to another.

She would surely hate him. For the second time in her life, he had flirted with her and then walked away.

Yet what else could he do? He could see no alternative but to marry Adelaide. It was the end of his chance of happiness. His marriage would be a loveless place, from which he would escape as often as he could—but wherever he went and whatever he did, he would never be at peace.

How cruel life could be. He'd lost Juanita when she'd died in his arms and now he'd lost Selina—before she had truly been his.

'Yes, I do insist on a doctor's examination,' Robert said, and knew that he sounded a cold, heartless brute.

'If his opinion is that the child was conceived while we were still together…'

'Darling!' Adelaide threw herself at him. 'I knew you could not refuse me. How happy you have made me. I shall be all you could want in a wife. You will have no cause to doubt me—at least until we have the heir and a spare.'

Robert put her away from him. 'This is a matter of honour, Adelaide. If you are carrying my child, I cannot abandon you, but I have no intention of setting up house with you. You will have your own establishment. I shall naturally wish to see the child sometimes, but we shall not live together.'

Adelaide's eyes snapped at him angrily, their green depths dark and reflective, like a woodland pool in winter. 'Very well, Robert. Have it your way—but you may be sorry…'

With that she flounced out of the room, slamming the door behind her. Robert remained standing at the window.

It seemed that Adelaide had won. He must write to Breck and ask him to find a decent home for Selina and her sisters somewhere far enough away that they would not meet by chance and cause each other pain. He would make certain that the rent was affordable, even purchase the house. If he thought she would let him, he would buy her a house and give her an income, but he knew that Selina's pride would forbid it. However, she need not know that he was her landlord, for Breck would keep his secret. There were other matters he might look into for Selina, and he would ask Breck to do all he could for her.

He turned towards the library, intending to write his letter, then realised that he had locked himself out. He must use the desk in the parlour or work in the estate office.

He was going to miss the company of Selina and her family when they moved out. Robert wasn't sure whether he would bother to restore the house now. He did not think Adelaide would care to live here for long as it was, and he had no intention of buying her a house in London. If she chose not to return to Italy, there was little he could do about it, but he would make sure that they had separate establishments.

Sitting down at the desk in the window, he opened the drawer and hunted for pen and ink. There was paper, but the ink had dried in the pot and the pen needed sharpening, for the quill had blunted. He would need to enter the library to fetch what was needed.

Once again he cursed himself for his careless behaviour in Italy. Had he not seduced the beautiful comtesse, he would have been free to pursue his own life.

Outside the door, Henry frowned. He had been about to seek Robert in the parlour, and had not been able to help overhearing the conversation. It seemed to him that his friend must be in something of a dilemma. Yes, he had asked the comtesse to wed him in Italy, but things had been different then.

Henry had his own thoughts on the matter. It was perhaps not his business to interfere in Robert's life—but he could not, for friendship's sake, stand by and see his friend lied to or cheated when a simple letter might bring the truth to the fore.

And if he were wrong, he would say nothing and no harm done.

CHAPTER EIGHT

'GOING to marry the comtesse?' Amy stared at her in dismay. 'Oh, Selina, surely you are wrong? I thought… after you nursed him when he was ill…and the way he looked at you…'

'Please do not be foolish, dearest,' Selina begged, and clasped her hands in front of her. 'What I did was nothing special. I would have done the same for anyone—as you would, my love.'

'Yes, well, of course,' Amy agreed. 'But you told me how you met before—and I know you feel something for him. You cannot hide from me, Selina. I know you like him…rather more than like, I think?'

'Yes, perhaps I do like him more than is sensible,' Selina admitted. 'But the comtesse told me that he had asked her to marry him, and he did not deny it. Now that she has come all this way to accept his offer, he would find it awkward to refuse her. She has the right to expect him to keep his word.'

'Perhaps…perhaps not,' Amy said, and frowned. 'If

she turned him down, he does not have to ask her again. I do not think he could prefer her to you.'

Selina smiled. 'You are prejudiced,' she chided. 'The comtesse is very beautiful, and I… It is a long time since I have bothered with my appearance. Had she not come, he might have been interested in a marriage of convenience, but—' She broke off and sighed. 'It cannot be helped. You do see how awkward it is for us now? I should like to move immediately, but Mr Breck was quite clear that the house would not be free until early next year.'

'But we were to have spent Christmas together! Millie was looking forward to singing carols round the Yule log and making kissing boughs for the great hall.'

'She can make one for us—and give another to Henry for the hall,' Selina said. 'I am sorry to disappoint you both, but if the earl is to make his own arrangements, I do not see how we can intrude on him and his guests.'

'Has he said he does not wish us to spend Christmas with him?'

'No…but it will be awkward, do you not see?' Selina bit her lip. She would find it almost intolerable to see Adelaide showing off her ring to everyone and presiding over the festivities like a queen. 'It will not be the same as we planned.'

'I wanted to be with Henry, and Millie has set her heart on it.'

'Are you fond of Henry, dearest?'

Amy's cheeks went pink. 'I like him very much,' she said. 'Tomorrow he is taking Millie and I to gather holly and mistletoe to make our decorations. You could come, too, if you wish. You do not expect us to cancel our arrangement?'

'No, of course not,' Selina said. 'I suppose if we are invited, we shall go for the ceremony of the Yule log—but we must not presume. The earl's plans may have changed considerably. We should make our own plans for a quiet Christmas.'

'I thought you meant to invite some of our neighbours?'

'Moorcroft said that he would send invitations. It is his house, and since we were to have celebrated together, I did not think I ought...' Selina turned away as stupid tears stung her eyes. 'Perhaps he will invite us, and if he does, you and Millie must go, of course.'

'Are you saying you will not?' Amy looked at her, a gleam of anger in her eyes. 'Are you just going to let her win? You have a perfect right to be here—we all do. If you had not taken the house, Moorcroft would not even be here. He intended to make plans for pulling it down and return to London. We are entitled to be at the Christmas Eve party—and I shall not let her drive me away.'

Selina sighed. 'No, you should not, and nor shall I— but it will not be the same...'

'I wish she hadn't come,' Amy said. 'I'm going to find Henry and ask him for the truth. He'll know what's going on.'

'You really shouldn't intrude,' Selina said, but her sister wasn't listening.

Staring at the door which had closed behind her, she took out her handkerchief and blew her nose. She hoped she wasn't going down with a cold, because she didn't want to spoil everything for her sisters.

'Do you believe her?' Henry asked the next morning, when Robert had finished confiding in him. 'Forgive me, Robert, but I think the lovely Adelaide would swear that black was white if it gained her what she desires.'

'She has agreed to have an examination by my doctor,' Robert said stiffly. 'If the evidence points to the child being mine, I do not see how I can refuse to marry her. I asked her to be my wife because we had been intimate and she had a right to expect it. She is a lady, not a whore, Henry. I should be less than a gentleman if I refused to stand by her in the circumstances.'

'Yes, that is undeniable—if you are the father,' Henry said, and frowned. 'But I heard rumours that she was seeing Bolingwood at the same time as you were visiting her, Robert. How can you be certain that the child is yours and not his?'

'If I thought…' Robert sighed. 'Surely she would have gone to him if she thought he was the father of her child? Why come to me if that is the case?'

'Because Bolingwood would tell her to go to the devil,' Henry said frankly. 'He would have been aware that she was also entertaining you—and he is a first-rate cad. If she threw herself on his mercy, he would tell her to get rid of the brat.'

'Perhaps,' Robert agreed. 'I'm trapped, Nor. I have no wish to marry her—but if the child is mine… I could not stand by and see her ruined or the child a bastard. She threatened to take her own life if I sent her away.'

'I see that you are in a difficult position.' Henry looked thoughtful. 'I know Bolingwood quite well. As a matter of fact, I saved his life once in Spain. He would tell me if she approached him before she came to you.'

'I suppose that would make a difference,' Robert said. 'If she is lying... I would arrange to have the child adopted for her, if she wished, and pay for her to go into seclusion until the birth. But if the babe is his, I should not feel honour bound to marry her.'

'She is hardly in need of your money, Robert. What she wants from you is a home and a father for her child so that she does not suffer a loss of consequence. However, you could help her find somewhere pleasant to stay where her secret might be kept.'

'May I ask you to write a letter?' Robert said. 'I should like to be certain that the child is mine before...'

'Before you break Selina's heart and your own?' Henry gave him a hard stare. 'I know you too well, Robert. You're in love with Selina. You may be prepared to sacrifice your own happiness—but what of hers?'

'You need not accuse me, Nor. I know that I may have aroused expectations, but I had no idea—' He broke off in distress.

'Amy has asked me to discover if you are to marry the comtesse. She told me that Selina would not allow anyone to see that she is hurt, but Amy is sure she is suffering. She has already spoken of leaving straight after Christmas, and although she will not forbid her sisters to share Christmas with us, she may not attend your party herself.'

'Damn her!' Robert exploded, his hands working at his sides. 'Not Selina—Adelaide. Had she accepted my offer in Italy, none of this would have happened.'

'Wouldn't it?' Henry arched his left eyebrow. 'Had you been married, I think you would still have come here after your uncle died. You would have met Selina and her family, but your position would have been irretrievable—as it is, all may not be lost. Make the comtesse no firm promise, Robert. Keep your distance and wait until we have our answer.'

'I must keep my distance from them both,' Robert replied. 'I had planned for a double celebration at Christmas, Nor. Pray keep that to yourself, if you will. At the moment Selina can hardly bear to look at me.'

'Yes, you must show restraint in both cases—but for different reasons, my friend.' Henry smiled at him. 'Do not imagine you are the only one struggling with an emotional problem. I had hoped to take my time getting to know Amy before I spoke to her, but in the circumstances I think I must speak now.' He shook his head. 'I daresay I am a fool even to hope that she might accept me.'

'We are not lucky in love,' Robert said wryly. 'What with this other business...it might be best to return to London at once and leave the house to Selina and her sisters. They would be free to enjoy Christmas, and at least I should not be on thorns lest one of them suffer some harm.'

'You are no further forward in solving the mystery, then?'

'No. I had hoped the vicar might show some light on the situation, but for the moment he has nothing to offer, it seems.'

'Well, Amy, Millie and I are off to pick holly and mistletoe for the great hall,' Henry said. 'Have you done your Christmas shopping, Robert? I am sending to London for a few things I need, and could include an order for you should you wish it.'

'Thank you, but I believe I shall ride into Long Melford. You must not worry if I do not return for dinner. If the weather is bad, I may stay at the inn until the morning, rather than risk the roads late at night.'

'Very well. I have been invited to dine with Selina and her family this evening. I think she does not wish to entertain the comtesse alone. I shall explain your absence, Robert.'

'Thank you.' Robert smiled. 'What should I have done without you these past years, Nor? If you decide to live at your estate, I shall miss you.'

'For myself, I should not think of leaving you,' Henry said. 'However, if I marry I must ask my wife for her opinion.'

'If you do marry, would you consider taking the east wing as your home? I should naturally have it repaired and refurbished to your taste, install a second kitchen to make you independent.'

'That is something worth considering. We should spend

some time at my estate—as I must occasionally, whether I marry or not—but it would be for Amy to decide.'

'Yes, of course. You have made up your mind to ask her, then?'

'Yes, I have,' Henry said. 'She is so good-natured that if her answer is no, I know she will not make things difficult for me. I believe that I shall ask her when we are gathering the holly.'

'I envy your freedom,' Robert said. 'And I sincerely wish for your happiness—even if it means that you will leave me.'

'I know you mean that.' Henry smiled. 'I may be a fool, but I want to look after her and Millie. Selina will make her own way in the world, but I could make things easier for her by giving her sisters a home with me. Millie could visit both of us, as I'm sure she would wish.'

'That was my hope, too,' Robert said ruefully. He offered his hand. 'I can only wish you good fortune— though if she refuses you, I shall think her a nonsensical chit.'

'Think yourself fortunate that I love you as my brother,' Henry jested. 'Any other man would find himself answering to my sword for that remark.'

'Ah, young love,' Robert mocked, and ducked the punch Henry threw at him. 'I shall not keep you—and I must leave at once or I shall not reach Long Melford before the day begins to close in...'

Selina stood at the landing window. She had watched the earl ride away earlier, and now her sisters and Henry were setting off with their baskets. Muffled with gloves, warm hats and scarves, they were taking the trap because it would be easier to bring back the greenery they planned to use in the hall. With only just over a week to Christmas Eve, they would be busy making kissing boughs and decorating the halls with holly. It was a time of year she had always enjoyed, even when her beloved mama had been unwell, as she had the past two years.

Her eyes stung with tears but she blinked them away. She had made up her mind that she would not dwell on her grief. Her sisters were entering into the spirit of things and she must, too—even though her heart felt as if it were breaking.

But she understood, and exonerated Moorcroft of all blame. Of course he must keep his word to the comtesse. Selina's throat was tight, and her heart ached, but she knew it was only right that he should honour his promise. She would think the less of him if he did not.

Selina had no claim on him. None whatsoever. He had been more than generous to her and her sisters. She had been given a period of respite, which had allowed her to save money she would otherwise have been forced to spend on rent. She was using it to give her sisters the best Christmas they'd had since her father fell into debt and then killed himself.

After Christmas they would pack up and move into the house Mr Breck had promised to find for her. Until then she would try to make the most of things as they were.

It was time to get on with her sewing. Wandering around feeling miserable would get her nowhere.

She went down to her favourite parlour, opened the door and entered, feeling a pang of annoyance as she saw that Adelaide was already there, and seated at her mama's spinet.

'Please do not play that, ma'am,' she said. 'It belonged to my mother and I do not like anyone else to use it.'

'I was not going to damage it,' Adelaide said, and stood up, twisting away from the instrument with a flounce of her silk skirts. 'Really—as if it would matter.'

'It matters to us,' Selina said, restraining her temper. 'No one has played it since Mama died. We could not bear to open it, and will not do so until our grief is sufficiently abated to make it possible. If you wish to play, there is a fine pianoforte in the west wing, I believe. Though Moorcroft has only recently had it delivered and I have not seen it.'

'I daresay you might have wished to play it yourself?'

'I might have taken advantage had it been here before the earl took up residence, but I do not intrude on his privacy,' Selina said. 'Although we are close neighbours, I do not treat his home as my own.'

'Do you expect me to believe that?'

'You may believe whatever you choose,' Selina said calmly. 'This is my private parlour. You are, for the moment, a guest in my home, and I would ask you to use the blue parlour—if you do not mind.'

'This house belongs to Robert, and since I am to be his wife, I see no reason why I should not go where I please...' Adelaide's eyes met hers in challenge and then fell. 'Oh, very well. Since you choose to be so unfriendly, I shall take myself off.'

'We shall meet in the other rooms, of course, but I need somewhere to call my own, ma'am. Do you not have a private parlour at home—somewhere your guests are not invited?'

Adelaide made no reply, shutting the door with a bang as she went out. Selina sank into her favourite chair, blinking hard. How foolish of her to be upset by the sight of a stranger sitting at her mama's spinet—but the comtesse had no right to intrude. She had forced Selina to take her as a guest and must accept the limitations that imposed. The house might belong to the earl, but this part of it was her home—at least for the moment.

She would not be upset. She would not break her heart over Robert Moorcroft again. She would be calm and work at her sewing, just as she had whenever she'd felt close to despair during the long months of Mama's last illness.

Picking up the silk handkerchief she was making for Henry, she began to hem it very carefully, with the tiniest of stitches. He was such a pleasant gentleman, and she had a feeling that he at least might become a part of her family in the future.

A few flakes of snow were beginning to fall as they finished gathering their holly and piled it into the back of the trap. Millie had been right to choose this spot, for there was a mass of holly and mistletoe, and even though they had cut a load, there was enough left for the estate workers to gather some for their own homes. Amy smiled as she looked about her. This had been so much fun, and it was mostly due to Henry.

'Amy, wait a moment.' He touched her arm as she would have followed Millie, who was about to gather up the last few sprigs of cut greenery. 'May I speak to you for a moment?'

Amy felt a little shiver of surprise as she looked at him and saw his expression. Her heart quickened and she felt suddenly shy.

'Yes, of course, Henry. Is there something I may do for you?'

'If we were alone I would go down on my knee, but as it is I shall just ask if there is any chance that you would consent to be my wife? I know it is too soon, but things being as they are—I wanted to ask rather than leave it and then find it was too late.'

'Henry… Mr Norton…' Amy stared at him, her breath catching in her throat. She had wondered, half hoped, but never dreamed that he would speak so soon. Lifting her clear eyes to meet his, she said, 'Why do you ask? Do you feel pity for us because we have nowhere to go and very little money?'

'No! Good grief!' Henry exclaimed. 'You must never think that, Amy. I know you are far above me. I am too old and ugly, and you are lovely beyond compare—but I love you. I am asking because you are the only woman I have ever wished to marry.'

'Henry…' Amy's eyes misted with tears, for she could not doubt his sincerity. 'I do not know what to say…'

'You must not be embarrassed, and you must not pity me either,' he told her quickly. 'I knew it was too much to hope for, but I felt compelled to ask. If you had gone away...'

'Hush, my sweet idiot,' Amy said, and touched her fingers to his lips. 'If we were alone I should kiss you, Henry, but Millie is already staring at us. I was simply shocked that you had asked me because I was not certain of your feelings. I had thought—hoped—but I was not sure.'

Henry stared at her, seeming frightened to move or speak, and Amy laughed. 'You need not look so stunned, my dearest Henry. I shall be happy to marry you, and when we are alone, I shall tell you why.'

'Thank you...' He took her hand, carrying it to his lips to kiss her gloved fingers fervently just as Millie approached. 'You have made me the happiest of men.'

'Oh, have you asked her?' Millie said, looking like the cat that had discovered the cream jug. 'I knew you would, of course. I told Amy you liked her a lot, but she just told me not to be silly. I'm glad you're going to be married. Especially if it means I can come and stay at Moorcroft with you.'

'I am not sure where we shall be living,' Henry replied, and laughed. 'Robert has offered us an apartment—in fact the whole of the east wing once it has been refurbished—but that is for Amy to decide. She might prefer to live at my own estate.'

'Pooh—fustian,' Millie said stoutly. 'Who would turn down a chance to live here? And everyone knows you are devoted to the earl. Amy wouldn't dream of dragging you away—would you, Amy?'

'You, miss, are too precocious,' Amy said, and her eyes were dancing with laughter. 'These things are for Henry and I to discuss—but wherever we are, there will always be a home for you.'

'I shall spend some of my time with you,' Millie decided magnanimously. 'However, I must tell you that I hope to go to school quite soon. The earl was telling me he knows of a good one that would fit my needs. He says that a mind like mine should be nurtured and given a chance to explore rather than allowed to stagnate with a governess.'

'Did he indeed?' Amy frowned. 'I am not sure what Selina would have to say about that, miss. I daresay she could not afford to send you to an expensive establishment.'

'Moorcroft intends to fund my education himself. He told me so only the other day.'

'And when did you talk to him?'

'I think it was the day before the comtesse arrived,' Millie said. 'I discovered him in the library—I did say I would go away if he was busy, but he told me to come in and talk to him about what I wanted in the future. So I did—and that's when he asked if I would like to go to boarding school or be tutored at home.'

'Indeed?' Amy glanced at Henry. 'Did you know about this?'

'Robert made no mention of it to me,' Henry said, hesitating before adding, 'His plans may have changed in some respects, due to circumstances beyond his control, but I am perfectly certain he will keep his word to Millie.'

'But would Selina allow it?'

'Why shouldn't she?' Millie asked, and then pointed at the folly. 'Look—someone is going in. Do you think it is the person who left the door open before?'

'I'm not certain. Stay here with the trap, both of you— and if anything happens, take the reins and drive away quickly, Amy.'

'What do you mean?'

'I must investigate…' Henry gave her an urgent look. 'We gave orders the lock should be repaired, but it has obviously not been done yet. Please…do as I ask. If you hear anything untoward, do not come looking—take Millie home and inform… Damn it, Robert isn't there. Tell the grooms to come—and tell them to come armed if you should hear a shot.'

Amy stared at him, her fingers trembling as she held out a hand. 'Please take care, Henry.'

'Of course. I have everything to live for.' He smiled at her, and then set off at a sprint towards the folly.

Whoever it was had gone inside. His heart was racing. However, he had come armed just in case—and if he discovered the intruder was dangerous, he would not be afraid to shoot.

Robert lingered over his purchases. If he were committed to Adelaide, he would be purchasing a Christmas gift for her, and he must do so out of politeness if nothing more, but he could not decide what to give her. His other purchases were all made, and he had changed his mind about not returning home. Snow had been threatening all afternoon, and if he delayed until morning, he might find the roads blocked and impassable. As yet the flakes were fine and dissolving almost as soon as they hit the ground, but the night might bring a blizzard.

This was simply wasting time. It hardly mattered what he gave Adelaide. He picked the most expensive necklace on show and saw the jeweller's satisfied smile.

'The lady who receives this will be most fortunate,' he said. 'There is no need to settle the account now, my lord. At the end of the month will do very well.'

'My lawyers in London will see to it.' He handed the man a card. 'In future you may send all your accounts to this firm.'

The man looked as if he might start to purr, insisting that he would have the gifts wrapped specially for the earl if he would care to wait.

'No, thank you, I prefer to do that myself. I shall take them as they are.'

He picked up the various boxes and placed them in the pockets of his great coat, thanked the shopkeeper for his help and went out. It was turning colder, and the snow was beginning to fall a little faster. However, if he left immediately, he should be able to reach home soon after dark.

He was thoughtful as he paid his shot at the hostelry and took his horse out into the bitter night, leaning forward to pat its neck.

'Forgive me, old fellow. I daresay you would have preferred the warmth of a stable tonight, but I have a feeling something is wrong. If we do not return at once…'

He shook his head. It was foolish, but something was calling him back, telling him that he should not delay. The rest of his purchases might wait for another time.

Selina was looking out of the window again when she saw the trap draw up in a hurry outside the house. From the way her sister jumped down and hurried round to the back, she could see something was wrong. Amy was shouting to the men in the courtyard.

Not stopping to watch further, Selina ran down the stairs just as Trent opened the front door to Amy. She entered the house, followed by Millie and Henry, who was carrying someone in his arms. For a moment Selina's heart caught and she feared the worst—then she saw that Henry was carrying a woman…a very young woman… hardly more than a child. On closer inspection she gave a cry of surprise as she saw that she knew the girl.

'I know her. She is called Sadie and she visits the kitchens here sometimes. Nanny says she is a wonderful cook, though not all she ought to be in her mind. What has happened to her?'

'It is a long story,' Henry said. 'This young woman has been hurt. We were at the top of the folly steps and there was a struggle. She fell. I swear I did not intend she should fall—I believe she is the person who stole Robert's horse and locked him in the folly the other day.'

'Of course you did not intend her to fall,' Selina said. 'She is scarcely more than a child. How could you intend her harm? Pray, bring her upstairs. She shall have one of the smaller guest rooms. Did she hit her head as she fell?'

'Yes—against the bottom step, I think. She has cut her head at the side and it was bleeding, though Amy bound it with my kerchief and I think the flow has stopped.'

'What on earth was she doing there?' Selina asked as she led the way upstairs to the room she had decided on for her unexpected guest. 'I thought it was dangerous?'

'We were told so, it is true, but Robert discovered there is nothing wrong with the stonework. However, when he went to investigate the other day, he was locked in and the culprit stole his horse. It was turned free not far from the estate, and since Robert was able to shoot off the lock, he was unharmed.'

'Why on earth would Sadie wish to lock him in and take his horse—particularly if she did not mean to keep it?'

Selina pulled back the sheets as Henry brought Sadie to the bed and placed her down as gently as he could.

'I fear I cannot answer your question, for it is a mystery,' he said. 'All we knew was that someone had been threatening Robert—a stone was thrown at the window, as you know. It may have been this young woman, though she seems unlikely to be a murderer.'

'I would say most unlikely,' Selina agreed. 'Well, this mystery may be solved once she is conscious again—we must hope that she has not been too badly harmed.'

'I know that you will care for her,' Henry said. 'Be a little careful when she recovers her wits, Selina. She may not be as innocent as she appears.'

Selina looked at the girl's pale face and the patch of sticky blood at her right temple, and her heart was touched.

'I do not know why she should lock Moorcroft in the folly and steal his horse. Nor do I know why anyone would threaten him. But I think this child has a story, and I am willing to listen when she is well enough to explain.'

'I am sorry to impose this on you when you have more than enough to do with Christmas just around the corner,' Henry said. 'If there is anything I can do to help, please let me know.'

'I believe we can manage to look after her,' Selina said. 'I was wondering when Moorcroft intended to return? It looks as if it may snow hard before the morning.'

'I am not certain of Robert's intentions,' Henry said, and frowned. 'He had some errands in Long Melford, I understand. He was not certain whether he would return or stay over until the morning. However, if he does not make the attempt tonight, the roads may be impassable by morning.'

'I hope he does not delay.'

Selina turned as her maid, Betty, came in, carrying a bowl of water and some dressings.

'Miss Amy said you would need these, miss,' Betty said, and tutted as she saw the girl's white face. 'The poor lass. She's had a nasty fall. Nanny is very distressed about her. Quite pale she was when Miss Amy told her what had happened. I made her sit down and have a cup of tea, but I daresay she will be here shortly and wanting to help look after the girl. I think this child has had a hard time of it, Miss Selina, and that's the truth.'

'Yes, she has,' Selina agreed. 'Amy and Millie—they are all right? This must have been a shock for them—and on such a happy day.'

'We had gathered our holly, and I believe they are bringing it in,' Henry said. 'If you will excuse me? I must speak to the bailiff. I am going to have a new lock put on the folly door immediately. In future we shall have no more accidents of this kind.'

'I think you are wise,' Selina said, and touched his hand. 'Do not blame yourself, Henry. I am sure you meant only to ask her why she was there and why she had locked Robert in…'

Selina blushed as she realised she had used the earl's Christian name, but Henry had not noticed. He thanked her, but she could see that the incident had upset him. If the girl were to die of her injury, he would feel himself to blame.

She returned to the bed and bent over the girl, looking at her face. She was very pale, but quite pretty, and something about her made Selina wonder where she had seen her before. She did not think they had met, but there was something familiar about her, though she could not place it for the moment.

'Her pulse is strong, miss,' Betty said, and offered the bowl as Selina began to bathe the wound at the side of her head. 'That looks a nasty bang she's taken. How did it happen?'

'She fell down the steps at the folly—that tower we passed on our way here the day we arrived.'

'Oh, yes, I remember it. Trent told us it was unsafe.'

'Well, it seems he was right, for she fell and hurt herself. It was as well that Henry had followed her in, for she might otherwise have lain there for ages.' Selina saw no reason to tell her maid that Henry might have caused the accident by startling the young woman. She was perfectly certain he would never have harmed the girl on purpose. 'We ought to put some salve on the wound and bind it,' Selina said as she carefully dried the nasty cut. 'I do not think her wound is deep. She may have been lucky.'

'Head wounds are unpredictable,' Betty said, and shook her head. 'Doesn't look much, but the bleeding may be inside where you can't see it—leastways so I've heard tell.'

'Yes, I've heard that head wounds are unpredictable,' Selina said. 'We must just pray that it is not too serious. I should be distressed if a young girl like this should take a fatal wound because of a fall. It would cast a shadow over all of us.'

'And just when you was planning a lovely Christmas, too,' Betty said, and sniffed. 'It ain't right, that's what I say. You don't deserve so much bad luck, miss, and that's the truth of it.'

'We must not despair too soon,' Selina said. 'I shall make sure my sisters keep Christmas whatever happens. We've had enough of sorrow and pain, Betty.'

'So you have, miss. We all thought you was about to be lucky for once and then that there foreign hussy turns up, and now this...' Betty clucked her tongue.

'The comtesse is as English as you or I, Betty. She married a foreign count but that doesn't make her a foreigner.'

'She don't belong here.' Betty sniffed. 'If his lordship has any sense, he should send her orf with a flea in her ear. He's a fool if he listens to her lies. Anyone can see what sort *she* is. He'll never know whether the child is his or not.'

Selina stared at her, her heart racing. 'What do you mean? Is…is the comtesse…' She could not bring herself to finish the question. 'Please go and fetch the salve, Betty. I can finish this alone.'

Selina's hands shook as she finished bathing Sadie's temple and then went to tip the water into a slop pail in the washstand. Was it possible that the comtesse was carrying the earl's child? If so it was no wonder that he felt himself honour bound to marry her.

Her throat caught and tears stung behind her eyes, but she blinked them away. She must not surrender to her emotions. Nothing had changed. Indeed, it only proved that Robert cared for the comtesse. Selina must forget him—forget the moment she'd looked into his eyes and believed he cared for her.

It would be ridiculous to give way to her emotions. She had this young girl to nurse, and Christmas to prepare for her sisters. Sadie had been living like a wild thing, and no one had bothered enough to discover why. It was time someone started to care for her welfare. Selina would not allow herself to grieve for a man who simply did not deserve her tears. She had other more important things needing her attention.

CHAPTER NINE

'WOULD you like me to sit with her for a while?' Amy asked on entering the bedroom later that evening. 'I've had my dinner and you must be hungry.'

'She has been very restless, calling out and tossing and turning,' Selina said. 'I should have left her to Betty and joined you for dinner, but I did not think I ought. Nanny came in for a while earlier, but she looked unwell and I told her she must rest, for I cannot have another invalid on my hands. I have been feeding Sadie a few spoons of the fever medicine Mama taught me to make, but it does not seem to have helped her. I have asked that the doctor might be summoned, but on such a night he may not able to make the journey. I think the snow has been falling hard this past hour or more.'

'Yes, it has,' Amy agreed. 'Henry had been worried for the earl, but he arrived home just a few moments ago. He was covered in snow from head to toe and asked for a hot toddy immediately.'

Selina's heart caught with sudden pain. 'He is hardly

up from his sick bed. What was the foolish man thinking of to travel when the snow is so thick?'

'He said he did not wish to be snowed in at the inn, but it snowed harder on the road than he had expected.'

Amy took the seat Selina had vacated. 'Go down to the kitchen. Cook has saved some supper for you. If I need you, I will send someone to find you.'

'Sadie began to settle a few moments ago,' Selina said. 'I hope she may rest now, though she has shown no sign of coming to her senses. She was raving before I gave her the last dose of medicine, talking so wildly that I could not follow what she said.'

'You've done your share. Go down now.'

'Thank you, dearest. I am sorry this happened when you were having such a happy day.'

'Happier than you know,' Amy said. 'No, do not stop now. I shall tell you later.'

'Very well…'

Selina frowned slightly as she left the room. Watching over the young girl who was raving in her fever, she had felt guilty. Since arriving at the house, she'd been too busy to pay much attention to the girl Nanny had described as 'different.' Why did Sadie have such a fascination with the Banford estate—and why would she lock Robert in the folly?

While in her fever the girl had called wildly for help, begging someone not to hurt her, and tears had wetted her cheeks. Although feverish, she did not seem as if she was dull-witted, more likely in fear of her life—or of someone who had threatened her.

Selina was convinced that there was a mystery here. Had Nanny deliberately deceived her—or had the girl herself been playing a game? She was clearly fascinated by the house and its occupants, and had probably been using the folly as somewhere to sleep—though she might also have other hideaways.

If Nanny knew more about Sadie than she was telling, it was time for her to share her secrets with Selina. If the girl was in danger or in need of protection, then she could not continue to hide behind the story Nanny had concocted to keep her safe.

An hour or so later, Selina left the kitchens carrying a tray with a jug of fresh lemon barley. She jumped as someone spoke behind her, and stopped, turning her head to look at the man who had called to her. Her heart raced as she waited for him to come up to her. Her anger with him had faded, and now all she felt was an overwhelming sadness that he was tied to the comtesse and would never know how much he was loved.

'Forgive me for intruding in your home when I know you must be busy,' Robert said, his eyes meeting hers with a look that she could only interpret as begging for her understanding. 'Henry was here with Millie and I came to speak to him—but I should like a few moments of your time, if you can spare them?'

'Of course,' Selina said. 'I heard that you were caught in the blizzard. I hope that you have been sensible and drunk your hot toddy?'

'Yes, thank you. I know I was ill recently, but I am normally robust and scarcely ever take a chill. Please do not worry about me. I am the least of your concerns.'

She flinched, feeling as if he had struck her. He was telling her that he was not her concern, which meant he did not want her involved in his affairs. Of course he would not now that he had a fiancée.

'I was merely concerned, as you have so recently risen from your sickbed. How may I help you, my lord?'

'It was I that wished to help you,' he replied, looking at her sadly. 'I know you must wish me to the devil—but I want to say that if you need more assistance in the house, I can send for a woman who is skilled in nursing to take the load from your shoulders.'

'There is not the slightest need,' Selina told him a little stiffly. 'I think Sadie is a very frightened girl, and I shall care for her myself.'

'Henry thinks she locked me in the folly. He says that she hangs about the kitchens and helps Cook with the baking. I have never seen her—except from a distance, as she made off with my horse. Is it true that she is not quite normal?'

'I was told that on my arrival, but I am not sure it is true. I believe there is a mystery here, my lord.'

'Robert—please,' he begged. 'If it was she that locked me in the folly, she must have had a reason. I cannot think that a girl like that would threaten me by throwing a stone through the window—nor do I think she could be concerned with other things that may have happened in the past.'

'Not directly,' Selina said. 'I believe her to be frightened—more a victim than a rogue. Perhaps she knows things that she ought not, or is indirectly involved in some unpleasantness and fears she will be punished—either by one of us or by the person who cheated your uncle.'

'Would you talk to her, please?' Robert asked. 'I have no right to ask you for anything, but I believe that if either Henry or I tried to question her, she would be terrified and she might run away.'

'When she recovers her wits, I shall try to discover her story,' Selina said.

She was also planning to speak to Nanny as soon as possible, because she suspected that lady knew more than she was saying, but she did not wish to cause trouble for her by suggesting that Robert speak to her himself.

She raised her eyes to his, meeting them with a clear, brave gaze. 'You may ask anything you wish of me, Moorcroft. Your personal life is your own, but you gave my sisters and me a home when we needed one, and I am grateful. If I may be of help, you have only to ask.'

'You more than repaid that debt when you nursed me.' His eyes seemed to glow with a sudden light that she could only interpret as passion. He stepped closer. 'Selina, I cannot speak as I would wish, and for that I beg you to forgive me. Circumstances lead me to do things I would rather not…'

Her breath caught, and for a moment her senses spiralled into an exquisite dance of delight. She almost swayed towards him, her body feeling as if she might have melted into his arms, but two things stopped her—

the tray she was carrying and the sharp, spiteful voice that shattered her dreams.

'Robert! What are you doing here? I did not know you were in the house.'

He sighed and turned to greet the newcomer. 'Forgive me, Adelaide. I returned chilled to the bone and have been taking a hot bath and changing into dry clothes. I believe you were changing for dinner when I arrived.'

'You might have sent word. I was worried about you.'

'Worried I had escaped back to London?'

Selina heard the faint sarcasm in his voice as she moved on up the stairs. It was not her business to listen to a private conversation between the earl and the lady he was to marry. If her heart told her that his feelings for that lady were not what they should be—could not be love because his affections were engaged elsewhere—she would not allow her mind to dwell on it. Such thoughts might raise hopes and aspirations which could not possibly come true.

Selina blinked away the sting of stupid tears. She was far too sensible to cry over something that could not be mended. Moorcroft had made her no promises—at least not in words—but his eyes…his eyes seemed to promise the earth.

No, she was being ridiculous. If Betty's insinuations were correct, the comtesse was carrying Robert's child, and that being the case, he had little choice but to ask her to be his wife. No matter that she had turned him down in Italy. If she was to be the mother of his child, that must mean that as a gentleman he was obliged to offer her marriage.

Even if his heart lay elsewhere? For a moment Selina allowed herself to dream, but then she quashed her foolish hopes. Whatever Moorcroft might feel, he was a gentleman and honourable. He would not allow a child of his to live as a bastard when he might marry the mother.

Opening the door of the bedchamber, Selina felt her personal hopes and dreams go flying as she saw that both Amy and Betty were struggling to hold their patient in the bed as she fought to escape them.

'Let me go!' the girl sobbed. 'I've done nothing wrong. I beg you, do not hurt me…do not let him take me again…'

'We are trying to help you,' Amy said. 'You have had a blow to the head. You must not get up yet.'

'He will kill me,' Sadie sobbed. 'He said if I told…if I came here…he would kill me…'

Selina put her basin down on the washstand and walked towards the bed.

'Let go of her,' she instructed. 'Amy, do as I tell you— and, Betty, stand back, please. Sadie isn't dangerous. She is just frightened.'

'I think she's mazed in the head, miss,' Betty said. 'She just told me the earl wanted her sent away to a house of correction, and if they got her again they would do terrible bad things to her.'

'Please leave me alone with Sadie,' Selina said. 'You, too, Amy. Sadie isn't going to harm me. She is afraid of too many people around her bed.'

'Are you sure?' Amy asked, but backed away from the bed, signalling to Betty to accompany her. 'I'll be outside if you call. If she attacks you, just shout.'

'Sadie isn't going to attack me. She thinks you mean her harm.'

Selina moved slowly towards the bed as the others left. Sadie had pushed herself up against the pillows, and her knees were drawn up to her chest. She hugged them to her, her eyes wide and frightened as she looked at Selina.

'I've seen you in the kitchen. Nanny says you're all right…'

'None of us would harm you, Sadie,' Selina said, and approached further, stopping short as she saw fear leap in the girl's eyes. 'Someone has hurt you badly in the past. I can see that. But it won't happen here. I give you my word.'

Sadie hunched over her knees. 'I'm in the house, aren't I? If he knew, he would skin me alive.'

'Who do you fear, Sadie? Why would he hurt you?'

'Because I know his secret,' Sadie said. 'I tried to tell the old earl, but he told him and they said I was a liar—they said I was mad and they sent me to that terrible place. They did things to me there…said they were driving out the devil in me…but I'm not a liar and I'm not possessed by the devil. I know what I saw and I know who I am…'

'I am certain you're not mad, Sadie,' Selina said calmly. 'You are in my house now and under my care. I swear to you on my darling mother's grave that I shall not let any-one harm you. You may tell me everything and I prom-ise you will be safe.'

'You won't let them take me back to that place?' Sadie asked, her eyes intense and pleading. 'If I tell you what I know and who I am, you won't have me sent to a house of correction? They do such cruel things…and he, the doctor, was the worst of them. He…' Sadie's eyes filled with tears. 'He violated me when I was drugged. I couldn't stop him. They thought they had broken me, but I didn't swallow my drugs, and one night when they thought I was sleeping, I slipped out and ran away. Nanny has been feeding me because she believes me—but the old earl thought I was lying…'

'The old earl is dead,' Selina said. 'The new one is a kind man if you get to know him, and if I believe you, he will believe you—and I promise you on my honour that you will never go back to that terrible place.'

'The earl…' Sadie blinked and then brushed away her tears. 'The old earl was my grandfather. His son married my mother in church by special licence when he was but seventeen. But she was only a tavern girl, and the earl refused to allow the marriage. He forced his son to give her up and she went away. When I was born she married again. She did not tell her new husband that her true husband was still alive. He believed she was a widow and he treated us both well until…' Sadie hesitated. 'Mam wanted me to know the truth about my father, but he heard her—and he was so angry! He raged at her and he beat her. She ran away that night and took me with her…'

Sadie stopped as Selina sat on the edge of the bed and reached for her hand. 'You think I'm lying, don't you?'

'No, not at all,' Selina replied. 'I had been wondering who you reminded me of—you are rather like your grandmother. When you are better, I shall show you her portrait.'

'Mama was ill soon after we ran away from him. We had no money and she needed medicine that we could not afford. When she knew she was dying, she told me to come here and throw myself on my grandfather's mercy—but *he* was here. My stepfather. He had become the earl's agent and he was cheating him. He told me that if I revealed who I was, he would see that I was locked away.'

'He was a wicked, evil man,' Selina said. 'I am so sorry that you lost your mama.'

'I miss her so—but I fear *him*.' The girl's hand trembled. 'He said if I told anyone, the earl would say I was a liar and they would lock me up. But when I knew what he'd done—what he planned to do to the old earl—I tried to tell him. He wouldn't listen to me. He told Nanny to send me away and then…then my stepfather said I was a mad, bad girl and they sent me to that terrible place.'

Selina held her hand tightly. 'You are safe now. I shall not let anyone send you away.'

'When the earl told my stepfather that he knew he had been cheating him, he swore he would get even,' Sadie said. 'He was so angry when he was dismissed. He said Mam had cheated him for years—that he was entitled to all he'd taken. And then…'

Sadie's hand fluttered in Selina's. She let it go, sensing that the girl was still nervous.

'He was so drunk one night that he told me… He yelled at me and told me he would kill me the way he had killed my father…'

'He killed your father…the earl's eldest son?' Selina

stared at her in horror. 'He told you that when he was drunk?'

Sadie nodded. 'I tried to tell the old earl, but he didn't believe me. He said I was lying and not right in the head. They had me shut away... But I escaped and hid in the woods. Then I stole the key to the folly...'

'So that is why Nanny lied to me. She wanted to protect you,' Selina said. 'What is the name of the man who did all these wicked things?'

'His name is Simpson—Harvey Simpson,' Sadie told her. 'If he knew I was here...if he knew I had told you all of it...he would kill you—and me, too. He is a dangerous man. He would kill anyone that stood in his way. He might even kill the new earl, for he is spiteful and cruel.'

'Yes, I see that,' Selina said. 'You are safe here with us. The present earl is a good man and he will keep us all safe. When I tell him your story, he will know what to do—and he will thank you.'

'Will he be angry?' Sadie looked at her nervously. 'Will he think I am lying or mad?'

'No, I am certain he will not. I believe you, Sadie. You will stay here with my family, and we shall tell the earl everything, so that he can take the necessary steps to have this man arrested for his crimes.'

'Will he be angry with me? I locked him in the folly and stole his horse.'

'I daresay he would have been cross had you harmed the horse, but he found his way home to his stable and I believe Moorcroft will forgive you.'

'I didn't mean to harm him, but he had found my hiding place and I was afraid of being sent away. I did it on impulse and then I was sorry—so I let the horse free near to its stable and it cantered home.'

'You must apologise to the earl, but when he understands how badly you have been treated, he will not be cross. I promise you that you will not have to hide or live rough again. I shall personally see to it that you are safe, and I know that the earl will want to help you. You are a distant cousin of his, and he will think it right that he should protect and provide for you.'

Sadie reached forward and took hold of her hand. 'You are an angel. I did not think anyone could be so good.'

Selina laughed and shook her head. 'I assure you I have very selfish thoughts sometimes. I am not an angel. But some of the people you have known are very cruel. You must try to forget them, because you are with friends now.'

'I shall try,' Sadie said, and tears trickled down her face. 'I did not know that there was anyone as kind as you, Miss Searles.'

'You must call me Selina, for we are to be friends. Try to rest now and eat a little of your soup—unless it has gone cold...'

'I will eat a little even if it is,' Sadie said. 'I've been grateful for a dry crust in the past, and if Nanny had not taken pity on me, I might have died.'

'You are certain this is what you want?' Selina asked, looking into her sister's face anxiously. The evening was advanced, and it was the first time they had had a proper chance to talk. 'Please do not marry for our sakes, Amy dearest. I assure you we shall manage somehow. I know we may continue here for as long as we need to find a new home.'

'Henry is the man I love—the only man I shall ever want,' Amy said. 'You must never pity him or think he is second best for me, Selina. I never notice the scars. All I see is the love in his eyes and I feel his goodness. I know that he will never hurt me or desert me, and I want to spend my life with him. If you say I must wait, I shall, but I would rather marry him as soon as the banns may be called after Christmas.'

'If that is your true wish, I could not refuse you, dearest. Indeed, I am truly happy for you. To find someone who is all that you could desire must be every woman's dream. Where will you live?'

'We shall spend some of our time at Henry's own small estate, but Moorcroft is to have the east wing renovated for us here and we shall live there most of the time. They are such friends, and Moorcroft relies on Henry for so many things. It would be a pity to part them, even though we could live quite adequately on Henry's income.'

'You will be living here?' Selina felt a pang of regret. Had things been different, she, too, might have lived in this wonderful old house, with her sister as her close neighbour. 'Millie will be delighted with the news. I know she will look forward to her visits here.'

'Yes, she is happy for us, of course,' Amy said. 'And Henry says you will always be welcome to stay with us— here or at his own estate.'

'How kind of him,' Selina said, and her throat caught with emotion. 'I shall certainly wish to stay with you sometimes.' She smothered a sigh. 'I am delighted for you both, my love. Give Henry my best wishes—and now I must speak to Moorcroft...'

'It is very late,' Amy said as the longcase clock in the hall could be heard chiming twelve bells. 'Will it not wait until the morning?'

'I think I should seek him out tonight. I doubt he will have retired, for I believe he and Henry had some business to discuss. I have sent Trent to ask if he will meet me in the library, and he will be waiting, I think.'

'Then I shall not keep you longer.' Amy kissed her cheek. 'Thank you for being so understanding, Selina.'

'I want you and Millie to be happy. Nothing else matters.'

Selina kissed her and then left her, making her way down the stairs and through the hall to the library. She knocked and then entered, her heart catching as she saw Robert sitting before the fire. He had removed his tight-fitting coat and was wearing just a waistcoat over his shirt, his tight breeches tucked into highly polished top-boots. As he did not immediately move, she glanced at him and then saw that his eyes were closed. The warmth of the fire had lulled him to sleep as he waited. She almost went away, but then decided that what she had to say was too important.

'Forgive me,' she said, and touched his arm, giving him a little shake. 'I am sorry to wake you.'

Robert's eyes flew open and his hand shot out, imprisoning her wrist. For a moment he stared at her wildly, and she thought he would strike out, but then his expression cleared and he released her.

'Forgive me,' he said. 'I was dreaming. For a moment I thought I was being attacked. My memories can be violent and ugly.'

'I should not have disturbed you. You are tired. Should I go away and leave you to seek your bed?'

'No, of course not.' He was on his feet now, his gaze narrowed, focused on her face intently. 'You would not have asked to meet me like this if it were not important. What have you to tell me, Selina?'

'I think I have solved your mystery for you, Moorcroft. It is a tale of wickedness, and quite shocking, but I must tell you that I believe it to be true.'

'You have discovered who this wild girl is?'

'Sadie has been cruelly mistreated. I know you will want to do the right thing by her when you learn of her sad history. She has told me everything at some risk to her own safety. Enough, I think, to enable you to bring an evil man to justice.'

'You intrigue me,' Robert said. 'Please sit down, Selina. Would you care for a drink—sweet sherry, or perhaps brandy?'

'Neither, thank you,' Selina replied and sat opposite him. 'We were right to believe that your uncle's agent had cheated him. What we did not know was that the man was also a murderer. He killed your cousin—who was Sadie's father—and he had Sadie incarcerated in a house of correction when she tried to tell the late earl the truth. She was treated abominably there and eventually escaped. She came back here and has been hiding wherever she could find shelter.'

'She locked me in the folly because she was afraid I would send her back to that place if I discovered she had been sleeping there?'

'Yes, I imagine that was her fear. She was sorry afterwards, and let your horse go near its stable.'

'She did not, however, release me.'

'No, because she was too frightened. It was a foolish reaction, Robert. Surely you can see that she is a vulnerable child and meant no harm? I have promised her she will be safe with us. I've told her you will find this rogue who harmed your uncle's family and deal with him.'

'You have a great deal of faith in me,' Robert said, and smiled. 'You called me Robert… You actually used my name as if you meant it.'

'I… Forgive me,' Selina said, and blushed. 'It was a slip of the tongue.'

'One I wish you would use more.' Robert moved towards her, his eyes intent on her face.

Selina was aware of the lateness of the hour and of the intimacy of the situation. She ought to leave but her feet were frozen to the floor.

'Selina, you must know that I…'

He moaned in frustration, reached out and drew her to him, then bent his head and kissed her with such tenderness that her flesh seemed to dissolve with pleasure. She leaned into him with a sigh. This felt so good. It was where she ached to be, where she felt she belonged.

Selina clung to him, her body melting into his. It was just as it had been on the night of that never-forgotten ball. She was boneless with pleasure, her lips soft and welcoming beneath his. All thought of duty and propriety fled as she surrendered to his kiss. How she wished she could stay here for ever, be his and he hers. Her hands moved into his hair, stroking the back of his neck, and she felt him shudder with an answering need and pull her in closer, the burn of his desire turning her to a flame of living desire.

His hand moved down her back, pressing her close to him so that she felt his extreme need, and she moaned, her head falling back, her lips opening on a breath of sweet ecstasy. This was paradise…the happiness she had for so long dreamed of without hope.

'Robert…' she breathed. 'Oh, Robert…'

'Forgive me,' he whispered as he released her. 'I've wanted to do that for so long but I have no right. It is such a mess, Selina. Adelaide claims to be carrying my child, and the devil of it is that she may be telling the truth— though I shall never be certain.'

'You think there may have been someone else?' Selina gazed up at him, her heart racing. 'Why would she lie to you?'

'Because she wants a father for her child and a wedding ring,' Robert said, his voice becoming harsh. 'She does not care for me in the true sense, Selina. We had a mild fling in Italy. I was bored, and she was looking for an affair that might lead to marriage. Because I had been intimate with her, I felt obliged to ask her to marry me, even though I was honest enough to tell her it would not be a love match. She refused me and I thought that the end of it. When I came here, I considered myself free. That day in your parlour—' Robert broke off and ran his fingers though his hair. 'It is the cruellest stroke of luck ever. I shall not lie to you, Selina. I never expected to experience love again, which is why I believed a marriage of convenience would suit me. As well Adelaide as anyone, I thought—but then I met you again. I was aware of something immediately, but I must admit it was a while before I remembered that night in Bath…'

Selina's heartbeat quickened. 'You did remember, then? I knew as soon as I saw you in the library that day. Had Mr Breck mentioned your name at the start, I might not have taken the chance to come here.'

'You would have avoided me?' Robert reached out, tipping her chin so that she looked up at him. 'Did I hurt you so much? Have I harmed you, Selina?'

'It was such a foolish incident,' Selina admitted. 'I knew you had been drinking, for I tasted the wine on your lips that night, but I could not forget you. I told myself a thousand times that you had merely been flirting—that it meant nothing to you—but for me it was special. I kept the memory enshrined in my heart for years. Until we met again…'

'And then you saw that I was not the bold young hero who had made love to you in the moonlight and promised to return and marry you?'

'You never meant to keep that promise. Of course I knew that…'

'But I did,' Robert said, and he was smiling at her in such a way that her heart went flying. 'I fell in love with an angel that night, Selina. However, I was young and selfish, and I thought I had all the time in the world. I wanted to win glory, and I thought only of the great adventure that lay ahead of me. I told myself that I would write to you and make you a formal offer—that when I came home on leave, we would learn to know each other properly. But then I was caught up in war, and reality drove the dream from my head. Though at the back of my mind, the image of an angel remained.'

'Yet you fell in love with Juanita?'

'No, I never loved her. Her story is bitter, for she was cruelly used—by men under my command. When I found her dying of her injuries, I held her in my arms until the last and can never forget what she suffered.' He paused, then, 'I was forced to hang the man who led the others into such a mad, evil act—and he was my friend.'

'Robert, that must have been so hard for you.'

'The reproach in his eyes as I sent him to the gallows haunts me still. So many deaths, so much pain—can you wonder I forgot a night when all was perfect and like a dream?'

'Yes, I understand. The life you had known in England must have seemed like another world away.'

'Yes, exactly. The horror of war, the pain and the smell of death…' Robert drew away from her and turned, staring into the fire. 'When Juanita was so cruelly raped and murdered, it devastated me. She died in my arms, beg-

ging me to help her, and I could do nothing but hang a
man who had once saved me from certain death.'

'I am so sorry. You must have felt such pain.'

'Yes.' He turned to her and she saw the anguish in his
face. 'I thought I should never recover from it. Too many
deaths, too many friends lost. Had it not been for Henry,
I think I should have gone mad from my grief.'

'Yes, I believe I can understand. The bond between you
shows in the way you are together—your complete trust
in each other.' Selina hesitated. 'You know that Amy and
Henry are to be married?'

'Henry is very fortunate. I wish I might be as fortunate
as he.' His eyes pleaded with her for understanding. 'If
I had my choice… You are the woman I wish to marry,
Selina. You must know that I care for you deeply?'

'I admit I have felt something between us.' Tears stung
her eyes and she could hardly speak. 'Yet I know that
you are not free, Robert. If the comtesse is carrying your
child, you must marry her. You do not have a choice.'

'No, I do not—if the child is mine,' he said, and his
mouth thinned. 'Henry believes Adelaide took another
lover at the same time as I was visiting her. He says the
person involved owes him a debt and will tell him the
truth. I know he has written a letter asking if this man
knows Adelaide is with child and if he believes it to be
his.'

'Surely she would have gone to him first?'

'That is my hope, but he must tell us if it was so,'
Robert replied. 'If he turned her down for reasons of his
own, I shall arrange something for her. I will help her to

disappear for a while and have the child adopted if she wishes—but if it is not mine, I shall not marry her.' His voice broke. 'How can I marry her when I love *you*?'

'Oh, Robert...' Selina's voice almost broke, too. 'I wish I could tell you that she did not matter—that we must marry despite everything—but I cannot. You are bound by your honour as a gentleman, and if you marry her, I must go away. I shall not visit my sister here, only at Henry's estate. We cannot meet once your decision is made because...' Tears trickled down her cheeks and she brushed them away. 'It would hurt us both too much.'

'I have hurt you again,' Robert said bleakly. 'You should hate me, Selina. I am a worthless fellow, not fit to worship at your feet.'

'Foolish man!' she chided, and smiled through her tears. 'Believe me, I would rather have loved you and known you than gone through life without ever knowing what love might be. I shall not hate you, Robert—I shall make a life without you, just as I planned before we met again.'

'You will allow me to help you? I can give you a home in a place of your choice and an income...'

'No.' She touched his lips. 'I shall make my own way, my dearest one. I am young and strong and well able to work. I shall apply to a lady who needs a companion and find contentment in looking after her.'

'I have a great-aunt who may need a companion. I believe her present companion is thinking of retiring. Would you allow me to do such a small thing?'

Selina hesitated, then inclined her head. 'You may mention me as looking for such a position, but you will not beg her to take me—or pay her to do so.'

'I do not think it necessary. She would be fortunate to have your services.'

'Then I shall look forward to Christmas, and afterwards...'

'We shall see what happens.' Robert reached out to touch her cheek with the tips of his fingers. 'Do not give up all hope, my love. I have not. I may still persuade Adelaide that she could do better than a man who intends to live his life in the country.'

Selina gave him a tremulous smile. 'I do not think she cares for the country much. She has not stirred out of the house.'

'We have a few more days until Christmas. Who knows? We may yet have a miracle. Perhaps she will decide she does not wish to marry me, and go away.'

'Perhaps,' Selina said—and yet privately she held out little hope. What woman in her right mind would not want to be Robert's wife?

'As for the girl—Sadie—I shall do all I can for her,' Robert said. 'Since you believe her, I must, too—and now that I know what her stepfather did, I shall make certain he is arrested and tried for his crimes.'

'We only have Sadie's word,' Selina said. 'I do believe her, but would a court of law?' She frowned. 'You have only to look at the portrait of your uncle's wife as a young woman and you will see the likeness. If that part of her tale is true, why should she lie about the rest?'

'I daresay she would not.' Robert smiled, but his eyes

were dark and angry. He was going to leave no stone un-turned in his efforts to find a solution to this difficult situation. 'This man will pay for his crimes. I promise you that, Selina. All we have to do is discover where he is hiding…'

CHAPTER TEN

'THANK you for helping me sew this for Sadie.' Selina smiled at her sisters. 'I do not think I could have managed it in the time if you had not given up your own pursuits to help me.'

'It was the least we could do,' Amy said. 'You have had more than enough to do, Selina. Sadie has needed nursing—though she seems much better now.'

'The doctor agrees with me that she will be well enough to join us for Christmas Eve, even though it is tomorrow,' Selina said as she snipped her thread and shook the folds of silk, holding the gown up against herself so that her sisters could see the effect. 'I believe this will suit her, and I am sure it will fit, for Nanny brought me one of her old gowns so that I could measure it without giving away our surprise.'

'That colour would have looked so well on you,' Millie said. 'It is a shame. That silk was to have been for your new gown, Selina.'

'I have other gowns that will do perfectly well for me,'

Selina said. 'Please do not begrudge Sadie anything we can give her, Millie. She has suffered far more than we can possibly understand. There was no time to shop for more silk, and I really do not mind.'

'You never do,' Millie said, and went to give her sister a hug. 'I do not begrudge Sadie anything. I like her, and I know she has been badly treated by that wicked man. It was lucky, really, that she fell down the stairs at the folly, for if she had not been brought here unconscious and feeling ill, she would probably have run away again.'

'Yes, I believe she would,' Selina agreed. 'Now she is with her family. Moorcroft has seen the portrait of his grandmother and he agrees she is very like her. He hardly remembers the lady, but the portrait is proof enough that she is his cousin's daughter—though not proof that her father married her mother, of course. He says that he shall settle a generous sum on her, whether or not the marriage is proven, and he means to offer her a home with him.'

'Sadie does not wish to live with anyone but you,' Millie informed her. 'She says she is grateful for Robert's offer—and she isn't frightened of him now—but she wants to live with *you*. At least for a while.'

'Sadie knows that she has not been brought up to be a lady,' Selina said. 'It will be some months before she is confident enough to go out in society—perhaps longer. She has been scarred mentally and physically. It will take time for her to recover her confidence.'

'She feels safe with you,' Amy said. 'Millie is to go to school in a few months, and if you are to work, I am not sure how you will manage.'

'Rob…Moorcroft has asked me to become her companion for a few months now he has heard what Sadie wants to do. He will pay her expenses and we shall manage perfectly well, for we do not plan to mix extensively in society. When I am settled, I shall invite friends to dine and to take tea. Sadie will need some new gowns, but Moorcroft will provide the money for her clothes. He will not force her to join him until she is ready.'

'He is to begin the renovations here after Henry and I are married,' Amy said. 'Our wing is to be done first and then the west wing. I think he may return to London until the repairs are finished.'

'Yes, perhaps.'

Selina laid down the silk gown she planned to give Sadie as a Christmas gift from the Searles sisters. The previous evening, Robert had sought her advice about his own gift to Sadie, and she'd asked if there was a small trinket that had belonged to his family—something his future wife would not consider a great loss.

'I do have a small pearl necklet that was my grandmother's. It was left to me with some other personal pieces in her will.'

'That sounds ideal,' Selina had told him with a smile. 'She would not wish for diamonds or rubies or any such jewel. It will take Sadie a long time to feel at home with her new family and the prospects that are now hers.'

'Adelaide must be prepared to take her under her wing when she is presented to society.'

'Have you spoken to her about it yet?'

'No, not yet,' Robert replied with a frown. 'I had

hoped we might have heard something positive from Bolingwood by now.'

'Henry has no reply to his letter?'

'None. I fear there will be none. Why should Bolingwood bother to answer? I daresay he thinks it an impertinence that Henry asked.'

'Yes, I daresay he might.'

Selina had not pushed her questions further. As yet Adelaide had not met her husband-to-be's new cousin. She was behaving as if she were already mistress of the house, paying only lip service to being a guest and throwing knowing smiles at her hostess. She was, of course, marking time until Christmas was over and Selina took her leave. How she would take to the idea of being required to introduce a girl like Sadie into society was an unknown quantity. There was also the question of whether Sadie would accept her as her mentor.

Somehow Selina felt that the two would feel mutual antipathy. Sadie had accepted Selina's sisters, and the assistance of her maid, but the only person she truly trusted was Selina.

'Robert says he will take me to school the first time,' Millie said now, as she put away her pin case and her silks. 'You will come with us, won't you, Selina? Amy will be on her honeymoon, but you will be in your new home by then.'

'Yes, I certainly hope—' Selina broke off as a light tap at the door heralded Trent's arrival. She looked at him and smiled as he entered, seeming a little uncomfortable. 'Is something wrong?'

'A…a guest has arrived, ma'am,' Trent said. 'At least he says he's your cousin, and he says it's important that he speak to you at once.'

'Cousin Joshua is here?' Amy looked at her in surprise. 'Did he write to you, Selina? Did you know he was coming?'

'No, I had no idea.' Selina frowned as she stood up. 'I cannot imagine why he should arrive the day before Christmas Eve without letting us know. Something must be very wrong for him to have made the journey. We have not had more snow, it is true, but the roads are frozen.'

'He says he is sure you will put him up for the night,' Trent told her. 'I wasn't sure you would wish to do so, ma'am.'

'It is very inconsiderate of him to make extra work for you all,' Selina said with a frown. 'I suppose I had better see him…'

'Do not ask him to come in here,' Millie cried. 'I don't want to see him.'

Selina looked at her in surprise. Her sister looked apprehensive, but Amy echoed her plea, and she smiled.

'What a pair you are,' she chided. 'If our cousin has travelled all this way, he must consider his mission important—and I can hardly turn him away if he wishes for a bed for the night. You must both be polite to him, if nothing more.'

'Why should we have him here, spoiling our Christmas?' Millie said, and pulled a face. 'He turned us out of our home and took all our things away from us.'

'Not quite all.' Selina frowned. It was on the tip of her

tongue to ask what was bothering Millie, but she bit the question back. 'Where is my cousin, Trent?'

'I asked him to wait in the other parlour, ma'am.'

'Was the comtesse there?'

'Not when I showed him there, Miss Searles.'

'Very well. I shall come now.'

Selina left the room. She felt annoyed with her cousin for arriving unannounced. If his mission was so important that it could not wait, he might have written to her in advance. She could not imagine what had brought him all this way so close to Christmas. Surely he must have guests invited over the next few days? If it should snow, he might be stuck here for days.

She silently prayed that the snow would hold off until Cousin Joshua had taken his leave. Pausing for a moment outside the parlour door, she heard raised voices.

'This is *my* parlour. Who are you, sir—and may I ask what you are doing here?'

Adelaide had returned and was clearly not in the best of moods. She did not care for a stranger in the parlour she had made her own.

'I thought my cousin was the tenant here?'

'I am to be mistress here when I marry the earl,' Adelaide replied frostily. 'Really, Miss Searles might have told me she had invited a male for Christmas. She seems in the habit of acquiring undesirable guests...'

Selina bit back the angry words that rose to her lips, managing to keep calm as she entered the parlour.

'Cousin Joshua,' she said. 'This is unexpected. I think your mission must be urgent or you would not have come unannounced at such a time.' Forcing a smile to her lips, she turned to Adelaide. 'Could I possibly ask you to remove to the library for a short time, ma'am? I think I need to be private with my visitor.'

'Well, really... You should remember that this is my house, Miss Searles. It is most inconvenient.'

'For the moment it is *my* home—and may I remind you that you are a guest, ma'am? I should be glad of a little privacy.'

'Be prepared to leave as soon as Christmas is over,' Adelaide hissed at her. 'I shall speak to Robert immediately.'

'Please do so, if you are unhappy with the situation.'

Selina held the door for her, her head up as she waited silently, proudly, for the other woman to leave. Her manner scarcely thawed as she looked at her cousin once the door was firmly closed.

'Well, cousin, to what do I owe your visit? I must tell you that I should have preferred you to write before coming here.'

'Believe me, I had no wish to make the journey,' Joshua said. 'Indeed, I was quite put out, Selina. At first I could not believe it had happened, and I made exhaustive searches before I decided that this could not be allowed to continue. Such a theft is a serious matter—very serious indeed.'

Selina's stomach clenched. She recalled the apprehension in her youngest sister's eyes and suddenly knew why her cousin had come here without bothering to give her notice.

'I'm sorry,' she said, playing for time. 'I'm not sure I understand you, Joshua. What theft are you talking about?'

'I think you know very well. Your sister has taken the *Book of Hours*. It was there when I visited you that day the lawyer came. Your servants tell me that it disappeared the day your sisters and you left the house. Since Millicent made her feelings known to me on the subject, I have no doubt who has taken it.'

'You are accusing Millie of stealing a book that belongs to the estate?'

'Yes.' Joshua stared at her belligerently. 'I know very well that your family considers *me* the thief—you feel cheated because the estate came to me—but that is the law, Selina. You may not like it, but that book belongs to the estate. It is part of the entail, and your father had no right to promise it to the child.'

'You are perfectly right. And Millie knows that, because I told her. How can you be certain she took it? I believe you have had builders in to restore the house? Are you sure none of them took it—or the servants may have packed it away...'

'You are protecting her, of course,' Joshua said, and his eyes glittered with temper. 'I should not enjoy making this official, Selina. If I am forced to go to court to recover my property, it will ruin you—destroy what little reputation your sisters might have. Your own reputation is distinctly impaired by your reckless behaviour. Do you wish Millicent to be known as a thief? She would never be received in society again.'

'How dare you threaten my family?' Selina suddenly felt the thread of calm snap inside her. She had tried so hard not to resent Joshua's behaviour, refused to rise to the bait as he gloated over their misfortune, but this—this was beyond bearing. 'You will leave this instant,' she said. 'Please go now. I refuse to listen to another word against my—'

'I have no intention of leaving without my property.'

Joshua's voice had risen, too. He took a step towards her, the glitter of menace in his eyes. Selina stood her ground, her tone cold as she repeated her request.

'Please leave my home, sir. I shall not give you a bed for the night. You may stay at an inn and—'

'Selina—what is this? Is this…gentleman annoying you?'

The door had opened unnoticed behind her. She spun round as she heard Robert's tone of enquiry, angry tears in her eyes.

'Will you please escort this gentleman from my home?' she said shakily. 'He has insulted my family and threatened my sisters with ruin. Now he refuses to leave.'

'I have every right to stay until I get my—' Joshua broke off abruptly as a hand closed over his arm. His eyes stared as he looked at the earl's face and saw his expression. Colour washed into and out of his cheeks, and he spluttered with indignation as he was hauled from the room, propelled through the hall and then thrust outside the front door.

'You will go to the local inn—The King's Head—and you will wait until I come there,' said Earl Banford in a tone that brooked no argument. 'I shall discover the truth of your accusations and I shall speak with you later.'

'That is all very well but...' Joshua's blustering tone faded as he recognised the iron will of his superior in rank. 'That book belongs to me—and I know Millie took it. I want it back.'

'When I discover the truth of the matter, you shall have your just deserts,' Robert said. 'Another word and I'll have my grooms take a whip to you and beat you off the estate.'

'You wouldn't...' Joshua had been about to say he wouldn't dare, but he realised this man would dare anything. 'You're welcome to the lot of them. Her reputation isn't worth a candle. Everyone knows what has been—'

At a movement from the earl, he took to his heels and started to run, forgetting to summon his horse in the sudden fear of his life.

Robert's eyes gleamed with satisfaction, then he turned and walked back into the house. The front parlour was empty. He knew exactly where Selina had gone, and frowned as he imagined the scene that was taking place in her personal domain.

'Millie—how could you?' Selina asked sadly as she saw her sister's look, which was half defiance and half fear.

'It isn't fair...' Millie said, tears beginning to well in her eyes. 'I love that book—and our cousin only cares about what it is worth.'

'And what *is* this infamous book worth?' a new voice asked, and three pairs of female eyes turned on the earl, who was standing in the doorway.

Millie went pink and looked down at the floor, making no answer.

'I imagine it must be worth somewhere between five hundred and a thousand pounds,' Selina said. 'Millie knows she did wrong. We must give it back, of course. I should have done so immediately if he had not threatened us in that way. I fear he means to ruin us and have his revenge.'

'He will do nothing of the kind unless he wishes to answer to *me*,' Robert said in a calm, firm tone that all three ladies recognised as the voice of authority.

'We cannot ask you to become involved...'

'Selina, you will allow me to manage this for you,' Robert said. He looked at Millie. 'You do have the book?'

'I...I hid it in the library,' Millie said. 'It is behind the books on the top shelf, which Henry has finished cataloguing.'

'Very well. You will fetch it and bring it here to me—now, Millie.'

'Yes, sir. I am very sorry.'

'Millie, before you go...?'

'Yes, sir?'

'I understand your feelings perfectly. The entailing of an estate is often unfair to female relatives. It is neither right nor fair that these things should happen, but it is the law. The book must go back—but you will not be labelled a thief. Trust me in this, please?'

'Yes, sir.' She twisted her hands before her. 'I am truly sorry.'

'No, Millie. I am sorry that these things have happened

to you—and your cousin might have been more understanding in this matter. However, I shall make certain he does not bother any of you again.'

'Thank you, sir.'

'Robert—I am still Robert to you,' he said, and the door opened and shut behind her.

'That was kind,' Selina said, and her throat was tight with emotion. 'I daresay she has learned a salutary lesson now.'

'Yes, I imagine she feels about one inch high,' Robert said. 'As it happens, I *do* believe these things are often unfair. Sometimes it is possible for an arrangement to be made. Your cousin might have done something had he chosen.'

'I should not have taken his charity.'

'No,' Robert said, and smiled oddly. 'I do not suppose you would.'

'I am grateful for your intervention.'

'There are things you should know, Selina, but for the moment I cannot reveal all. Fear not, the situation is not as desperate as you believe.'

'What do you mean?'

'Later. Please trust me, Selina.'

'Robert…'

'Excuse me—I have something more to say to Millie, and I think it best said in private.'

'Well!' Amy breathed deeply after he left, shutting the door softly. 'Thank goodness Robert heard what Cousin Joshua said to you. I can hardly believe he was so spiteful—but I suppose I should have known. No one with an ounce of decent feeling would have turned us out of our home so soon after Mama died.'

'I think I may have been partly to blame. I did lose my temper with him.'

'Had he spoken to me as he did you, I think I might have shot him,' Amy said hotly. 'He is a thoroughly unpleasant man. I could wish that Robert might thrash him.'

'He came close to it, I think,' Selina said, and smiled. 'You should have seen the look on our cousin's face when Robert took hold of him and propelled him out of the house.'

'I think that some small recompense,' Amy said, and laughed. 'We shall not let him spoil Christmas, Selina. Robert came here to make sure that we would all attend his lighting of the Yule log tomorrow. I assured him that Millie and I would be there. I think he intended to ask you, too—which was why he was outside the front parlour.'

'Yes, of course I shall be there,' Selina said, forgetting that she had cast doubt on it some days earlier. 'Sadie is so looking forward to seeing the log and the decorations in the hall. I think she has never been to a Christmas party, and she would not dare to attend without me.'

'How fortunate,' Amy said in a low voice, and smiled as Selina stared at her. 'It gives *you* an excuse, dearest.'

'If I needed one…'

'I know how you feel about him,' Amy said. 'Did you really think you could hide it from me? We both know you love him, Selina. Millie wanted to put a frog in the comtesse's bed, but I told her if she did she would not be allowed to attend the party.'

'I do not think it would drive her away—and Millie is already in too much trouble,' Selina said, and sighed. 'Cousin Joshua is spiteful, but I think he was about to repeat gossip he'd heard. I think my own reputation must have suffered when I took this house.'

'How could you have known that the new earl would return home sooner and decide to take up residence? Besides, we live in separate residences.'

'Do we?' Selina smiled. 'In truth we have been forever in each other's pockets. When I nursed Robert…' She shook her head. 'I made my decision and I do not regret it. What can it matter now? You are to marry Henry, and by the time you introduce Millie into society, I shall have been long forgotten.'

'You will *not* just run away and allow her to win? I thought you had more fight in you, Selina.'

'You do not understand, Amy dearest. If it were a matter of fighting for Robert's love… But it is not. He is bound by his code of honour. I could not ask him to turn away from it for my sake. Besides, if the child is his, then it must be born in wedlock. If I demanded that he forget everything he believes in for my sake, I should not be true to him or myself.'

'Surely you do not believe her story? She is lying, Selina. I would wager all I have on it.'

'Please do not,' Selina said. 'We may believe she is lying—but how can we know? Only Adelaide knows the truth.'

'Perhaps even she is not sure.'

Selina shook her head. 'We shall not discuss this again. I am going upstairs to see Sadie, and I shall give her the new gown. She will wish to wear it for the party tomorrow evening.'

'Yes, I daresay she is wondering where you are. She said she might join us for dinner this evening. I have loaned her one of my dresses. It was something I had the year before last and I believe it will fit her—it is not as fine as her new dress, of course, but she seemed pleased.'

'That was kind of you,' Selina said. 'Do not scold Millie when she returns, Amy. I think she knows she has done wrong.'

'Robert has something he wishes to say to her when she gives him the book. She will feel shamed enough.'

Selina nodded and left her sister alone. She was thoughtful as she walked upstairs to Sadie's room, the new dress over her arm. Millie was young and impulsive, and this lesson had been a hard one for her to learn.

She could only hope that Robert could contain the affair before it became a terrible scandal.

'This is the book you wished returned, I believe?' Robert placed it on the table in front of Joshua. 'I do not think it has been harmed.'

'I *knew* she had taken it,' Joshua said, and pounced with such glee that Robert's lip curled in a sneer of disgust. 'The little thief…'

'Some would consider that you and the law of this land that protects the entail are the thieves.'

'You know the law is on my side,' Joshua blustered, his cheeks heated. 'It is my duty to preserve the estate library as I inherited it—as it was when my uncle lived.'

'Yes—to an extent,' Robert agreed. 'However, we both know there are ways of breaking the entail. Unless you have a son, it ends with you, does it not?'

'Yes.' Joshua's eyes narrowed. 'If you are suggesting that I should give the book back to her…'

'I do not suggest you give anything away. However, you do know that as there are no other beneficiaries at present, it *is* possible to break the entail on this matter—for a sum of money.'

'Yes, I suppose. It is worth a lot of money—at least six hundred pounds…'

'I daresay it might be worth more. You could sell it if you reimburse the estate with either goods or money to the value of the thing you dispose of—that is perfectly legal.'

'Yes…' Joshua looked at him warily. 'It has not yet been valued. It might be worth as much as a thousand pounds—or even guineas.'

'A thousand guineas or fifteen hundred pounds,' Robert agreed pleasantly. 'Would you sell it for the right price?'

'Perhaps… Would you give fifteen hundred pounds for it?' Joshua asked, still uncertain of where this was going.

'Would you sell for that amount?'

'Well, I… Yes.' Greed was too much for Joshua. 'Yes. As you say, there is no other male relative. I would take fifteen hundred. I could invest it in land, perhaps.'

'Very well—fifteen hundred it is.' Robert put his hand into his coat pocket and pulled out a piece of quality vellum with his seal on it. 'Here is a bill of sale. Please sign and this is yours.' He placed a draft on his bank for fifteen hundred pounds beside the deed.

'You would pay so much just to please a child?' Joshua seemed stunned, but picked up the pen supplied by the landlord on the table in front of him and signed without bothering to do more than skim the deed of sale. 'No… it's for *her*—Selina—isn't it? Payment for past favours, I daresay?'

'At another time you would meet me for that,' Robert said quietly. He picked up the sheet of vellum and blew on it. Then, when it was dry, he folded it and put it inside his coat pocket. 'However, it is Christmas, and Selina would never forgive me if I killed her cousin. It would cast a shadow over the festivities.' He smiled as Joshua pocketed the bank draft. 'I am persuaded you will mind your manners in future—unless you wish to find yourself in trouble.'

'What do you mean?' Joshua demanded as Robert picked up the book. 'You may threaten to shoot me, but you cannot command my opinions or my tongue.'

'Your cousins are under my protection. If you do them harm, either now or in the future, you will find me a bad enemy. Believe me, you would soon wish that you had never been born. I do not make idle threats, and if anything happens to destroy Selina or her sisters, you will feel the full might of my vengeance.'

Joshua stared at him sullenly. 'I suppose you intend to marry her? I wish you joy of the cold bitch.'

'What I intend to do is none of your affair. You may

rest assured that you will not be invited to the wedding if she should accept me. I shall wish you good day, sir.'

Slipping the small but very expensive book into his coat pocket, Robert left the inn. It would soon be back with the person who loved it most in the world. Robert was smiling grimly as he walked to his horse and mounted. One obstacle overcome. He only wished that the next might be as easy…

'Are you sure that you wish to walk as far as the folly?' Millie asked, and looked uneasily at the girl beside her. 'It is your first day out of bed. I know you had dinner with us last night, but you haven't been out of the house since you fell.'

'I feel perfectly well. If you are afraid of being scolded, I can go alone.'

'Certainly not,' Millie said stoutly. 'Selina would tell me not to let you go alone—but I think she would not have let you come had she known what you intended. You said a little walk in the gardens.'

'Yes, I know. I did not mean to deceive her, but there is something I hid near the folly. It is all I have in the world, Millie. Your sister has been so kind to me. I want to give her something pretty as a gift.'

'She doesn't expect anything,' Millie said. 'Selina has only done what she thinks right. I agree with her. That terrible man deserves to be punished. I hope they catch him soon—and I hope he hangs.'

'I am not sure they can prove he is guilty of murder,' Sadie told her, her eyes shadowed with memories. 'He told me in a drunken fit and no one believed me. They thought I was a mad girl.'

'Well, we know you are not,' Millie said. 'We are your friends, Sadie. You do not have to give us gifts just because we made that dress for you.'

'Selina gave me more than a dress,' Sadie said, and hugged her arm. 'She believed in me. Nanny has been kind, but I don't think she truly believed everything I told her. You are so lucky to have Selina as your sister.'

'Yes, I know.'

Millie looked fearful as they came in sight of the folly. She caught at Sadie's arm.

'Look—someone has just tried to enter the tower but it's locked. See—he is looking round now... Do you think he has seen us?'

Sadie's face went white, and she stopped in her tracks as she followed Millie's pointing finger. 'That is *him*... He must have followed me here. He knew I sometimes went to the Folly as it is where my mother and father met... their special place.'

'He must have come looking for you but could not get in because Henry has had the lock repaired.'

'Yes...' Sadie was pale, and she let go of Millie's arm suddenly and ran to a bush near the folly. She scrabbled around the base and then stood up, clutching a small bundle wrapped in a scarf. At once she started back towards Millie. 'We had better go quickly.'

Even as she spoke, the man recognised her and yelled, then started to sprint towards her.

Sadie screamed at Millie in panic. 'Go back!' she cried. 'Tell them he is here!'

Millie hesitated. Then, taking her silver penknife from her coat pocket, she opened the small blade and ran towards them. Sadie was screaming as the man grabbed her, struggling and trying to pull away from him, but he had her by the arm and was dragging her with him. What he had not bargained for was the whirlwind that was Millicent Searles in a rage. As he fought to hold on to his quarry, he was suddenly set upon by a fireball of yelling female form who stabbed at his cheek with her knife, drawing its sharp blade across his flesh so deeply that he screamed in pain and let go of Sadie.

'Run!' Millie cried, and grabbed Sadie as she hesitated, forcing her to run with her.

Behind them their assailant gave another scream— of rage this time—and clutched at his face, which was bleeding profusely. However, the wound was more painful than dangerous, and after a moment of stunned surprise, he shouted after them and began to pursue them.

'You go on,' Sadie gasped as they heard his pounding feet behind them. 'He's gaining on us. I can't run much further. I feel unwell. Go on—save yourself…tell the earl what has happened.'

'I won't leave you,' Millie said, breathing hard. She kept hold of Sadie's hand and kept on pulling her, even though it slowed her down and she knew the man was gaining on them. 'I won't let him take you—I won't.'

The man was almost upon them. Sadie pulled away from Millie, turned to face him, pushing Millie behind her, urging her to go and leave her. But Millie refused to leave her.

'Touch her and I'll kill you,' Millie said, and darted out from behind Sadie, penknife in hand. 'I'll slit your throat, you wicked rogue. You won't take her again. She has friends.'

'You evil little brat,' Harvey Simpson snarled. 'Think you can mark me and get away with it—I'll see you sold into slavery. We know how to deal with a troublesome child like you.'

Ignoring Sadie for a moment, he pounced on Millie. She screamed like a banshee and started kicking and stabbing at him with her knife, but he grabbed her wrist, twisting it until the tiny knife fell from her grasp. Then he grabbed her by the throat, lifting her off the ground, his narrowed eyes glaring at her as he spat into her face.

It was the last thing Harvey Simpson was to do in his life. Even as his other hand came out to strike Millie, a shot rang out, and he stared in shock, a trickle of blood coming from the corner of his mouth. His grasp on Millie opened and she fell to the floor. He crumpled at the knees and then fell forward across her. Millie screamed at the horror of being trapped beneath his twitching body, but in another moment it was yanked off her and she was being scooped up into a pair of strong arms.

'Thank God,' Henry said as he looked down at her. She was streaked with blood but he could see it was not her own. 'You brave girl, Millie. You're all right now. I've got you. You are safe with me.'

'Is she hurt?' Robert asked. He had bent over the body

of his victim, smoking pistol still in hand. 'He's dead. I hoped he might live to hang, but it seems my aim was too good.' He stood up and looked at Millie, who was now standing on her feet but clinging to Henry for all she was worth, and then at Sadie, who looked as if she might faint.

'Brave girls,' he said, and strode to Sadie's side, scooping her up even as she tried to protest that she could walk. 'I won't ask why you were all this way from the house. I shall just thank God that we happened to ride this way.'

'It's my fault,' Sadie said, and promptly swooned.

'She wanted to fetch that bundle,' Millie said and, shaking off Henry's supporting arm, darted forward to pick up the little parcel Sadie had dropped. 'Something for Selina, I think. That man…he's the one who hurt her. The one who did all the terrible things—cheating the late earl and murdering your cousin…' Millie blushed as they looked at her in shock. 'Well, if you don't listen at keyholes, no one tells you anything if they think you're a child.'

Robert smiled. 'Just as well you have a mind of your own, isn't it, Millie? You must remind me not to get on your wrong side. Had you been a little better armed, I think our friend here would not have stood a chance.'

Millie drew a sigh of relief and looked at him shyly. 'You're not angry with me, then?'

'No,' Robert said. 'I am not in the least angry. I might have been months trying to find this fellow. You and Sadie have saved me a lot of trouble. But you must promise me one thing…' He glanced at Sadie, who had begun to come to her senses. Setting her down on her feet, he held her until he was sure she was steady.

'Anything. We'll do whatever you say,' Millie promised. 'Won't we, Sadie?'

'Yes…' Sadie said a little doubtfully.

'Please do not mention this to Amy and Selina until after the celebrations. We wouldn't want them to worry, would we?'

'Oh, no,' Millie agreed instantly. 'This will be our secret. You must promise, too, Sadie. We shan't tell my sisters because they want Christmas to be special this year—and we don't want to spoil it for them, do we?'

'No.' Sadie smiled as she met the earl's eyes and read his amusement. 'No, Millie. We don't want to spoil things for Selina. She doesn't need to know any of this.'

'I shall tell her when I'm ready,' Robert said. 'Now, I have to take care of this—the magistrate does need to be told. Henry will take you home.'

'No,' Sadie said, and took Millie's arm. 'We are both all right now—aren't we?'

Millie nodded.

'Henry must stay with you, Robert. You will need a witness—and I'll swear to it that Harvey Simpson was trying to kill us both. He would never have let Millie go after what she did to him.'

'You'd better give me that knife,' Robert said. 'I'll see you get it back when they've finished with it, Millie.'

'Papa gave it to me. He told me that if I was ever attacked, I should use it.'

'Which you did—to good effect,' Henry said. 'I think perhaps I shall teach you to shoot, Millie. A girl like you should have her own pistol—just in case.'

'Good grief, Henry!' Robert exclaimed. 'What will you teach her next? If she gets her own pistol, I think no rogue in the country will be safe.'

Millie went into a peal of laughter. She handed over her knife, took Sadie's hand in her own, and the pair of them put their heads together as they walked off, the sound of their laughter bringing a smile to Henry's face.

'God help the man that marries Millicent Searles,' he said.

Robert smiled. 'I almost envy him, Henry. One thing I'm certain of: he'll never have a dull moment…'

CHAPTER ELEVEN

'I DO not see why you had to invite that family for the party this evening,' Adelaide complained as she met Robert by his request in the great hall on the afternoon of Christmas Eve.

The medieval hall had been decorated with greenery, and the grate was prepared for the huge Yule log that was waiting to be dragged in that evening and lit. It would be kept burning throughout the Christmas period, for if it lasted the whole twelve days, the household would have good luck the next year.

However, its romance was lost on Adelaide—especially as she had discovered that Robert was not alone, as she'd expected. 'We shall have nothing to do with them when we are married.'

'Is that your intention?' Robert looked at her, barely able to conceal his dislike. 'Personally, I shall miss them— and I certainly intend to see Sadie often. She is my second cousin, after all.'

'Can you be certain? You only have her word for it.'

'As a matter of fact, it is on record. The vicar called this morning to tell me he had found the special license amongst his registers. He recalls that my uncle refused to accept the marriage, but tells me it was quite legal—though my cousin lied about his age, pretending to be older than he was. In truth he needed his father's permission to marry, but despite that, the license was granted and they were married in the sight of God. Had she not run away, Sadie's mother would have been my cousin's true wife. Her marriage to Harvey Simpson was, of course, not legal.'

'Which was why he was so angry when he discovered the truth,' Henry said. 'He had thought her a widow. He must have been bitter when he learned that his wife had never in fact been his—and was still married to a member of the aristocracy.'

'He hated that. He was a Republican and belonged to a group of fanatics.' Robert frowned when he saw the look of disgust on Adelaide's face. 'I am sorry if this bores you, Adelaide, but it is a matter of interest to me. My uncle, his wife and his two younger sons died of natural causes—but my eldest cousin was murdered, and his daughter was treated abominably. My uncle was in part at fault, because he would not allow the marriage—which just goes to show how wrong things can go when you allow convention to overcome true feeling. My uncle worried too much about the opinions of others and the honour of his family.'

'What are you saying?' Adelaide's gaze narrowed as

she looked at him. 'Why are you looking at me like that, Robert? I do not understand.'

'I wanted you to have this.' Robert presented her with a dark blue leather case.

Adelaide gave a cry of surprise as she opened it and discovered the diamond necklace lying on a bed of velvet.

'It is my Christmas gift to you.'

'You should have kept it for tomorrow,' Adelaide said, all smiles again. 'It is beautiful, Robert—very expensive.'

'I am glad you like it.' Robert hesitated, then, 'It comes with my apologies. I must ask you to forgive me, Adelaide—but I cannot marry you. I fear it would be a terrible mistake. Even if you are telling the truth, I cannot live a lie for the rest of our lives. I shall, of course, do all I can to help you. It should be possible for you to have the child in secret, and I can arrange—'

'No! I shall not listen to this!' Adelaide cried. 'You promised me marriage, Robert. I shall sue you for breach of promise. I shall let it be known that I am with child, and I shall drag your name in the mud. You will never be able to raise your head in society again. See if she wants you *then*!'

'It is my belief that Selina would take me even then,' Robert replied. 'But I cannot believe you would truly be so spiteful, Adelaide. If you destroy me, you destroy your own reputation.'

'Not if I swear that you raped me...' Adelaide's eyes glittered with hate. 'I shall never allow you to be happy if you throw me off, Robert.'

'You must do your worst,' Robert said. 'I am truly

sorry that it has to end this way, Adelaide. Naturally I shall still help you, despite all you say, but I hope you will think better of it.'

'I demand that you keep your word and marry me.'

'I am afraid that I cannot oblige you,' Robert said. 'I realised recently that the chance of true love only comes once in a lifetime. If I throw it away...' He paused. 'I would feel honour bound to wed you if I were sure the child was mine, but I do not think you have been quite honest with me, Adelaide.'

'So now you will call me a liar? By what right do you reject the child I swear is yours?'

'By the right I gave him, Adelaide,' a strong voice said from the doorway.

Adelaide started, her face draining of colour as she turned to stare at the man who had just entered.

'You look shocked, my dear. Did you imagine that I meant it when I said I would not marry you?'

'Bolingwood?' Adelaide's expression was stunned. Her next words showed that she had forgotten everyone else in the room. 'But I pleaded with you, and you told me I was... You said you were finished with me!'

'Because you demanded—as you always do.' Bolingwood walked towards her, a stern look on his handsome face. 'I knew you were not always faithful to me, Adelaide, but I also knew that the child was almost certainly mine. I visited your bed more than most of your lovers. You made me angry when you assumed I would snap to attention. I know that my fortune is not as large as some you might have had—had you been less careless with your favours—but I shall not be dictated to even by the woman I love.'

'The woman…' Adelaide stared at him, a look of wonder on her face. 'Bolingwood, are you truly saying that you love me?' Her voice had died to a whisper.

'Do you imagine I would have put up with your tricks for so long if I did not care?' he drawled, a look of amusement on his face. 'I danced to your tune for a long time, but when you told me you were with child, I decided to teach you a lesson. I did not imagine you would try to blackmail Moorcroft into marrying you when the father might have been at least two others I could name.'

Adelaide put her hands to her face as it flamed with colour. 'They meant nothing to me,' she whispered, her shoulders beginning to shake. 'You should hate and despise me…'

'Perhaps I should, but I have always loved you the way you are,' Bolingwood said. 'However, I am going to tell you my terms, Adelaide. We shall be married, and I will give you all you could hope for as my wife—including my love and respect. But if you ever betray me with another man, I shall divorce you, and you will never see your children again.'

'Bolingwood…' The colour had drained from her face. 'Do you accept my terms?'

'I think we are no longer needed,' Robert murmured to Henry, and they left the room just as they heard Adelaide's tearful acceptance and her abject apology.

'Well, that seems to be the end of that,' Henry said as they looked at each other outside the hall. 'Bolingwood is determined to carry her off with him immediately, and I think there is little doubt of who will wear the breeches in that marriage.'

'Oh, I do not know,' Robert said, and smiled oddly. 'He is in love with her, after all, so I daresay she will know how to get round him.'

'In small ways, perhaps,' Henry agreed, 'but I am certain his threat was genuine.'

'It is not our affair. I am very grateful to him for coming in answer to your letter, Henry.'

'He thought it as quick to come in person as to send a letter—and twice as effective. The lovely Adelaide knew that protest was useless once he appeared.'

'I think she truly cares for him. Had he not tried to teach her a lesson, this little episode need never have happened.'

'Well, it is over now—and that other business is settled. We may relax and enjoy the party this evening.'

'Yes.' Robert touched his shoulder. 'You intend to announce your engagement, I know, so we shall keep ours for another day—but I shall ask Selina to be my wife tonight.'

'Then I hope I shall be wishing you happy before too long.'

'I hope so, Nor. I cannot think there is anything now to stand in our way.'

Selina put the finishing touches to her parcels. The sisters had decided they would take their gifts into the great hall and place them on the long table at the far end, away from the hearth where the log was to be lit that evening. It was a family tradition, so Trent had told them, and belonged to the days when it had been a happier house.

'In the old days, the family left their gifts there, and then, after the Yule log was brought in and the wassail drunk, the gifts were handed out by the children of the family.'

'Then that should be your task, Millie,' Amy said. 'For there are no other children in the house.'

'I am no longer a child,' Millie said with a trace of indignation. 'I am thirteen and a young lady now.'

'Of course you are, miss,' Trent said with a wink at her sister. 'But if there are no children, then the youngest member of the family carries out the present-giving.'

Leaving her bedroom, Selina made her way downstairs. To visit the great hall so that she could deposit her gifts, she must go through the library. She had seldom ventured into the west wing since Robert and Henry had taken up residence, though she knew her way well because she had enjoyed exploring the house before they came. It was as she reached the bottom of the stairs and turned towards the library that she saw Adelaide. The comtesse was coming towards her, and she looked happy and excited.

'Ah, Miss Searles,' she said. 'I am glad to have seen you. Will you wish me happy? I am to be married.' She held out her left hand, showing Selina the magnificent diamond ring on her third finger.

'It is settled, then?' Selina felt a lump in her throat. 'I hope you will be happy.'

'Thank you.' Adelaide hesitated, then, 'I am sorry for

the spiteful things I said to you. I hope we shall be friends in future. Now, if you will excuse me, I am in a hurry. My fiancé is waiting…'

Selina felt unable to reply. The change in Adelaide's manner was amazing, and she wondered if she had misjudged her. Perhaps her spiteful attitude had been a front because she had felt vulnerable and uncertain of her position. Now she knew she was to be married and she no longer felt the need to strike out with her sharp claws.

Selina's throat was tight as she first knocked at and then entered the empty library. Tears burned behind her eyes but she held them back. Robert had told her that he must do his duty by the woman who carried his child, but he had hoped it might be avoided, and she—she had been foolish enough to allow herself the hope that she might find happiness with him after all.

Her heart was racing as she went through the library and into the west wing. She found herself in the anteroom just off the great hall and was fortunate enough not to encounter anyone as she walked quickly to the table at the far end. It had been decorated with greenery, and she saw some parcels had already been placed there. Some she recognised as being Amy's handiwork, and others besides. Scrupulously avoiding looking at anything that did not concern her, she left her parcels and ran swiftly back to the library, closing the door behind her and standing with her back towards it. She was breathing hard, her chest tight with pain.

Millie and Amy were both looking forward to seeing the Yule log brought in later that evening and attending

the party, as was Sadie. Had she been able to cry off,
Selina would have been glad to do so, for the evening
could hold nothing but pain for her. Adelaide would be
there, showing off her diamond ring and shining with
happiness.

As she hurried back to her own room, Selina's thoughts
went sliding and skidding as she tried to think of an excuse to absent herself that would not spoil things for her
sisters and Sadie. There was none that she could make
without casting a shadow over the celebrations. She must
simply paint on a smile and get through the evening as
best she could—and yet her heart felt as if it had broken
into a thousand pieces.

Sitting down at her dressing table, Selina picked up her
brush and began to smooth it over her hair. She would
wear her best yellow gown. It wasn't new, but she'd only
worn it a few times before her dearest mama became ill.
After that it had remained in her armoire and was therefore almost new. Her mother's pearls would set the gown
off, because it had a modest neckline which skimmed
above her breasts and bared her shoulders, ending in little puffed sleeves.

Both her sisters and Sadie had new gowns for the evening, but hers was a favourite, and she did not feel in the
least deprived. Indeed, had the news of Adelaide's marriage to Moorcroft—she must cease to think of him as
Robert now—not cast a shadow over her, she would have
been completely happy.

It was just as she had finished dressing that a knock
came at her door. When she called out that whoever it was

might enter, Sadie entered, wearing the pretty silk gown that the sisters had made for her. Betty had dressed her hair into ringlets, taming its usual wild tangle, and she wore a blue ribbon about her neck from which hung a little pearl that Selina recognised as having been Amy's.

'Oh, my dear, you look beautiful—really lovely,' Selina said, and went forward to take her hands and kiss her cheek. 'You look so much like your grandmother when she was young, dearest. No one could doubt that you are Moorcroft's cousin.'

Sadie touched the pearl at her neck. 'I had nothing to wear so Amy lent this to me,' she said. 'I know it belonged to your mama—you do not mind me wearing it this evening? I shall return it safely.'

'No, of course I do not mind,' Selina said, and smiled. 'You need a little ornament of some kind, Sadie, and that is perfect for a young lady.'

'I prefer something simple. Amy is wearing a necklace of silver and moonstones that her grandmother left to her. It is very pretty, but I do not think it would suit me. This is just right.'

'Perfect,' Selina agreed. She felt a little tremor run through the girl. 'You must not be frightened, my love. People may stare at you a little this evening, because they will be curious about the new addition to the Moorcroft family—but no one with a heart could fail to love you.'

Sadie clung to her hand. 'I do not think I could have managed this evening without you. Millie and Amy are both my friends—and Millie...' Sadie blushed and cleared her throat, as if she had meant to say more. 'But you are like a sister to me.'

'I am glad to have you with me,' Selina said. 'When I settle in my new home, it will be just be the two of us—and the servants, of course. Millie will visit us, and we shall visit Amy and Henry, but I am not sure that I shall be invited here.'

'If you are not then I shall not visit either.'

'You must not be stubborn, Sadie. This is your family home. You will want to visit Ro…the earl and his children sometimes.'

'Not without you,' Sadie said. She looked puzzled. 'I thought you and he… He seems to like you very much. Why do you have to leave?'

'The earl is to be married to the Comtesse Adelaide de Saracosa. When that happens, I must leave here…perhaps sooner—after my sister's wedding.'

'Are you sure?' Sadie frowned. 'I thought I saw…' She shook her head, as if deciding that silence was best. 'Whatever you do, Selina, I shall be with you. I never want to leave you.'

'You think that now,' Selina said, and laughed softly as she squeezed her hand. 'But one day you will meet someone you can love and then you will be married yourself, my love.'

'I do not think any man will wish to marry me after what happened at that place.' For a moment shadows gathered in the girl's eyes.

'You must not think of it,' Selina said. 'One day a man will love you so much that he will not care—except that he will be angry and he will want to hurt the people who hurt you. Put it all behind you, dearest. Someone will love you truly one day, and then you must not be afraid to tell him your secret. I know it will not matter to the right man.'

'Do you really think so?'

'I know it,' Selina said, and kissed her cheek. 'Now, put that smile back, please, my love. We shall not allow anything to spoil our evening. This is the eve of Christ's birth—a time to be joyous and to show love and understanding to our neighbours as well as to those nearest to us. Come along, Sadie. We must go down and greet our friends…'

Selina stood watching with Sadie and her sisters as the men carried in the huge log. It was so big and so heavy that it took several of them to carry it between them, and the cheers, laughter and applause that greeted their efforts were given generously.

Once the log had been satisfactorily placed, and everyone had finished offering advice about how best to ensure that it continued to burn throughout the festivities, a taper was placed in the wood shavings beneath the log. They caught with a little whoosh, and as everyone gasped and clapped, Selina guessed that the shavings had been primed with something to make them catch hold quickly—perhaps a little brandy? The smell that gradually began to permeate through the hall was wonderful, spicy and warm with a hint of the wood itself.

Immediately everyone started wishing each other the

compliments of the season. Trent and his small army of helpers began to circulate with trays of drinks from the hot punch bowl, which complemented the wassail cup. This was merely sipped and passed on from hand to hand, but the punch was drunk heartily, and eager hands reached for more. Plates of tarts, pies, pastries and sweet biscuits, marchpane treats, nuts and cakes of almond with hot jam inside were passed round, too. Down one side of the hall, a table had been set with plates of cold meats, pickles, bread, larger tarts and messes of meringues with cream and fruit. There was something to suit all tastes—from the tart and spicy for the gentlemen to the sweet and light for the ladies.

It was as well that Moorcroft had employed his chef to help with the celebrations, Selina thought. Her cook would have found it difficult to cope even had Selina helped prepare the feast—and some of the fancy trifles might have been beyond her.

Glancing about her, Selina frowned as she noticed that Adelaide was not present. Caught up in the excitement of the ceremony, she had not noticed that the comtesse was missing. Where was she? It was rather odd that she had chosen not to attend the party, since she must wish to show off her ring and take her place as the hostess.

Her gaze travelled on to the earl. He had been making the rounds of his friends, welcoming them to the party and exchanging greetings with everyone. Now he had seen her, and she knew instinctively that he meant to make his way to her. Amy and Millie had gone up to the high table and were making plans for the distribution of gifts.

Without knowing exactly, Selina guessed that every guest would receive a small gift from the earl. Moorcroft was reviving the old traditions, and he meant his neighbours to know that his home was once more open to visitors.

He had this evening put off his dark coats and was wearing a beautifully tailored coat of royal blue cloth that fitted his broad shoulders like a second skin. His shirt was pristine white and his cravat was simply but elegantly tied. Selina found that she could hardly bear to look at him and turned away, moving to the window to look out at the night sky. It was dark, but as she glanced up, she saw a bright light suddenly appear and shoot across the sky before it disappeared.

'Have you wished?' a voice said at her side, and she knew without turning that it was him. 'On such a night your wish is bound to be granted.'

'Is it?' Selina curled her nails into the palms of her hands. She knew that her wish was impossible, even though she had made it without thinking. 'Sometimes we cannot have what we want.'

'Is that so?' he asked, and there was a soft, husky, teasing note in his voice. 'This is Christmas Eve, Selina. Do you not think it a time for miracles?'

'For some, perhaps,' she whispered, her heart aching. He sounded happy, and she must do nothing to spoil his newfound happiness. Her own pain must be hidden. 'I believe I am to congratulate you.'

'Indeed? What makes you say that?' Now he sounded surprised, a little uncertain.

She turned to look at him, her feelings under iron control. 'I saw Adelaide earlier, when I came to leave my gifts with the others. She showed me her ring and told me she was to be married.'

'Ah...' Robert smiled, a huge grin spreading over his face. 'Was that all she said?'

'She apologised for having been spiteful and said she hoped we could be friends in future.'

'I imagine she took great pleasure in confusing you,' he said, the smile leaving his eyes for a moment. 'She did not tell you that she was engaged to Lord Bolingwood, I daresay?'

Selina's heart jerked and then did a dizzying somersault. For a moment the room seemed to spin around her and she thought she might faint.

'The comtesse is to marry Lord Bolingwood—not you?'

Robert reached out, his hand taking her chin and tipping it so that she looked up into his eyes. 'Not me, Selina. Her child is his child, it seems—or so he firmly believes. He is aware that she took other lovers, but it appears that he is able to overcome his hurt at her betrayal because he wants her no matter what she has done.'

'He must love her very much,' Selina said, and her breath caught in her throat as she looked into his eyes and saw the love and laughter reflected there. 'I thought... It almost tore me apart, but I could not stay away and let everyone down tonight.'

'Of course you couldn't,' he said, and stroked his fingertips down her cheek. 'Damn her for hurting you with her careless words. It is like you to think of others instead of yourself. I had no idea you had spoken to her or I should have sought you out sooner. I wanted to speak to you later, when the party was over and we could be alone so I could ask you to marry me. Henry is going to announce his engagement to Amy this evening. This is their night. We shall have ours another time.'

'Shall we?' Selina smiled as she moved closer to him, her heart beating wildly. 'I recall you once asked me to wait for you, Robert—but I do not think I gave you my answer.'

'You did not,' he said. 'But I hope that you will do so now. You know that I adore you—that my life without you would be empty and useless.'

'Would it?' Selina moved closer, a little teasing smile on her lips. 'You have been a long time in returning for your answer, Robert dearest—but now that you have...'

'Yes?' He moved in closer, suddenly tense.

'My answer is what it has always been. Yes, I will marry you, Robert Moorcroft. Because I love you and I have never stopped loving you from the first moment you kissed me.'

'My sweet angel,' Robert said, and bent his head, kissing her lightly on the lips. 'I adore you, and very soon now I shall show you how much...but I think they are going to begin the ceremony of the present-giving.'

'Then we should join them.' Selina offered her hand. 'This is Millie's big moment. We should not spoil it.'

'My gift to you this evening is only a token,' Robert said. 'Later, when we are alone, I shall give you the gift I want to give the woman I love...'

* * *

'Millie, I have another gift for you,' Robert called to the young girl just as she was leaving the hall after most of the guests had departed. 'This is special, and I know you will treasure it.'

Millie hesitated, looking at him uncertainly. He had been a little cross with her over the *Book of Hours*, and she'd thought he might be disappointed in her because she had stolen it, even though she felt it belonged to her by right.

'A gift for me, sir?'

Robert handed her the package. She took it with trembling hands, guessing what it was even as she stripped away the brown paper and ribbon. Her eyes widened as she took out the precious book and then she gazed up at him.

'Is this really for me? How did you persuade Cousin Joshua to part with it?'

'Let us just say that I made him see things from my point of view.' His eyes smiled, though his mouth remained stern. 'This doesn't mean I condone stealing, Millie—but I happen to think that yours was the better right. Had your cousin been a fair man, he would have given you the book. '

'I do not know how to thank you.' Millie choked on her tears. She brushed furiously at her eyes because she was too old to cry. 'I shall always love it and—and I love Henry and you, too.'

'I thank you on behalf of Henry and myself,' Robert said with a twinkle in his eyes. 'Off to bed with you now—and don't keep Selina, for I have unfinished business with her.'

'Are you going to ask her to marry you at last?' Millie asked with a cheeky look. 'It's about time—that's all I can say…'

Robert laughed as she sped away, clutching her precious book. There went one happy lady—now to make another Christmas wish come true…

'That is lovely, thank you,' Selina said as Robert slipped the beautiful daisy-shaped diamond ring on her finger.

It fitted her hand as if it had been made for her, the stones large and pure white. She smiled, because it was exactly right for her—for the woman she was. Robert had already told her that all his family jewels were hers to choose from when she wished to wear them, but this ring was special.

'You have given me three wonderful gifts this evening, my dearest.'

'The glass angel was but a trinket,' Robert said. 'Yet when I saw it I knew that it was exactly right for you—my own special angel.'

'It is a Christmas angel and I shall treasure it,' Selina said, lifting her face as his head came down towards her. 'I am the happiest woman alive, Robert. I truly have all I could ever want.'

'Then you will be my wife and be content to live here?'

'Live in this beautiful house with you, as your wife?' Selina's smile came from deep inside her. 'I could not ask for anything I should like more. You have decided not to pull it down?'

'And enrage everyone from Henry to Millie? You have made it a home,' Robert told her with a smile. 'Wherever you are—that is my home, Selina. We may live here, but we shall visit Paris, and of course we shall spend some time in London. I may even buy another house somewhere—but that is for you to choose. Our family home will remain here in this house.'

'This is such a perfect house,' Selina said. 'The way the hall came to life with all those guests this evening—the music and the laughter and the food. That is the way Christmas should be spent—with friends and those you love, Robert. I do not think you could have a more perfect setting than this house—and it's where I should like our children to grow up. They will spread their wings and fly, but they will know they can always return to this house.'

'Because you have made it come alive again,' Robert told her. He drew her closer, his eyes tender as he bent his head to caress her lips once more. 'My sweet love—my angel.'

'I am just a woman,' Selina said, and laughed. 'But do not underestimate me, Robert darling. We shall argue, and I can be as stubborn as Millie when I choose—but we shall be happy because we love each other.'

'I adore you,' he murmured, his lips seeking her throat as he kissed and nudged at her with the tip of his tongue, sending little tremors running down her spine. 'I have been wanting to do this for an age. Do you think we could continue where we left off all those years ago? If you will promise not to run away this time…'

'Robert…' Selina's breath came faster as she leaned into him and felt the heat of his body and the urgency of his need. 'I think if you were to take me upstairs to your room so that we can be alone…that might be my very best Christmas present of all.'

'I should be delighted to do so—if you are certain you do not wish to wait for our wedding night?' His eyes caressed her softly, conveying the depth of his love and need.

'Robert, my dearest…' Selina touched his lips with her fingertips '…I have been waiting for such a long time. Please do not…'

Whatever she meant to say was lost as he scooped her up in his arms and headed swiftly for the stairs.

* * * * *

Governess Under
the Mistletoe

ELIZABETH BEACON

Elizabeth Beacon lives in the beautiful English West Country and is finally putting her insatiable curiosity about the past to good use. Over the years Elizabeth has worked in her family's horticultural business, became a mature student, qualified as an English teacher, worked as a secretary and, briefly, tried to be a civil servant. She is now happily ensconced behind her computer, when not trying to exhaust her bouncy rescue dog with as many walks as the Inexhaustible Lurcher can finagle. Elizabeth can't bring herself to call researching the wonderfully diverse, scandalous Regency period and creating charismatic heroes and feisty heroines *work*, and she is waiting for someone to find out how much fun she is having and tell her to stop it.

Previous novels by the same author:

AN INNOCENT COURTESAN
HOUSEMAID HEIRESS
A LESS THAN PERFECT LADY
CAPTAIN LANGTHORNE'S PROPOSAL
REBELLIOUS RAKE, INNOCENT GOVERNESS
THE RAKE OF HOLLOWHURST CASTLE
ONE FINAL SEASON (part of Courtship & Candlelight)

Dear Reader,

It's such a privilege to be invited to share a small part of your Christmas with you and I really hope you enjoy Peter and Sophie's story. A Regency Christmas seems to have been very different from the festival we enjoy now and finding out as much as I can about the traditions lost and carried on has been a wonderful experience. This is a story about rediscovered hope and joy and I wish you both, and a Very Happy Christmas and New Year.

Elizabeth Beacon

Mike and Marion, Katherine and Petra
with many thanks for your friendship, gentle
encouragement, dog-sitting and excellent coffee.
I couldn't have finished this one without you!

CHAPTER ONE

PETER Vane, Lord Sylbourne, blinked snowflakes from his eyelashes and cursed the storm and the early darkness that came with it. They were in the middle of nowhere in this dratted blizzard, and might as well be in the Alps instead of so-called temperate England.

Trying to stifle his impatience with the obstacles in their path, and the odd sense of unease that had dogged him since the outset of this journey, he glanced at his coachman through the thickening veil of snow and an early dusk. Muffled heavily against the cold, Merryweather looked like some spectral visitation from a frozen underworld. The poor man couldn't do anything to avoid the worst of the weather, stuck up there on the box of the swaying coach as he urged, wheedled and commanded his team to go on when instinct urged them not to.

Peter knew they could go no further by Merryweather's absolute silence as he surveyed the steep descent in front of them, and it would be criminal to risk the horses' legs and necks in such conditions. Still, some instinct told him to hurry on—as if there were wolves on their trail and they were so hungry as to be beyond either fear or mercy. But there had been no wolves left in England for many years now. He had the warmth of his horse between his legs to keep him from freezing in his saddle, and he felt even more guilty about his coachman and the groom up on the bench seat facing the worst of this appalling weather when he recalled how he'd given in to his sister's desperation to get home.

Any sane man would have called a halt to their journey at the last posting house and settled in to wait out a storm that had been signalled by the yellowing clouds and heavy silence even then. If only he'd had the sense to read the signs…

'Merryweather!' he yelled above the noise of protesting horses and the coachman and grooms' shouted reassurance. 'Pull the rig up under the shelter of yonder trees, if you can get it there, and I'll go look for help. You're nigh spent, man, as are these poor beasts. We can't go any further.'

'True. We can't take them down yonder hill, and there ain't room to turn and go back, even if there was a mort of shelter to be had for miles. But you'll hurry about it, won't you, my lord?'

'That I will, Merryweather. Besides not wanting to lose Lady Edwina myself, my sister's fiancé will kill me with his bare hands if we don't get out of this damned snow before she takes an ague—although I'm not sure Captain Wroxley would mind if we left his brother buried head down in the nearest snowdrift,' he added more softly, and nodded to the well-sprung and once-gleaming coach body already disappearing under a covering of snow now it was still at last.

Merryweather muttered something uncomplimentary under his breath that ended with a heartfelt wish that Mr Cedric Wroxley might pitch head first into the nearest ditch, then wake up somewhere very warm indeed. He drove the now quiet team through a farm gate and onto the faint hint of a roadway that seemed to lead to a small wood offering the only shelter within reach until Peter could find better.

'Quite,' Peter agreed with a grimace, just as the window of the carriage was pulled down and said Mr Wroxley put out his head to complain, despite the driving snow.

'We appear to be driving into a field,' he observed querulously, as if they might not have the sense to realise.

'No—are we really?' Peter couldn't help asking, with a look at the high hedges around them as if he had no idea where they had come from.

'This is not the time for misplaced humour, Sylbourne,' his bugbear said coldly.

'Nor for sitting about with the window down like that, losing what little warmth is left inside the carriage. Have some consideration for my sister and aunt and at least try to behave like a gentleman for once,' he ordered the Honourable Cedric irritably.

'Shall you go look for shelter, Peter?' Lady Edwina Vane asked, pushing her supposed escort aside and doing her best to pretend all was well with her world. 'Maybe I could come, too?' she offered a little less hopefully.

Peter had no doubt that after so many hours of Cedric Wroxley's company, even a snowstorm as fierce as this one might look almost attractive, given the alternative of enduring the wait for rescue with that worm complaining about his own discomfort the whole time.

'No, I need to know we can find somewhere safer and warmer before I dare risk you and Aunt Hes wandering about in a blizzard, Dina. For now you will be better off here—for all it's not the ideal spot for sitting out a storm. You had best huddle together as close as you can under all the rugs and falderals you have in there between you to keep warm, and if there's any heat left in the bricks, then bundle them in there with you.'

He gave his sister what he hoped was a reassuring smile, then turned to the man sitting across the way from the ladies. All hint of softness left his stony grey eyes.

'Cedric, remember that your brothers will slay you very slowly and then feed you to Seetley's hunting dogs in little pieces if anything happens to Giles' betrothed—if I manage to restrain myself from killing you before they get the chance, of course. So don't make the mistake of annexing any available warmth for yourself if you wish to see the New Year with a complete skin,' he told him coldly, and hoped he looked even fiercer then he felt at the thought of any harm coming to Dina or Aunt Hes at the selfish little worm's hands.

The Honourable Cedric was quite capable of letting Peter's sister and aunt freeze if it saved him doing so himself, and Peter wished now he had been able to withstand the pleading look Cedric's own sister, Lady Leticia

Durronde, had sent him when she had begged the Vanes
to take her brother with them since the Durronde coach
would be full, with her husband, three young offspring
and the nanny. Leticia's maid and her husband's valet
had threatened to resign and stay in Bath if they had to
endure her youngest brother's company for even another
mile after their journey from London the week before,
with him moaning and pontificating the whole way.

'If you hadn't got us lost, I wouldn't need to,' Cedric
said and put the window back up with a bang.

'Ar—'

'No, Merryweather, you may be perfectly sound in
your judgement of yonder so-called gentleman, but don't
forget young Jem here is still relatively innocent, and
he doesn't need to learn any more backstreet curses to
shock his poor saintly mother with when he gets home,'
Peter chided with forced cheerfulness—for even to him
their situation suddenly had the potential to be very dangerous indeed. 'Do you think you three can keep from
freezing while you unharness the team and huddle them
into the corner of the field over there? Near that stand of
trees and as far out of the wind as you're likely to get?
I wish I could offer you a better billet, but I need you to
stay within earshot of the carriage in case Lady Edwina
or Miss Willis should need your help, and the poor beasts
deserve as much care as we can give them after I have
dragged them out on a fool's journey on such a day.'

'We'll do right enough huddled together in that corner with the horses, my lord. You go find somewhere we
can light a fire and bed down for the night without risk-

ing dying of cold, and don't worry yourself about us in the meantime.'

'Aye-aye, Merryweather—anything you say,' Peter replied with a mocking salute and set off to see if the faint light he'd seen from the road just now would lead him to shelter.

Somehow he had to save Edwina and his aunt from spending a wretchedly uncomfortable night sleeping in a cramped carriage, with his sister's appalling brother-in-law-to-be whining away endlessly about the weather and the cold as if everything was Edwina's fault. Nobody could understand why he hadn't stayed in his comfortable chambers in the Albany in the first place. It wasn't as if he had any love for his elder brothers, so staying away from Captain Giles Wroxley's wedding to Lady Edwina Vane wouldn't be rendered unthinkable.

Giving up on plumbing the murky depths of Cedric's mind, Peter concentrated on being able to see the will-o'-the-wisp light up ahead every now and again as the snow swirled another way for a brief moment. He prayed he would find shelter before he was irretrievably lost and confused by the storm and the deepening darkness.

Sophie Rose did her best not to sigh as she watched her eldest charge toss her embroidery frame on the floor in disgust. As that young lady's one-time governess, she decided philosophically that the fine lawn clamped in it would fare no worse there than it had in her companion's unskilled hands.

'It's no good, Miss Rose. I can't sew for toffee,' Imogen Frayne admitted on a sigh to rival the gusts outside.

'I know, dear. When you said you intended to embroider a handkerchief for your brother Lysander, I refused to lay odds with Viola against you getting halfway through since I never bet against a certainty,' Sophie said with a rueful smile.

'Zander has become so perfect since he took holy orders, I dare not buy him something new to wear on Twelfth Night lest I be accused of tempting him with luxuries or some such nonsense. But I'll never find a husband while I'm so bereft of feminine accomplishments, Rosie,' Imogen reflected rather gloomily.

Sophie shot her former charge a thoughtful look. 'Do you suppose your brother will notice if I finish this?' she asked, and at Imogen's shrug and unrepentant grin picked up the frame and began undoing what had already been done because she was glad to occupy her restless fingers. 'I really don't think there's much danger of you staying on the shelf while the young gentlemen you meet once you're officially out have full use of their eyes,' she went on, sparing an amused glance at her fair-haired, almost angelic-looking young friend.

'You're entitled to your opinion, I suppose,' Imogen allowed, not inclined to believe a word. 'But as for that sewing you seem to find so annoyingly simple, Rosie dear, I doubt if my middle brother will even notice if I suddenly learn to sew, since he's so preoccupied with being the perfect curate nowadays he'll soon be stuffy as poor Dr Tombs down in the village. For the rest, why on earth would I encourage any man to try to wed me when you set me such a poor example?' demanded eighteen-year-old Imogen.

And since Sophie was determinedly single at five and twenty, she probably *wasn't* a good example for such a lovely and lively young girl to follow. She frowned at the very idea.

'My example should encourage you to accept any personable, good-natured gentleman who offers for you, since I provide a fine illustration of what happens to young ladies who prove too finicky,' she managed to reply, equably enough—even if the subject of marriage was a sore one at the moment.

Luckily Imogen knew nothing of the dilemma rattling about so relentlessly in Sophie's head that she felt the threat of a headache gnawing away at her patience—and, whatever else a governess should be, in Sophie's opinion she should always be patient—if only to confound a defiant pupil. Imogen was hardly that, even if it had been very hard to convince her she needed a governess eight years ago, when Miss Rose had arrived at Heartsease Hall.

'My big brother has set me an example I prefer *not* to follow by asking Miss Garret-Lowden to marry him. She will make us all miserable.'

'Miss Garret-Lowden is a very pretty young lady. Only imagine how odd it must have felt to be thrown straight into a family drama the very day she and her mama arrived to spend the Christmas season, and how awkward that was for them.'

'Poor Aunt Helen could hardly have expired at a more

inconvenient time, could she?' Imogen agreed, in an excellent imitation of Mrs Garret-Lowden on hearing that her host had received news of his elder sister's sudden death that morning and was off to Ireland posthaste with his other sister. They'd hoped to be in time for the funeral or to be able to offer help and comfort to the grieving widower and his vast tribe of children, even if they were not. 'It's almost as if they thought the poor darling did it on purpose to inconvenience them—which makes them a pair of heartless cats.'

'Not necessarily—and I at least intend to try to give them the benefit of the doubt,' Sophie asserted with gentle irony, trying to lighten the brooding frown now marring her ex-pupil's smooth brow. 'Especially as I wish to keep my place, and Miss Garret-Lowden will be Mrs Timon Frayne one day.'

'Papa would never turn you off on her say-so, Rosie. How can you think he would be so spineless? Even if Timon *has* become her willing slave and would very likely do whatever she says without thinking of the consequences for the rest of us.'

Glad Imogen had no idea of the turmoil that conclusion had caused her governess, Sophie wished she could honestly tell her she was mistaken in her future sister-in-law. Unfortunately Sophie thought Miss Garret-Lowden probably *was* shallow and silly, and her mother devious and ambitious under all her frills and furbelows. Evidently Sir Gyffard Frayne agreed, since he had invited Sophie into his bookroom before his hasty departure for Ireland and made her a purely practical offer of marriage.

'That woman and her daughter have clearly decided my son is a fine match and will provide them with a comfortable home for life. With the knowledge that he already has his share of his mother's fortune and that my title will descend on him one day, I find it difficult to disagree with them, Miss Rose. Miss Garret-Lowden might make the boy a decent enough wife, but I can never be easy about my girls' future if they have to depend on her and her mother's goodwill if aught happens to me before they wed. I beg you will ponder a marriage of pure form between us whilst I am away, Miss Rose—and please don't dismiss the whole idea without considering it properly. You have the strength of character to prevent that harpy ruining my daughters' lives if I die before they come of age. Don't give me an answer now, for I know the idea of marriage to such an ancient husband must revolt you. I doubt I'll be back before spring is well on its way, so you'll have plenty of time to consider my offer. Weigh up that disadvantage against the love I'd be a fool not to know you feel for my girls, and the knowledge you would have an assured place in society once more.'

'I'm overwhelmed, Sir Gyffard,' she had said. Looking back, she decided it had lacked a certain eloquence. 'I have no thoughts of marriage, and this is unexpected, to say the least.'

'Surely that's all the more reason to give it consideration?' he had argued in his usual wry manner. 'You don't appear to cherish the usual girlish dreams of marrying for love, since I never saw you flirt with a single one of my neighbours in all the years you've been with us, so perhaps you could be content to be tied to an old breakdown if it helps you avoid the unenviable lot of the governess for the rest of your life?'

'You are very far from such a state, sir,' she had protested, but he'd shaken his head and told her not to be mealy-mouthed.

'I'm nearly thirty years too old for you, and if you agreed to wed me, it would cause a good deal of spiteful gossip, but I can think of nobody who would look after my girls as devotedly as you have done since you came to us. I thought my darling wife had run mad to take on such a child eight years ago, but she told me to be patient and not to interfere, and time has proved her right—as usual.'

'I can never thank you both enough for giving me a chance when I was so very young and clearly unsuited to the post,' she'd answered, but he had waved her thanks aside with the self-deprecating smile that had made her wish one of them was decades older or younger, so they could indeed patch some sort of marriage together out of loneliness and fellow feeling.

'Don't accept my offer out of misplaced gratitude, young lady, for you have more than repaid us for that opportunity. Take the security of being my wife, and one day my widow, along with the assurance you will be surrounded by stepdaughters who'll love you until your dying day. But don't accept my offer out of duty, my dear. That would prove a very hard bedfellow for us both to live with.'

'I always wanted children,' she carelessly let slip.

'Then I must take it all back, Miss Rose. Forget I ever

spoke. One day you might find yourself a husband who will give them to you and make you happy into the bargain,' he urged generously.

'I loved a man once, Sir Gyffard. No, he was hardly more than a boy at the time. But he loved me back with all the headlong passion of youth until he saw me as he thought I was deep down and decided he loved me no more. Unfortunately for me I can never picture myself loving another, however hard I have tried to forget him over the years. Your offer would give me the only family I can have, since I can't bring myself to care for another man as I did for the one I would have wed if life had been a little less cruel and circumstances not quite so appalling.'

'Then we had best both consider a closer connection whilst I am in Ireland, for I suppose I'm not yet quite too old to give you the babes you clearly long for—if you could bear the thought of such a plodding and weary old man after your wild young lover,' he said, with that warm, wry smile of his that surely she could come to love if they both worked at it hard enough.

Her inner heroine raged at her for even considering the idea, but she did have such a deep need for a child that even the faint promise of one drowned her out for the moment. 'Let it just be an idea and no more on either side, Sir Gyffard. For you might meet a suitable lady in Ireland who would make a far more ideal wife than a simple governess of five and twenty without connections or family.'

'We both know there is little plain and simple about you, Miss Rose. My Marianne always told me there was a broken love affair behind your decision to hide in this backwater with us, as well as your refusal to entertain the idea of staying here as a distant connection of her family instead of our governess.'

'If we go ahead with your idea, I will tell you all there is to know, Sir Gyffard, but please allow me to keep my counsel on that subject otherwise.'

'Of course. Your family and connections haven't impinged on us these last eight years—I doubt they will do so in the next few weeks,' he concluded comfortably.

The very idea of either catching up with her made her shudder now, in the snug and comfortable old room, but this wasn't the right time to think about such unlikely conundrums, and Sophie knew she was putting off that time even as she put it aside and made herself concentrate on the here and now.

'I'm very happy with my lot,' she told Imogen. 'Before you take it into your head to throw me at any elderly single gentlemen, you should consider that I'm not well suited to marriage, Imogen, but a single life would not suit you half as well.'

'If I were a better, kinder creature, I would probably regard it as my mission in life to teach other people's children, as you do.'

'But not if they wanted to learn needlework,' Sophie teased.

'Watercolours and the French language for me, then— oh, and use of the globes, since we all follow Ferdy's ship around the world so closely I could recite most of the places he's been without having to think about it,' Imogen argued blithely.

'Even with your youngest brother's epic voyages to call on, there's really no need for you to think about going out as a governess,' Sophie said, quite certain Imogen would be followed up the aisle by Viola and Audrey in their turn.

If she refused Sir Gyffard's offer, she supposed she would have to find another post, which must be less agreeable than this one, since she loved her pupils and had been accepted by the family and their servants with a generosity she knew was unusual.

'Papa would never turn me out, and nor would dear Timon—even though his betrothed would probably hold the door wide open for me to leave and then slam it behind us girls if he could be persuaded to send us away. Once she is living under our roof, we shall never be allowed to forget my mama was "naught but a vulgar actress"— at least according to Livia's mother, who was far less respectable than Mama before she wed Mr Garret-Lowden, if rumour is to be believed. I suppose some noble families would say Papa diluted his ancient line by marrying Mama in the first place, but she was more of a lady than any of them.'

'I don't believe anyone among the *ton* would say any such thing—especially in your papa's hearing,' Sophie argued.

Sophie thought of the steadfast, obviously ill lady who had given her seventeen-year-old self the post of governess because she'd thought Sophie was young enough to teach and care for her girls as if she were their elder sister, rather than just drum a set of accomplishments into them and not care a rap for their happiness. Lady Frayne had died three years later, and Sophie had indeed cared for the Frayne girls. Meanwhile Miss Garret-Lowden had Timon Frayne under her steely little thumb. Perhaps it was time for Sophie to prove it and accept Sir Gyffard's proposal so their future could be secure.

'You're probably right, Miss Rose,' her one-time pupil replied with suspicious docility.

'You really should not pretend to be meek and mild when we all know how far from that desirable state you truly are, Imogen.'

'And how am I to reply to that unjust accusation, Rosie? If I agree, I'll be accused of playacting. If I argue, it will confirm your prejudices. I truly can't do right for doing wrong today.'

'Something you would do well to remember whenever you are trying to pull the wool over my eyes,' Sophie said with an affectionate smile.

'Shall I offer to rub lavender water into your temples and order you a purely medicinal glass of Papa's best cognac to soothe your much-tried nerves, then, Miss Rose? That is what dear, dutiful Livia Garret-Lowden does for her darling mama whenever she wants to silence her continuous flow of tittle-tattle.'

'Not if you value your gown or your papa's best brandy.'

'I thought not. So you will just have to forgive me for being human and resign yourself to the fact that your eldest pupil will never do you credit, Miss Rose.'

'That I won't. You have a quick understanding and a

decided character, Imogen, and can prove yourself a fine example of a young lady of birth and education whenever the fancy takes you. Even if some of us wish it took you in that way a little more often.'

'Being ladylike at all times is so boring—you must admit. But Mama was very much a lady, wasn't she, Miss Rose? Although she took part in a few strictly private performances of the most respectable parts of Shakespeare's plays as a girl in Dublin, I can't see how that made her an actress.'

'Of course not—and Mrs Garret-Lowden is foolish to claim otherwise. Your father will withdraw his consent to the match if that lady is not careful. We all know how truly he loved your mama, and he will not tolerate such spiteful nonsense talked against her.'

'I wish he *could* bring himself to forbid it.'

Since Imogen was 'out,' and could no longer be dismissed as too young to have any opinions of her own outside the schoolroom, Sophie cast about for a topic to divert her former pupil on such a gloomy and snow-laden evening, which was coming in far too early this afternoon, even for late December.

'We were talking about your future rather than your brother's, were we not? I would be very sad to think there was the least likelihood you would ever follow in my footsteps, Imogen dear. In most households the governess leads a very narrow and restricted life, since she is not fish, flesh nor good red herring and doesn't seem able to fit into either her employers' world or life below stairs. Such a life would smother even a person of your happy and determined nature within a month. I was so very fortunate to be employed by your mama, Imogen, for I shudder at the very thought of the half-life most of my kind are forced to endure in order to earn their bread.'

'I agree it was lucky—although more for us, the Fraynes, than for you, Rosie. But I do have two little sisters waiting in the wings, and I might have to step aside to let them have their chances in a couple of years. I might not *take*, whatever you say to the contrary,' Imogen said earnestly, and Sophie wondered if she had done too good a job of raising Lady Frayne's daughters to be modest and unimpressed by their own looks, unstudied charm and considerable intelligence.

'There never was a more pampered governess than I, Imogen dear, and I'm lucky enough to like my pupils very well. But I'm certain you will never follow in my footsteps, nor should you seek to do so.'

'Yet you're held to be a very superior example of your kind, Miss Rose. Although I suppose it's not the same as being mistress of a house and raising daughters of your own, is it? I really can't see how you expect me to meekly wed when you're so determined not to. It seems a very odd expectation indeed—and most illogical in you,' Imogen said cunningly.

'Ah, but I have no expectations, nor do I possess a doting family who are more than eager to introduce me to suitable gentlemen I might like to marry one day. Which is all very fortunate, since I'm five and twenty and quite ineligible, so perhaps we could stop discussing *my* future and get back to considering yours, my dear? Now, *I* propose that you hurry up and marry a fine gentleman, with a prosperous estate in an agreeable part of the country, and raise your own daughters instead of someone else's. By the time your little sisters are out of the schoolroom and old enough to find their own handsome and brave husbands in their turn, I shall have found myself a neat little house equidistant from all three of you and will make a school there for your daughters and a few carefully selected young ladies of good birth in need of an education to go with it. I shall then be well set up for the rest of my days as a fine educator of lovely and modest young ladies without very much effort.'

'You're trying to divert me from my woes in a most underhand manner, Miss Rose,' Imogen informed her severely. 'But I will find a gentleman you can't resist and insist that you marry him somehow or other—even if I have to drag you to London with me to track him down.'

'Not if you bound and gagged me and then enlisted some wild horses. I'll be far too busy teaching your sisters and then all those daughters of yours to step out of my proper place and racket about town, even if I wanted to.'

Sophie paused and wished they could get off the uncomfortable subject of her marriage, or lack of one, and then listened intently to a faint, out-of-place noise she suddenly thought she had heard out in the inhospitable dusk that was now descending so rapidly.

'Hush a moment, Imogen. Did you hear something outside? I thought I caught the faint noise of a bridle on that last gust of wind, but surely nobody would choose to venture abroad today, when they could stay safe and warm at home?'

'Any rider out there tonight would have a hard time seeing the hand in front of his face—let alone being mad enough to try to pay Christmas visits to a house on the side of a hill and miles away from the nearest village in a snowstorm in the first place.'

'I suppose I must have imagined it, then, since your neighbours all appear to be perfectly sane. I had hoped your brother Lysander would find time to ride over and give us a Christmas Eve blessing, now he's taken holy orders, but of course it's quite out of the question now,' Sophie said thoughtfully.

But she moved away from the glowing fire to go to the window and stare out at what little she could see of the scene outside through the snow-veiled dusk all the same, wondering at herself for imagining things as she strained her eyes to see beyond the flurries of snow and the gathering darkness.

'No, this time I'm sure I saw something move out there. I wonder if Cordage can have ventured out on some errand he suddenly considered vital and has lost himself in the snow.'

'Not even *he* is that devoted to duty. He wouldn't go out in this weather tonight unless it was a matter of life and death, Miss Rose. You probably only heard a deer coming down from the hilltop to seek shelter in the woods. You have such sharp ears—and most inconvenient I've found them at times as well. That reminds me—I must remember to ask Cordage to get the woodsmen to cut holly as soon as it's fit to be out tomorrow. Ti is sure to forget, since he's so grumpy nowadays and is being forced to stay with Lysander now Livia and her mama have insisted on staying for Christmas. Anyone with any manners would have called for their carriage as soon as the messenger came from Uncle Porthdown, telling us about poor Aunt Helen's death.'

Sophie was beginning to think social niceties would only get Imogen and the Garret-Lowdens through the supposedly festive season in her dreams. Still, young enough to hope the spirit of the season would prevail, she shut the heavy curtains behind her to cut out the distractions of reflected candlelight and flames from the fire and knelt on the broad window seat in an attempt to penetrate the blizzard and the too-early dusk outside.

'Good heavens!' she exclaimed, then scrambled up and ran for the door.

'Whatever is it, Rosie?' Imogen demanded.

'A horse and a rider who looks more like Hannibal coming over the Alps than a mortal man,' Sophie muttered half to herself as she ran into the hall and shouted for Cordage and whoever else was within earshot. 'You must go and reassure your sisters all is well and see they stay in the schoolroom and finish their letters to your father, Imogen. On no account should *any* of you follow us out into the blizzard,' she said sternly as her former pupil threatened to plunge out into the snow without a thought for her own welfare.

'But, Miss Rose, someone may be freezing to death out there.'

'Then there is no earthly reason why you should be obliged to do the same. Please go comfort your sisters as I ask, and I'll come tell you what's to do as soon as I know myself.'

Muttering darkly about pots and kettles, Imogen went nevertheless. Sophie knew her well enough to be certain she would make sure her little sisters were reassured, even if she would much prefer to be at the centre of the action herself.

CHAPTER TWO

WEARILY slitting his eyes as close to shut as he could manage against the constant onslaught of driving snow without actually closing them and riding into a tree, Peter decided he was seeing things now to add to his miseries. He swiped an impatient hand across his face in the snow-blurred twilight and dared open his tired eyes a little wider to look harder. But the illusion was gone from the lighted window he could see ahead of him, so maybe he was still sane.

He let out a deep sigh of weary relief at being spared delusions and decided he might be a mere ten feet from sanctuary or even half a mile for all he could see through the shifting flurries of snow that seemed one minute as wild as dervishes and the next as soft and life-stealing as death itself. He shook his head and muttered encouragement in Hannibal's flicked-back ears, for the poor beast had borne him as stalwartly through this white nightmare as a docile cart horse instead of the high-bred hunter he really was.

So why had memories of Sophie Bonet come back to haunt him at such a desperate moment? He would have thought a man might see angels if he was on the verge of death, not hard-hearted, self-serving little devils like that one had proved herself to be. Once upon a time he had thought he loved her, of course, but he'd been a young fool who had known so little of the world that he looked back on his younger self with pity. He should have been locked up for his own protection until he had grown enough common sense to see the devious little adventuress for what she was. It must be eight years since he'd last set eyes on her, but exotic rumours of her fate since she had marched out of Holm Park for the last time, with her pert little nose in the air and a couple of expensive bandboxes in her hands, were legion.

He liked best the one about her setting up as a pirate queen in the unsuspecting Caribbean and charming all the renegades into running about doing her bidding. Once upon a time, Sophie Bonet had been his friend, almost a relative and an intrepid playmate. That Sophie had been so eager for life and adventure that he'd almost forgotten she was a girl and had led her into all sorts of unsuitable mischief. He smiled wryly at the thought of that wild young version of Sophie Bonet taking on the world and winning, then wondered what he'd seen to recall her so strongly to mind that he could almost hear her voice in his freezing ears.

'I'm getting lost in more ways than one, Hannibal old boy,' he muttered, and as his gallant mount seemed to like the sound of anything other than eerie, snowbound silence or howling, snow-laden gusts of wind, he murmured a commentary on his own folly in giving in to Edwina's pleas to get her to her wedding despite the fact going on in such weather was madness.

There it was again—the snatched hint of a few words buffeted about on the wind. He recalled he'd once heard that a man could hallucinate if he was on the verge of death by exposure to extreme cold, and fought a deep shudder of disquiet that would scare even his brave mount.

'Over there, Cordage!'

He caught that Sophie-like voice beckoning him on—a siren's deceptive call.

'There's not going to be anybody about out here on such a night, miss, and you really need to go back inside before you take an ague yourself.'

The masculine part of the duet yelled this in a strong country voice, and Peter began to wonder if help might not be at hand after all. He didn't recognise even the timbre of *that* voice. If he was back in the past with Sophie, his imagination would conjure up his father or Brimble, the butler at Holm Park—not a gruff West Countryman who sounded excusably annoyed about being outside on such a night on a wild-goose chase.

'No, I'm sure I saw someone,' the Sophie voice insisted, and Peter almost believed she was real, and shuddered at the monstrous idea of meeting her now he was all but spent and at his most vulnerable. 'Over there, I tell you. There really is a rider heading straight into the ha-ha, Cordage.'

Halting Hannibal, lest she was real and right, Peter

wondered at himself for believing in the impossible at such a time. He hesitated between jumping down and risking floundering, or staying up here and hazarding Hannibal's knees. Deciding on the lesser of two evils, he heaved himself out of the saddle and sank to his hips in drifting snow as he fought to push his horse back from the ditch. All the poor animal wanted now was to take the quickest route to shelter and the stable he seemed almost able to scent on the howling wind.

Very well, Peter told himself with determined logic, *since the ha-ha clearly exists, the voice that says it's there must be real as well*.

Even if that voice sounded perilously close to that of a female he never wanted to set eyes on again so long as he lived, he had to believe his senses or risk being on the edge of madness. There was nothing for it but to believe the siren voice would find a way to rescue him before he and his horse expired from sheer cold and exhaustion, and Edwina, Aunt Hes and Merryweather had to kill Cedric for being possibly the most annoying man in England— or make a bonfire out of the coach in order to keep themselves warm and try and attract attention to their plight.

'Over here!' he bellowed, as loudly as he could over the howling wind.

Lights flared through the murky darkness, sometimes blotted out by driving snow, sometimes clear as will-o'-the-wisps in the sudden breaks in the curtain of white as it swirled another way.

'Rouse the grooms and stable boys, Miss Imogen,' the

man roared over his shoulder. 'We'll need help to carry him inside if he's been out in this for very long.'

'Imogen, do as Cordage says and then go inside and do me the courtesy of staying where I asked you to in the first place,' the Sophie-like female ordered some poor soul beyond Peter's faltering vision. He sympathised with the poor girl, whoever she might be, since she clearly lived under the cat's paw.

'And you should get inside in the warm as well, miss,' the man called Cordage argued rather desperately.

'Don't be ridiculous,' the shrew ordered her companion impatiently.

At the sound of her voice growing louder in his ears, Peter decided he ought to be grateful she was nigh as ungovernable as the woman he remembered so reluctantly as the most indomitable female he had ever met, since this one had evidently seen him from the window yonder and set out to rescue him.

'Catch this!' the woman ordered him, and he put out a hand without even thinking about it and caught the end of the leather belt she threw him more by chance than any skill on his part. 'Now, pull yourself back onto the road with it,' she went on, as if in charge of at least a battalion of rather stupid men lost in the snow. She prepared to lean back against his anticipated weight on the end of it.

'With one hand?' he demanded crossly, and thought he heard her gasp at the first sound of his suddenly hoarse voice—as if he reminded *her* of someone she didn't want to recall as well.

'Let your horse go and he will surely follow us. There

seems little doubt he has more sense than you do,' she said brusquely, and a dreadful suspicion began to dawn on him that this wasn't a female who sounded like opinionated, sneaky, lying, felonious Sophie Bonet, but the real thing.

'Why would I trust you to pull me onto the road?' he shouted, and if she chose to think he meant she might not be strong enough, then she was as good at deceiving herself as she was everyone else.

'What choice do you have at the moment? Or do you actually like it in there?' she asked, and there was a husky note in her voice now—as if she knew whom she was rescuing as well as he knew who she was.

'Between the devil and the deep blue sea, as I am?' he quizzed her.

'Geography really isn't your strong subject, is it?' she mocked.

He preferred that to the shock and almost welcome she'd seemed about to betray just now, when she'd realised exactly who she was rescuing from his own folly.

'Hence my reliance on straws,' he muttered, and discovered she had reeled him in to such effect she not only heard every word, but seemed about to prove him right by pulling him over the brink and on top of her with all her slender strength.

Out of the numbing snow, Peter finally reached the road to wherever it was he was going, feeling perilously like a huge fish on the end of her line as he stumbled on the kerb of what felt like a gentleman's drive and only managed to right himself and not fall on top of her by willpower alone.

'Have you got him safe, Miss Rose?' the earlier voice barked out of the dusk, and its owner waded towards them as fast as he could through the settled snow.

Peter caught glimpses of warmly dressed minions dashing about in the man's wake to no great effect through the flurries of snow he hoped really were growing less fierce. There was so much still to do before he could rest and dream of being properly warm at last.

'Yes, so pray tell Thomas to lead this stalwart beast to the stables for a thorough cosseting. Then if you would ask Mrs Elkerley to warm bricks and make a hot toddy, while the maids fetch warm blankets and start boiling water for a bath.'

'In a minute,' the brave Cordage argued, and he took Peter's arm and thrust it over his shoulder even as Sophie propped him up rather ineffectually from the other side.

She was petite as ever, and he fought another tranche of memories as he somehow found enough breath and energy to tell a bemused Hannibal to find the stables. With a snort half of apology and half of eagerness, the weary horse allowed himself to be caught by the hurrying groom who suddenly loomed up out of the light-reflecting snow ahead of them. Hannibal left behind a bemused master, who shook his head in disbelief and wondered how in Hades he'd managed to wander into one of his worst nightmares as he lurched through knee-high snow between his ill-assorted rescuers.

'Maybe I'll wake up in a snowy ditch any moment now and find out it's all been a terrible delusion,' he murmured, stumbling between one small yet very determined prop and one large and burly manservant.

'If it is, I sincerely hope I'm sharing it, then—and what on earth are you doing out here in the worst storm we've endured in years?' Sophie demanded.

'Looking for sanctuary,' he said dryly, wishing he could come up with something wise and witty to show her his defences were firmly in place and that she would never hurt him again.

Hopefully only he knew how good it felt to have the warmth and reality of her arm clasped about his torso. Even through the numbness threatening to overtake him after tramping through all the snow, he felt as if a fire leapt wherever they had contact with each other to burn away the chill of eight years of aching absence. He felt her body shift lithely against his as she insisted on taking some of his weight on her shoulders—as if she knew how close to failing he'd been when she'd seen him through the snow, as if some last pull of connection between them told her he was on the edge of freezing to death. He felt his shivering body respond to the only female he'd ever believed he passionately loved and cursed it bitterly.

'So was I,' he thought he heard her murmur, as if to herself, and suddenly the fact she was here, no more than twenty miles from Holm Park, hit him and hurt him like a savage blow. Suddenly it felt as if he was living in a world where none of the usual rules of geography applied. How could he not have known she was so close? And, since she had mentioned 'years' just now, she'd probably been here ever since she'd left him feeling as if his heart and soul had been hollowed out so she could take them with her and leave him a talking automaton instead of a man.

'How long?' he asked, in the sort of shorthand they had communicated in when they were young and supposedly so in love with one another that each had known what the other was thinking without needing more words.

'Eight years,' she told him, and he could hear the defiance in her voice even as she refused to look at him, staring determinedly through the shadows at the venerable manor house that was now growing ever closer—thank heaven.

'How devious of you to hide in plain sight, Princess,' he muttered softly as they finally reached the step up to a stout oak side door and shelter.

It could no longer be the sanctuary he'd dreamt of, since this noble old house sheltered Miss Sophie Bonet within its walls, and must therefore be considered enemy territory. She had been so close to his home all this time and never come to him—nor even thought of him alone without her. Somehow that physical closeness hurt more than if she'd been a thousand miles away with her pirates.

As they finally came within the circle of light cast by a flaring torch hastily set in the sconce by the door by Sophie's hurrying acolytes, he realised his other rescuer wore the dark and respectable dress of a butler, rather than that of the yeoman farmer he'd taken him for. Peter hardly dared look at the female who'd once dominated so many of his wasted dreams and youthful frustrations while he was still weak and cold and shaken. He had two far more worthy females to worry about out in the snow.

'It was necessary—and delusion my foot,' Sophie muttered direly, as if that barb had finally managed to penetrate her armour and actually hurt her. He wondered fleetingly why she hadn't left him to freeze to death.

'A man can hope,' he said tersely, while mentally begging her pardon for believing she'd leave anyone in danger when she could prevent it. Even eight years on, she clearly didn't have enough coldness to allow her worst enemy to die in a ditch.

Sophie gritted her teeth and reminded herself there would be plenty of time for hysterics once they got the frozen idiot inside and made sure he would survive his reckless ride into a blizzard despite his worst efforts.

Trying not to let herself fully know that this was Peter Vane she was helping to stagger through the heavy blanket of snow and spiteful little flurries of wind that seemed intent on landing them all in a drift, seeing off rescued and rescuers together, she had somehow managed to plod steadily on with the fact of her nemesis solid and heavy against her. Now he was suddenly too real.

'Idiot,' she chided breathlessly, and imagined she saw his familiar boyish smile of long ago in the uncertain light of the flambeau.

In that moment he looked exactly as he'd always done when he'd laughed off some reckless act of mischief when they'd been adoptive family, then friends and then—oh, so briefly—far more to each other than a very young lady and gentleman should be. All that was dead and done with, she assured herself. Somehow she had to rout

out all she remembered about him from the old days—all she'd foolishly allowed herself to cherish ever since, when living without him had become nigh unbearable.

Occasionally she even sat and dreamt of her young love, when she needed to reassure herself she'd once been loved so magically, and it sometimes seemed as if his touch and voice and image were stamped on her senses so deep he might be standing next to her. Then she would hear someone coming, or see one of her pupils look up from their work at their dreamy-eyed governess, and thump back to earth with a jarring thud. On those occasions reality stamped its heavy and uncompromising feet all over her memories, much as it did now, as he glared down at her with winter in his grey gaze, as if he'd have preferred a snowdrift to Sophie Bonet's help.

'Not quite as big a fool as I used to be,' he said, frowning darkly in the flaring light of the torches as they battled against the last angry flurries of snow and the wind bundled the light, deadly stuff about like a fractious child.

At last they stumbled up the steps and into the side hall, where Cordage could finally slam the stout oak door on the cruel weather outside and Sophie could survey the snow-encrusted figure of the Earl of Sylbourne without flying snowflakes distorting everything about him but his voice and the feel of his now mighty frame against her slighter one. And if his body had felt far more honed and solidly masculine than her traitorous senses remembered it being against her softer, much smaller one, she told herself she was beyond making such comparisons and owed him no more than the care any stranger might expect on being snowbound so close to Christmas.

Later she would examine the totally astonishing fact of Peter Adam George Fitzroy Vane, Earl of Sylbourne, wandering about a remote Worcestershire hillside alone in a snowstorm—preferably when she was totally alone herself. For now, there was no need to feel properly warm and alive for the first time in eight years, despite the fact her hands were stinging and her frozen feet argued otherwise. There was no call to think her world had swung back into kilter from the first moment she'd known Peter was the man she'd seen wandering out in the snow either. Certainly no need to suffer the delusion he'd come for her at long last. There was no call for fairy tales at all; this wasn't fairyland, and he certainly hadn't set out to find her—she had seen his revolted reaction when he'd actually realised who she was.

Ordering herself to accept truly cold reality, and not give in to the buzzing in her ears or the rush of hot blood thundering into her frozen extremities as they began to warm into painful life again, she made herself steadily inspect Peter's powerful, if visibly shivering and snow-caked, figure as dispassionately as she could.

'It would be best if we hurry through to the kitchens, lest Mrs Elkerley throw us all back out into the blizzard for ruining her maids' hard work on these floors,' she suggested prosaically, and she scrunched gingerly in that direction on her sodden and probably ruined indoor shoes herself, hoping they would all follow into the bustle and life of the kitchens before his lordship began to ask awkward and personal questions of the Fraynes's respectable governess in front of Cordage.

'No,' Peter argued, and she felt the familiar snap of her once ready temper as she took in his mulish expression and impatient frown.

'Do you prefer making work for the staff to showing consideration for how much they have to do at this time of year, my lord?' she asked—then could have kicked herself as she saw Cordage's intelligent gaze flit from one snow-covered figure to the other at her tacit admission that she knew this fugitive, and in fact numbered a member of the peerage among her acquaintance.

'No, I prefer not to have the death by exposure to the cold of my sister, my aunt and my coachman, groom and coachman's apprentice on my conscience. Nor risking the image of my best team being eaten by whatever predators run wild in this confounded frozen waste you inhabit haunting my nightmares as well,' Peter informed her sharply.

Sophie was glad the Garret-Lowden ladies were not present.

'Where did you carelessly mislay so many of them, then?' she asked, as if it was *his* fault such a heavy snowfall had blocked their path and led him to search for shelter in the last place he might have been expected to come upon by accident.

'How would I know? I don't belong in this benighted land,' he snapped back, as if she was occupying some outlandish arctic waste out of contrariness, instead of living in rich and rolling countyside barely an hour's ride from his own estates.

'Then how are we going to find them, pray?' she asked.

'By getting out of my way so I can consult someone with enough common sense and local knowledge to go back out with me and fetch them into warmth and shelter before they all freeze to death.'

'And you're godlike in your immunity to the elements nowadays, are you?' she asked sarcastically.

With a significant glare at his snowy person, and the soaking-wet greatcoat and once-immaculate beaver hat that now looked as if it would empty a snowdrift on Mrs Elkerley's immaculate floor all on its own if he took it off, Sophie let herself feel how desperately cold he must be. Yet he looked stubborn and immovable as ever, and she wouldn't give much for the chances of anyone who tried to tell him he should stay here while they went to find his party in the snowy treachery of a December night without him.

She sighed at the hostility fizzing between them, shrugged her own shoulders and unintentionally dislodged a snowball. Never mind their abraded feelings towards each other. Never mind for now that he clearly hated her and would prove a very uncomfortable house guest to go with the ones they already had. All that mattered at the moment was getting his family and servants safely back to Heartsease Hall without the Earl of Sylbourne managing to kill himself along the way.

'Why don't you come through into the warmth of the kitchens and at least get that snow brushed off whilst we consider how best to rescue your party?' she suggested practically.

Time for old grievances later. No, there would only be the odd chilly nod in her direction from such a mighty lord of the land.

'Aye—very well, then,' he conceded reluctantly.

Grasping his hand, and ignoring his gasp of shock or perhaps even revulsion at the contact, Sophie allowed herself a sigh of relief as she tugged him into the kitchens and told herself this really wasn't the time to search Peter Vane's face and form for the changes eight years had wrought. The maids were staring at this apparition of something like a walking snowman, and Cook stopped in mid grumble at the bootboy for forgetting that the spit still needed turning whatever was to do outside.

'Heaven preserve us,' Cook said faintly as she eyed the unlikely trio in front of her as if she couldn't believe her normally reliable senses.

'It might have to if you go and let the dinner burn while you're too busy gawping at your betters to bother with it, Nan Burton,' Cordage cautioned gruffly, and his voice seemed to wake the watchers from their trance. Cook snapped out orders with abrupt authority and searched her mental reserves for something pithy enough to say in reply to such provocation while the gentry were listening.

'Don't just stand there dripping all over my clean floor. You might as well take them wet clothes off and hand them over to the housemaids, since they've got nothing better to do on a night like this than stand about with their mouths open,' she managed to rap out convincingly enough, even while her eyes lingered on the strangest and most snow-covered figure of the three.

If she let herself, Sophie felt she might be intimidated by the grim-looking nobleman impatiently stripping himself of his outdoor clothes with hands obviously too cold for the task. He cursed colourfully under his breath and had to accept her help undoing buttons and unknotting his muffler. How he must hate the fact he couldn't remove his gloves for the clumsiness of his icy fingers.

The sheer grim determination it must have cost him to forge his way here against driving snow and biting cold tugged at her, as if an old love might be simmering dangerously under the calm veneer she somehow managed to maintain, but she told herself it was not possible. This man was nothing like the young and carefree Peter Vane she'd once fallen headlong in love with, and he clearly thought there was nothing left of tender, starry-eyed Sophie Bonet in her either.

She left off dreaming about days that would never come again and occupied herself with noticing the impressive breadth of shoulder that had been revealed now his snow-caked greatcoat had finally came off under Cordage's encouragement instead. The well-cut riding jacket beneath it did little to conceal how physically powerful Lord Sylbourne had grown in the past eight years, and the rigid control he was managing to keep over his stern face argued that his mental powers had been tested and refined as well. A formidable aristocrat now stood in front of her.

Command sat so easily on his wide shoulders even she found it difficult not to concede the running of this whole situation to him—but he didn't know these hills, nor which of the house's staff could best be relied on for the task ahead. Nor could he judge the lie of the land when he was a stranger to the area. Something in her refused to let him take over Heartsease Hall as ruthlessly as he had no doubt taken over Holm Park since his father died. Sir Gyffard would certainly have something pithy to say about even an earl stepping into his house and ordering everyone about as if he owned it—if only he was here to object.

'Oh, you poor soul,' the housekeeper exclaimed as she bustled into her rival's domain to bat at whatever snow still dared attach itself to Peter's lordly person.

'Have done, Mariah,' Cordage ordered, and as usual she took no notice.

'Why didn't you have the gentleman's coat and hat off him as soon as you got him inside the house? Aye, and his boots as well, since they must be wet through, Joseph Cordage?' she demanded of her dour colleague.

Sophie decided she would have to intervene before one of their famous arguments broke out and Peter stamped back out into the snow to rescue Edwina and Miss Hester Willis on his own.

'Sukey, please fetch the master's spare greatcoat and a beaver hat from Mr Timon's room. I suppose Sir Gyffard's spare boots will probably fit his lordship best, since he's determined to go out again and get in everyone else's way while we do our best to rescue his companions. Lucy, see if you can find some riding gloves that will fit our guest, and, Beth, please concoct the hot toddy Mr Cordage

taught you to make. Then you'd best find a goodly length
of flannel and a flask to keep some broth warm for the ladies. I suggest the grooms send for the home farm plough
teams, Cordage, and whatever vehicle they think might
be able to get across country safely in all this snow.'

'I doubt such a vehicle exists,' Peter objected as he
tugged off his ruined top-boots with the awed bootboy's
help. He still managed to look annoyingly composed and
somehow elegant even in his sodden stockinged feet when
he took the timidly offered hot lemon, honey and whisky
with a warm smile of thanks for Beth—who promptly became smitten with such a polite and magnificent gentleman. He downed it in a few hasty gulps.

'You forget that we live on the side of a hill not infre-
quently snowbound or icy in winter, my lord,' Sophie told
him tersely, and tried not to notice how awed the servants
were by their unexpected guest—and maybe by the governess's sudden change to commander of the household as
well. 'We're not unprepared for such weather at this time
of year, although this is extreme even by our standards.'

'Very laudable,' he said dryly, but he took the towel
Lucy shyly offered him with another smile of gratitude
and a polite thank-you and rubbed his moisture-darkened
hair impatiently. He emerged with his shock of wildly
curling tawny locks in the sort of disarray Sophie suspected it had not seen for many a long year, if his fashionable Brutus haircut was anything to go by.

'Will you see to the preparations while I change, please,
Cordage?' Sophie asked.

'Don't be so daft, woman,' Peter barked, in contrast to

his meticulous thanks for all the servants who had carried out her orders.

Somehow Sophie managed to hide her wince at his obvious revulsion at the very idea of her company.

'You would slow us down and endanger the whole rescue into the bargain. No, you will stay home and look to the young ladies who appear to be under your care—if their fear about coming out of hiding in the hall yonder is any indication of the state of tyranny they live under in *your* charge.'

Sophie's temper threatened to boil over at his implication that the Frayne girls were so frightened of her wrath they didn't dare show their faces, even as she heard a muffled giggle and saw Audrey, the youngest daughter of the house, peep round the door with eyebrows raised in a question. Sophie could not resist her, if Peter Vane did but know it, or care to note it with those sharp grey eyes of his hard on her.

'Very well, girls. Pray come into the kitchen and meet his lordship, who will be staying with us until the snow has abated sufficiently for his party to travel onwards,' she said somewhat ungraciously, struggling to pretend he was a mere acquaintance she had recognised from the past and didn't particularly care about one way or the other.

'Ladies,' Peter said, with an elegant bow that made Sophie snort with derision at his would-be exquisite manners and wonder that Audrey, Viola and Imogen could really be so instantly blinded by such flattering attention from a lord of any complexion as they appeared to be from their delighted smiles and the odd giggle. 'Since nobody has introduced us I shall have to do it myself. I am Peter Vane: a very foolish earl who has led his sister, aunt and an extra gentleman we acquired along the way, plus a coachman, groom, stable lad and a prime team, into the worst weather he can recall experiencing this side of the Atlantic Ocean and then lost them all so comprehensively in this blizzard he must now beg for rescue.'

'Yes, but which earl are you?' Audrey asked, as if the rest was obvious.

'Sylbourne, ma'am. And which lady of consequence am I addressing, if I might be permitted to ask such an impertinent question?'

'Of course you can, your lordship. I am Miss Audrey Frayne. The tall, skinny one trying to hide behind me and not managing it is my elder sister, Miss Viola Frayne, and that's Imogen, the eldest of us girls. She tells me she should be addressed as Miss Frayne because my aunt is absent—except she won't come out of the hallway to be called anything, despite being as close to out as makes no difference.'

'Yes, I will—and don't be such a horrid little rattle,' Imogen protested, emerging from the shadows and blushing like a peony.

Sophie knew she was right about her former charge's excellent prospects among the *ton* as soon as she beheld Peter's look of stunned awe at such unselfconscious beauty, before he pulled himself together and inherent good manners made him strive to set this obviously diffident girl at ease.

'Miss Frayne,' he said, with an admiring look and a

smile Sophie tried very hard not to feel wistful about, since *she'd* once been the lucky recipient of that look herself on a daily basis. 'I'm honoured to make your acquaintance—and if you had made your official debut already, I'm quite sure I would have heard about riots in Mayfair as the bucks and beaux competed for your smiles. I'm even more honoured to have met you before any of them could outflank me.'

'You are very kind, my lord,' Imogen claimed, recovering her composure under the influence of his lighthearted nonsense and that nigh-irresistible smile. 'I don't believe a word you say, but you're still very kind.'

'Merely perspicacious. But if you'll excuse me, I, too, have a sister I'm quite fond of—despite the fact she regularly gets me into trouble very much as your own evidently do you. I really need to go back and find her before she falls into some outrageous piece of mischief while my back's turned or runs off with a highwayman.'

'Oh, yes, you must indeed fetch her into the warmth. The poor lady must be very cold and frightened out there in the cold and dark,' Imogen agreed with a sympathetic shudder.

'My sister Edwina is more likely to think it's all a splendid adventure and will make a fine preparation for her new life on campaign with her husband-to-be. At least she will pretend to do so, whether she's scared or not, since she's a stubborn Vane as well. But my aunt will be furious if I don't hurry up and bring her back to civilisation.'

'Let's hurry up and do so, then,' Sophie urged, only to

receive Lord Sylbourne's best stern glare and a scathing invitation to 'see sense.' 'Why?' she asked mildly, and glared back until her eyes threatened to water. Luckily he looked away before her nerve failed, and she caved in and did as she was bid like everyone else.

'Don't you trust the men of this household to help me and mine?' he countered coldly, and how could she argue that she did, then demand to go with them anyway?

'Of course I do. But won't your sister and aunt feel re-assured to see you return with a lady to keep them company on their return journey?' she argued feebly.

'They're more likely to think I've run mad to permit one to imperil herself and their would-be rescuers with her headstrong determination to garner as much attention to herself as she can contrive at all times,' he snapped harshly.

'You're clearly not at all well acquainted with Miss Rose if you believe *that*, my lord,' diffident Viola spoke up to defend her governess, and Sophie knew how badly his judgement hurt when she had a strong urge to hug her brave young defender.

'You're quite correct, Miss Viola,' Peter said with a wry smile that held a hint of sadness. 'I know your Miss Rose very ill.'

'Then you should wait until you do know her before you're in any way qualified to make scathing judgements about someone we all value very dearly, my lord,' Audrey piped up, with an emphatic nod that told him he was in danger of losing *her* good opinion as well.

'Would I had such stalwart defenders,' he said ruefully.

'But, however wonderful your Miss Rose is, she would be very much in the way if she was to hold up my sister's rescue while a pony is tacked up with a ladies' saddle and she changes into a suitable habit for such a ride. She would slow us down on the way back to my carriage with my worrying about her welfare as, well.'

'You really don't know me at all, do you, my Lord Sylbourne?' Sophie said with a direct look that she hoped reminded him of how little she'd *ever* slowed him and his friends down when they were impulsive youths and she was the burr in their boots who refused to be left out of any misadventures going.

'Only by repute,' he said harshly.

Luckily he'd already turned away before she flinched and paled at the implied insult, so he didn't see how squarely that shaft had gone home. Not that she had a stinking reputation, but the fact he believed she should have was enough to make her feel almost physically wounded.

'Then we're in the same position,' she managed to reply as the maids finally came back with the outer garments she'd asked them to look for.

Cordage guided Peter to his own parlour, where he could change into warm, dry clothes in front of the fire and in private, before submitting his poor chilled body to the biting wind blowing up outside.

CHAPTER THREE

THE last of the snow fluttered almost disconsolately outside, and the sight of it made Sophie shudder. Fear and
compassion for Peter, stubbornly pitting his will against
the elements and the night, warred with hurt and anger.

So he thought he had the right to judge her harshly
across the almost unbridgeable lapse of time between
the Sophie Bonet he'd known and quiet, respectable Miss
Rose, did he? His view of her was obviously set, and there
was little point attempting to change it. No, there was no
point at all, she thought on a private sigh. In the end she
had decided she didn't need to go with him. Nor could
she face his dark looks and unspoken disgust while she
got her defences safely shored up against him for such a
frozen odyssey. So she had withdrawn into her previous
quiet persona and let the whole uproar of plans and preparations for his rescue party carry on a little apart from
her as soon as Peter was recovered and more than ready
to direct operations himself.

She watched them leave from a side window, where

there was no distracting light to make it impossible to see outside and where she couldn't be seen either. She felt so reluctant to stay behind while Peter risked himself again, but she had to remind herself that Sir Gyffard Frayne trusted her with the welfare of his daughters. Her earlier need to go with Peter through the now rapidly freezing landscape had felt more like a premonition that he was in some sort of danger rather than any desire to interfere. And the stubborn feeling that she belonged at his side might have persisted from the old days, even after that stony greeting. So somehow she made herself stay behind, like a meek little woman waiting at home for a warrior to return after some great manly quest, complete with tall tales of dragons, damsels in distress and ghostly foes to pour out to anyone gullible enough to believe them.

No, if there was any danger out there, beyond that of being frozen to death if he missed his way, Peter would insist on facing it with *anyone* other than Sophie Rose at his side. The lighthearted and deeply-in-love Peter and Sophie of eight years ago were as far from Lord Sylbourne and Miss Rose as they would be if the entire Arctic wastes lay between them with awe-inspiring glaciers and un-crossed ice floes to make sure they could get no closer. Mature and aloof Peter Vane obviously felt no connection to the Fraynes' governess, but fear for him nagged at her as she made herself join the hasty preparations to welcome a party of cold travellers to the hall.

Sophie bustled about the gracious old manor house with all three Miss Fraynes, helping Mrs Elkerley and the maids while part of her still pondered the incredible feel of mature and impressively muscular Peter Vane struggling against the knee-high snow next to her. For that short time he'd needed her, whether he liked it or not, and a part of her she did her best to ignore exulted in every step they'd taken side by side. But that part of Sophie was a fool, and she did her best to ignore her insistence that fate had led Peter Vane to her door on such a night, so he would be marooned here for as many hours or days as the snow lay thick on the ground.

Fate had an odd way of working if it took eight years to lead Peter to Heartsease Hall for her to find floundering in a snowdrift. She would have to have words with such a fickle deity, if she believed in it in the first place—and she was fairly sure she did not. If there was only one truly right man for every woman, then fate had made very sure she couldn't have hers. No, this was nothing to do with her and her once broken heart, so sensible Miss Rose must fade back into her role and hope the wind veered back to the mild southwesterly of the past few weeks, so Lord Sylbourne could spend Christmas by his own hearth instead of Sir Gyffard Frayne's.

Almost warm, and in blessedly dry clothes that fit him wherever they touched, Peter set out to fetch the people he cared most about in the world—and Cedric Wroxley—back to the warmth and safety of Heartsease Hall. He felt as if the world had shifted on its axis since he set out on his desperate quest. Part of him had wanted to stay in the warmth of the hall and get truly comfortable for the first time since he'd risen from his warm bed at the posting inn in Gloucester that morning, ready to face an overcast but otherwise benign-looking day. Then he'd had the beckoning prospect of being at home and watching the echoing barn of a place it had become to him come alive for Christmas and his sister's wedding. Now he must endure however many days it took for the roads to be clear stuck here in the middle of nowhere, forced into the company of the last person he'd ever wanted to see again.

Little wonder he rode a little apart and didn't even try to make the rest of the rescue party forget he was an earl and the rest of them were not. He was a stranger to these men, and they were risking cold toes and chilblains at the very least to fetch a party of fools into the warmth and shelter of their home, and Peter felt vaguely guilty about his preoccupation with one of their household. He felt as if he'd taken a blow sharper than any the cold and misery of that confused ride about their hillside in driving snow could throw at him. Sophie Bonet had rescued him from slowly freezing to death, or tramping about for hours only a few hundred yards from warmth and shelter, but he hadn't been able to thank her, and he frowned into the night as he brooded on the curmudgeon she'd made of him.

He must prepare himself to share a roof with Miss Bonet-Rose and shore up his defences against the conniving little adventuress. The Heartsease Hall servants would just have to think him high and mighty while he wrestled with dark thoughts. They'd think far worse if he ranted at the family's governess for vanishing like a summer mist with his youthful heart in her greedy little hands all those years ago. Calf love, he chided himself. It had been mere infatuation and that was all. And if he'd never experienced such joy and happiness as he had for those few heady days in high summer, then neither had such exquisite agony clawed at him either, once he'd finally realised she'd gone for good. She couldn't have loved him—had probably felt nothing beyond the animal attraction of his youthful passion for her and the satisfaction of knowing a supposedly dashing young lordling was so deep in love with her he would make her a countess one day and to hell with the consequences.

His mouth twisted in a parody of a smile, and he felt the thoughtful gaze of the head groom, as if he wore his thoughts on his face for all to see. No, he was too good at hiding his feelings nowadays to wear them on his sleeve, so he forced his face blank and locked the most bitter of them to the back of his mind. The man was perceptive, and Peter was impressed by the absent owner of Heartsease Hall for hiring and keeping such excellent senior servants, since he knew very well it was the secret of running an efficient and happy household. Perhaps the man had left the hiring of a governess and the education of his daughters to his wife, Peter speculated as he fought the notion that whoever had employed Sophie was equally shrewd, since the Frayne girls seemed delightfully unspoiled and untainted by the usual affectations of young ladies with little else but a fine marriage on their minds.

The ease with which Sophie Bonet appeared to fit into the household argued she was a long-established member of it. Again he wanted to frown as it occurred to him that nothing about this Sophie meshed with the picture he'd had in his mind all these years of a careless little adventuress with only her next easy pleasure on her mind. He sighed in tune with the wickedly cold wind blowing in on the coattails of the snowstorm and scented Jack Frost waiting to freeze and petrify this icy kingdom Old Winter had made at this far edge of the Cotswold Hills. Tomorrow the snow would carry a crust of ice, and even the stream he could hear burbling down from the hilltop would either be full of icicles or frozen in its tracks. They would be stuck here as if they'd been enchanted by some evil spell. There would be no escape without a Russian sleigh and specially shod horses to run over the hard-packed snow—and how was he going to get hold of those in the middle of nowhere?

Peter found it difficult to decide who would be the least happy when the sun rose on Christmas Eve tomorrow. His sister would not be marrying her love on Christmas morning, as they'd planned since Giles Wroxley had come home on leave the day before Advent began. There was no chance of their marriage taking place on Christmas Day itself. Nor would his intrepid aunt be hunting with her beloved pack of like-minded friends on Boxing Day. And Cedric Wroxley would not be in London, and would therefore be unhappy by definition. He cared very little if Cedric was content or utterly miserable, but they would all be forced to endure his miseries since Cedric didn't seem the type to suffer unseen or unheard.

Peter Vane would rather wake up in any house in England than the one that sheltered Sophie Bonet under its broad roof, and from her pale face and shocked eyes when she had peered up at him in the full light of the Heartsease kitchens just now, Sophie herself wasn't pining for his company over the next few days either. Good. He was glad that she would suffer even half the discomfort he felt at the thought of spending hours, let alone days, with a woman who had betrayed and deserted him when he was scarce more than a boy.

He ought to be ashamed of himself for hating a lone female once part of his family and his own hope of happiness, but he smiled grimly into the night and rode on. At least brooding about Sophie's unlikely hiding place had stopped him being quite so conscious of the biting cold nipping at his fingers and toes. Now he was back to noticing the world about him, and he wished he hadn't bothered to shrug off Sophie's many mysteries. It felt as if his thick jacket, borrowed greatcoat and heavy wool muffler might as well be made of tissue rather than best British wool, as the cruel cold beginning to set in now the snowstorm was finally dying away began to bite. His muffler was supplied courtesy of the absent Ferdinand Frayne, or so the little scullery maid who'd brought it to him had shyly told him. Apparently Master Ferdy was a midshipman on the Java Station, and, "He don't need it there cos it be 'ot as 'ades, my lord." So Peter was glad of its thickness, even if it told the tale of a young man used to a warmer climate and feeling the cold in his native land.

There—he'd managed to divert himself from his slavish preoccupation with Sophie Bonet for almost a minute now, and was surveying all he could see of the hillside by the light of their lanterns and the fast-clearing night skies. He must stop himself brooding over her all over again. The half-moon would serve very well to light the way with its own reflection off the snow, and the whole of nature seemed now to go still as the wind finally died and the last dark cloud cleared the moon. At least the increased light would help them find his stranded carriage, but he winced at the thought of his sister and aunt having to battle against this deadly cold all the way back to Heartsease Hall and safety and comfort, if not necessarily peace of mind, since both of them had been deeply attached to Sophie Bonet, too, once upon a time.

Damnation take the woman! Here she was, dominating his thoughts and chipping away at his hard-won self-control once more. He made himself think about his lovely and sweet-tempered mistress instead, in the hope that *la belle* Kitty might turn his thoughts from a less obliging and, in his eyes, far less worthy female. But he found to his acute annoyance that he couldn't even form a picture of the statuesque blonde beauty in his head for the intrusion of a little dab of a female who barely reached his chin on tiptoes and looked as if a strong wind might blow her away. It annoyed him how acutely he'd noted, when she'd supported him out of the storm and into her lair, that Sophie had far more womanly curves now than she had been blessed with at seventeen.

This was going to be the worst and most frustrating Christmas season ever if he didn't learn to master his baser impulses, so Peter made himself calculate ways and means of escaping Heartsease Hall before a thaw set in and the roads became a sea of mud for days afterwards. Maybe he could ride for home by one of the old packhorse routes tomorrow? Or somehow wade through the snow to the nearest mail-coach route, since the mail had to run even if the post boys must walk it to its destination. It didn't matter if he ended up in the next village or the nearest town and no further on with his journey, because if he wasn't *here*, he couldn't be drawn in by a lying little witch masquerading as a respectable governess. If that made him a coward, so be it.

The Garret-Lowdens were conspicuous by their absence while all the fuss of getting Heartsease Hall ready for its influx of important if unexpected visitors went on around them. Unable to believe they'd suddenly discovered tact, Sophie concluded they must think a merchant had been silly enough to set out in such weather, or a farmer and his wife had come back too late from market and needed rescuing. If dressing for a quiet country dinner took precedence over their interfering with the household then thank goodness for vanity, Sophie concluded, and hurried to get everything done before the ladies emerged resplendent.

Telling herself she was glad to be housed on the second floor herself, with the younger Miss Fraynes and their schoolroom, so they could sleep soundly well away from the guests and all the fuss they would cause, Sophie helped light bedroom fires and hastily air mattresses before beds could be made up. She hoped warming pans and flannel-wrapped hot bricks would take the chill off the crisp linen sheets by the time they needed to be occupied. The laundry maid had been fetched from her cottage nearby and was supervising a vast washing day's worth of hot water in her kingdom as fires were lit under the coppers and a fleet of buckets set ready to be deployed when the travellers finally reached the hall and needed warm baths to truly thaw out before assuming fresh clothes or taking to their beds.

'Cordage says the men will retrieve the luggage from Lord Sylbourne's coach in the morning, but do you think the ladies will have valises, Miss Rose?' Imogen asked, as if being without her own clothes was the most serious problem a lady might face on such a night.

Sophie was pleased her one-time pupil didn't realise how serious the travellers' plight was. Her young friend's imagination wasn't offering a host of dangerous and highly unlikely mishaps to fret over as her own was.

'I doubt they will risk weighing down the horses with anything not strictly necessary tonight, Imogen,' she replied, ruthlessly raiding the housekeeper's stillroom for sweetly scented washing balls, lavender water and some of the elder Miss Frayne's precious Denmark Lotion, in case Edwina or her aunt had found time to become concerned about their complexions after exposure to the bitter frost now rapidly following the heavy snowfall.

'Aunt Matilda will be furious at us for using up her Denmark Lotion,' Imogen observed with considerable satisfaction.

'No doubt. But since the unlucky ladies will arrive here in the clothes they stand up in, they will need some of the

comforts they are accustomed to. Your aunt will hardly
begrudge her things to make life more bearable for them,
considering Lady Edwina is the daughter of an earl.'

'Oh, *she* would complain if Queen Charlotte herself
was benighted here and stood in need of them, but doubtless Papa will tell her not to be uncivilised and ignore
her, and she will get over it in time—especially as he
will then send to town for half a dozen of everything she
has been deprived of in her absence,' Imogen said with
easy cheerfulness.

But Sophie pictured the squire's faded yet ever-hopeful
sister and shivered at the very thought of her hysterics
when she discovered someone had dared trespass among
her things, even in an emergency.

'We should take chemises and some nightgowns as
well,' Viola put in, with happy anticipation of some excitement to liven up the coming festive season. It had seemed
to her such an unpromising Christmas up to now, with
the sadness of bright and lively Lady Porthdown's death
in childbed, along with her seventh child. 'None of us has
anything half as fine as Aunt Matilda's night attire and
underclothes,' Viola added.

Sophie wondered if Viola had taken a few envious looks
at the finely made things on washing day and longed for
something a little less workaday herself.

'I daresay the ladies will be too glad not to be sleeping
under a hedge to mind if we donate some of our plainer
items, my dear. While your aunt might forgive us for
filching her lotions and potions in time, she would never

abide the thought of another woman wearing something as intimate as her chemise or night attire.'

'Let's hope they're not large, then, since we're all too small to supply any Junoesque ladies. Even Audrey's taller than you are, Miss Rose. I really don't see why we have to hand our things over without a second thought either,' Viola said resentfully.

Sophie sighed and realised she had a long way to go to resign her younger charges to their maiden aunt's querulous ways after all.

'And what will they do about gowns, Miss Rose? If the ladies are well enough to dine with us, I don't think they should have to stay in their bedchambers for want of a suitable gown. We can hardly donate those, since we don't have any,' Audrey said, as if the biggest dilemma the ladies might face tonight was not being able to sit down to dinner in suitable clothes.

'True—so why don't you go and see if you can find something suitable for them to wear from among your late mama's belongings in the attics? I suspect my gowns will prove far too short and plain for both ladies, and Lady Frayne would have been the first to lend whatever was needed to any lady in distress,' she suggested, knowing the late lady's daughters would be practical about their visitors' plight.

Now the sharpest edges of grief for their beloved mother had abated, Viola and Audrey loved any chance to go through the sweetly scented trunks of clothes stored carefully in the attics so their father should not be reminded of what he'd lost. Luckily Imogen shared the late

Lady Frayne's practical approach to life, and allotted her little sisters the task of searching for anything that would make their enforced visitors comfortable from among the items interleaved with tissue, lavender and spice-heavy moth bags.

'Be very sure the lantern is hung up safely out of your way,' Sophie admonished as they dashed off to carry out their quest. 'I don't want to camp on the lawn for the Christmas season in the cold whilst we think up ways of informing your papa how you burnt down his house whilst he was away from it.'

'We'll be very careful—don't be such a worry-wart, Rosie,' Viola told her with an impish smile, then dashed off in her little sister's wake.

'At least that should get them out from under everyone's feet for a while,' Imogen muttered, as if she found their high spirits wearisome, and Sophie managed to hide a smile at this show of sophistication.

She knew how odd it felt to suddenly be considered grown-up at Imogen's age, when a girl often felt so much less mature than she ought to in the face of the abrupt change from schoolgirl to young lady. Wishing she could explain how it seemed to be a lifelong struggle not to hide one's head under the bedclothes and hope the complex problems of maturity would go away, Sophie sighed and decided there were certain things about life you had to learn for yourself.

'While your sisters are busy, perhaps you would check the bedchambers that are being got ready for the ladies in case any details have been missed, Imogen? Once Viola

and Audrey select a couple of likely gowns and a set of
underclothes and a nightgown apiece, we must make sure
it all gets ironed as best we can. With such a pother going
on, there will be no time for the details later, since your
visitors should be upon us very soon now,' she said, and
she turned towards the older part of the house, ignoring
Imogen's grimace at the idea the newcomers would be *her*
guests, as she was the only available lady of the house not
in the schoolroom, and biting her lip on a wrongheaded
impulse to take that burden off Imogen's shoulders and
onto her own.

Sophie shuddered at the very idea of putting herself
forward like that in front of the Vane family.

Now she was in the oldest part of the house, a rambling
warren of bedchambers, closets and somewhat makeshift
corridors added when the fashion arose for privacy among
the great and the good. Mrs Elkerley was far too busy
to cast her critical eye over the gentlemen's allotted bedrooms, now her maids had done with them, so Sophie had
rashly offered to check all was as good as it could be at
such short notice. The ladies must have the best remaining guest rooms in the newer wing of the house, since
they could hardly turn the Garret-Lowdens out of their
rooms, and the gentlemen must take the twists and turns
and eccentricity of the medieval parts of the hall and be
grateful not to be sleeping in the abandoned coach or a
draughty old barn, she decided militantly.

Peter had been allotted the best room available in the
old wing, as befitted an earl, and it seemed an intrusion

on his privacy for her to be there at all—but he would never know. Even if he did, he would have to put up with her presence after landing himself on the doorstep at what should be a most joyous time of the year. If it had been left to her, he would have been lodged in a nice draughty garret, but her opinion didn't matter very much, so the blue bedroom it had to be.

Holding her candle high, she surveyed royal-blue-painted plaster with quaint depictions of heraldic beasts picked out in white to lighten the whole effect, and then the elaborately carved dark oak bedposts almost swathed by richly embroidered hangings. She whisked away the last torn trail of a dusty old cobweb and removed a neglected speck of dust from the venerable Venetian mirror with her handkerchief. The billowing feather mattress looked inviting enough under its silk brocade cover and hastily-turned-back snowy sheets, and Sophie decided his lordship would be more comfortable here than he deserved to be.

The late Lady Frayne had taken great pains in turning a decaying, if historic, old house into a welcoming home without ruining its unique character, and Sophie shuddered at the very thought of all the alterations Miss Garret-Lowden seemed hell-bent on making when it finally came into her fiancé's possession on the death of his father. Every time she managed to stop herself thinking about Peter, unease about the Frayne girls' future and Sir Gyffard's proposal plagued her in a familiar strand of niggling anxiety. Sophie ordered herself to concentrate on the here and now and set aside that conundrum for later.

Somehow she must avoid Peter Vane, Earl of Sylbourne, as much as she could, until the harsh weather abated and he could leave. In an ancient house like this, with rooms often leading off each other or tucked away in odd corners where the house had been altered to fit more modern tastes over the years, it was going to be a challenge. Unless she hid in the schoolroom until the weather changed—and that would be an admission of cowardice she wasn't prepared to make. She listened to the howl of the wind around the venerable oriel window and decided she'd imagined that tingle of fear for him earlier. Lord Sylbourne would never permit harm to come to anyone in his care, least of all his little sister, so how could she be fool enough to think him vulnerable to danger from any human agency abroad tonight?

She wondered how it might feel to trust herself to his mature care, to be gently bullied in the interests of making him feel better about her safety, and told herself her shiver at the very thought was one of revulsion. Miss Rose stood on her own feet, fought her own battles and much of the time managed to enjoy a life that most young ladies would avoid with horror. There was no need to look back at what might have been and wonder why she had walked away from him all those years ago.

No, there was no need to do that, she decided dreamily as she eyed the finely etched carafe on the ancient oak table next to the bed. She decided a very particular moment in one's life could seem like a breathtakingly lovely piece of blown glass. Once, very briefly, her existence had been full of fragile light and sparkle, but she'd been far too young to realise how precious and breakable it truly was. Her beautiful bubble had been made by the finest of craftsmen, she recalled, with a reminiscent smile it was as well she couldn't see on her own lips, since it revealed so much regret and nostalgia she would be horrified. That lovely glass vessel had been finely etched with Arcadian dreams and beautiful promises exchanged by two painfully young lovers on that last, perfect June night. Her young love had made it so delicate and exquisite that she shivered at the very thought—not with cold but with remembered warmth—on this December night when not even the glowing fire lit in the grate and quantities of flannel-wrapped hot bricks could quite banish the chill of an unused bedchamber.

Yes, it had been almost too beautiful, and the next day Peter's father had taken it in his careless, destructive hands and shattered it into sharp little shards that still seemed to be lodged somewhere deep inside her even now—all the more painful because their source had been made of such yearning hopes and dreams she wondered she'd ever been innocent enough to believe they could come true. She wouldn't let herself recall that every line and whisper had been made with love, because Peter no more loved her now than he would Morgain le Fay or Lady Macbeth.

No, she reminded herself robustly, and she didn't love him either. This Peter—this granite-hard nobleman with contempt for her in his rigidly controlled mouth and cold-as-iron eyes—wasn't her young love any more than she was his.

Sophie heard Audrey calling her name and told herself it was a relief to escape painful memories of a time when she had been naïve enough to think the world well lost for love. The next few hours would be quite difficult enough without dwelling on how different her life might have been if she'd ignored her conscience and eloped with the merry boy who'd become the dour Earl of Sylbourne.

Riding on through the ghostly almost-darkness, Peter felt weariness tug at his limbs and the beginnings of a headache threaten. Not that suddenly feeling ill at ease in his own skin had anything to do with Sophie Bonet—more likely it was caused by squinting so hard into the driving snow while he'd been looking for shelter. Now the rapidly chilling air threatened even greater danger to his family than the blinding whiteness he'd battled earlier, and he had good reason to feel uneasy. He did his best to forget he'd stumbled on Sophie Bonet's hiding place after eight years of not looking for it and to concentrate on finding his sister, but Sophie was constantly on the edge of his thoughts. And very annoying he considered it as well. He tried to tell himself the eerie darkness now lit by a faint, clear moon reflected off the snow was warmer and more appealing than the chilly little mercenary's heart, and that she wasn't worth a pang of regret for the eight years of separation yawning between them now.

Except Sophie Bonet *wasn't* sailing the Caribbean with some pirate king in thrall to her charms, robbing innocents to satisfy her lightest whim, and nor was she coldly card-sharping with a lover in some silken den of iniquity as he might have secretly hoped. She was a respectable and apparently highly valued governess to a well-established family of country gentry. None of which chimed with her pose of ambitious and amoral adventuress the day she'd left Holm Park. So how could he carry on loathing a female who'd schemed to so little effect? Particularly if she'd never schemed at all but used it to cover her running away from those who loved her for who knew what reason all of her own?

No, he *hated* Sophie Bonet; it had been the anchor to his rocking world ever since she'd left—the goad that had driven him on every time he'd been tempted to marry money to pay off his father's massive debts, after all. He had to hate her; if he stopped doing that, he might have to remember how desperately he'd once loved her. He couldn't endure such pain as he'd felt when she had betrayed him and left, as if nobody at Holm Park had ever mattered to her in the first place.

He would accept this Sir Gyffard Frayne's hospitality in his absence, then leave without a backward look as soon as the first icicle began to melt. Now he knew the place to avoid as if it was cursed, he and Sophie could pretend to be as oblivious to each other as if they'd never met again.

'You're quite certain you came this way, milord?' The Fraynes' burly head groom interrupted his brooding thoughts as he peered into the eerie night to find the way.

'Aye. I may be a fool for being out in such weather in the first place, Cox, but I'm a fool blessed with a keen sense of direction, and I recall yon riven oak looming up at me out of the blizzard on my way to the hall,' he replied as civilly as he could.

It wasn't anyone else's fault but his own that he'd permitted Edwina's urgings to overcome his judgement and had carried on with the journey when he should have considered their safety over Dina's pleas and sulks and insisted on stopping. He was responsible for them being caught in this parlous state, and his punishment seemed to be enduring Sophie Bonet's company until some sort of thaw cleared the way and freed him. A week in the local lockup on bread and water even in these conditions would have been preferable, but that wasn't Cox's or anyone else but Sophie Bonet's fault.

'Sounds like you were at the top of Badger Hill, then, my lord, and I wouldn't take any team of mine down there in a tricky storm like this one was neither.'

'My coachman told me in no uncertain terms that he'd rather lose his job than risk his team on it.'

'Quite right, too,' Cox said robustly, and Peter wondered if the man thought he had the least intention of dismissing Merryweather for not doing what he'd never have let him do in the first place.

'I ordered the horses unhitched and taken as close to a copse at the corner of the field we turned into as they could safely get, so they'd be sheltered from the worst of the weather. Does that give any clue to where they will be?' he asked, doing his best to banish Sophie from his mind and concentrate on his sister and his aunt.

'Aye, milord, and if I'm right we should come on them any minute.'

'Odd that it took me so long to find the Hall when we were so close all along.'

'Very likely you wandered about and got lost along the way. For all some think we live in a soft sort of country, these hills are hard on strangers at this time of year.'

'My own home is barely twenty miles off,' Peter defended himself rashly.

'Then you should have known better than to set out on a day like this, your lordship,' the groom chided, with no apparent fear for his own job if his master heard of him scolding this foolish nobleman forced to seek shelter while he was away.

'You're right,' Peter admitted ruefully. 'But you can blame my sister and her fiancé for that particular folly. They were to wed on Christmas Day, and she couldn't endure the wait for better weather if there was the slightest hope she could get home to marry him in time.'

'I expect it's a love match, then,' the head groom said sagely. 'My daughter is due to wed Christmas Day as well, and she's been driving me and her mother barmy with her sighing and her dreaming. Don't seem able to hear a word that ain't about weddings or setting up home afterwards or some such nonsense.'

'You have my heartfelt sympathy. It was probably just that sort of absentminded idiocy that led my sister's affianced husband to fall off his horse and break his ankle and dislocate his shoulder two days before he should have set out to fetch his bride home from our grandmother's house in Bath.'

'Which accounts for you being here instead, I suppose, my lord?'

'Indeed it does,' Peter agreed, his gaze sharpening on a glimpse of restless movement in the shadows.

CHAPTER FOUR

SUDDENLY the snow-swathed hillside was eerie and the night almost uncanny as the fitful moonlight struggled against ragged wisps of cloud. Peter could imagine this land in former times, wild with wolf packs and outlaws roaming the frozen hills in search of easy prey. A vivid imagination was more a curse than a blessing at such times, and he tried to fight a shiver of foreboding.

Telling himself not to be a fool, he let his mount pick its way towards the place where he'd seen that hint of movement, and could have shouted with joy at the sound of an enquiring wicker—a *who goes there?* from one of his carriage horses.

'Be that you, my lord?' Merryweather's gruff voice challenged out of the dark.

'I sincerely hope so,' he replied, with a lifting of his spirits even the threat of many hours, if not days, in Sophie Bonet's company couldn't quite destroy.

'Aye, that's his lordship's voice, all right, Jem. You can put the blunderbuss away and stop your worriting now. We'll need to be ready to move the cattle as soon as his lordship has the ladies and Mr Cedric safely out of yon coach, and you'll need both hands for that.' The irrepressible Joe Merryweather's voice boomed out of the darkness.

'Lady Edwina and my aunt must be our first concern, Merryweather,' Peter told him. 'I believe it'll be safer for her ladyship to ride double with me than try to ride alone when she must be perished with cold by now. Mr Wroxley's already informed me that he's a very poor horseman, so could you bear to carry him pillion after the hard day you've already had? That sturdy animal yonder looks well up to your combined weight.'

'My Titan's fresh and needs something to do, my lord. He could plough all day and still carry two men for as long as anyone could ask him to, so the gentleman might as well ride with me, since I ain't been driving all day,' Cox offered, as if sensing Merryweather's reluctance.

'When I say Mr Wroxley's a poor horseman, Cox, I really mean he's no sort of rider at all. He'll probably do his best to unseat you both.'

Hearing Merryweather mutter something scathing about Wroxley's inability to ride a donkey into hell, Peter couldn't suppress a bark of laughter, even though he knew he shouldn't encourage the rogue's pungent opinions in front of the awed Jem and most of Sir Gyffard Frayne's stable lads.

'I don't know what you can find to laugh about in this disastrous predicament you have managed to land us in tonight, Sylbourne,' Wroxley's reedy voice informed him from the hunched shadow that was all they could see of the coach until they got a little nearer to the hedge where it now rested.

Peter concluded the damn fool had put down the carriage window once again, to lecture the world about his own discomfort, causing far more to those around him, as usual.

'Only the prospect of seeing you tip yourself into the nearest snowdrift when you try to ride back with us, Wroxley,' Peter said cheerfully, knowing there was no point pretending he didn't detest the little worm when the worm in question had done his best to break up his sister's engagement to his own brother and, once he was warm and fed, would gloat unbearably that the wedding could not now take place as planned.

'Now, that really is too bad of you, Peter,' Edwina said, with an irrepressible mischief in her voice that told him she would secretly love to see it happen all the same.

'I know, but it's been a trying day one way and another, and I don't know how much more querulous disapproval I can stand from that particular quarter,' he confided for her ears only as he lifted her down from the carriage and onto his saddle so she didn't have to get her feet wet.

'Of course it has. And after you gallantly came to my rescue in order to escort us home as well, it really is too bad of us to get ourselves into a pickle and then blithely expect you to get us out of it.'

'No, it isn't,' the dishonourable Cedric said as he emerged from the belly of the coach. 'It's the least he can do after getting us into this mess in the first place.'

'No, the least he could do was ride off home in order to avoid your constant carping and criticising. Pray be quiet for once, Cedric, and stop making everything so much worse,' Lady Edwina told her soon-to-be brother-in-law severely.

Peter silently cheered her on, knowing this was one relative by marriage she would never win over, since her advent in Captain Giles Wroxley's life would push the not very Honourable Cedric even further down the line of succession to the Seetley title than he clearly felt he deserved to be.

'Let's have you out of there before you freeze to death, Aunt Hes,' he said, ignoring Cedric to concentrate on a far worthier person.

'How far must we ride, my boy? I really am ridiculously cold, and I don't know if I can stay in the saddle for long,' Miss Willis declared, and the lamps picked out the pallor of her anxious face as Peter approached.

He was shocked by the sight of his usually redoubtable aunt so clearly shaken. She was in no state to ride an unfamiliar horse more used to the plough than the saddle, despite her famous ability to ride to hounds long after everyone but the master and the hunt servants had given up and gone home.

'Would it offend your dignity to ride pillion behind our absent host's head groom, Aunt Hes?' he asked, consigning Cedric to the indignity of being led from the back of one of the other grooms' horses, so he couldn't do the horse or himself permanent damage.

'Since I don't want to stay here and freeze to death,

I'd accept a ride behind the devil himself to get under a warm, dry roof tonight,' Miss Willis said fervently.

'That's settled, then,' he declared, and made sure it was so before Cedric could argue.

After gruffly denying the prancing little dandy any luggage, he gave his horse the office to be off and left the fool to look after himself for once in his life.

'How the devil will you put up with sharing a house with him when we finally get you married off to his brother, Dina?' he asked, when they were safely on their way back to Heartsease Hall in the wake of Cox and his chilled and weary pillion passenger.

'By telling myself it's only until we leave for active duty once Giles is fit again,' she admitted, and Peter could tell what a strain today's dash for home had put on even *her* stalwart courage from that weary admission.

'And now you'll have yet more of his company because I have made a mull of things,' he said apologetically.

'Yes, your ability to arrange for adverse weather conditions, a blocked main road and then this road that was apparently free but turned out to be perfectly designed to make the very worst of these hills is indeed culpable in *you*, brother mine,' she informed him so solemnly he had to chuckle at her gentle mockery.

'I'm going to miss you, brat.'

'As I will you—when my initial elation at such blessed freedom from your fussing and nagging has worn off after a year or two, brother dear.'

'All for your own good, little sister,' he said half seriously.

'And I could never have wished for a more careful guardian, Peter. Even when you weren't actually in the same country,' she told him almost solemnly.

Peter didn't want to think how much he'd miss her presence in his home or his life tonight and risk becoming maudlin. Not when Sophie Bonet was preparing to welcome a pack of benighted travellers to Heartsease Hall and Edwina would certainly recognise her one-time playmate and adored cousin by marriage.

'Now you've tamed that rogue Giles Wroxley, and clearly intend to be happy with him, he can worry himself about what starts you're likely to get up to next instead of me. Under all that cavalry swagger and "Aren't I a fine fellow?" manner of his, I know he's a good man and almost deserves you. I'm truly glad you found your ideal husband under your nose before you rashly agreed to make a lesser man unhappy for life, Dina,' he said, frowning as the flaring torches lit to guide them back cut through the darkness at last and they crested the gentler slope up to Heartsease Hall.

'All Giles and I need to make our happiness complete is to know you'll make an equally happy marriage, brother dear, so we can leave England with an easy mind when the time comes,' she said, with a determination to do Peter good that made him stiffen in the saddle for a moment, before he forced himself to relax and sit easy for the sake of the noble hunter who'd borne them both so stalwartly. He wondered fleetingly if this Sir Gyffard Frayne he'd never met but owed a lot might part with what was apparently his favourite mount for a tempting enough sum.

'There's no need for me to worry about the succession just yet,' he argued distractedly as those lights loomed ever closer. He wished this strange ride through the snow-haunted darkness might be longer as he readied himself to meet Sophie as if it didn't matter.

'The succession, Peter—is that truly the only reason you would wed?'

'Aye, it's an honest enough one for a man in my position.'

'Not for you, my dear! Not when you're every bit as headlong and passionate as any of us Vanes under all that elder-brother starch and lordly dignity you assume these days to keep the world safely at bay.'

'When I finally bring myself to wed, I intend to take a quiet and proper countess who will in due time present me with an heir and some girls to dote on and spoil as foolishly as I have my little sister. Heat and passion are for idiots and adolescents who know no better.'

'That writes Giles and me off as mad or immature, then. Such a lukewarm existence would never do for either of us, thank heavens.'

'Luckily for you, your fortunes match very well, and you both have elder brothers to take responsibility for passing on the family honours. At least you can wed purely because you want to, rather than having to suspect your title or fortune is more of a draw than you are.'

'Oh, you poor dear. How very unfortunate for you to be born a man as well as one of the lords of creation; you must find it *such* a heavy burden,' his sister mocked.

'I live with it,' he said solemnly.

'You trade on it whenever it suits you, and don't pretend you don't. I've seen you play the remote and dignified earl whenever some silly young debutante decides she would like to be a countess—until she learns how frosty Lord Sylbourne can be and rapidly changes her mind.'

'There you are, then—it works,' he said with a shrug.

They eyed the looming bulk of Heartsease Hall, and even he couldn't help but admire what he could see of the ancient honey-grey stone and the rambling bulk of the grand old manor house in the torchlight and the snow-reflected gloom of what was going to be a very long December night.

'Yet once upon a time you were so deeply in love even I thought you were bound to be happy, Peter,' his sister observed impulsively.

The weary animal under them jibbed at the involuntary tightening of knees into its flanks as Peter jolted at the very idea of his sister and Sophie setting eyes on each other again and either of them trying to turn back the clock to his foolish youth. He *had* thought the world well lost for love back then, and Sophie Bonet the most wonderful female on God's good earth—which only went to show how foolish extreme youth could be.

'All the more reason to be wary, since I know what a folly love is,' he managed to respond tersely.

Somehow he must arm himself against the deceiving jade until he could get himself and his responsibilities back to Holm Park for Edwina and Giles's wedding. Sophie Bonet had taken a boy's dreams and turned them into nightmares, and if Miss so-called Rose thought she could use that long-ago Peter Vane to her advantage, she would soon discover her mistake.

'It would be a shame if you let one blighted love affair ruin your whole life, Peter dear. And must you look so very grim about it just now? The poor people who have taken a pack of strangers into their house will think twice about their kindness if you show them such a thunderous countenance,' Edwina chided.

'I'll endeavour to be as cheerful as an alderman's banquet from now on,' he lied, and luckily the bustle of their arrival diverted them both from that particular subject. 'You had best prepare for a shock when you see who is part of the household about to take us in for the night, Dina,' he warned, even as he felt his sister jolt with surprise when she recognised the petite figure of Sophie Bonet waiting at the top of the steps to welcome them to Heartsease Hall.

'Please hurry inside and get warm and dry, everyone. We might as well wait to introduce ourselves in form until after you have changed out of your cold, wet clothes and feel more comfortable,' Sophie urged as soon as the weary travellers were safely off their horses in various fashions—awkward and unwieldy in the case of the thin gentleman with a look of discontent about his narrow countenance; annoyingly easy and assured as Peter Vane swung out of his saddle as soon as he could after making sure the enchantingly pretty young lady riding behind him was safely on the ground.

He only let Edwina wobble on numb feet until he had his own feet under him, then swept her up in his arms to run up the newly cleared steps, as if a laborious trek through snow twice in one night was a little light exercise as far as he was concerned.

Could this slender and elegant young lady be the Dina Vane she remembered as an endearing little girl with her silver-grey Vane eyes forever full of mischief? Sophie tried not to look for signs of her one-time playmate in this vision of chilled elegance in Peter's arms, and told herself she was a governess with nothing in common with the daughter of an earl.

'We have bedchambers prepared, if you will trust the young lady's welfare to Sir Gyffard's housekeeper, Lord Sylbourne?' she heard herself say uncertainly.

He glared at her, then listened to his sister protest that she was quite capable of standing on her own two feet now the worst of the cold was shut outside.

'Don't come downstairs again until you're sure you haven't taken a chill, then,' he demanded as he set his sister down.

'Whatever sort of wife do you think I'll make Giles if I can't withstand a little hardship in safe old England, Peter?' she asked merrily, and turned her enchanting smile on Mrs Elkerley whilst sending Sophie a look that warned she was reserving judgement about *her*.

'Good evening. I'm Lady Edwina Vane,' she said, and Sophie could see the little girl she remembered had indeed grown into a lively young woman with a mind of her own.

'This is Miss Frayne, the eldest daughter of the house, Lady Edwina. Her sisters are the urchins peering at you from the upper gallery when they should be in the schoolroom,' Sophie said—calmly enough, considering the ridiculous rush of emotions she was doing her best to keep to herself on seeing the people who had once been the closest thing she had to a family standing there like strangers.

'In their shoes I know *I* wouldn't have meekly retired to learn French verbs until I had found out exactly who was riding out of such a night to look for shelter either,' Lady Edwina said, and prepared to climb the stairs as Peter carried their aunt up, despite her protests that she could walk as well.

'Perhaps they will do as they're bid now that they have, then. If they expect to come downstairs for the sweet course tonight, they might condescend to listen to me for once, I suppose,' Sophie suggested, and heard a whispered consultation followed by the rush of ascending footsteps.

'And pray what is the name of the Miss Fraynes's governess?' Lady Edwina asked coolly.

'I am Sophie Rose,' Sophie declared without a pause.

'Of course you are,' Edwina murmured sardonically, after Imogen had rushed ahead to be sure all was ready to make these awesome beings welcome. 'If you wish to be Miss Rose, I'm quite sure you have earned the privilege.'

'Indeed, my lady,' she said, and as Edwina eyed her speculatively Sophie realised her one-time friend believed the worst of her.

'It is your choice to keep whatever secrets you choose, Miss Rose, but my fiancé's brother makes it his business to sniff out gossip of all kinds. I should confess from the outset, if I were you, and save yourself a deal of trouble.'

'Maybe I should,' Sophie agreed stiffly. 'Except my employer and his younger sister are attending another sister's funeral and will be in Ireland until well into the New Year. Miss Matilda Frayne, who normally resides here, and chaperones her nieces as well as lending me whatever countenance a governess needs, should hear that gossip first, don't you think?'

'We will have to hope she returns before it reaches her anyway. It's just as well *my* aunt is here to chaperone us all now, is it not?' Lady Edwina remarked, and left Sophie in little doubt that Miss Willis would prove as hostile as Edwina appeared to be.

'Since Mrs Garret-Lowden and her daughter, Mr Timon Frayne's betrothed, are staying with us, Imogen and I do not lack respectability,' she replied flippantly.

'Should Mr Frayne not be our host, then, instead of forcing *you* to take on the duty, Miss Rose?'

'Mr Frayne is staying with Mr Lysander Frayne, who recently took holy orders and is curate to a nearby parish. He felt it was more proper than staying here with his fiancée in his father and aunt's absence,' Sophie said blandly, and she opened the door to the rose bedchamber and gestured her ladyship inside.

'How very restrained of him,' Edwina said absently as she gazed round at the glowing fire in the hearth and the well-fitting shutters keeping out the freezing night. 'This is enchanting,' she said at last, and even Sophie couldn't doubt her sincerity.

'The late Lady Frayne had a way of making her house

welcoming as well as comfortable,' Sophie replied a little stiffly.

'Yes, Mama loved to entertain, and always claimed her visitors deserved the best she could offer them—despite the age of the hall and all the twists and turns some people seem to despise,' Imogen put in, and Sophie frowned at this reminder of Miss Garret-Lowden's open contempt for her predecessor's taste.

'Well, I think it a charming house, obviously full of stories. I'd love to explore and hear some of them, if only you might be free to guide me tomorrow, Miss Frayne?' Edwina asked, and Sophie had to admire Dina's social aplomb and her genuine good nature, despite her clear dislike of the Fraynes' governess.

'I should be delighted—even more so if we manage it without my little sisters tagging along to chatter us into the headache,' Imogen agreed.

Sophie suddenly felt ancient and unneeded.

If Imogen was about to become a lovely and confident you woman, surely *she* would see to the welfare of her little sisters once she was suitably married and able to take them into her own house if their father should die prematurely? Then all this fuss about the future would be for nothing, since Sophie would either go with them or find other employment. Yet for eight years she'd coaxed, ordered and persuaded the Frayne girls to learn suitably ladylike skills, and she'd come to love them dearly.

The idea of being thirty and seeking a new place made her wistful as she turned to leave the room. 'We should let Lady Edwina rid herself of her wet things so one of the maids can help her bathe and change before dinner now, Imogen. You will have plenty of time to quiz her ladyship on the latest London fashions and who's in and who's out in the wider world once she's warm and dry again.'

'I suppose so,' Imogen conceded, obviously reluctant to be parted from this wonderful new friend so soon.

'I am so glad you were there to divert Peter's fire. I was dreading an abrupt order to get into bed and stay there from my formidable brother, Miss Frayne. He has such a decided character, we quite despair of him ever finding a lady brave enough to take him on,' Lady Edwina said, and Sophie was fairly sure Imogen took her words at face value and wasn't immediately planning the best way to become the next Countess of Sylbourne, despite such blatant encouragement from his sister to do so.

She was puzzled over that declaration that Peter was unwed. How on earth could he not be? When she'd left Holm Park, early on that beautiful June morning, the scheme for Peter to marry Miss Diamantha Rivers, with her vast fortune and her desire for a title, had been so far advanced it would have taken legal action to renege on it. The old earl had pleaded with her to disappear and rescue the Vanes from a debtors' prison, and yet here was Edwina, declaring her brother a single gentleman.

It would be extreme to lie for the sole purpose of making Sophie squirm, but Dina evidently thought her desertion unforgivable. Sophie added the memory of once seeing Diamantha pointed out as Countess of Sylbourne to puzzle over once she was alone, and did her best to keep her expression blank.

'We will leave you alone now, then, my lady. If you change your mind and require dinner in your chamber, do inform one of the maids, and Mrs Elkerley will see it is sent up to you' was all she said in response.

'I'm not as chicken-hearted as all that, Miss Rose,' the lady replied.

'I never thought you were, Lady Edwina,' Sophie replied coolly, then ushered Imogen out of the room ahead of her, advising her to see to her own toilette as she would be hostess for the evening.

'You won't desert me, will you, Miss Rose? The very idea of having to play lady of the house when I'm not even quite out yet makes me shake in my shoes,' Imogen admitted, and Sophie bit back a reluctant sigh, knowing she could not do as she so badly wanted and confine herself to the schoolroom for the evening.

'Of course I won't,' she reassured her. 'Although Mrs Garret-Lowden is sure to remark on my presence at the dinner table when you are entertaining important guests.'

'A fig for that. If she really wanted to interfere in our domestic arrangements, she should have come to help when we were all of a tizzy and trying to get everything done in time for our guests' arrival. She and Livia clearly think more of their hairstyles than they do of the domestic affairs of Livia's future home.'

'You probably made it a little too plain that you would not welcome their interest when Mrs Garret-Lowden declared her intention of going through the menus for the Christmas season with Cook this afternoon,' Sophie said mildly, as they had now entered Imogen's room and could be sure of privacy.

'Cook would have resigned on the spot.'

'And a fine pickle that would have left us all in at such a time, I agree. But one day both you and Cook will have to resign yourselves to your eldest brother's choice of a wife, my dear,' Sophie chided halfheartedly.

'Not until he's resigned *himself* to it as well,' Imogen said militantly, and Sophie decided she had enough battles to plan without this one as well.

'Just remember the duties of a hostess for tonight, then, my dear, and let's hope the morning brings fine weather so that our visitors may depart.'

'Better if it doesn't, as far as I'm concerned, since Timon will then be able to compare the behaviour of a true lady like Lady Edwina with the cattish pranks of his Livia. That might make him think twice about actually marrying her.'

'As the lady is his choice of wife, Imogen, you might as well accustom yourself to the idea and get to know her better. Why don't you go and change into your best muslin and let Tilly put your hair up in that new style she's been experimenting with? You'll look as fine as fivepence then, and that will help you to feel better about playing hostess tonight,' Sophie said encouragingly, and left Imogen in the capable hands of her maid.

Next she made sure Viola and Audrey hadn't given in to temptation and escaped to roam gleefully about the house until dinnertime, and then went to her own room to re-dress her hair in a ruthlessly correct chignon then cover it with a neat lace cap. She donned a dark grey gown that screamed *governess*, and told herself it didn't matter if nobody could mistake her for anything else tonight.

'You're not really going to keep company with an earl and his sister in *that* hideous old thing, are you, Miss Rose?' Audrey asked when she re-entered the school-room.

'I'm a governess, Audrey. It's not right to push myself forward as I fear I did earlier today. So now I'm trying to put myself in my place,' Sophie replied.

'That's ridiculous,' Viola said gruffly. 'You shouldn't pay so much heed to Mrs Garret-Lowden's ill-natured attempts to set you at nought. She only does it because she thinks you're far too pretty to be a governess, Miss Rose. She's a bad-tempered cat and so is Livia,' Viola told her defiantly, and Sophie sighed.

'I have to listen, Viola, and somehow you must accustom yourself to your brother's fiancée becoming part of your life, my love. She will be your sister-in-law and the first lady of this house in all but name.'

'*No!* She could never stand in Mama's shoes, and Timon is an idiot if he even thinks that she might be able to.'

'That's quite enough, Viola. You have to accept what is in life and live with it as best you can. Miss Garret-Lowden is your brother's choice and must be respected as future mistress of this house. If you refuse to offer her that respect, you will hardly deserve any in return, and it will reflect very badly on your governess. I shall very likely be dismissed, and I shall miss you sorely if I have to look for another place before you and Audrey are ready to leave the schoolroom.'

'It would horrify *me*, Vi, for goodness knows what sort of dragon they would employ if they ever manage to persuade Papa to get rid of Miss Rose.' Thirteen-year-old Audrey spoke up with a pleading look for her fierce older sister.

'I will try to be polite to them, then—but only for your sake, Miss Rose. I think Timon has lost his wits, and he doesn't deserve that I should try and accustom myself to Livia or that horrid woman for his sake,' Viola replied sulkily.

Viola had adored her eldest brother until he'd brought his betrothed home to meet his family and inspect the home he and his wife would one day call their own.

'You must do so for your own sake, Viola. Mr Frayne is your father's heir, and he and his wife will probably live here after they marry,' Sophie said uneasily, wondering if she should accept Sir Gyffard's offer in order to provide a buffer between the girls and the Garret-Lowdens even they couldn't ignore.

'Papa must outlive both Livia *and* that miserable mother of hers, then, since Ti will do anything she asks of him just for the sake of a quiet life, and we'll be miserable as sin if he abandons us to her so-called care,' Viola burst out.

Sophie frowned for the strife and misery her pupil would endure if she didn't learn to hide her feelings a little better. 'How disappointed your father will be if he returns home and finds you have been cap pulling with your brother's betrothed instead of making her welcome.'

Viola's face fell at the thought of her adored father hurt and upset because his daughters had shown hostility to a lady staying under his roof. 'Did *you* never want to shout your feelings out loud, Miss Rose, instead of pretending to be calm all the time as you insist we should be?'

Yes, tonight, a rebellious voice whispered in Sophie's ear, but she told it to go away rather than risk making the disaster of Peter's coming here into something even worse.

'That's a wilful exaggeration of the graceful deportment I want you to learn, Viola. Nobody can be controlled at all times, but you have to realise that actions have consequences, and sometimes hurt those you care about most.'

'Then saying how I feel about Livia would reflect badly upon you. Is that what you mean?'

'In part, perhaps, but I wonder how your brother would feel if his future wife and little sister were at daggers drawn?'

'Serve him right for asking her to marry him in the first place,' Viola said mutinously.

Sophie frowned again. Reasoning with her fiery young charge was ultimately futile, since her hot temper would probably break through and the truth come spilling out regardless. She decided she could only hope she was wrong. 'Nevertheless, he did ask her to do so, and he could not be so ungentlemanly as to jilt a lady on your say-so even if he wanted to end his betrothal—which I doubt.'

'Better than ending up married to her,' Viola persisted, fidgeting under her governess's best stern-eyed gaze all the same.

'He would be shunned by polite society and considered a man who refuses to honour his word by everyone else if he cried off from their betrothal. I thought you had your brother's best interests at heart, Viola, but clearly I was mistaken.'

'Better for him to be an outcast rather than end up wed to the wrong person, Miss Rose,' Viola said, with a steely determination that she was right.

'Perhaps we could persuade Miss Garret-Lowden she is about to wed the wrong man instead, Vi. For she does like a lord, and I'm sure she would love to wed one. Considering a real, live earl has just dropped into our lives, and must stay here at least until the snow has melted, perhaps she will decide there are better catches than Ti to marry if only she exerts herself a little more,' Audrey said, and managed to look angelically innocent when Sophie frowned at her reproachfully.

'Yes, if there was the slightest chance of netting an earl, she would drop poor Ti like a hot coal, for all he will be able to make her a baronet's lady one day. The rest of us might wish Papa could live to be a hundred, but I really don't think Livia does,' Viola said thoughtfully.

Sophie groaned silently at the idea of the schemes two budding Machiavellis might come up with to throw Miss Garret-Lowden and Peter Vane together if they got the chance. Since they had driving snow, knee-high drifts and a killing frost outside to make the roads icily impassable by morning as formidable allies in their campaign, she suddenly dreaded every moment of the next few days even more than she had been already.

'I don't wish to hear any more ill-natured speculation from either of you,' she made herself say sternly, refusing to listen to an urgent inner voice screaming that Miss Garret-Lowden was about as wrong for Peter as a woman could be. 'For all we know, his lordship is married, and that would ruin your reprehensible scheming at the outset.'

'No, he would have mentioned it if he had a countess waiting anxiously at home by now,' Audrey declared, and Sophie supposed she was right.

He would have said so with a significant look in her direction to tell her he was beyond her reach in every way possible now, and Edwina had already said he was unwed. Yet *why* wasn't he wed to Diamantha Rivers? Perhaps he had been and now Diamantha was dead? If so, it was little wonder he appeared able to afford the very best in attire and horses, since the Rivers fortune could probably have bought out the Royal Mint with change to spare. Shaking her head at the very notion of Peter's marriage to such a ruthless golden dolly, she told herself it didn't matter to her what he'd done or not done and tried to wrench her thoughts away from him.

Telling her pupils to be sure to eat up their dinner and then come downstairs only when Cordage sent to say the sweet course was being served, she reluctantly left them to their own devices and went down to Imogen's room.

'You look truly beautiful,' she told her erstwhile pupil sincerely.

'I feel like the cook-maid got up in her mistress's clothes, Miss Rose, and I can't tell you how much I'm dreading tonight.'

'Nonsense. You know exactly how to behave. All you need to do now is put it into practice. Your mama would be so proud of you tonight, my love,' Sophie said with a slightly wobbly smile. 'Come, we had best get it over with and face our demons, for I doubt wishing them away will work all of a sudden,' she added, and wished she had kept quiet when Imogen eyed her speculatively.

'Why is this evening an ordeal for you, Rosie?' she asked as they stepped onto the half-landing where their staircase joined the one from the older wings, before descending into the hall below in a stately twist.

'Yes, pray enlighten us as to exactly why there should be any difficulty in entertaining a few strangers for you, Miss Rose?'

Peter's voice rumbled from the other branch of the staircase, and Sophie felt her heart jolt and her nerves scream.

'Your lordship,' she greeted him coolly, and sank into a curtsey, hoping the everyday courtesies would distract him from asking unanswerable questions.

He gave her a perfunctory bow, nicely designed for governesses he didn't much approve of, then turned to offer a much more reverent one to Imogen. 'You promise to be the most enchanting hostess any foolish traveller could hope for. Although I fear we have thrust ourselves on your family in the most scrambling fashion, Miss Frayne,' he said with a warm smile.

'Thank you, my lord,' Imogen replied shyly, and swept him a curtsey Sophie hoped he noted was exactly right for his rank.

He offered his arm to Imogen, and they progressed downstairs in fine style, and even Sophie had to concede they were a well-matched pair. His now neatly styled hair was a shade darker, and his height exactly right for a lady of Imogen's inches to feel protected but not overwhelmed. She should be relieved her former pupil had come across a man so well suited to become her future lord if the fates dictated it should be so, instead of on edge and almost physically sick at the very idea, Sophie chided herself fiercely.

'What about Miss Rose?' soft-hearted Imogen protested as Sophie fell into step behind them.

'No doubt your governess prefers my room to my company,' Peter said austerely, and went back to coaxing Imogen out of her nervousness as if Sophie and anything to do with her was as irrelevant to him as the newel post at the bottom of the great staircase or the stableyard cat.

'No doubt she does,' Sophie echoed almost silently, yet she saw his shoulders stiffen at even that whisper of sound—and why should she care if she hurt him when he was doing his best to show her that she meant less than nothing to him?

CHAPTER FIVE

'GOOD evening, my dear, and don't you look enchanting tonight all tricked out in your best?' Mrs Garret-Lowden's rather harsh voice greeted Imogen from the hall below them.

She gave an artistic start at the sight of Peter at Imogen's side, as if she had not the slightest idea he'd been there all along. And with Peter looking magnificent even in his borrowed evening clothes, Sophie silently gave Mrs Garret-Lowden the palm for amateur dramatics.

'I really had no idea you were entertaining guests tonight,' she went on, with an assumption of lighthearted intimacy with the eldest daughter of the house that Imogen was too good-natured to refute.

'Oh, you can lay that omission at my door, ma'am.' Peter intervened to rescue his young hostess. 'We are a party of benighted travellers who were silly enough to set out for home on a day when all sensible folk would stay safe and warm in the nearest hostelry and thank their stars they need go no further until a thaw sets in.'

'Well, I'm sure you're all very welcome, sir, whoever you might be,' Mrs Garret-Lowden returned, with a fine pantomime of the gracious hostess she'd have no right to be even if her daughter had already been wed to the son of the house.

'My lord, may I introduce Mrs Garret-Lowden and her daughter? Miss Garret-Lowden is betrothed to my eldest brother. This is Lord Sylbourne, ma'am, Miss Garret-Lowden,' Imogen said, calmly enough.

'Mrs Garret-Lowden; Miss Garret-Lowden,' Peter returned, and bowed with such formal politeness Sophie could tell he had read them a little too easily as they simpered and looked utterly charmed to make his acquaintance.

At least Sophie knew why the Garret-Lowden ladies hadn't interrupted the frantic preparations going on around them now. Every piece of finery they jointly possessed was arranged about their persons. She thanked her stars they had been too busy to interfere, while wondering wickedly if puce satin went quite as well with rouged cheeks and a parure of garnets as Mrs Garret-Lowden thought it did.

'Good evening,' Lady Edwina greeted them regally as she swept downstairs and followed them into the family sitting room that was warm and aired. The statelier rooms in the house were anything but. Poor Imogen had to perform formal introductions all over again.

'My aunt sends her apologies, Miss Frayne, but she feels too chilled and tired to come downstairs tonight, and has decided to take a light meal in her room as you so kindly offered,' Lady Edwina Vane went on, after one long, cool look at Mrs Garret-Lowden and her daughter that silenced both for almost a minute.

'Of course Miss Willis must not come downstairs after such a daunting experience if she feels in the least bit weary,' Imogen agreed—so earnestly that Peter looked more charmed by her than ever. But that was no reason for Sophie to feel he'd kicked her somewhere tender and vulnerable.

Mrs Garret-Lowden and her daughter considered governesses a lower order of life altogether, and Imogen didn't know Peter, so they didn't realise what a snub it was when he made no effort to acknowledge Sophie's existence. She really hoped he knew that if Imogen didn't need her support, she would be delighted to stay upstairs and keep to the strictest definition of a governess's position—to be unseen and unheard as often as possible to all but her charges.

Refusing to be intimidated by his coldness, she did her best to pretend he didn't exist either, and smiled cautiously at Lady Edwina. How she wished she was easy with this polished young woman she'd once been as close to as any sister. But this was no time to sit about moping. With Peter's sceptical glances at her buttoned-up gown and screwed-back hair under its concealing cap harder on her than the frost outside, memories of another life could wait until she had time to air them in private.

'So far as I can tell, my aunt is only chilled and weary,' Edwina assured her very young hostess, then settled into a seat in the comfortable sitting room to await whatever came next with a composure Sophie could only envy.

A few moments of awkward silence ensued while Sophie sat as far away from the fire and the company as her role of Imogen's silent supporter allowed and the Garret-Lowden ladies weighed up their strategy for captivating noblemen.

'What a pretty picture these three young ladies present, do they not, my lord?' Mrs Garret-Lowden said with a proud smile at her daughter that said the inclusion of the others was mere form.

'It's as well for a gentleman to nod and smile and say nothing at times like this, Peter dear, since you might be invited to pick which one of us is fairest and trouble will surely follow,' his sister declared lightly, and Mrs Garret-Lowden's smile became forced.

'I do so agree, sister dear,' he replied, with a quick, wry look at Imogen that probably made her heart beat faster as well as earning him a shy smile.

Sophie let her shoulders droop a little in her dark corner, and even that slight movement earned her a quick frown as Peter glanced at her and then looked swiftly away, as if the sight of her threatened to ruin an already disastrous day for him. She made herself sit up straight and apparently undaunted as she noted Edwina's clear grey gaze skim past her on its way to Livia Garret-Lowden and a slight frown mar her smooth brow in turn.

Unless Dina Vane had changed out of all recognition, she was uneasy about Sophie's newly humble role in life, and wondering if she had been a little harsh in ignoring a former friend and almost-relative, whatever her past sins. Knowing how sharp Mrs Garret-Lowden's eyes could be, Sophie kept her face impassive and willed Edwina to forget she was there. Would she was not, she decided. However hard she tried to be indifferent, it still pained her to watch Peter go about his daily life as if he'd never met Sophie Rose Bonet before and wasn't the least bit interested in her now he had met her again.

It was all so confusing—for hadn't she fled Holm Park and launched herself on the betwixt and between life of a governess to achieve exactly this result? At seventeen it had been perfectly plain she would never marry if she couldn't marry Peter Vane, then Viscount Deerbourne, and since his father, the Earl of Sylbourne, had lost her own modest portion along with everything his family owned in that last wild attempt to recoup his fortunes in trade, the only alternative to marriage had been to earn her own living. She shuddered to think what society had thought she was doing to pay her way when it heard Sophie Bonet had run away from her adoptive family and launched herself on a weary world unprotected.

Probably exactly what an almost-naïve girl like her *would* have done if not for Sophie's Aunt Hermione, late Countess of Sylbourne, having met Lady Frayne when they were incarcerated together at a Queen's Square boarding school in Bath. Sophie shuddered. Yes, she told herself militantly as she risked a baleful glance of her own at Peter's strong profile, he should be grateful she *wasn't* the adventuress he clearly thought she'd become. Rumours that a close connection of his late stepmother had been forced into a life of crime to keep herself from starvation would have put a dreadful blight on his prospects as a fortune hunter.

'I wonder if Cedric is planning to eat in his room as well as my aunt,' Lady Edwina speculated as the minutes ticked by. A waiting silence prevailed now Mrs Garret-Lowden's attempts to set up her daughter as Lord Sylbourne's preferred partner for the evening had fallen so sadly flat. 'My affianced husband's younger brother is travelling with us to Holm Park for the wedding, Mrs Garret-Lowden,' Edwina explained opaquely, and Sophie almost felt sorry for the lady and her daughter as they tried to unravel the complex web of connections between the *haut ton* and decide precisely who was marrying whom.

'Apparently your beloved captain's brother *is* planning to grace us with his presence tonight after all, Dina.' Peter helped the Garret-Lowdens out with part of the puzzle. 'I believe I hear his voice in the hall—and he would have rung the nearest bell and summoned dinner to his room if he did not fully intend to come downstairs tonight, since he clearly believes answering bells is the sole occupation of any servant he happens to come across in his travels.'

'True,' Edwina said, with a rueful glance at her brother and an encouraging smile for her young hostess. 'Your papa must be very proud of you, Miss Imogen, since you could hardly be a better hostess to such a demanding party of strangers if you had twenty years' experience at your back,' she said, and on seeing Imogen's daunted expression as she rose to meet Cedric's ungracious entrance, Edwina stood up at her side in a united front that left even Cedric looking a little daunted.

'Good evening, Mr Wroxley. I bid you welcome to my father's house for as long as you stand in need of our hospitality,' Imogen managed, with a gracious nod of the head Sophie recalled Lady Frayne using when doing the pretty to her husband's less attractive friends.

If she had known Imogen would be so ably supported by Edwina, she could have stayed in the schoolroom and been more comfortable herself, she decided wearily, and wondered whether to ring for candles so she could work on Imogen's Twelfth Night gift for her middle brother while the rest of the company ignored her.

'My thanks, dear lady,' Cedric drawled, as if a royal welcome should have been no less than his due, but he was going to be lenient and ignore the lack of one just this once.

He sat stiffly on the chaise by Peter's side, so he was opposite the ladies and could eye them critically. Clearly he had noted that Imogen was a very pretty girl it might be diverting to pursue if boredom threatened to smother him completely in such a quiet country house; Lady Edwina Vane he passed over, as if he'd already decided she was unworthy of his attention or perhaps was too frightened of his elder brothers and Peter to risk bringing their fury down on his head if he gave her a second glance. His rather protruding eyes, of a sludgy brown that reminded Sophie of river mud, lingered on pretty Miss Garret-Lowden. Sophie decided Mrs Garret-Lowden was more than capable of protecting her ewe lamb from third sons of viscounts who might decide it would be diverting to prey on her.

Sophie felt a shiver of unease slip down her spine as Cedric's gaze seemed to sharpen on *her*, as if something had made him take a second look at a mere governess, before Peter unexpectedly intervened, as if he was still trying to protect her from the petty enmity of the Cedric Wroxleys of this world.

'Will our unexpected arrival put too much strain on your cook's resources, Miss Frayne?' he asked Imogen politely.

'Not in the least, my lord. Her kitchen, larder and any other available storage space have been full of vast quantities of puddings and pickles and salted this and jellied that, as well as sugared whatever else she could find to sugar, for weeks now. I daresay we could entertain an army here and hardly notice the difference for at least a fortnight. In fact you have saved Cook from having a truly miserable time over the Christmas season. We received the sad news of my aunt Helen's death only the day before yesterday, and Papa and my other aunt, who usually lives with us, left for Ireland immediately, in the hope of getting there in time for her funeral, or at least helping her poor husband and my six young cousins cope with her loss if they were not,' Imogen explained.

Sophie felt proud of the quiet dignity with which Imogen played hostess to these unexpected guests, despite her youth and inexperience.

'Dinner is served, Miss Rose,' Cordage announced

dolefully, after opening the heavy oak doors as silently as a ghost.

Not sure how to feel at his obvious designation of her as the most senior lady of the family present, if certainly not the most important one, Sophie got to her feet wondering how she would solve the problem of two gentlemen and five ladies arranging themselves around the dining table, and sincerely wished she hadn't been needed to give Imogen moral support tonight.

'I hope we're not going to process in strict order of precedence, Miss Frayne?' Lady Edwina asked. 'It would feel odd to stand on such ceremony when we would be starving in a snowdrift right now if you hadn't been kind enough to send us rescue.'

'It would be a relief not to stand on ceremony, I admit, since we are only using the family dining room. The state rooms are nearly as cold as the icehouse at this time of year if fires have not been lit in them for days on end,' Imogen admitted. 'Oh, Miss Rose, you *will* carve, won't you?' she protested, as Sophie tried to slip into the seat furthest from the one set for the lady of the house to apportion the roast duck Cook had somehow conjured up, along with a stuffed bream and a tempting array of lighter dishes suitable for an Advent dinner.

'Or shall we dispose of formality and allow my brother to do so, Miss Rose? He naturally gravitates to the head of the table, as you see, being a managing sort of man at the best of times,' Lady Edwina teased.

'No, this is the place for one of the ladies of the house,' he protested, and seemed so horrified at the idea he might end up sitting next to Sophie that he took the place fur-thest from the blazing fire she had been doing her best to slip into until Imogen had stopped her.

'I am not of their number,' she protested as Imogen whisked herself into the seat next to his lordship in order to give Sophie no chance of changing her mind.

'The ducks will be cold by the time you have cut them up at this rate, Miss Rose,' Imogen told her cheerfully, and Sophie shrugged in a rather inelegant surrender and did so rather than argue any further.

Even Cedric Wroxley ate with a will—after he had spent a few moments eyeing the feast in front of him as if he was being offered leavings from a shambles. His initial pose was to satisfy himself he was superior to all the rest of them in good taste and fastidiousness, what-ever social rank they might lay claim to.

'Your father evidently has a very fine cook in his em-ploy, Miss Frayne,' Peter told his young hostess lightly after he had savoured the perfectly roasted duck with Cook's famous cherry sauce. 'Should he ever tire of her talents, I will be very happy to offer her a new post at Holm Park.'

'For once I really hope Papa will not oblige you, my lord,' she responded, calmly enough, but Sophie could see what a strain the evening was proving for such a young hostess, even if the rather overwhelming idea that an ac-tual earl seemed to be gently flirting with her was bol-stering her flagging confidence.

'The Swiss magician you employ would be furious if he thought he was going to be scouted from his precious

kitchen, Peter, despite his outspoken contempt for everything he's experienced in this country since descending
onto our very inferior shores,' Lady Edwina put in, and
she and her brother encouraged a light patter of conversation until the sweet courses were set out and Viola and
Audrey arrived to lighten the whole atmosphere.

At last the time came for the table to be cleared and
the port and brandy decanters introduced, so the ladies
could return to the cosy family sitting room and leave the
gentlemen to their own devices.

'You will tell us all about your adventures, won't you,
Lady Edwina?' Audrey urged eagerly as soon as the tea
tray had been brought in and Imogen was gracefully dis-
pensing tea under Mrs Garret-Lowden's critical eye.

Sophie was very pleased to see even that lady could
find nothing to criticise in Imogen's behaviour as hostess, although she clearly thought her darling Livia would
perform any of the tasks very much better. In Sophie's
opinion she was so wrong in that conclusion that it almost
beggared belief—even for a doting mama.

'All of them? From the year of my birth onwards, Miss
Audrey? Such an odyssey would take up rather more time
than we have to spare before bedtime,' Edwina teased
gently.

'Of course not. For tonight could you just tell me the
story of your journey here and why you were out in the
storm, please? I think it must have been very exciting.'

'Hardly that, Audrey; consider how frightening it must
have felt to be lost out there in such a sudden and disori-
entating blizzard,' Sophie protested from the shadowy

corner she had retreated to after Mrs Garret-Lowden's latest repressive glare in her direction.

'It's all right, Miss Rose. I suppose it *was* exciting with hindsight. Or at least it was until it suddenly began to seem dangerous as well, and I started to wonder if we might end up with our necks broken. That was when it seemed impossible for poor Merryweather to tell the difference between the road and the ditch any longer. My wedding was to take place on Christmas Day, you see, and it was like dashing through the wilds to meet my one true love and marry him—if you will excuse me calling your lovely Cotswolds the wilds, Miss Frayne?'

'It would be so much easier if you could bring yourself to call us by our given names, Lady Edwina,' Imogen summoned up the courage to suggest, and Sophie wondered if the convention of naming her the eldest still seemed strange to Imogen. She was accustomed to her aunt Matilda being known as 'Miss Frayne.'

'Then of course I will—if only you younger ladies will name me Dina as my brother does in return. I am always called that by my friends, and I find Edwina such a formal mouthful,' Edwina Vane invited.

Sophie wanted to shrink into her corner of this cosy room and disappear. Once upon a time she would have called Edwina so and not had a second thought about it, but she was clearly being lumped in with Mrs Garret-Lowden as far too mature and dignified to call unrelated young women by their informal nicknames.

'I must speak to Mrs Elkerley and Cook about menus for tomorrow before panic breaks out in the kitchen.'

Sophie muttered this feeble excuse to escape the suddenly oppressive position of governess and ghosted out of the room.

Once outside it she wrapped herself in a shawl one of the girls had left carelessly draped over an ancient oak chair in the hall and grabbed a candle, before speeding towards the kitchens where it would at least be warm. But before she could reach sanctuary on the other side of the green baize door, Peter stepped out of the shadows. She supposed she should have known he and Cedric wouldn't stay together, happily drinking Sir Gyffard's best cognac, since they clearly disliked and distrusted each other.

'Scurrying off to hide from the big, bad wolf?' he asked, with the merest suggestion of a sneer on his handsome face.

'Of course not,' she lied, yet the candle wavered in her suddenly unsteady hand, and he took it impatiently from her and set it safely down on the vast Spanish chest nearby.

'Well, don't,' he went on, as if she hadn't spoken, and she felt her temper stir at him for finding her so unimportant he didn't even bother to listen to her. 'What you choose to do, where you decide to hide and why you pretend that Sophie Bonet never existed is a matter of no importance to me.'

'And is my presence such a matter of indifference that you demonstrate it at every turn, my lord? That makes it an odd variety of unconcern in the first place, don't you think?' she taunted—a little unwisely, considering the cold fury in his icy grey eyes she had never seen before, even when he was in the foulest of tempers. He had obviously sought her out to threaten her with who knew what retribution if she revealed the closeness of their former association to anyone here tonight.

'My sister is with me,' he said flatly, and she flinched at the implication that she might seek to do damage to a girl she remembered only with affection and a bitter regret they were now estranged.

'I had noticed.'

'She knows,' he told her tersely, and this time Sophie winced visibly. 'Not by my doing—or at least not consciously,' he added, then frowned all the harder—probably because he had to explain himself to her, she supposed.

'Then how?' she asked, discovering she was not as guarded against his open dislike of her as she'd hoped.

Tired and angry and uncomfortable as he was, he reminded her a little too poignantly of a much younger Peter Vane. A Peter Vane she had hurt and infuriated until he had believed her exactly what she'd wanted him to. Back then it had felt as if her life was as good as over when he had finally thought her a lot worse than she ought to be. Now she felt… Just how *did* she feel?

Confident it was better not to analyse any personal feelings she still had for him until she was strictly alone, she held her tongue and hoped he'd hurry up and be done with her.

'She heard us arguing.' Even in the faint light of that flickering candle and the snow-reflected moonlight beyond the uncurtained window he must have seen her pale. 'No,' he said impatiently, 'not you and I. My father and I raged at each other for days after you were gone. Apparently Dina couldn't believe you would have left me voluntarily and was listening at doors to find out where you were. Needless to say she found out a little too graphically for a schoolgirl what *had* actually happened between us—something I find it very hard to forgive myself or my father even now.'

'So you and your father discussed me in such an ungentlemanly and heated fashion that you could not fail to be overheard by anyone who happened to be passing by and it is *my* fault? Considering I wasn't even there, I was very clever indeed to do such damage by proxy.'

'Yes, you were. A clever little minx who fooled me she was an angel in human form and as deep in love with me as I thought myself to be with her—young fool that I was. You pulled all our strings and made us dance to your own bizarre tune so very cleverly back then—did you not, Sophie Bonet?'

'Indeed, I must have been a very accomplished schemer at an early age to have put myself out in the cold so completely, must I not?' she asked ironically, wondering how he thought her ending up virtually penniless and a governess was a success for that young girl who might have had so much more if she truly was the vicious adventuress he clearly thought her.

'Why did you do it, then?' he asked impatiently, clearly too tired and worried about his sister and his aunt to care about her motives for a desertion long past.

'Oh, for fun, of course,' she answered facetiously.

'Of course,' he replied flatly, and turned away as if

too weary and indifferent to care if her argument made no sense at all, since she got singularly little 'fun' out of her position here.

After the first terrible sting of absence had faded, she had learned to value her young charges and her employers as she had never thought she could when first exiled from the love and security she'd known at Holm Park—before her aunt had died and the old earl had gone to the devil. Better not to think of those first hard weeks and months here, when she had cried herself to sleep every night. How she'd longed for him then, almost sick in heart and mind at the tearing lack of this insensitive great oaf to hold her all night long and whisper sweet words in her ear until she slept on a cloud of soft dreams that never came true.

She fought that younger, sillier Sophie now, as she watched him turn towards the sitting room where the other ladies were taking tea, and told herself it didn't matter what he thought of her. How odd, then, that tears threatened and she had to order herself once more to go and discuss those menus with Cook and Mrs Elkerley before she could return to the sitting room, where she would brazen out the rest of the evening until she could escape to her own rather spartan sanctuary a significant floor up from the adult family and their guests. She couldn't shirk her duty just because being in the same room with Peter made her feel so uncomfortable she might risk fighting her way out of the governess chrysalis she'd built round herself if she wasn't careful. She shuddered at the very idea of the furore *that* would cause.

She reluctantly made her way back to the sitting room

ten minutes later, wishing she could indicate to Imogen that it was high time the ladies were in bed. The gentlemen must do as they pleased, of course, but the household would be very grateful if they would do the same and let the staff take plenty of rest before their busy day tomorrow. Since it was still barely nine o'clock, such a suggestion would seem inhospitable at the very least, so she would have to slip back into her dark corner and endure this farce a little longer—unless the Vanes suddenly became overcome by fatigue after their strenuous day. But she doubted either of them were feeling that obliging.

'What a very fine performance you give as the stern and reserved governess, Miss Rose.'

Cedric's reedy, gloating voice came out of the shadows in the entrance hall, and she did her best not to jump half a yard and give him the satisfaction of knowing he made her nervous.

'And your manners are a little odd, to say the least, in making personal comments about a stranger, Mr Wroxley,' she said coldly and went to step round him—only to shiver with shock and a deep-down whisper of fear when he snaked out a hand to stop her. She couldn't shake off a mature man, even if he was a poor and thin specimen of the breed. She was barely five feet tall, and no longer honed and fit from tearing about the countryside on her pony, or walking for hours whenever the fancy took her, so she supposed she would have to think up some strategy for repelling so-called gentlemen like Cedric Wroxley now Imogen was out and likely to attract suitors of various sorts—some of whom might well consider the governess fair game.

'I don't need manners to deal with the likes of *you*, Miss Rose.'

'Would that be a threat, Mr Wroxley?'

'More a simple statement of fact,' he said, looking down his nose at her as if she had suggested he might have fleas. 'There's some secret you don't want known nagging at me. Some connection or resemblance to a person far more important than you pretend to be that I cannot quite pin down. I intend to get to the heart of it before I'm done here. It will be something to do, after all.'

'You lack both manners and honour, then. If I had anything to hide, I might be worried by such threats, I suppose, but since I do not you may tell your tales if you wish to, Mr Wroxley. I wonder how well you will be received in polite society when it's known you would trifle with a lady's reputation for your own amusement,' Sophie managed to say, with a cool contempt that belied her fast-beating heart and the pain of his hand crushing her wrist so hard she was hard-pressed not to cry out and give him the satisfaction of admitting he'd hurt her in more ways than one.

'Let her go.' Peter's icily controlled voice interrupted whatever vitriol Cedric Wroxley had been about to spew at her in reply. 'Do it now, Wroxley, or I'll break your arm,' he added.

And if Mr Wroxley lacked the basic common sense to shiver at the silky menace in his voice, Sophie did it for him, then crossed her arms across her body in a vain attempt to feel warm even after Wroxley abruptly dropped her hand as if it might poison him.

'No need for such passion, Sylbourne. I was only making the lady's acquaintance. I didn't know you were interested in such a dull little doxy or I'd never have laid a finger on her in the first place.'

'I have an interest in any lady you decide to turn your repellent attentions towards, and Miss Rose is a connection of mine—irrespective of your prurient opinion of our dealings. The lady has chosen to live by her own efforts and on her own terms, but that doesn't mean you won't have the entire Vane interest ranged against you if you try and do Miss Rose harm of any kind, Wroxley.'

'Hoping she will warm your bed for you while you're marooned here in the middle of nowhere, are you?' the wretched man mocked from a safe distance.

Sophie stepped warily between him and Peter as the latter let his temper loose long enough to lunge threateningly towards his bugbear, as if the urge to hit the little worm despite his weedy size and cowardly temperament was becoming nigh uncontrollable.

'I don't care what his opinion is of me, Peter,' she declared, as coolly as she had it in her to do, with the racing of her heartbeat and the damnable feeling she had that every blow and kick landed on Peter would hurt her acutely—even if an inadequate enemy like Wroxley was the one trying to land them. 'Apparently Mr Wroxley's thoughts rarely rise above the gutter, and I'm too small to punish him for it, but unfortunately he's not up to your weight. You'll only feel guilty once you've recovered your temper if you hit him, although he clearly deserves to be hit by someone.'

'Until then it would be my pleasure to teach him some manners—even if his acquiring a little honour is clearly too much expect,' Peter argued, even as the fury died out of his grey gaze and he brought his awesome temper fully under control.

Wroxley did not know him well enough to see that the fiery edge had gone from his fury, however, and took advantage of being light and quick on his feet to scurry up the stairs as if he thought Peter wouldn't be able to resist the temptation to come after him, despite her reasoning and his own self-control.

'I'm going to bed. The company is so poor in this benighted ruin I'll be better off in my own company.'

He smirked from his safe place on the landing above, and Sophie only hoped he'd trip up on one of the many changes of level the old part of the house rejoiced in before he got to his bedchamber and probably bolted the door as a precaution against Peter throwing her aside and running after him to finish the fight they'd almost started.

CHAPTER SIX

'YOU should have let me hit him,' Peter grumbled.

'And give him the satisfaction of knowing he'd won a moral victory when his head finally stopped ringing? I think not,' Sophie said firmly, and did her best to evade him and join the other ladies in the safety of the family sitting room.

'Better than this, perhaps,' he murmured, and he stopped her by taking her upper arms and holding her with a surprising gentleness so he could kiss her hungrily.

At first there was only anger and urgency and heat—nothing of the aching sweetness she recalled from those long-ago kisses they'd used to exchange before both of them realised the world wasn't well lost for calf love. Then his true instincts and the familiarity of her uncontrollable urge to respond to him, even after eight years apart, seemed to take over. His mouth softened and his hands coaxed and soothed rather than trying to control her. Her whole body seemed to sigh as he truly seduced her, as if it remembered all they'd once been to each other in a long, heady moment that almost made her believe in their fools' paradise again.

She felt herself melt from the inside out, sighed a desperate plea for something she didn't understand wanting deeply and instinctively, and kissed him back. *He even smells right,* mused the small part of her not occupied with feeling. *Such a tempting mix of clean-shaven man, along with something citrusy and yet spicy and pure essence of Peter Vane—the only man I ever willingly kissed. The only man I ever want to kiss me...*

The thought brought her to terrified clarity.

'No...' she managed to moan between lips that felt as if they had forgotten how to speak anything intelligible, horrified by the very idea she might slip back into the agony of loving and losing him all over again.

'No?' he murmured, and he raised his head to peer down at her through the dimly lit gloom.

Any moment now one of the servants might leave their supper and discover them locked in each other's arms as if they weren't passionate enemies nowadays rather than lovers. Or perhaps Wroxley might find the courage from somewhere to creep down and catch them, making such kisses seem ugly and furtive, traded between cynical lovers bent on the most basic of pleasures. She doubted Wroxley knew any other sort of wanting a woman, self-obsessed as he clearly was.

'You really need to put in a lot more work on your denials if you expect them to be honoured in future, Miss Rose,' he said flatly, and released her as if he couldn't imagine how he'd come to be holding her in the first place.

'And *you* should learn the difference between wanting and hating,' she managed to find breath to counter.

'Ah—there you reveal yourself to be still far too like the not-very-grown-up seductress I remember so well, my dear. At least I have learnt there isn't much room between the two when it comes to my dealings with you,' he said, as if discussing the weather.

And he turned about face and left her standing gazing after him with her mouth agape and nothing to say.

At first she had to blink back tears as she made herself acknowledge that he'd just admitted he hated her. Well, she'd seen it in his eyes the first moment they'd met out in the snow, she told herself, so it should come as no surprise. Then she let herself take in the other half of his driven declaration, and the lingering feel of his mouth and hands hot and urgent on her eager body. He wanted her—wanted *them*—nearly as much as she did, despite their past disasters and all the misunderstandings that must blight any future they could have. If only they had met as lovers now, instead of years ago when it had all been impossible, she concluded wistfully. And why did his wanting her as badly as she yearned for him make her feel better about the throb of unrepentant, frustrated wanting at the very centre of her? The notion she could be so vengeful made her frown.

The feeling of almost being scorched by the heated longing between them lingered about her hot nipples and breasts that suddenly felt full and rebellious under her prim bombazine. In this needy, shaken guise she hardly knew herself—didn't want to know herself. All the same, she had an awful feeling this was the real Sophie—the one she'd blithely thought dead and buried these last eight years. Wanting, wanton Sophie, who only needed a hot look and a few careless kisses from my Lord Sylbourne for her to long to be even hotter; begging for far more than an earl and a governess should ever dream of being to one another.

'Ah, there you are.'

Edwina's voice interrupted her confused reverie. She had put her head out of the sitting room in a probable effort to find her brother, and she didn't look too pleased to see Sophie there instead, even though she came outside the warmth and comfort of the room and shut the door behind her.

'Yes, here I am,' she replied idiotically.

'I suppose I really *did* see my brother outside in the snow, blowing a cloud just now? If you and he have been arguing that accounts for his frustration at not being able to make the world dance to his tune, as well as his trip outside into the arctic air to cool his temper, Miss Rose.'

'It does?'

'Oh, decidedly,' Dina said, with an almost feline look of sisterly wisdom.

'And you're pleased about it?' Sophie asked incredulously.

Edwina shrugged philosophically. 'You two might as well be miserable together as apart,' she said, as if that explained everything.

'Has he been miserable?' she asked impulsively, then could have kicked herself for revealing she might care whether he was happy or not.

'Of course he has. You left him so cruelly how could he not be? But he's got over it, I'm pleased to say. Now, come back in the warmth, instead of hovering out here like a hen in a fox's lair, and we'll leave him to cool his ardour and his temper out there in the snow,' Edwina said placidly.

Sophie felt like reminding her one-time friend she couldn't like her, not after the way she'd treated Edwina's beloved elder brother, but decided Edwina needed no such reminder.

So she went meekly back into the sitting room to meet Imogen and the girls' welcome, even if she also had to patiently endure Mrs Garret-Lowden and her daughter's perpetual looks of puzzlement over how she could intrude on the family and their unexpectedly important guests like this.

She wondered if she was the only one who blessed the sudden silence when Mrs Garret-Lowden finally ran out of inane things to say to the daughter of an earl. Her rather obvious attempts to find out what His Lordship's financial and marital status might be from one who knew him so very well became almost desultory, and she began to nod in front of the fire after her demanding day of criticising all and everything about Heartsease Hall and its inhabitants, despite her successful scheme to make Livia mistress of it one day.

Livia seemed as relieved to watch her mama wind

down as the rest of them were, and carefully ignored the occasional snore as Mrs Garret-Lowden shifted in her chair. Sophie was almost in danger of liking the girl as she listened to her chat with Imogen about Christmas Eve, and how on earth they would get to church on Christmas Day if the weather didn't let up. Perhaps Livia would make Timon Frayne a perfectly good wife after all, once she was away from her mother's unfortunate influence. Sophie wrestled with the hope that they'd misjudged the young lady and she was merely under her ambitious parent's thumb. If so, Sophie would not need to consider Sir Gyffard's unexpected proposal and all could go on more or less as it always had.

She was torn between instinctive revulsion at the idea of wedding any man when she still felt so tied and torn by the haughty and dismissive Earl of Sylbourne Peter had become, and a feeling that it was her duty to protect the girls from a woman who would do her best to push them as far to the edge of her daughter's new family as she could without actually putting them out into the world with nothing and making a scandal.

If Livia would become a woman of character one day it would free Sophie of the need to put Viola and Audrey's future before her own and wed their father. So much hope to rest on such a frail set of shoulders, she decided cynically when she spared a glance from her sewing to see Livia watching her gently snoring mother as if waiting for a sleeping tiger to awake and start roaring and devouring. She felt a stir of pity for the girl, who'd clearly grown up with such huge hopes resting on her securing a good husband that Sophie wondered anew how strong the family's position in polite society truly was. If only Sir Gyffard had not been forced to go away at this very time he would have had the chance to assess Livia and her mother's characters for himself. Maybe then he would never have made that awkward offer of marriage to *her*.

Sophie very much wished he hadn't done so—had at least given things time. If Timon truly loved Miss Garret-Lowden he was quite right to marry her. If she loved him back, or even liked him very well, then perhaps Miss Garret-Lowden should be permitted to follow her own path through life—preferably without further interference from her mother. Who was Sophie to judge the depths and shallows of another person's heart when she'd lost her own at too early an age ever to get it back? Then there were the mysteries that lurked in a certain pair of ironic grey eyes whenever he let them rest on the unworthy person of Miss Sophie Rose, and who knew what *they* might be?

'For goodness' sake come inside and close the door quickly, Peter,' Edwina urged her brother rather sharply when he finally reappeared. 'You have brought the cold air back in with you as well, you wretch,' she told him brusquely, and she nodded rather severely from him to the fire as Mrs Garret-Lowden came back to life with a snort they all pretended not to hear.

'There you are, my lord,' she said with dazed bright-ness, and blinked up at him as if she secretly found him more intimidating than she ever intended to admit.

'Here I am,' he agreed calmly, and took up a typical male posture, warming his borrowed coat-tails in front of the fire while he surveyed the cosy parlour as if he owned it.

'Perhaps we could play whist now there are four of us again,' Mrs Garret-Lowden suggested hopefully, and Sophie wondered if *she* was one of that four or outside it, along with her pupils past and present.

'Oh, no, Mama, you know I abhor it. I cannot keep the suits in my head, let alone all that nonsense about trumps and cross-trumps and the stratagems that delight you,' Livia Garret-Lowden protested fervently, despite the presence of the formidable Earl of Sylbourne.

'Then why don't you join myself and my sisters in a game of spillikins, Miss Garret-Lowden? Miss Rose is a formidable card-player, and my brothers vie to have her as their partner in games of skill because they know there is a strong chance they will win,' Imogen said artlessly.

Sophie supposed she ought to applaud any attempt the girls made at getting to know or even like one another—even if it left her where she least wanted to be.

'Miss Frayne exaggerates,' she said colourlessly, and hoped her inclusion would be enough to put Mrs Garret-Lowden off the whole idea.

'I doubt it. You always found it easy to pick up any game that required quick wits rather than luck, Sophie,' Edwina said impulsively—then cast Sophie a look of half apology and half defiance when she realised she'd let slip that she knew the Fraynes' governess far better than either of them had admitted. 'Miss Rose is a distant relative, and we often played together when I was Miss Audrey's age,' she finally said with a shrug, as if the foibles of the aristocracy were above explanation.

'Why on earth did you never say so, Miss Rose?' Mrs Garret-Lowden demanded, her nose twitching like a terrier on the track of a doomed rat.

'I would rather not trumpet my connections,' she replied, with what she hoped was dignified reserve.

'But what folly is *this*, Miss Rose? Such relations must improve your own consequence—and that of the family who choose to employ you. You're related to a *lord*, however remotely,' Mrs Garret-Lowden informed her majestically, and failed to see the distaste for such snobbery in the very people she wanted to impress the most as she laid down her own philosophy of life.

'Perhaps it would be best if I made the family who have chosen to employ me aware of the fact before I advertise it about the neighbourhood,' Sophie said unwarily, more interested in Imogen and her little sisters' wide-eyed reproach at her secrecy than whether Mrs Garret-Lowden or her daughter might choose to think she was setting her own manners and standards of behaviour above theirs.

'And perhaps it would be best if you recalled you *are* a governess—a servant who may be trusted with the upbringing of the young ladies of the house one day but dismissed for impudence and seeking to put herself above her betters the next.'

'Perhaps so, madam,' Sophie said, in as noncommittal a tone as she could summon. She sent a warning glance at Imogen not to fire up in her defence.

'Yet neither you nor I employ Miss Rose—do we, Mrs

Garret-Lowden?' It was Peter, rather surprisingly, who came to her defence. 'And you could hardly expect Sir Gyffard Frayne to thank us for putting a perfectly good governess to his younger girls and the cherished companion of his elder daughter out in the snow in his absence just because Miss Rose has the misfortune to be numbered among *my* vast tribe of relatives and connections by marriage—could you, ma'am?' he ended, a little more genially, as if he was puzzled as to how he should categorise Sophie now the truth was partly out about their family entanglements.

'Well, no, I suppose not,' the lady agreed doubtfully, struggling with the fact that she disliked and distrusted Sophie for being passably pretty and under the age of thirty, which now had to be weighed against the fact she was clearly a lot better connected than Mrs Garret-Lowden had realised when she had been doing her best to set the governess down as a nothing to be got rid of as soon as her own daughter had her feet firmly under the table at Heartsease Hall.

'Clearly you are to be spared a trek through the snow to the nearest inn tonight, then, Cousin Sophie,' Peter informed her with an apparently genial smile.

'How you do relieve my mind, Cousin Peter,' she responded repressively, and raised her sewing suggestively towards the working candles Imogen had ordered to be lit in order for her to work in comfort, as if she would really like to continue with it if only he would stop bothering her with his ill-timed humour.

'Good. Then why don't we continue with our plans

to entertain ourselves?' he said, and she was tempted to glare at him for his insensitivity—except he was perfectly aware of what he was doing and that would satisfy him all the more.

'Yes, why don't we?' she echoed, with a mouse-like humility that won her a sharp, uneasy glance from Edwina and another bland smile from Peter that Sophie knew perfectly well was intended to punish rather than placate her.

Doing her best to concentrate on her cards, whilst very conscious that the younger girls were whispering more about her than the game they were supposed to be busy with in their own corner of the room, Sophie very soon found herself battling a headache as well as two formidable opponents in Mrs Garret-Lowden and Peter.

'Really, cousin, one would imagine you had not played cards since last we engaged in battle at Holm Park all those years ago,' Edwina reproached her as they finally lost the first game.

'If you recall, Miss Frayne got me into this situation by revealing otherwise just now, Lady Edwina,' Sophie replied with would-be lightness.

'So she did. We shall have to blame it on your tiredness, then, or an inability to concentrate all your attentions on the cards tonight, shall we not?'

'Since you and Lord Sylbourne had a far greater ordeal to endure today than any I can lay claim to, I really can't fall back on that flimsy excuse, can I? It seems to me that I'm merely guilty of playing very badly indeed. Lord Sylbourne and Mrs Garret-Lowden would be well on the way to beggaring us both by now if we were not playing for penny stakes.'

'Cousin, surely you can't intend to continue addressing us so formally now your foolish insistence on keeping our connection secret has been found out? It's laudable in many ways that you so stalwartly refused to trade on the Vane name to gain an agreeable position, but now you have one there really is no need to carry the desire to keep your self-respect to such extremes any longer,' Edwina informed her, with a look that spoke of her ambiguous feelings towards Sophie.

It was a look made up half of angry provocation and half of regret they should all have come to this, and it made Sophie bite her lip and consider her words very carefully before she replied.

'Perhaps you are right. I do have more than my fair share of foolish pride.'

'You always did,' Edwina agreed, and held Sophie's gaze steadily for the first time all evening. 'Much of it misplaced. I only know of one other person with more idiotic nobility than you possess—and more ability to drive the rest of us distracted.'

'How trying of me,' Sophie said with a wry smile.

'It is indeed trying. But how much of it is deliberate and how much instinctive I shall probably never know. Now, do you think you could concentrate a little harder this time, cousin? Mrs Garret-Lowden has just cut for trumps and I don't believe you have the slightest notion what suit she came up with.'

'I will try,' Sophie agreed, humbly enough, and did

so from then on—because at least if she fixed her attention on the cards she could not spare so much for my lord Sylbourne and his inquisitive sister.

By the end of the evening at least honours were more or less even in their battle of cards. Mrs Garret-Lowden went to bed reasonably happy with a world that held good enough card players to keep her amused and a real live earl to boast about to her friends.

'How could you keep such an important part of your life as being connected to the Earl of Sylbourne and his family hidden from us for so long, Miss Rose?' Imogen demanded, as soon as Audrey and Viola had finally gone to bed in a state of weary over-excitement.

Sophie was exhausted herself, and somehow it had been easier to let Imogen drag her into her comfortable but quite sparsely furnished bedchamber so she could interrogate her than argue.

'It wasn't something that seemed likely to crop up in day-to-day conversation, Imogen,' she said a little limply, but it had been a trying day, and it seemed high time she was excused from making up ingenious tall stories.

'You could have said something when Mrs Garret-Lowden was forever puffing her own acquaintance while setting you down as a nobody—even when you were in the room and very obviously able to hear her. How could you have just sat there and let her trample over you in that awful meek way, as if it was all you deserve, when all the time you're related to an *earl*?'

'Because it would have been ill-bred and foolish to

argue with a guest under your father's roof. Mrs Garret-Lowden's daughter is engaged to be married to your eldest brother, and I would prefer to stay in my post until your sisters do not need me any more.'

'Yet you have never seemed like the stuff martyrs are made of before now, Rosie,' Imogen declared, with a loud sigh that told Sophie she had at least half forgiven her sins. 'I do wish you'd seen fit to tell us about your connection to the Vanes when we were preparing to receive them under our roof this afternoon, though. It would have come as far less of a shock then than it did just now.'

'I agree. But it was a huge shock for me to see Lord Sylbourne stumbling through the snow at the time. I truly didn't know whether he and Lady Edwina and Miss Willis would choose to acknowledge our remote relationship after so many years. We have had no contact with one another these last eight years, and your knowing about the relationship would have added to the awkwardness if they had wanted no more of me.'

'Why should they not want to know you? You can hardly help it if your own circumstances mean you have to seek paid employment, Miss Rose. I would think a great deal less of His Lordship and his sister than I do at the moment if they had chosen to ignore an old friend out of such cold snobbery.'

'No, that would be unfair. There is far more than a mere gulf in circumstances dividing us nowadays,' Sophie admitted unwarily.

'Lord Sylbourne is very handsome,' Imogen declared, a little too innocently.

'Indeed he is *very* handsome, very noble, and somehow he seems almost rich with it nowadays, if the quality of his team and the stable boys' description of his coach and hunter are anything to go by,' Sophie replied, unable to conceal her own puzzlement at his apparently comfortable circumstances.

When she had left Holm Park with her two bandboxes and Lady Frayne's address in her pocket she had probably been the wealthiest person in the household, with the twenty guineas she'd had sewn into her petticoats to keep them out of the last Lord Sylbourne's hands and a whole five shillings' worth of change in her purse. It might have been all she'd been left with after the last Lord Sylbourne had flung her little fortune to the four winds, but at least she hadn't been in debt. The Vanes had been so deeply mired in it their position had seemed almost irrecoverable.

'I think there is something more than a vague family connection between you and Lord Sylbourne, Miss Rose,' Imogen informed her sternly. 'Please don't try to deny it, as if I'm still a schoolgirl. I don't know him very well, but it seems to me that His Lordship wouldn't be so cold and ironic to a lady obliged to became a governess—particularly a lady he seems to have known very well in the past—if there hadn't been some sort of falling out between you once upon a time.'

'Perhaps there was a slim chance of something more all those years ago,' Sophie admitted, 'but that is private, as well as very much in the past.'

'So you don't mean to tell me another word about it?'

'Not if I can help it. It was only boy-girl silliness, and

it lasted barely a week before wiser counsel and common sense prevailed.'

'Maybe His Lordship felt less sensible than you about it all, then, Rosie, for I really wouldn't call him indifferent to you now.'

'Perhaps not. But I doubt veiled dislike is a cover for the sort of romantic nonsense you are hinting at, Imogen. Lord Sylbourne and I parted worse than strangers to each other, and we have met again in much the same frame of mind. Now the fact of our past connection is publicly acknowledged I hope we shall go on comfortably enough together while he keeps to his place and I stay in mine.'

'And how I wish you would stop acting as if that's slightly below Cox's humblest stable boy. You are my sage counselor, as well as my little sisters' beloved governess, Rosie, and I want you to stop pretending to be an antidote. It really does our credit in society no good at all when you refuse to grant us the place in your affections I think we have earned over the last eight years.'

'Very well. I shall try to be a little more self-satisfied from now on, if that will please you better.'

'And isn't that just like you, Rosie? I say how much we love and value you as our friend, and you turn it back on yourself and imply you would be guilty of false pride if you accepted how fond we Fraynes truly are of you. No wonder Lord Sylbourne didn't try and persuade you to stay with him at Holm Park if you threw his affection and respect for you back in his face as you are trying to repulse ours.'

'I shall attempt to have a little more faith in myself and

in your family as well, then, Imogen, but please don't ask me to go over long-dead ground and do the same with the Vane family. It may be Christmas, but I'm not a saint, and there are some things in the past that should stay there, safely dead and buried.'

'Or perhaps you cherish them as reasons not to make a good life for yourself now, Miss Rose?' Edwina's voice said stonily from the doorway.

Sophie smothered a groan at the very idea that she had been overheard musing out loud.

'I beg your pardon. I did knock, but you were evidently too busy to hear me. I'm sorry to trouble any of you again tonight, but my aunt is restless and running a slight fever. I wondered if there was any feverfew or suchlike in the house that I might give to her.'

'Of course. I'll make up an infusion of gentle herbs that should soothe her to sleep instead of trying anything more drastic for now. I will bring it to her room as soon as I have it ready, Lady Edwina. Meanwhile I'm sure Imogen will be delighted to find one of the scented herb cushions we made up in the summer to tuck under Miss Willis's pillow.'

'If you will do so, and then sit with my aunt for a while, I would be deeply obliged to you, Imogen. One of us will be needed to help Sophie in the kitchen—or the stillroom, if you have one. I know there will be fires to light and pots to watch from having seen your Miss Rose and her aunt work together on such remedies in the past. We certainly never needed a doctor at Holm Park when either of them were available to physic us,' Edwina confided.

Sophie stopped herself meeting her acute gaze, silently agreeing that it was as well she had learnt so much from her aunt, since after her death and her husband's decline the Vane household hadn't been able to afford a physician.

'I knew you were skilled in making up potpourri and pomanders, Miss Rose, but I never realised you could treat the sick as well,' Imogen said interestedly, and Sophie flushed as she realised the poor girl was finding out a great deal she hadn't known before about her one-time governess tonight.

'The need never arose for me to do so while your mama was alive to carry out any healing the household needed,' she excused herself, but she shifted under Edwina's gaze. 'And what use was their knowledge to Her Ladyship or my aunt when all is said and done? Both of them died despite their skills.'

'Losing your aunt and your employer gave you good reason not to even try to help the sick any more, didn't it?' Edwina asked as they sped down the stairs together, wrapped in as many shawls and rugs as they could safely carry against the creeping cold taking over the old house now most of the fires were either extinguished or banked for the night.

'Good enough.'

'And you've been trying hard not to care about your fellow human beings for longer than either of us want to ponder, haven't you, Sophie?'

'Maybe I have. But I don't see why it matters to you if I use or don't use whatever Aunt Hermione taught me. I still recall how to concoct a simple cure for restlessness and stress, and hopefully that's all Miss Willis will need to set her to rights after her chill and have her tearing about the countryside on horseback once again when the snow has cleared.'

'It has to matter to me, or I might become as buttoned up and isolated from my fellow human beings as you appear to have made yourself, Sophie. I should hate to feel I had to close myself off from the world like that to feel safe.'

'Touché,' Sophie said flatly, and perhaps she *had* done just that to survive the isolation and misery of leaving Holm Park and her youthful love for the odd existence of young governess to a lively and close family. 'Although I really do care about my pupils—past and present,' she defended herself weakly.

'A trio of motherless girls who are inclined to love anyone who takes an interest in them in return? How could anyone not love them if they happen to share a roof with them? Come, Sophie, surely you can do better than that?'

'I admired their mother very deeply too. Lady Frayne helped me at a time when I felt totally friendless and forsaken, so don't judge me, Edwina—or at least don't do so until you know what it has felt like to walk in my shoes these last eight years,' Sophie said dourly.

They finally reached the more workaday part of the house and she turned thankfully towards the stillroom.

'You didn't need to be alone; we would have stood by you whatever you did back then. You were far more like my sister than merely the niece of my father's second wife, Sophie, and I certainly loved *you* enough to be broken-hearted when you left without a word. You stayed away with not even a letter once a year at Christmas to tell us how you were and what you were doing all these years.'

'Because it was better you didn't know,' Sophie said bleakly—then started violently when Peter loomed up out of the darkness behind them.

He must have caught at least that last sad statement, judging by the puzzled frown he turned on her as she swung her flickering candle towards him to see who was there, even though the fast-beating of her heart would have told her who it was in the pitch-dark, but how she wished she knew how long he'd been creeping along so silently in their wake.

CHAPTER SEVEN

'AH, PETER, there you are. I tried to find you, so you could help me soothe Aunt Hes, but you were not in your room when I looked, so I found Sophie instead. You might as well stay here and help her brew one of her potions while I go and send Miss Frayne off to bed. Aunt Hes doesn't know her and might believe all sorts of odd things if she wakes up and is still wandering in her mind as she was when I looked in on her just now,' Edwina said, and was off upstairs before either of them could argue that Peter could relieve Imogen of her task just as well.

'I suspect we're being left here to resolve our differences, Miss Rose, since my sister has become a very managing female nowadays—although even she probably doesn't realise how profound our differences truly are,' he said with a manly shrug.

He took the large old key she was holding as if she hardly knew what it was for and opened the ancient oak door of the stillroom, then he raised the candle he'd taken from her slackened grip to coolly survey the neatly labelled bottles and the impressive range of little spice drawers Lady Frayne had acquired to hold her pharmacopeia of ingredients.

'You should certainly be able to find whatever you need in here—although if it has lain untouched since the mistress of the house died I'm not sure the remedy will be quite so effective as it ought to be.'

'Mrs Elkerley replaces whatever needs replacing once a year. We go through the entire cabinet together when we can snatch a few moments to ourselves every summer, to see what must be kept and what thrown away. We take whatever we can from the herb garden, and there's a very good apothecary in Worcester who sends us reliably pure herbs and cures from further afield if we need them and neither of us has the time to fetch them ourselves.'

'You have not resigned your healer's skills altogether, then?' he asked, and thus revealed he'd heard far more of that whispered conversation with Edwina than she would have wished him to.

'I have little enough need of them here, since my late mistress trained her housekeeper to be nigh as fine a herbalist as she was herself. I'm not withholding necessary care by not practising all my aunt taught me while I live under this roof. Indeed, I only agreed to do this tonight so Mrs Elkerley can sleep. She is so busy trying to make Christmas as normal as possible for the girls she might succumb to exhaustion well before Twelfth Night if we don't help wherever we can.'

'Then we're privileged indeed to have you prepare a remedy with your own fair hands, are we not? Has it occurred to you that by not teaching some of what you know to your pupils you could be withholding important benefits from their future families?' he pointed out, finding the flaw in her argument.

'They learnt some things from their mother, and the practice of medicine is improving all the time,' she excused herself limply, and she touched the candle he'd finally put down on the sturdy oak table to others in well-placed sconces round the walls. Then she lit the central lamp, since it was very necessary to see what she was doing if she wasn't to do more harm than good.

'If you truly intend helping me, please light the fire. We'll need it, and even if we didn't I'd like to work without gloves to make my fingers clumsy. When that's done you could find the kettle and fill it from the water jar over there, if you have time before you leave me to get on with my tasks. Mrs Elkerley has it filled with fresh water every morning, in case she needs to make up a remedy in a hurry, so you can trust it to do your aunt no harm. I shall need the small pestle and mortar as well,' Sophie told him distractedly as she opened drawers, sniffed the contents to make sure they were good and in their rightful place, then began meticulously to weigh and measure dried flowers and leaves while he began doing as she asked.

'Yes, Miss Rose,' he said with mock meekness. 'I can see how you manage to be such a formidable governess to those unfortunate girls now. They must line up to say their lessons by rote. I suppose it is, "Yes, Miss Rose. No, Miss Rose. Three bags full, Miss Rose," for the poor things from dawn to dusk. Why *do* you call yourself Miss

Rose, Sophie? It seems an odd sort of a name for a governess—unless you set out to be a rose with a great many thorns from the outset?'

'It's my last given name,' she said, trying to sound distracted and far too busy to answer idle questions in the hope that he wouldn't prod that particular wound any deeper.

In truth, she had called herself by that name in a fanciful attempt to keep the memory of their last night of complete love and hope and breathtaking happiness alive in her heart—despite the cold reality that had frosted the petals on that particular dream. They'd used to meet in an almost forgotten rose arbour down by the lake. His mother had caused it to be planted as a new bride, when she'd first come to Holm Park as a hopeful young woman herself. In the full flush of midsummer twenty years on it had been covered by a rampant canopy of heavy-flowered growth, and the scent of the first Lady Sylbourne's beloved Bourbon and Provençal roses had been so heady even a strict abstainer from alcohol might have got drunk on fragrance alone.

The memory of those magical nights of breathless first love, as they'd dreamed away the darkness in each other's arms, had kept her sane through the pain of losing all she had so longed for and then finally had for so short a time. To take it all out and expose it to his cynical gaze now would leave her without even that comfort, when he left her behind and went back to Holm Park and his sister's wedding festivities without a backward look, so she shrugged off the need to remind him how much he'd once loved her and carried on with her tasks.

'Is it?' he asked with almost insulting uninterest. 'I really can't recall ever knowing your other names in the old days, Sophie.'

'No, you wouldn't,' she replied, almost as carelessly, as if she didn't remember each one of his as if they had been engraved on her heart as poor Mary Tudor had claimed 'Calais' was on hers.

'There—the wretched stuff has finally caught. Let's hope it warms this ice house up before you're done and don't need to work in here,' he said, and he sat back on his heels to watch the flames lick over the pine cones and well seasoned kindling and wood he had found in the box beside the grate. 'Why shouldn't I remember every detail about you, Sophie?' he asked, as if he'd been the one left with nothing but memories to keep cold reality at bay and not her.

'Because when I first came to Holm Park you disliked your new stepmother nearly as much as you did her scrawny little niece, and once you had decided you could put up with us both after all, if you worked at it hard enough, there seemed little point in sharing confidences with a boy who thought more of his schoolfriends than he did about mere females of any sort.'

'Including my little sister, I'm ashamed to recall. You tolerated having her follow you about like a little lost puppy far more readily than I ever did, so I suppose it's little wonder Dina finds it hard to forgive your desertion. I promptly left her alone at Holm Park with my father soon after you departed, closely followed by most of the servants. Aunt Hes finally took Dina away from him and paid for her to go to school when the constable caught the poor girl stealing from the local baker because she hadn't eaten properly for days.'

'I should have brought her with me,' Sophie reproached herself, and felt bitterly ashamed of leaving Edwina to the care of a man who had seemed to lose all tenderness for those he'd once loved once the grip of drink and gambling closed so tightly on his mind it became like a mania. She'd thought he'd still cared enough for his daughter to take care of her, but evidently she'd been mistaken. '*You* left as well?' she asked incredulously, when his words finally hit home. She turned to look at him fully, so surprised she had stopped worrying about what she might give away.

'How could I stay? He was insisting I must wed a girl I would have cheerfully crossed any street in the land to avoid.'

'You didn't marry Diamantha Rivers after all, then?' she asked, and told herself it wasn't dignified to stand here staring at him with her mouth open like this.

'Why on earth did you ever think I would, Sophie?' he said silkily, as if she was far worse than Diamantha—with her arrogant demands and chilly heart—for running away.

She should have known he would never wed a female he had come to hate when she was thrown at him as the woman he must marry, even though he'd been still under-age and legally his father's chattel.

'Because I once had her pointed out to me as the Countess of Sylbourne perhaps? Or is it the fact that her father was rich as Golden Ball and had promised to pay off all your father's debts? And she was pretty enough, in all conscience, so I can't believe you refused to wed her when I was gone.'

'Then you obviously had very little faith in my love for you. Only imagine how it would feel if *you* had been told to wed a man you couldn't abide to keep your family from a debtors' prison. Put yourself in my shoes for once. Why didn't you do just that and believe in me, Sophie? You were supposed to love me to distraction, yet you thought I would shrug off everything you were to me, what I stupidly thought was our true love, solely for the sake of money. God knows I thought I was disillusioned before, but this trumps even my wildest speculations about why you left me with nothing more than a terse little note wishing me goodbye and godspeed, as if you were saying farewell to a distant acquaintance.'

'They said the settlements were signed and contracts exchanged. At first I wouldn't believe you could agree to such a cynical match, however desperate your father's finances might be. Then the banns were read the Sunday before I left. How could that be done if you hadn't given your consent to the match, Peter? I didn't hear from you the entire time you were away in London, trying to come to terms with your father's creditors, so I thought you had decided there was no other way out than the one he had found you—or rather the one he found at your expense. How could I stay and watch your father and Mr Rivers force you into marrying Diamantha? I had no money. There was nothing I could do to help you out of their trap but make it worse for you. I had to leave, don't you see? I loved you too much to stay at Holm Park and watch everything we'd dreamed about die.'

'An odd sort of love without any faith in the strength of your lover's feelings it must have been, then,' he condemned bleakly.

If she'd had even the faintest glimmer of hope left in her heart that he might one day forgive her for giving in to circumstances, even when he refused to do the same, it finally flickered and died.

'I thought nothing except that your marrying a rich wife could keep your father and the family from complete ruin. You know as well as I do how he was. He was so much worse after Aunt Hermoine died and there was nobody left who could keep him from the gaming tables and those wretched clubs of his. It seems to me the gentlemen there are so spoilt and bored with all the finest things their money and prestige can buy that they lack the sense and morals of ten year old children, let alone grown men.'

'I hope you're not expecting me to argue. My fellow earls seem to find me a deeply peculiar creature for refusing membership of those august temples to the finest ways in life a man can contrive to rid himself of his family, fortune and self-respect.'

'Then at least your family will know *you* never intend to drag them down the same path Uncle Hart seemed so determined to follow.'

'Is that yet another reason why you left Holm Park like a rat leaving the sinking ship, Sophie dear? I suppose you thought it wasn't worth the risk that you might find yourself wed to a fool ready to bet his wife and his children's future on the turn of a card, or the passage of a raindrop down the window pane? At last I'm finally beginning to be glad you left, since I might have found myself wed to a woman with no faith in my integrity or my determination to rule my own life. If you'd stayed, I wonder if you would have watched me for signs I was about to tumble into a state of drunken debauchery, where I cared not a snap of my fingers for those around me. If so, thank you for leaving when you did, my dear. It would be worse to marry such a wife than be incarcerated in the Fleet or the Marshalsea for debt.'

'You would have married me anyway? Despite the banns and the fact we couldn't afford to hire a carriage to elope to Gretna since we were both under age?'

'I would have found a way—fool that I was back then.'

'Uncle Hart and Mr Rivers would have caught us and brought us back home in disgrace. You would have had to marry Diamantha after suffering the indignity of being dragged back to Holm Park, and I would have had to watch them do it to you.'

'Is that why you went?'

'Yes—if you will have it in words with no frills left on. I could not endure the threat your father had made to force me to stand at his side and watch you marry Miss Rivers, while Mr Rivers stood at *your* side and made sure you went through with it. And that was in order to have my dowry restored to me, so I would become eligible enough to wed the man they had already picked out for me. I couldn't wed a man I'd never love for the pain of loving you and having to live without you—don't you see, Peter?'

'If I had my father in front of me now I think I might finally find it in myself to put a bullet in him after all,' Peter said, in a coldly furious undertone that made Sophie shiver at the hatred that had grown up between two men who had once had an easy relationship—before Aunt Hermoine died and Hartley Vane gave up on love and life.

'He was a weak man.' She excused the man who had once destroyed all her hopes and dreams as casually as others might swat a fly.

'Weak men inflict as much pain and suffering as wicked ones; of the two I think I would prefer to be wicked.'

'If your father had died before my aunt he'd have been mourned as a good man.'

'No, he would have died an untested man, with good intentions that soon failed. Don't excuse him, Sophie; I don't think I could endure it now I've found out exactly what he did to rescue himself from his own ridiculous folly. I never knew he had gambled away your money as well as everything else he could lay hands on by fair means or foul. How the hell did he manage to persuade your trustees to release capital to him like that? Of all the unsafe and untrustworthy men they could find to look after your future wellbeing, he carried off the palm.'

'I don't know, but somehow he did. It was lost in that wild scheme he invested in. Perhaps he really did hope to double or triple what my parents had managed to save from my mother's inheritance, and what little money Papa had managed to send me before he died to make a decent dowry. It was a small enough fortune in all conscience, so I suppose it would have made little difference in the long run.'

'You'll have it back threefold once I speak to my man of business,' he insisted.

'No, I won't have you put Dina's fortune at risk for the sake of a few hundred pounds that could be better spent elsewhere. I'm content here, and should I ever find myself in need of funds I promise to inform you. Please don't risk undermining the recovery of your estates and fortune for the sake of a dowry I shall never need.'

Which was true enough, Sophie thought uneasily, since if she did decide to wed Sir Gyffard for the sake of his daughters' future welfare, and perhaps even her own, she would have no need to provide such a wealthy man with a dowry—and she had little inclination to be an extravagant wife, or indeed any wife at all.

'What do you think I've been doing for the last eight years, my dear? Sitting on my hands and getting ready to follow in my father's shaky footsteps straight to Hades, perhaps?' he asked with a humourless smile.

'I truly have no idea,' she snapped, and pounded the dried herbs together into such a fine powder she then had to throw the dust into the fire and begin all over again before the infusion could be strained through the muslin she had ready for the task and not become a fine sludge poor Miss Willis would not be able to swallow.

The room was filled with the smell of crushed herbs for a moment before the flames flared and they were gone.

Counting to ten, Sophie carefully ignored her companion for long enough to measure it all out again meticulously and cautiously crush the dried leaves just enough for them to release their essential oils when the water was hot enough to extract all that was needed from them.

'Ready?' he managed to ask, as if they had been discussing the weather.

She nodded. 'I think the kettle is hot now. Please pour enough boiling water into that jug to half fill it for me,' she said politely, since she doubted *her* hand was steady enough to get the amount right, and it would affect the strength of her potion if she did not.

He frowned in concentration. Sophie found his intent focus on the task in hand almost painfully endearing as His Lordship the Earl of Sylbourne poured water into an earthenware jug as if his very life depended on it. 'Will that do?' he asked as he presented her with the steaming vessel.

'Perfectly, I thank you,' she said solemnly, and poured the hot water over the dried and roughly pounded herbs, then stirred until she was satisfied they were releasing their essence into the water. 'Now we must leave it to cool, then strain it and halve it, so there will be a dose for Miss Willis to take in the night should she awake after a while and still be restless.'

'I will sit with her. I won't have Aunt Hes wake up too soon and find it, then overdose herself by accident.'

'You have been lost in snow, endured a long and exhausting ride, and now you intend to stay up all night to prove you really are an idiot then, my lord?'

'Certainly not,' he said, sounding offended that she should even think he was less than invincible.

'Then go to bed. I have no mind to treat you for exhaustion—or to trouble Cox and the stable boys to come and carry you down one flight of stairs then up another because you've collapsed from it either. Once you've given your aunt half this mixture and got her to sleep I shall watch her until I'm sure she's in no danger. Since I wasn't out in the worst of the weather, as you two were, I expect you and Edwina to go to bed and sleep.'

'I look after my own,' he insisted dourly.

'A general must make sure he's fit for action so his troops don't mill about uselessly and lose a battle because he's pretending to be invincible.'

'Stubborn chit,' he accused her grumpily.

'Stupid man,' she countered, every bit as crossly.

'You're right,' he admitted very reluctantly. 'I hate the fact, but I still can't deny you're the best person for the task—even if I didn't feel as if I'd been beaten all over with sticks by your faithful cohorts before they brought me into the warmth and safety of this fine old house tonight.'

'I hate to break this painful fact to you, my lord, but you are only human.'

'Don't I know it?' he informed her irritably.

She met his eyes unwarily and something warmer than distrust and dislike lurked in the clear grey depths of them now.

'I feel far too human whenever I'm with you, Sophie.'

'Even now?' she whispered, with an incredulous glance

down at her grey clad form and a self-conscious pat at her still firmly tied spinster's cap.

'Always—despite the ridiculous disguise you seem to think will keep any self-respecting rake at a distance,' he said, with a wry twist of his sensual mouth that might have been a smile if she was another female. 'What it does is make you more intriguing, my dear, so I suggest you abandon it—lest I feel the need to unwrap those layers to see if Sophie Bonet is still hiding under them, despite your attempts to stifle her in stern grey bombazine.'

'She isn't,' Sophie made herself say bleakly, certain she'd left that silly little creature behind at Holm Park, when she'd left to be an independent woman.

'If you say so,' he replied, with a cool look that told her he didn't believe her.

'I never want to be that needy again. Please accept my word that Miss Bonet is no more and leave me alone, my lord.'

'No. Even if I had never loved that Sophie I wouldn't let you do this to yourself. You live your life through your pupils, cut yourself off from your friends and family and seem to think you're not subject to the grief and joys that's make up daily life for the rest of us.'

'Just because I don't wear my heart on my sleeve any more, don't assume I'm incapable of feeling,' she defended herself hotly—and then wished she hadn't when he smiled at her as if that was exactly the response he'd been after. 'You think you're so clever, don't you, Lord Sylbourne? Has it never occurred to you it might just be *you* I've no feelings for? And isn't it as well I'm not eating my heart out for a man who doesn't want me?'

'No, Sophie, oddly enough it's not at all acceptable to me that you might have forgotten all we ever were to each other,' he informed her brusquely, and fitted his mouth to hers in a kiss that might have taken place only seconds after the last time he had loved her. It was gentle, warm and seductive.

No! the barely healed part of her heart that remembered how it felt to be so open and vulnerable to him screamed protectively. *Don't let him do this to you again, Sophie Jeanne Rosalind Bonet. Remember the agony it cost you to part from him last time and push him away.*

Unfortunately the rest of her wasn't listening. If he'd seized and taken, instead of seducing and asking, she supposed hazily that sensible Sophie might have shouted loudly enough to drown out the Sophie who had loved this man to distraction. Instead his mouth teased, and this mature and tested Peter seemed to know exactly the right ways to seduce her wits away from her—which she supposed he did, since he had only to remember how they'd been together and she would be an open book to him...a very easy one to read.

'Ah, Sophie,' he murmured, as if he couldn't help himself.

Her lips parted to say something nonsensical, except he took advantage instead, and deepened their kiss. His tongue dipped between her teeth and played wickedly, until she moaned an incomprehensible something and felt her heartbeat race and her skin heat under his gentle touch, as if the fire inside her had only been waiting for him to fan it into an inferno all these years.

'Peter...' she gasped when he lifted his head long enough to pull in a much needed breath, 'I remember,' she said, without much connection between words and meaning, so dazed was she by the fact of him, here with her, after so many years apart, so much the same and yet so different.

Her eyes darkened as she gazed up at him and she felt the breath check in his powerful torso, as if he too felt the awe of this moment as well as the weight of heady memories. She raised her hand and gently smoothed his dark gold hair where she'd mussed it in memory of her wild young lover. The muscles in his lean cheeks worked as he reacted to her touch. It was as if they were enchanted by an indelible spell that made them always sensitive to each other, however little their minds might want them to be.

She could feel him drawing away from her even as he took in a heavy breath and clenched his hands in a brief, betraying gesture when they shook with the feeling and the fever of what they'd unleashed between them so recklessly.

'Aye, too well,' he agreed, and for a moment there was that old enchantment in his dear grey eyes after all. 'I've never hurt so much in my life—either before or since— as I did when I got home and found you gone, Sophie. So determinedly gone I finally realised you hadn't the least intention of coming back,' he told her. The truth of it was stark in his gaze as he went back into the past and used it to put distance enough between them to hold off any more hurt at her hands.

'I'm so sorry,' she murmured, suddenly full of regret for her lack of faith in both their loving and their love.

Part of her still insisted she'd done the right thing, trying to free him from the reckless promises they'd made each other—all that headlong loving they'd been too young to deal with—except perhaps they would have learned to temper it for the real world? she decided regretfully, and the awe of it woke her to what a fool she had been not to believe in him back then, and at least try and cling to love despite everything in their way. Life apart from him had been so dim and dull she felt as if she was only herself again now he was here—and it was eight years too late.

'I expect you are,' he said bleakly as he eased himself away from her.

She discovered he'd lifted her and sat her on the venerable oak table to even up the difference in their heights and make love to her more comfortably without her even noticing her feet were no longer on the ground—exactly as he'd used to do all the time to her dazed young self when they were so in love with each other.

'Much as I want you, I'm not prepared to live in a fool's paradise and then find myself pushed to the far edge of your careful little life again, Sophie. The second time I fall in love will be with someone who can love me back with all her heart—not the niggardly little bit of it you allowed me.'

'I did love you,' she assured him earnestly. 'I loved

you so much, Peter,' she told him, and cynical Miss Rose would have been jumping up and down in the corner if Sophie hadn't banished her to the attic long since.

'Not enough, Sophie,' he told her a little unsteadily.

'Maybe not,' she said, and felt tears sting. A great weight seemed to settle in her chest as she took in the very different life she might have led, if only distrust and self-sufficiency hadn't been written into her character as certainly as pride. 'I was wrong not to hang on to our love with every breath in my body,' she admitted at last, then shrugged as if to pretend the knowledge didn't cut into her like acid etching its way across her heart. 'I wish you all the luck we never had, and great joy with your second love, Peter Vane,' she managed to say.

She met his eyes with little more than a sting of tears in her own behind all the pride that still wouldn't let her break down and admit how little her life would always be without him.

'Then you're a better woman than I am a man, since I can't honestly wish you love or happiness with another man even now, Sophie Bonet,' he admitted, with a smile that seemed to have all the humour left out of it somehow.

'Don't worry—I don't think there will be either,' she muttered, so softly she had no intention of him hearing her.

But his senses were apparently at the almost superhuman level they had always been, since he picked up those unwary words and seized her by the shoulders to glare down at her as if he'd like to read through to her very soul and find out what was in it.

'There is some man, then?' he demanded hoarsely, as if she had struck him a heavy enough blow to knock the wind out of him. 'Who the hell is he?' he snarled.

It demanded she look at him, she supposed, because he thought the truth more likely to be clear in her eyes than it was upon her tongue.

'Not really,' she heard herself say weakly, and felt furious with herself for being so meek even with him. 'It really is none of your business anyway,' she told him, meeting that blazing look of his with what she hoped was cool composure.

'You'll always be my business until we're both cold in our graves,' he gritted between clenched teeth, as if she was sorely trying his temper on purpose.

'Not if you intend that second love of yours to be true and steady in return,' she told him, with as much dignity as she could summon when she had to bend her head back so far to look at him directly.

She wondered angrily why she'd ever fallen in love with a man so much taller than she was. Any fool could have told her it would give her a crick in the neck at the very least. Maybe the discomfort would distract her from the pain in her heart while she considered if he might be right in saying she would always be his, however many years they spent apart.

'You really think either of us can blithely live our lives with another and pretend not to know what we could have had together would have been so much more, Sophie?' he asked, as if discovering she was a new and not particularly pleasant form of life.

'I think we will have to,' she said, and wished that dratted pride of hers would let her look away.

'It sounds as if you intend to do so a lot sooner than I do,' he muttered grumpily.

She had to grasp her hands behind her back to stop herself reaching up to soothe the frown from between his brows or the grim line of his dear mouth. 'No, I don't really intend to wed anyone. It's just that I had a proposition to consider, and I have considered it and cannot accept.'

'A proposal?'

'More a proposition than a proposal,' she confirmed carelessly, and saw a blaze of fury in his eyes that made her step back in awe. 'Not *that* sort of proposition,' she assured him hastily.

'Good. I don't really want to end my life at Tyburn, dangling on the end of a silken rope after murdering the rogue for daring to make you one of those.'

'If you don't know by now that I'm quite capable of fighting off undesirable advances without some man lurking in the background to frighten off the wolves for me, Peter Vane, then you don't really know me at all.'

'Yes, I do—you're a fierce little thing and always have been. But you still don't acknowledge how big an advantage a man's strength gives him over a tiny slip of a creature like you.'

'What I lack in inches I make up for in vigour—as I'm sure you would recall, if you set your masculine mind to reasoning instead of reacting.'

'Aye, you were an unholy terror when you first came to Holm Park; that much I do remember. But a determined man can still overcome most women if he really sets his mind to it, and I can assure you, Sophie, you would be well worth an unscrupulous rake's worst attentions— even if he had to fight his way through all that wretched stuff,' he said, with an emphatic wave at her grey bombazine armour.

'You should know,' she told him impulsively, and watched the beast in him roar and then submit to the curb he exerted with an impressive self-control he'd not possessed in the old days.

Yes, this was a new Peter Vane—a stronger and more determined man than he'd promised to be even as a dazzling youth of not quite twenty. She wouldn't be able to prod and push this Peter in a direction he didn't already want to take.

He noted her involuntary step back at the sight of the potential temper in his eyes and gave her a very straight look. 'Don't think you can manage to bait me into forgetting what you have just said as you could once upon a time, Sophie. Who is he?'

'There is hardly even a "he" for us to talk about.'

'Who is he?' he asked implacably, and leant on the heavy oak door and folded his arms across his chest as if he had all day—or all night, which was even worse.

'My employer asked me to consider making a marriage of convenience with him before he left for Ireland.' She saw fury snarl and snap under his apparently impassive expression and held up her hand to stop something she didn't quite comprehend. 'He offered me a white marriage at first, if that makes you feel any better,' she said, with perhaps a little too much irony in her voice, since the flare of temper still burning in his eyes told her it hadn't helped very much at all.

'Since he has to be at least twice your age to have a grown son of five and twenty, no, it really doesn't help at all. What the devil were you thinking of even to consider such a May and December offer, Sophie?'

'Because he's right to have made it.'

'Right to offer you a travesty of a marriage? To ask you to chain yourself for life to a man who lacks even the basic sense to want you mercilessly in his bed if he's proposing to marry you? What's right about him thinking a hopeful young woman like you would even dream of accepting him when you might yet meet a man close to your own age and make a normal marriage with him? What sort of a man is this Sir Gyffard Frayne of yours that he'd dare even suggest such a fiasco to a fabulous creature like you?'

'An honourable one—a man who cares for his family before anything else and would see his daughters safe from the kind of situation I was placed in when Aunt Hermione died and your father decided he'd only ever promised to care for me to make his wife happy. Sir Gyffard is a good man who loved his wife deeply. It was my letting slip I would have liked children that made him consider a true marriage.'

'How very magnanimous of him,' Peter said insufferably, and leaned on his prop now with the look of a Bond Street Beau eyeing up the village idiot. 'What a terrible burden it would prove for such a man to have a young and lovely creature like you in his bed.'

'Yes, since he doesn't love me, or lust after me as you appear to believe he should, I think it probably *would* be a burden to him. Which is why I shall not accept his offer, although I should be telling him so and not you, my lord. He will find another way out of his difficulties when he returns home and we should not suit.'

'Those "difficulties" being Mrs Garret-Lowden and her too obedient daughter, I suppose?'

'It is not my business to discuss it,' she said defensively.

'But I can assume, can I not? If not for Sir Gyffard being so in love with his late wife you would have considered his offer more seriously, would you not?'

'Perhaps,' she lied.

'No perhaps about it. You want children and don't particularly care who sires them so long as it isn't me.'

'Of course not. That's a terrible distortion of what I said.'

'Prove it, then, Sophie. Marry me and let *me* give you those brats you evidently want so very badly, since you seem to have spoiled me for loving any other woman as I once loved you.'

'I could never marry you on such terms,' she said unsteadily, for to bear his children and share his bed, knowing he could never forgive her or let himself love her back, would be worse than knowing some other lucky female was his countess.

'Why not? It's exactly the sort of offer you seem to be considering nowadays.'

'Not for long—and only because I suddenly felt so stricken at the idea of never being part of a family in the truest sense of the word.'

'Then I see no difficulty in your accepting my proposal. After all, you would be very much a part of my family, since you would be providing me with most of it now there is only Dina and Aunt Hes left for me to glory in otherwise. Accept me, Sophie. Provide me with an heir and a few pretty daughters for us to give a more steady life than either of us ever had growing up, even when your aunt was alive and my father was almost happy for a time. One man is very much like another if all you need is a sire for your children, after all.'

'No, they're not. I won't live in such an unequal marriage, and I won't share a marriage of convenience—especially not with you, Peter.'

'You, of all people, are worried about the differences in social status between us?' he said and shook his head as if that was the last straw. He stood aside so she could leave whenever she chose to, almost as if he was weary of sharing the same air with her. 'Go to bed, Sophie. I will persuade Aunt Hes to drink half your potion and then drink the rest myself. Otherwise I'll find myself staring into the night for as long as we have one, wondering how on earth lovely, laughing little Sophie Bonet ever grew into such a hard, dry and humourless antidote as Miss Rose is proving to be. Go dream of your besotted baronet, Miss Rose, while I thank my stars for a lucky escape in those far-off days when you hadn't quite grown into your thorns.'

Taking a last look at his shuttered face and deliberately careless pose, she pulled her shawl a little closer about her body as a defence against the coldness that was way beyond the merely physical and gave him a tight little nod. Then she unlatched the door and left. Trailing up the stairs by the light of the well risen moon, she refused to go back and grab his candle because she might stop to rage and rant at him while she did so, and there was no point ruining the quietly dignified exit that had cost her so much effort.

This promised to be the coldest night she had ever experienced, and she dearly wished governesses merited having their fires banked to burn all night, when normally she would have been horrified at the notion of such unnecessary pampering.

CHAPTER EIGHT

PETER looked round the now almost warm stillroom without seeing much of it, and tried not to feel as if he'd lost the woman who had haunted his dreams these last eight years twice over. Evidently she had never truly been his to lose if she could consider marrying a man so much older to beget brats with him. His fists tightened until they were rock-hard and his knuckles stood out white against his tanned skin. He had to fight the urge to bring them down on the ancient and iron-hard oak table until the pain distracted him from this feeling of sick revulsion and the bellowed *No!* that was screaming through his very soul at the idea of her tying herself into a farce of a marriage.

'Fool,' he accused himself. 'Cursed, deluded, beef-brained idiot; how could you allow her to lead you round by the nose like this a second time?'

Shaking his head as even those soft, savage words echoed about the cooling chamber, whispering mockingly that he'd lost her all over again, he picked up the cooling jug full of honey-sweetened infusion. He took one last look round to make sure the fire was doused and everything safe before lighting a new candle from the one that was guttering and telling himself he'd been there far too long already.

Peter sighed at the idea his life would forever feel empty without even this cool and self-contained version of his warmly loving and passionate Sophie in it, and carefully followed in her cooling footsteps up the stairs, then along the branch of this rabbit warren that led to the bedchamber his aunt had been given, to deliver his burden before seeking sleep himself—courtesy of Miss Rose's skills in the stillroom.

'I thought Sophie's draught was never coming,' Edwina whispered as she tiptoed towards him with a rueful nod at their peacefully sleeping relative. 'Not that we appear to need any help getting Aunt Hes off to sleep now she's finally warm and in full possession of her senses again— thanks to our youthful hostess. Miss Frayne reassured her how welcome she is to stay here for the entire Christmas season if need be, then she sat and read her some rolling passage from Gibbon's history that was enough to put a regiment to sleep. Aunt Hes was lost in dreamland before she finished the first paragraph.'

'Yes, Miss Frayne is a delightful girl, and, yes, I like and admire her very much, and, no, I really don't think I'll be asking her to marry me if that's all right with you, sister dear? Does that answer the questions I sense wavering on the tip of your busy tongue, Dina?'

'Enough of them for tonight, I suppose. It's a pity,

though. Miss Frayne would make you a fine countess, and I think you'd be lucky to win her.'

'Very lucky indeed. But she deserves better than I could offer as her husband.'

'So you *are* still in love with Sophie Bonet,' she said.

He wished it wasn't a statement. He couldn't let it lie as if it might be true.

'No,' Peter argued, as coolly as he could contrive, when he wanted to shout that denial out loud to make it feel more real. 'But I once loved her so much the memory of it would prevent me being the passionately ardent husband Miss Frayne deserves to find herself one day, when she is a little older and knows a bit more about the world than she does now. For myself, I promise to make more of an effort to find a woman I can admire and hold in affection this coming season. Hopefully I can then marry her on that understanding, and we'll make ourselves a family together. I truly think I'm done with love, Dina.'

'And I truly think you're as great an idiot as you ever were, brother mine,' she told him with a sad, affectionate smile, then patted his cheek and shut the door in his face with a whispered, 'Goodnight, you darling great fool,' to speed him on his way.

'I wonder if Sophie would give me an antidote to loving unwisely and then brew another potion to make me forget I ever did so in the first place if I asked her nicely?' Peter muttered to himself as he cast a rueful look at his haunted eyes and wryly downturned mouth in the fine old mirror in his room, before downing half the soothing

mixture she'd made for his aunt and shrugging out of his
borrowed clothes.

Finally letting weariness slow his racing thoughts, he
felt vaguely ashamed of his murderous impulse towards
his absent host when he was taking advantage of his hospitality on so many fronts. It seemed wrong to want to
kill the owner of the coat he now made himself lay tenderly across the back of the chair in the dressing room.
Glad that at least the starched neckcloth about his throat
came from one of the sons of the house, and his evening
breeches belonged to an altogether more slender man than
Squire Frayne clearly was, Peter still pictured himself
punching Sir Gyffard satisfyingly on the chin before he
renounced the idea reluctantly.

If he went about hitting all the men who had the good
sense to want a female as young, pretty and full of potential fire as his Sophie, he'd soon pound his fists bloody
and find himself incarcerated in the local lock-up.

No, he had to forget his vengeful instincts towards his
unwitting host and accept life as it was. If he could come
up with a scheme to put the Frayne girls out of the reach
of the female shark Sir Gyffard's elder son seemed intent on saddling himself with as a mother-in-law, without having to wed Sophie himself as she wouldn't have
him, then he'd rack his brains for one while he waited to
be released from the heaven and hell of staying under the
same roof as Sophie Bonet.

Yes, when he was back in his right mind again he
would think of something other than the wicked fantasy
of tugging a deliciously passionate and wildly responsive

Sophie into this wide old bed with him and shutting the bed curtains on the world until it went away.

He sank against the bank of down-filled pillows with a weary sigh and waited for it to feel as warm and as comfortable as it should be when it had been so meticulously aired and warmed. Pity that the lack of Sophie in it made him feel as if it was stuffed with discarded horseshoes rather than feathers, he decided sleepily, and then he felt the dual effects of Sophie's mild soporific and his strenuous trek through a blizzard overtake him at last and sank into dreams. There he felt truly warm and content at last as he curled protectively, possessively, about Sophie's fine-boned and temporarily sated form, with the silky feel of her heavy dark hair and the unique scent of her in his nostrils as he held her to him as if he would never let her go. Dared never let her go now he'd found her again.

'Oh, Rosie, you don't mind if I come and talk for a few moments, do you?' Imogen asked, after knocking on her door when she heard Sophie return to her room.

How could she refuse to answer when Imogen was unlikely to sleep without some reassurance that she was doing a fine job of welcoming strangers into her father's house in his absence?

'I really can't think how on earth we're going to keep everyone happy until the roads are passable and they can all go home, can you? How long do you think they might be forced to stay?' Imogen whispered anxiously as soon as Sophie opened the door to her.

'Come on in, do, my dear; it really would be too bad

of us to wake the girls now they're settled at long last,' Sophie replied, and did her best to smile reassuringly at her young friend as she went back to brushing her long hair as if nothing untoward had happened down in the stillroom with Peter. It had, though, and she felt her hand shake even as she did her best to look as unruffled as a plaster saint.

Imogen slipped off her light slippers and dived under the covers of Sophie's bed to keep warm. It seemed as if she'd managed to convince her all was well with her former governess, even if Sophie wasn't as certain herself.

'And I suppose the answer to your last question is that it depends on the weather and is thus beyond our control.'

'Cordage says the snowfall is not over yet, and that if it were only Lord Sylbourne and his sister to consider we would get along merrily enough over Christmas and hardly notice they hadn't been invited for the season in the first place.'

'I think I might,' Sophie argued faintly, but luckily Imogen was too wrapped up in her own concerns to hear the strain in her voice as she forged on with her own concerns.

'It's Mrs Garret-Lowden, Livia and that awful Mr Wroxley who're sure to make life difficult for us all,' Imogen said, with a fierce frown at the counterpane on Sophie's bed that was now stretched over her steepled knees as she hugged them, looking more like the schoolgirl she'd been so recently than the self-possessed young hostess of earlier tonight. 'However shall we contrive to amuse people who so clearly don't want to be amused, Miss Rose?'

'Have you considered that not being amused could be their favourite form of entertainment?' Sophie suggested wryly. 'Although I suppose we will just have to rely on Christmas itself to keep them occupied, if not actually pleased with life. Anyone who refuses to even try and be happy at this time of year is clearly living in the wrong country and ought to take up residence in one that doesn't celebrate the birth of Jesus. Even your most awkward guests must at least pretend to be happy at such a joyous time, don't you think? It would never do for them to appear un-Christian. We shall have to rely on appearances to guide our guests through tomorrow and then onward to Christmas Day itself with the odd smile or two on their faces. Meanwhile we will have to hope a thaw sets in, so they may all leave on St Stephen's Day and we need worry no more about their state of mind.'

'At least if that happens sooner rather than later we needn't care about Mr Wroxley's amusement or lack of it. But I can't help but wonder if the Garret-Lowdens intend to stay until the Last Trump,' Imogen confided gloomily. 'Do you think Mrs Garret-Lowden could have designs upon Papa, Miss Rose?'

Sophie thought it very likely indeed, but could hardly say so. While Imogen might be embarrassingly determined to marry Sophie off to any personable gentleman of her acquaintance, she doubted Sir Gyffard was on her list. She could only hope she never learned of his offer.

'I don't know, Imogen. We mustn't speculate on the

hopes and aspirations of a guest under your roof in such a gossiping fashion.'

'Maybe not. But going about a little in society, as I have been doing of late, and meeting ladies like Mrs Garret-Lowden, has made me realise Papa is quite a catch. Until I began to put up my hair and attend quiet country parties he was just Papa. Now I realise he's Sir Gyffard Frayne, and quite a desirable *parti*, as far as widowed ladies in less than comfortable circumstances like Mama Garret-Lowden are concerned.'

'Don't call her so, Imogen, it's neither kind nor lady-like.'

'Never mind correcting my manners, Rosie dear. If you can't be confident I won't disgrace your teachings in public by now you might as well give up being a governess and look about you for a husband of your own instead,' Imogen teased.

Sophie was too tired and too confused by Peter's arrival and Sir Gyffard's offer to pass it off as too ridiculous to be worth arguing about as she usually did. 'I'm not eighteen years old, nor a young lady of good family and excellent prospects, Imogen,' she said wearily.

She recalled wistfully how heady it had felt to be a year less than eighteen and on the brink of such promise of love, life and laughter with Peter. It had seemed more like a natural disaster than a broken love affair when it all ended in heartbreak and lost dreams.

'Maybe not, but you *are* a very pretty, youngish lady of five and twenty who refuses to look about her for a more secure position in life whilst she's still young enough to enjoy it. Whatever you say about family connections and knowing little of each other nowadays, Lord Sylbourne watched you very closely all evening, Rosie. Every time he thought nobody was looking at him his eyes followed you as if he couldn't help watching your every move.'

'Nonsense. His Lordship is a gentleman of considerable address and doubtless has a good deal of experience of the world; he may look as high as he likes for a bride. If he's conscious of my existence at all it must be as a curiosity.'

'I don't think he regards you as a novelty,' Imogen insisted stubbornly.

No, he knows far too much about me for that, Sophie thought uneasily, and pretended to watch herself serenely in the square of mirror above the fireplace as she carried on brushing her long sable hair even more thoroughly than usual.

'No, because I doubt he regards me as anything at all,' she insisted, in the teeth of all the evidence, and evaded her own dark eyes in that mirror in case she should read too much in them.

Peter disliked her, and after tonight's arguments and revelations he might even hate her, but he clearly wasn't as coldly detached from all they had been to each other as he'd like to be.

'Well, he seems like a very acute and perceptive gentleman to me, so I daresay he managed to see through all that awful bombazine, screwed-up hair and your awful fright of a cap to realise you're nowhere near the frumpy old maid you were doing your best to appear tonight.'

'I really hope not,' Sophie lied, almost convincingly.

But the unwanted memory of that hurried kiss in the dark hallway, and then their much more intense and bittersweet embrace just now, intruded on her and made her wonder if she was lying to herself on more than one count.

It would have been better, with hindsight, if she'd dressed in her usual quiet style and brazened out the evening as a lady with some small pretensions to looks and breeding even if she was forced to hire herself out as a governess. By guying herself up so absurdly she had probably achieved the opposite effect from the one she'd intended and made herself singular rather than inconspicuous.

Next time she had to endure such an ordeal she'd make sure she was serenely unaffected by Peter's unexpected presence in her employer's house. Maybe then he would accept that she'd made a comfortable enough life apart from him and leave her alone for the remainder of his time at Heartsease Hall. The very idea of many more days like this one made her wonder if she might not put herself out in the snow to fend for herself before Mrs Garret-Lowden insisted on doing so instead.

'Why *did* you dress in your worst and pretend to be such a quiz all evening, Miss Rose?' Imogen asked inconveniently, and she watched Sophie with earnest and much too innocent blue eyes.

'To add to your dignity as daughter of the house, of course.' She was uneasy under that steady scrutiny.

'I think it was because Lord Sylbourne disturbs you; he is a most decided and vital gentleman, is he not?'

'Almost a stern one nowadays,' Sophie admitted ruefully.

'Except when he laughs, and when he was teasing Audrey and Vi he seemed quite ready to do so, don't you think?' Imogen said thoughtfully.

'Perhaps he has children of his own from a previous marriage,' Sophie said unwarily, then heard the wistful note in her voice.

'Lady Edwina did not say so, and I doubt they could be anywhere near my little sisters' ages, for he cannot be more than thirty or so.'

'He is seven and twenty,' Sophie corrected impulsively, then gave a wry grimace as she realised how badly she'd given herself away this time. 'His birthday is in June,' she added flatly.

'You know Lord Sylbourne and his sister very well indeed, do you not, Miss Rose?' her merciless interrogator insisted ruthlessly. 'You must have been intimately acquainted with them at one time to remember his birth date so readily, despite managing to pretend you're only distantly connected through marriage when Lady Edwina let even that secret drop unwarily.'

'Details of the Vane family's births, deaths and marriages are listed in the Peerage for anyone to look up.'

'And you expect me to believe you make a habit of slavishly studying it as light bedtime reading, I suppose?'

'No, I doubt you'll allow me that much privacy.'

'Nor should you be allowed it when you have evidently been keeping some very deep secrets indeed from us Fraynes all these years, Miss Rose; I'm deeply shocked.'

'No, you're not; you're thrilled to have tripped me up in a stretching of the truth, even if it wasn't a downright lie.'

'Perfectly natural in a poor deceived innocent such as I find myself to be,' Imogen declared, with a display of something uncomfortably close to her late mother's dramatic talent.

'We don't live in a melodrama, Imogen, and kindly remember how difficult you have always found it to draw me into your theatricals.'

'You have clearly been living out a drama of your own for years, and I scent a mystery, Rosie. You know how much I love having one of those to solve.'

'There's nothing sensational for you to find out about me. I'm a very ordinary and boringly respectable creature who happens to have been acquainted with the Vane family in my youth and that's all,' Sophie lied uneasily.

'And they happen to be one of the most powerful and respected families in the land, yet you don't declare the relationship openly? With such friends you could be more gainfully employed, or even very respectably wed by now—couldn't you, Rosie?'

'No, because we are no longer on such terms,' Sophie forced herself to admit. Though it should be quite obvious to any but the most self-absorbed or indifferent observer that there was no warmth in the relationship any more, shouldn't it?

'Even more intriguing,' Imogen replied implacably.

'No, my dear, only deeply uncomfortable, I'm afraid,' Sophie said stiffly. And it *was* downright painful to know

Peter and Edwina Vane would probably sleep uneasily under this roof tonight because she shared it with them.

'Well, it was perfectly obvious to me you knew Lord Sylbourne as soon as you came upon him in the snow. You were so taken aback to find him struggling against the elements alone out there. Even having to watch you both through a snowstorm, since you forbade me to go with you, I thought you were about to faint at the sight of him and might have to be rescued as well, Rosie. I never actually saw anyone visibly shocked before. It really is a blessing that for once Mrs Garret-Lowden was too wrapped up in dressing grandly for the evening in order to depress our pretensions to watch you like a hawk, because even *she* would have known Lord Sylbourne wasn't a stranger to you.'

'Sometimes I can't help wishing you were back in the schoolroom, young lady, so I could administer a scold for your impudence.' Sophie did her best to speak sternly, but knew it was a poor effort even before Imogen grinned unrepentantly, so she went back to brushing her hair unnecessarily and cravenly avoided Imogen's too-acute gaze while she did so.

'As I have told you before, you really should have more faith in your own teaching, Rosie. You must know I would never dream of saying such things to anyone else but you.'

'I'm not quite sure if I ought to be glad or sorry you say them to me.'

'Oh, I think you ought to be pleased that I know you won't repeat every word I say to the nearest receptive listener, as my little sisters might, or reproach me for being light-minded, as Aunt Matilda does every time I open my mouth in front of her.'

'Clearly I have not been stern enough with you, miss, but I fully intend to be so now. It's high time we were both in bed and fast asleep. We have a very long day ahead of us tomorrow, and all the excitement of Christmas Eve to weather as well as everything else. I don't like to turn you out when you're obviously so comfortable in my bed, Imogen dear, but I want that bed rather badly myself now, and would prefer you weren't in it,' Sophie declared as she finished plaiting her long dark hair in preparation for what she was quite certain would be a restless night.

'Very well, then, but you can't put me off for ever, Miss Rose,' Imogen told her smartly, and reluctantly re-moved herself from the warmth of Sophie's bed so she could dash downstairs to her own. 'I hope you sleep well, Rosie, despite what ought to be your uneasy conscience about deceiving us so shamelessly all these years,' she said, blowing Sophie a kiss farewell before scurrying off to her own bedchamber and the sleep of the innocent.

CHAPTER NINE

SOPHIE slept eventually, but her dreams were nowhere near as innocent and untroubled as Imogen's must be. She tossed and turned for a time, struggling to come to terms with how her life was with Peter back in it. Trying to calm herself for sleep, she did her best not to think about him. But it was like telling water to flow uphill, or the sun not to shine, so she finally let herself remember instead.

It had really begun the day he'd returned from his first year at Oxford, grown tall, sophisticated and as exquisitely dressed as any fashionable buck she'd laid eyes on when Aunt Hermione had still been alive and she and Uncle Hart had given delightful summer parties for their London friends. Until then Peter had been an awesome but distant figure in her life.

Three years her senior, he had been far too mature to have much to do with a harum-scarum dab of a girl with pigtails and a restless desire to be involved in everything girls shouldn't do. She had tagged along when he rode out with his friends, sneaked away from her lessons to watch them fence and box, and had always given herself away somehow, by wriggling at the wrong moment to get a better view or once, she recalled with a rueful smile, falling out of the tree she'd climbed to study them learning the so-called noble art of fisticuffs in enough detail to remember how to practise it herself.

Then he'd left Eton and gone on to university and come home a man—or at least they'd both thought so at the time. She recalled him in those absurdly high shirt points and fanciful neckcloths he'd favoured back then, although his rather theatrically cut coats certainly hadn't needed the buckram and padding some of his narrower-chested contemporaries had had to resort to. As for his waistcoats, she remembered with a tenderness that ought to worry her, they had been exuberant poems to the silk-weaver's art.

Since she had hardly had time to note his travelling clothes today, she shouldn't be quite so well acquainted with his mature style as she was, but as she considered the soberness of his collars now, the plain elegance of the knot he used to tie his neckcloths and the austerity of his stuff waistcoat she knew how young he'd really been back then. Lord Sylbourne would probably wince at the suggestion he'd once been a dandy, but she recalled being as dazzled by the new Peter Vane as he'd clearly been by his own splendour at the time.

So, at sixteen to his nineteen, she'd fallen head over heels in love with a splendid young lord, and he'd continued to be almost as oblivious to her as he'd been the previous year, or any of the other years since Sophie had come to live at Holm Park. He hadn't been *quite* as unmindful of her, since she hadn't let him ignore her—although he'd clearly wanted to. That summer she had sighed artistically over him at every turn, drifting about Holm Park's increasingly dilapidated rooms in what she had imagined was romantic disarray, putting up her hair and doing her best to refashion Aunt Hermione's most spectacular gowns to fit her own much shorter, slimmer and largely undeveloped figure. He had looked at her whenever he hadn't been able to avoid doing so with scornful irony, and gone on with his life as if she was a part of it he would prefer to forget if only she would let him.

Sophie had furtively watched him ride away at the end of summer from the schoolroom window and realised it was high time she grew up. Used to running wild about Holm Park without a governess, or any interested adult to tell her to mind her lessons, she had realised at last she was behaving like a would-be gothic heroine, dramatising her own passions and dreams until they became reality—if only to her. She had decided that day that Aunt Hermione would be ashamed of her niece if she could see her drifting about Holm Park like some childish tragedienne. Her skewed and silly view of herself as centre of her own melodrama made her a figure of fun, and it clearly had to change. So she had enlisted the help of the local ladies by asking for it sincerely, instead of glaring at them and running away, and had learnt slowly and painfully to be a lady.

It had made her a lot more popular, and had led to her introduction into the grown-up world—despite Uncle Hart's increasing poverty and uninterest. The local vicar's daughter, a kindly and practical young woman Sophie had learnt much from, had helped her remake some of Aunt Hermione's quieter gowns properly, and had taught her the value of self-discipline more by example than through nagging her to mend her wild ways. Sophie wished she could have stayed in contact with her.

The next time Peter had set eyes on his late stepmother's inconvenient niece, he had been visibly startled at the change in her. That time he had stared incredulously and then looked again to make sure he hadn't imagined it. She had smiled and secretly preened herself at the look in his grey eyes as they dwelt on her neat cambric gown and smooth and restrained dark locks. It had been as if he couldn't get over the differences in her.

It wasn't even as if she had made all those changes because she *wanted* him to look at her with admiration hot in his youthful gaze, she had told herself. She'd done it because she'd suddenly realised she had to grow up. Uncle Hart had been whistling the family fortune down the wind, and it had become clear she was nothing but an encumbrance to him. There would be no brilliantly hectic season followed by a suitable marriage for her. Perhaps she reminded Uncle Hart too painfully of the second wife he'd lost.

Any future she had to look forward to must be of her own making, and until Peter had come home with his splendid coats grown a little shabby, and his shirt points showing signs of much washing and ironing, Sophie had told herself she would be happy in a good enough marriage. She would contribute birth, connections and a pretty enough face, her logic went, and her husband would provide wealth for them both to live contentedly and the stability she had lost when her father died.

And then Peter had come home with a glint of masculine admiration and something a little hotter and less familiar in his suddenly intent gaze, and common sense had flown out of the window as if the last hard twelve-month of teaching herself to be a lady had never been. Even then he must have known things were going very wrong at Holm Park, she decided now, as she lay in her governess's bed in her neat little room and let the past overwhelm her for once. Uncle Hart must have cut Peter's allowance for such a brilliant young beau to still be wearing the same coats and slightly yellowing linen he had the year before, and she could just imagine how humiliating proud young Peter Vane, Viscount Deerborne, must have found such outward signs of poverty.

Still, he'd looked magnificent to *her* as she had stared back at him, noticing the new maturity of his harder features and finding him even more manly and exactly as he ought to be than ever. She'd fought it for all of a day, that rush of infinite possibilities waiting to be seized and explored. As Dina had excitedly run downstairs and swooped on her brother with wild whoops of joy he'd returned with a gruff hug, she had made herself stand by with an indulgent smile and pretend she didn't want to be in his arms far more urgently.

'Why have you come home so soon, Peter?'

Edwina had asked the question Sophie wouldn't let herself say in case he thought she cared passionately what he did and how long he was to be there for.

'You can ask me that, brat, when you know perfectly well it's my birthday next week?' he'd chided, with a smile that hadn't quite convinced Sophie, even if Dina had seemed perfectly happy with his explanation.

Of course his father had sent for him, Sophie reflected now with something like hatred in her heart for the weak man who had ruined his son's future as lightly as he had turned the next card. A hasty marriage of his son and heir to an heiress of vast fortune got from slavery and cotton mills had been supposed to mend the Vane fortunes and give Hartley Vane more credit at the gaming tables. Yet apparently that wedding had never taken place—and what on earth had Uncle Hart done to keep himself out of the nearest clink after that?

Deciding she would never sleep if she lingered on her then guardian's many sins and omissions, Sophie wriggled restlessly against her feather mattress and shifted on the usually cool linen pillowcases. How on earth she was to sleep after such an upheaval in her life was a puzzle to her, despite her heavy eyes and weary limbs.

In the week it had taken Hartley Vane to tear himself away from the green baize tables and his current mistress Sophie and Peter had tumbled into love and loved headlong and fervently, as if they'd somehow known it was all the time they would have. After all her plotting and scheming for some sort of future for herself based on good sense and logic, Sophie had abandoned practical common sense and embraced madness. Oh, how she'd loved that young and urgent Peter Vane; loved her fate, her stars, her everything, as she'd whispered in his ear that night in the arbour down by the neglected and overgrown lake at Holm Park and the nightingales had sung both literally and figuratively for them.

Suddenly she plunged into her memories and was back there, vibrantly responsive and way beyond any notion that she should hold back in the face of such magic. He'd lain with her supine on top of him after they had made fiery, driven love, having been out of one another's arms for a whole three hours while they had dinner with Edwina and allowed a very little space for propriety. The cushions and quilts they'd brought down there over the last heady days to cover the creaking old daybed had formed themselves to their bodies, and for a moment their passion had seemed spent as he'd let his breath slow at last and drawn her back against his lithe, bare torso.

Sophie had sighed with total contentment and gloried in the feel of the lightly dusted masculine curls under her naked shoulders, feeling him stroke her thick dark locks into something approaching order against her scalp. His very touch through the heavy weight of her hair had made her tingle and fizz with love and life. She'd sighed with the joy and tenderness of it all and snuggled a little more surely against him, murmuring something unreadable and wordless only he had been able to interpret as luxuriant satisfaction and a sensual question.

'Yes, soon,' he'd told her, his touch teasing and light as he'd moved on from adoring the feel of her long silken hair alone to laying locks of it over her bare skin and admiring the feel of both under his gentle, not all that soothing touch.

He'd moved her a little, so he could admire the sight of her sprawled back against him as the moon shifted and picked them out between gaps in their rosy canopy. Her svelte curves and slender lines against his more angular and muscled thighs, hips and chest had felt so different from the way they had last week—before he'd come home and loved her. She felt as if she'd learnt the deepest secrets of what it was to be a woman and he had become her man—the only man—whilst she did so. There was no inequality of one being more in thrall than the other. They had been as they were born to be: in love, full of love and very bound up in loving each other.

Then his almost idle touch had changed and intensified. He had reached for her high breasts and cupped them in his hands with a purely masculine grunt of approval. 'Like ripe little peaches, just ready to pick,' he'd murmured in her receptive ear, and she had pretended to bat him with a hand that had felt almost too heavy with sensual longing. He wriggled his long, sensitive fingers a little higher and tweaked the eagerly proud nipples into even more tight arousal than she'd thought they were capable of, well loved and eagerly tended as they had already been that night and every night since he'd come home.

Somewhere a sneaky little voice of caution had chided her that she shouldn't have fallen so eagerly into his arms at the first sign he might return her passionate curiosity about how rightly they might fit together, but she'd moaned a protest and slammed the door on sensible

Sophie. He'd taken it as a sign he'd been too rough, and had gentled his touch until his finger pads on her hot and shameless nipples had been little more than a sensual whisper. Those burning, impudent little peaks of sensation had given her away every time she'd tried to pretend he might want her more than she did him.

And it had only ever been a pretence, she recalled now, as her cheeks heated and her breath quickened just from the memory of how it had been between them when everything had seemed right and possible. Then, she had felt the quickening of his loins under her, giving away how acutely he wanted her, just as her wanton nipples and the fiery desire between her thighs had refused to by coy about her need of him, and soon they had loved as if it was for the last and best time once again.

'Peter,' she had murmured thickly, with a mouth that had wanted to kiss and rouse and tease far more than it wanted to speak.

'Princess Sophie,' he'd replied, his voice lingering over each syllable as if he would love even that insubstantial part of her.

'Touch me there,' she'd demanded, as huskily as some exotic Cleopatra who expected the most extreme physical satisfaction from her lover as her royal right.

'Here?' he'd teased, stroking an appreciative hand down her flanks to smooth the lovely line of them, then back up to the slender waist he'd found in the last few days. It had been tiny enough for him to span it with his long-fingered hands and lift her up to kiss him from above as she laughingly told him that at last she'd found a way to look down on him for a change.

'You know where,' she'd chided, and had writhed back against his rigidly demanding manhood and parted her hips to invite him to find out for himself how warm and eager a welcome awaited him there.

Instead he'd somehow summoned up the iron will to override his need and smooth that teasing hand up to her intent, rather cross face, exploring it with his index finger as if he hadn't already catalogued it in every way she'd thought possible this week—and even in one or two ways that would not have occurred to her if he'd never shown her how sweet novelty could be. Catching a huge breath of wonder and want and demand into her labouring lungs, she had told herself she could resist the drive and urge to completion if he could. She'd let her breath out and told her senses to wander, to capture what he was weaving for them against her skin.

Yes, it was there, and it had felt as if it always would be so—the feather-light touch of his one sensitive finger padding against her lips, so full and kissed and slick with need of him. Heat and a kind of warm, slow shiver of absolute desire had followed his fascinated digit over her skin, outlining her chin, drawing a picture in the shadows of her rather firm jawline for them both, until she'd laughed breathlessly at his implied mockery of its latent determination. Then he was air-inscribing an invisible code against her satiny sensitive cheek, letting his finger wander into the intriguing curlicues of one ear. Afterwards he had done the same all over again on the

other side, until he'd reached the opposite ear and confirmed for them both how sensual and arousing a lover's
touch there could be.

Sophie heard herself whimper even now at the memory
of his touch on so everyday an item as her ear, and was
suddenly almost as hot with embarrassment as she had
been hot then with passion and heady, about-to-be satisfied desire for her lover. Deciding there was little point in
fighting the spell of that long-ago love when all she had in
her future was an empty bed and a body that would only
get her from place to place with as little fuss as possible
now she couldn't have him, she gave herself the night off
from reality and tumbled back into what had once been.

'Peter!' she'd demanded then, as his gentle, relentless
exploration had continued to the back of her neck and
teased her tender nape, just under the hairline, where
the finest hairs on her head stood on end at attention for
him. And her voice had been so husky and wanting she'd
hardly known it herself, but he'd heard all there was for
him in it and had run that teasing finger back to her neck,
soothing it for a brief moment before playing over her
mouth with such eager fascination she'd gone beyond patience and grabbed his finger with pearly little teeth and
emphatically insisted on more.

And she'd got it, she recalled now, helpless under the
spell of that long ago banquet of the senses, that feast
of true love he'd served up for her on their last night together—even if they hadn't known it was all they would
ever have back then. *Good,* a feral voice insisted in her
head. If they'd known it was to be the end they would

have been so sad, so lost in the misery of parting, that the joy and hope and sheer exultation of loving so completely would have been lost to them.

Instead of flipping her over and plunging into her as he had the other night, after he'd chastely bade her goodnight in front of his little sister and the few remaining servants who'd stayed at Holm Park, then climbed up the ivy to her bedchamber as soon as everyone else was asleep, he had urged her to flip over and then spread his arms invitingly, lying lazily prone and not at all passively rampant.

'Take me, my wild love, I'm all yours,' he'd invited with a wicked smile.

For a moment she had knelt above him, with the moonlight caressing first one part of her shamelessly bare body then another as she shifted speculatively, as if judging which way she could best drive him mad with needing her. His smile had become a little less triumphant and his eyes had almost pleaded with her as the silence stretched and she had enjoyed every second of having such a vigorous and driven young lover at her mercy. Then she'd taken one more longing look at his masculine perfection and want had undone her. She'd smoothed her own teasing line along narrow hipbones and lithely long legs, then swooped, trailing her silken locks, still warm from his touch, over his straining manhood and then following with an exploring index finger. She had allowed one swift luxury of touch over his mightily aroused member, then laughed joyously as it seemed to twitch with his powerful need of her and even grow a little more rampant under her fascinated gaze.

'See what you do to me?' he'd said huskily, in a voice that had sounded as if all the gentlemanliness had been sieved out of him so only pure essence of Peter Vane remained, stripped as naked and undefended as was Sophie Jeanne Rosalind Bonet. 'Give me yourself,' he had demanded on the coat-tails of all that humility, revealing he could never leave himself completely behind—even in her. Nor would she have wanted him to.

With a hasty wiggle, intending to do just that, she'd knelt up with her knees either side of his narrow pelvis, leaning forward to take his mouth in a passionate kiss even as she eased his desperate sex into her own and sank down on it until he was fully engaged and she was full of wonder—and Peter Vane. The luxury of his tongue in her mouth, his manhood in her, her heart and body fully open and yielding even as she took, had made her moan with the sharp arousal of everything she was and that she now knew had been so rare.

Miss Rose wriggled protestingly in her lonely bed and told herself she should be thankful she'd been privileged to feel such love and heat and satisfaction even once in her life, without wishing she could go downstairs now, find her way across to the old wing of Heartsease Hall and somehow coax and seduce and plead with Peter to do it all again.

No. She had had *then*; there was little hope of *now* when Peter was so aloof and sceptical he might never have been the wild young lover who had fought off the merciless goad of his own passion to see hers satisfied extravagantly first. Again she was back with her young lover, learning the novelty of riding their mad dance to its wild, wide, joyful conclusion on *her* terms. She'd felt him cup her buttocks as she'd strained to catch the full, strong rhythm of lovers and had smiled against his desperate mouth in welcome and satisfaction as she'd finally got the way of it and had risen and fallen on his rigidly straining member.

For the first time she had been in control of the slip and friction and drive of their lovemaking, and she'd savoured each rise and fall and added the occasional provoking squeeze of inner muscles that flexed and loved and revelled in his potent manhood inside her wildly pleasured femininity. It couldn't go on at such intensity. Nothing could last long at that pitch of heat and fervour. And at last she'd felt the huge power of their mutual climax and spun into the infinite space that they always seemed to explore together at the end of their intense enjoyment of each others' bodies.

She'd convulsed into ecstasy with her eyes wide open, to share it with him, and he'd striven under her, clasping her lithe hips with his big hands as he held her in the mutual rhythm of life. Her long, sharp moan of ultimate pleasure had blended itself with his unrestrained shout of triumph and she'd bucked with the delicious spasms of her own climax, feeling his whole body clench with the wondrous power between them as he poured himself into her and she into him.

Lying sated across his mighty torso, the other way up this time, she had watched his dear grey eyes melt into silver by the light of the setting moon and felt everything she could ever want out of life was there, inside her still, under her, around her and forever with her.

'I love you,' she'd whispered, with all the intensity she'd had in her in that infinitely intense moment. 'I love you, Peter Adam George Fitzroy Vane, and I will never love anyone else as long as I live.'

He'd run a lazy, contented hand down her still heaving torso, sent the other one to pull her even closer and smooth down her back and along the column of her spine, finally grasping her nape and pulling her close, nestling her head into his neck where she could count his racing pulse.

'Always and for ever,' he'd vowed into her receptive ear as she'd naughtily slicked that pulse at the base of his too tempting throat with her neat little tongue. 'I will always love you, Sophie Jeanne Rosalind Bonet soon-to-be-Vane—until the day I die and beyond it there will be no love for me but you.'

She had sighed her absolute satisfaction at that sensible conclusion and dreamily murmured something idiotic he'd seemed to understand perfectly well, then gone to sleep in his arms.

Sophie shook her head against the lonely night now, and sighed for the fragility and preciousness of that wondrous time when the night had hardly darkened the sky at all in high midsummer. At least they'd had that last day together, his twentieth birthday, before it had all ended and the nightingales had sung no more for Miss Rose. Now even the scent of summer roses in full reckless bloom carried such a weight of sadness she could barely tolerate the task of gathering petals for pot-pourris in the garden, beloved though that scent had been of the woman who had taken her in when Sophie had come to Heartsease Hall so destroyed by losing love that she hadn't cared one way or another if she lived or died.

As the long ago, impossibly young Sophie and Peter had wandered home in the dawn light they had been absorbed in each other and as careless of the rest of the world as all young lovers should be. Lost in the sharp joys of loving, of mutually wanting and being one with the only being on earth they could ever possibly want like this, they'd been frighteningly oblivious to what was to come. So lost in watching the play of tenderness for her on Peter's beloved face as they'd walked arm in arm through the wild and untended gardens of Holm Park, how could Sophie have known that Hartley Vane, Lord Sylbourne, had come home with the dawn as well, and stood watching them from his vantage point?

Apparently he'd been almost rigid with fury as he'd stood within the generous range of windows that lit the lord's bedchamber and cursed the day he'd ever set eyes on his late wife's half-French, pitilessly orphaned niece rescued from the Terror following the French Revolution. Once he'd recklessly promised Lady Hermione Arcourt he would take the brat in and raise her as his own if only she would marry him, and *this* was how the little whore repaid him.

The Fifth Earl of Sylbourne had successfully broken those two young lovers apart, although both of them had thought it impossible. If he'd still been alive he might still curse her for ruining his plans, since Peter must have refused his father's ingenious solution to all his woes. The Hartley Vane she could first remember might even have felt a pang of pity for the hopeful, reckless girl she'd been when she had loved his son so impulsively and fiercely if he could have seen self-contained Miss Rose finally fall into an exhausted sleep with a trail of hot tears still soaking the pillowcase.

'Good morning,' Sophie offered softly as she did her best to slip into the breakfast room without attracting notice next morning. She sighed wistfully and knew she should have known better as a circle of interested faces looked up from their various plates to eye the tardy governess.

'Good morning, Miss Rose,' Lady Edwina greeted her, with an ironic smile.

'Miss Rose,' Peter observed, with a frown for her shadowed eyes and pale face—as well he might, Sophie decided militantly, since *he* was responsible for putting them there.

'It's snowing again, Miss Rose. Perhaps we'll be marooned here for days and days and have to eat Mr Wroxley,' Audrey exclaimed happily, and bounced out of her seat excitedly to check on the weather once again.

'Well, really, Audrey…' Sophie began, only to be overridden by Peter's frown, which made very clear he thought poorly of the governess's scold she was about to administer to her lively charge. How did he think Audrey and her sisters had survived what he clearly thought crushing care with that sunny disregard for her authority fully intact? Sophie wondered wrathfully.

'There's not enough meat on him,' Peter pointed out laconically.

'True. Then we'll just have to put up with him and starve, I suppose,' Audrey said, with the cheerfulness of a child who had never been truly hungry in her life.

'I very much doubt it when the household is all but ready for Christmas, Miss Impudence—and don't let Cook hear you casting aspersions on her ability to feed a small town at the briefest of notice,' Sophie chided mock seriously, and looked up to find Peter staring at her, as if astonished she *wasn't* a cold-hearted dragon to the three lively girls who had filled so many empty places in her heart these last few years.

'No, indeed. Papa would be most displeased if he got back from Ireland after spending so many days with Aunt Matilda weeping all over him and then moaning about her nerves, only to find you were forced to do the cooking, look after my two unruly little sisters *and* help play hostess to our guests whilst he was away, Miss Rose,' Imogen joined in, as Sophie attempted to help herself to breakfast without seeming discomposed by all this unwanted attention.

'I'm only the governess, Imogen. I daresay Sir Gyffard will have a great many more important matters on his mind when he returns than worrying about who was doing what while he was away. And Cook would run me out of her kitchen if I so much as suggested she wasn't able to cope with anything a mere house-party of ten could demand of her,' Sophie pointed out mildly. But she felt Peter's glare as if a brand had scorched her skin even with her back to him, and met his cold, interrogating look when she turned and made her way to the table.

He could think what he chose about her relationship with her employer, she decided, and hoped he *could* read her mind, for once.

'No, you're far more than just our governess, Rosie. We'd be lost without you,' Audrey protested, and wriggled into the small gap at Sophie's side so she could briefly share her chair and give her a fierce hug, as if to comfort her for even thinking she could be spared.

'How touching,' Peter said flatly, and Sophie saw his sister shoot him a sharp look, as if speculating about his feelings towards her humble self far too acutely for her comfort.

'It is indeed, Lord Sylbourne,' Imogen said sternly, and it was obvious to Sophie he'd lost some ground in her youthful eyes, even if he was now pretending to be all charming attention in the hope of regaining it. 'Our mother died five years ago, and Papa shut himself up in his library for weeks on end after she died. Since our Aunt Matilda, when she's not ordering us to leave her in peace, is more given to stern lectures on our duty than she is to offering comfort and support, Miss Rose has earned our affection and respect by being there and listening when we needed her the most—even if she sometimes feels the need to give us the benefit of her common sense whether we want it or not in return.'

'Thank you, my dears...I think,' Sophie said, with a hug for Audrey, who had attached herself to her side as if she knew her governess needed the warming proximity of a friend in more ways than one, and a grateful smile for Imogen.

'You have three very fine supporters in the Misses Frayne, Miss Rose, if you should ever need a reference for your next position,' Peter told her, with a hint of reluctant admiration in his eyes.

Sophie met those eyes for a long moment—before letting her gaze fall as the Honourable Cedric Wroxley sauntered into the room and gave its comfortable shabbiness a contemptuous look, bowing perfunctorily to Lady Edwina and the eldest daughter of the house and then ignoring the rest of them.

'There's the most infernal draught in the bedchamber someone decided was fit to be mine, for some odd reason,' he announced, and seemed surprised when his complaint was met with a careful silence rather than an abject apology.

'Like the rest of us foolish travellers, I'm sure you're thanking your overworked guardian angel that you didn't have to spend the night in an abandoned coach in the middle of a snowdrift,' Peter observed cheerfully, as if he had no idea Wroxley meant to be unpleasant.

The irritable dandy shot him a killing look, before summoning up a watery smile and aiming it in Imogen's approximate direction.

'Miss Frayne, it is not what I am accustomed to, of course, but I am deeply grateful for this port in a storm,' he added, with a more ceremonious bow, as if he had now recalled the fact that she was not only the eldest daughter of the house but very pretty with it.

'You are welcome, of course, Mr Wroxley,' Imogen lied, a little uneasy under the stare of his indefinitely coloured eyes, and Sophie managed to muffle a groan at the idea of protecting her eldest responsibility from the advances of an icy would-be rake.

'Thank you,' he replied, with a sort of vinegary simper Sophie couldn't imagine enchanting even the most foolish of maidens. It certainly hadn't impressed any of the Frayne girls, if their carefully blank expressions were anything to go by, and she rather thought they were.

'To what do we owe the pleasure of your company before noon, Wroxley?' Peter asked lightly, and Sophie gave him a grateful half-smile for relieving the pall on conversation the Honourable Cedric had caused.

Cedric would be astonished to know he was the instrument of peace between them, as well as disappointed at not having managed to heighten any discord around him, on the principle that seeing others unhappy seemed to be one of his greatest pleasures.

'I hoped we might be able to depart before the weather closed in again, but I see you were not quick enough to take advantage of the brief break in the weather.'

'This is only a respite—not a change in the weather,' Peter informed him rather gruffly, and Sophie was once again surprised at the control under which he kept his once fiery temper nowadays.

'Having spent so long among the savages in the Colonies these last few years, I doubt you yearn for sophisticated society as you might have done if you'd stayed in London,' Wroxley replied, with a sneer that ruined any good looks he might have had if only he'd possessed a more amiable temper to gild a not particularly impressive lily.

'My time in the American States made me value a people who accept a man for what he is,' Peter said quietly, and Sophie thought any other man would have been silenced by this implication that he was rather less than he might have been.

'How very rustic,' Wroxley said with a shudder.

'Some of us prefer rural simplicity to urban complexity.' Peter obliquely defended Imogen and her household as Wroxley sat in the only available seat—next to him, the one Sophie had carefully avoided when she'd sat down by Imogen and Audrey.

Seeing the dark look Mr Wroxley shot His Lordship, Audrey decided to ignore their most unwelcome guest and ask the question she'd clearly been burning to ask while less important matters were aired.

'Does being in mourning for poor Aunt Helen mean we can't bring the Yule Log in and deck the great hall with evergreens the way we always do on Christmas Eve, Miss Rose?' she asked apprehensively.

Sophie gave the idea some thought, then decided her employer wouldn't want his daughters to endure a more miserable Christmas than necessary, with him away from home and their brothers all busy elsewhere for most of the season.

'I don't know what you think, Lady Edwina, but it's my belief nobody would condemn us for bringing the Yule Log into the house. Many of the staff here would be most upset if we didn't, since they think good fortune will leave the house if we don't light the new log with the remains of the old as usual. And we could hang some evergreens up to celebrate Christ's birth and the promise of evergreen life he brings with Him. But perhaps the scarlet ribbons and gilded pomanders we usually add would seem a touch too brilliant in the circumstances.'

'As far as I can see it would be more of a *faux pas* to deprive yourselves of the true spirit of Christmas than it would be to defer to a few killjoys who might object to a little glitter and joy to celebrate this wondrous time of year,' Edwina said, looking endearingly surprised to be appealed to as an authority on polite behaviour.

'Oh, we can manage without the glitter I daresay, but it wouldn't seem like Christmas at all without the holly and ivy and mistletoe,' Audrey declared artlessly.

Sophie privately thought that if the weather didn't let up and allow their visitors to leave very soon, it would be an odd sort of a Christmas anyway.

'Let's hope the snow stops long enough to allow us to gather up the vast amount of greenery we need to satisfy you, then, Audrey,' she said, and exchanged an indulgent glance with Edwina when her youngest pupil again leapt to her feet to inspect the weather through the sash windows that lit this newer part of the house with the odd reflective lightness of too much snow outside them.

CHAPTER TEN

THIS time at least the snow seemed less heavy from the outset, and more like a desultory reminder that winter wasn't done yet than a serious blizzard like yesterday's more businesslike one. It was enough, however, to keep them in the house all morning and to demolish all hopes the travellers might be able to set out for home following some miraculous change in the wind or enough rain to wash away all the snow and ice.

As it was Christmas Eve, and she couldn't bring herself to re-impose lessons on her pupils in order to hide in the schoolroom like a coward, Sophie had to finish hemming Imogen's handkerchiefs for her in the sitting room with Peter, Edwina and Imogen, as well as Mrs Garret-Lowden and Livia—when they finally felt splendid enough to dazzle an earl with their fashionable finery.

Sophie managed to stay quiet enough in her seat by the window, where she could catch the light, and avoid being part of the intimate circle by the fire that would remind her too poignantly of days gone by. Then she and Dina, and often Peter as well, if he was home from school, would huddle over the fire in the old day nursery—the cosiest and most easily warmed room in the vast chilliness of Holm Park in winter, once there wasn't enough money to heat more than a few rooms. Seeing the fascinated glances Livia seemed unable to help herself casting at Peter, Sophie felt forgotten enough to enjoy the illicit pleasure of doing the same thing.

He truly had grown into a mighty man, she decided in an attempt at impartiality; a formidable man, even. Who would have thought light-hearted, laughing Peter Vane should grow into this rather self-sufficient and thoughtful gentleman? Whatever she had done to him by refusing to believe their love for each other strong enough to weather adversity, at least she hadn't managed to weaken him in any way. She wondered what they would have been like now, if all had gone as easily as they had so mistakenly thought it would when they had tumbled so headlong into love all those years ago.

By now she would almost certainly have been mother to a growing brood of children, and he would be my lord Sylbourne, sometimes solemn and responsible as he spoke in the House of Lords, or took up the offices of a powerful nobleman, while he gradually repaired the chaos his erratic sire had wrought on the Vane fortunes. Perhaps sometimes he would cast all that aside and be as light-hearted as ever—laughing with their children and teasing his wife that her expanding girth made her as wide as she was tall when she was growing big with his child…

She had to stop that particular thread of what-might-have-been, because of the almost physical pain that shot through her at the feeling of vast emptiness at the lack of all that with him. Their children would never be born; the love that would have brought them into the world was as cold and dead as the weather outside, and she was the one who'd killed it. She shivered, and decided the heady warmth and delirious sense of promise during that last brief summer at Holm Park seemed as unlikely now as a heatwave in January, despite all her futile remembering last night.

She also decided it was little wonder Miss Garret-Lowden let her eyes rest on the Earl of Sylbourne with awe and a touch of hunger, since she still had the use of her own. Sophie could sympathise with that after last night—especially when she'd hoped she might be immune to him until he'd set out to prove what a myth that was by kissing her.

What really made her frown, and unconsciously drop her hands into her lap to sit staring out into the dwindling snow to try and calm herself, was the roar and fury of possessiveness that rocked her at the thought of Miss Garret-Lowden daring to go further than look a little longingly at Peter, maybe tempting him to dally with her. It was simply anger that the girl might flaunt herself so shamelessly under Peter's nose in the midst of Timon Frayne's family, under what would one day be his roof and with his little sisters present to watch her, she assured herself. Sophie tried to truly look at the snowy landscape, rather than gazing blindly ahead, seeing all sorts of appalling visions of Peter kissing Livia instead of herself. At last she blinked away tears she assured herself were of fury at the very idea, and noted only a few snowflakes were actually swirling about on the air now.

'It looks as if we shall be able to denude Sir Gyffard Frayne's woods of all available greenery exactly as Miss Audrey wants us to this afternoon, does it not, Miss Rose?' Peter asked, far too close to her for comfort, and Sophie turned to look up at him so unwarily that his rather stern mouth lifted into a wicked smile. She was so dazzled she smiled back before her brain could order her not to.

'Yes, indeed,' she agreed, then shook her head as if trying to shake some sense back in while she told herself to stop gazing up at him like an idiot. 'I had better order a quick luncheon made up for us ladies, then find Viola and Audrey and tell them the good news. I hope I can manage to stop them galloping off into the snow without so much as a pair of gloves between them to keep out the cold.'

'Whatever would you do without so many reasons to be busy all the time, my dear Miss Rose?' he asked ironically, and she felt herself blush.

She wished she didn't know Mrs Garret-Lowden and her daughter were straining to hear every word the Earl of Sylbourne and the Fraynes's governess were saying to one another, even if they could no longer demean and snipe at her so openly now, given Sophie's newly discovered connections to the very earl they were trying to fascinate.

'I should have to make them up, I suppose,' she managed, with something much closer to her usual serene composure.

'I shall suspect each one you come up with from now

on,' he said softly, with a wry smile that made her want to say something sharp and starchy to banish it, so she wouldn't be tempted to reach up and tenderly smooth it away as she would have done so casually once upon a time.

'At the moment you need not, since we will all need to be busy if we're to have the house looking suitably festive by the end of the day,' she told him, and she rose to her feet to carry out the first of her tasks, telling herself to be glad it would take her out of the room and away from his dangerous company as she did so.

'Then I had better go and see if Cox has managed to get a cart out to Badger Hill to fetch our belongings. It seems ungrateful of me to live in my host's or one of his sons' clothes, as well as his boots all day, then take them outside and get them soaked with snow.'

'I'm sure Cox was glad of something for the stable boys to do, since he always says they're more trouble than they're worth when the weather stops them exercising the horses and themselves properly,' Imogen remarked from her perch by the fire, and seemed disinclined to leave it and Dina's excellent company.

'How gratifying to have done them so much good as well as ourselves, then, if the job turned out to be straight-forward enough not to have caused them more trouble than it was worth,' Peter said solemnly.

Sophie contrasted his easy good humour with Cedric Wroxley's bad manners and sulks, when in truth Peter had far more to try his patience at every turn. Those sulks had led Wroxley to retire to his room in a snit, some time ago to write letters about his appalling situation to more sympathetic people, and the rest of them had heaved open sighs of relief and happily gone on without him. Sophie doubted he would reappear to join them in the woods this afternoon—no doubt he was penning highly coloured accounts of the total lack of refinement shown by everyone but himself to be sent off at someone else's expense as soon as the mail got through.

'Do you think Mr Wroxley is *ever* happy?' Viola whispered later, as they crept by the place where the staircase from each wing converged, so he wouldn't hear them and come out to glower at them bundled up in the oldest clothes they could find to protect them against the cold while they scrambled about in the undergrowth.

'I have to hope so, my love,' Sophie said noncommittally, not willing to scold Viola for asking a perfectly valid question.

'Perhaps we should ask him if he'd like to come and gather holly with us this afternoon after all, then. It *is* Christmas Eve, and everyone should be happy on such a day, shouldn't they, Miss Rose?'

'I believe Mr Wroxley will be far happier in a warm room writing to his friends than he would be outside in the cold, considering he keeps telling us how much he hated travelling through the snow last night. Sometimes you have to let others to be happy in their own way, Viola, and accept that we are not all the same,' Sophie cautioned softly.

'I suppose so, but it seems a pity to be alone and miserable when he could come with us and be happy.'

'True, but not everyone enjoys being cold, wet and up to their knees in snow.'

'Lord Sylbourne won't be so faint-hearted.'

'Let's hope not—or he'll lose your admiration as surely as I would if I refused to venture out in the cold and get my skirts draped in snow until they're wet through and my boots are so wet my toes forget they belong to me, just to keep you and your sister happy and Heartsease Hall shrouded in greenery.'

'You know perfectly well you love Christmas as much as we do, Miss Rose, and wouldn't miss it for the world,' Viola told her happily as she jumped off the last stair in excitement and ran off to find Audrey and hurry her into her outdoor clothes, so they could all get outside sooner.

'Would you not, Miss Rose?' Edwina asked, with a pretend frown down at the ancient gown the girls had found from the attics for her to ruin instead of one of her own fashionably narrow ones. 'Now, that really is very odd in you, Sophie, to actually *enjoy* dashing about getting wet, cold and dishevelled in such a hoydenish fashion,' she said, in a wicked parody of Mrs Garret-Lowden that made it feel like the old days for a moment, as if their old, easy relationship was salvageable despite all the years of cold silence in between.

Telling herself not to build her hopes up as she met Edwina's coolly ironic gaze, Sophie agreed meekly that it was very peculiar of her. 'No doubt I shall change my mind before the afternoon is out.'

'Not with your lively charges so determined to be merry despite all the efforts of surprise visitors and my future brother-in-law to put them off the idea,' Edwina said, with a shrug at the inevitable fact that Cedric Wroxley would always do his best to ruin the happiness of others if he could out of sheer perversity. 'What could be keeping Peter, I wonder?' she added, with an impatient look at the stairs from the older part of the house, as if that ought to make him appear all the sooner.

'I doubt he's hesitating between bonnets or which fob goes with what coat,' Sophie suggested, as some of her old mischief emerged from beneath Miss Rose's more solemn persona.

'Can you imagine him standing in front of his mirror wondering if *this* coat would better bring out the colour of his eyes or *that* one?' Edwina asked, with a breathless giggle at the very idea.

'No, never,' Sophie replied, struggling with her own laughter at the thought of large, manly and confident Peter Vane fussing about his appearance like a dandy—or indeed a Garret-Lowden. Suddenly some of the joy in the season she had felt so lacking until now made her want to launch herself into the day and forget about tomorrow or next week, when the thaw would surely set in and let the Vanes depart with the snow.

'Oh, look, Miss Rose! Lord Sylbourne has been outside with Cox all the time you were making us put on enough clothes to cover a Bath seminary full of young ladies,' Viola cried from the garden room, where she'd dragged her sister to add a few more despised garments than Audrey altogether approved of wearing.

All three Frayne sisters dashed into the hall to watch

ELIZABETH BEACON

the float that was being driven round to the front of the house in great style by Peter and their father's head groom. The home farm cart followed it, and another smaller one, clearly intended for people rather than evergreens, all fitted with runners to make it slide over the snow rather than drag through them behind the stalwart farm teams. Both the heavy horses and the grooms walking alongside them looked glad to be out of their stables and doing, rather than eating their bedding and polishing harness respectively.

'Come *on*!' Audrey ordered, and dashed through the door as soon as Cordage got it open, with an impatient look back at less impulsive older ladies, who were clearly wasting precious time in her eyes.

Sophie paused for a moment on the doorstep to enjoy the air of holiday about the scene in front of her as laughing grooms threw snowballs at each other whenever Cox's back was turned and the girls jumped up and down with delight at all the bustle and jollity. The carts were bright in their harvest colours, and red ribbons had been tied on here and there because it was Christmas Eve and the lads were determined to celebrate despite the weather and the grief their elders felt for 'Miss Helen,' who'd gone off to marry her Irish lord nigh on a quarter of a century ago, before most of them were even born. From what Sophie recalled of that vivacious lady, having seen her on her one visit to her brother's house during Sophie's time as governess, she would have been first to insist her family didn't make themselves miserable at such a time, and would have loved to join in the fun if she'd still been there.

Sophie jerked out of her reverie when Cox jumped down from his perch and bowed to her as reverently as if he was conducting a princess from her castle: 'Your carriage awaits you, Miss Rose,' he told her solemnly, and proceeded to hand her up onto the bench seat beside Peter before it even occurred to her to argue.

'But this is your seat, Cox,' she objected idiotically, and he grinned as if he knew how much she wanted to be exactly where she was.

'You don't think Farmer Furkiss would trust anybody else but me with his plough team, do you now, miss?' he asked, with a nod at the grinning stable boy who was currently holding the reins of said team between the shafts of the cart and perfectly willing to be 'just anybody' today.

'Probably not. But I can't help wondering how you persuaded him to trust His Lordship with his prize team, since they must be even more precious to him,' she said, but she settled in her seat anyway, because it was the place she most wanted to be and hadn't she just told herself to seize the moment?

'It wasn't easy, I can assure you,' Peter told her, and gently gave the horses his command to move off while she made a great play of settling herself comfortably on the padded cushion she doubted the cart usually enjoyed. 'I had to drive Farmer Furkiss round the hillside in this contraption until he was satisfied I wouldn't lame them or drive us into a ditch. I did wonder if Merryweather might take offence at being given a mere float, but he's so fallen under your youngest pupil's spell he'd probably consider it a privilege to drive a muck cart if she was beside him.'

'However did Audrey manage to make such a strong impression on him in so short a time?' Sophie asked rather apprehensively, far too familiar with Audrey's daredevil ways to think she'd flashed a winning smile and her wide blue eyes in the coachman's direction and won his ever-lasting devotion by being sweetly pretty.

'That might be giving too much away for her comfort.'

'You must tell me now, or I'll have nightmares tonight and wake the whole house with my screaming as I imagine what she's been up to in my dreams.'

'Promise not to scold her, then?'

'Why? Is it so very bad?'

'Unusual, perhaps, but not bad,' Peter replied with a baffled smile she recognised all too easily as coming from yet another victim of Audrey's peculiar brand of charm.

'Tell me,' Sophie demanded, bracing herself for something dreadful.

'Promise first.'

'Very well, I won't scold her—in the probably vain hope that someone else already has,' she conceded.

'Apparently when Merryweather had finally got himself warm and dry last night, and should have been fast asleep himself, he went down into the stables to check on my team and Hannibal, my favourite hunter, and found your Miss Audrey already there, wrapping up his charges in all the blankets she could manage to carry out of the house. She said she couldn't sleep for the thought of them in a draughty stable, shivering with cold—not that her father's stables seem to me to be particularly uncomfortable. I've lodged in less comfortable wayside inns at various times myself over the last few years.'

'That little monkey,' Sophie said despairingly, thinking of all the mishaps that might have happened on the trip from Audrey's room on the second floor through the dark house to the stables. 'Mrs Elkerley must have been furious when she found out her best blankets were being used for horses—even noble ones as she is sure to think yours, since they are yours and you seem to have impressed her mightily for some odd reason.'

'Luckily she didn't discover it, since Merryweather coaxed one of the maids into taking them out into the drying yard and beating them secretly, then brushing them clean of all traces of horse hair until they looked almost like new. I fear the poor maid has fallen under Merryweather's unlikely spell and might stow away in our carriage when we leave in order to follow him back to Holm Park if we don't watch her carefully.'

'I shall make certain I do so, then,' Sophie claimed, priming her mouth in pretend severity.

'You are far more likely to give the girl most of what you have and the clothes off your back as a dowry to tempt him into actually marrying her,' he said, not altogether approvingly, and Sophie wondered exactly when she'd gone from hard-hearted adventuress to mawkish sentimentalist in his estimation.

'Does he deserve her?' she asked half seriously.

'Probably. He's an honest enough rogue under all his brashness and bluster.'

'Since they only met yesterday I shall wait on events,

then, before putting my personal fortune at risk again for the sake of future happiness.'

'Don't even joke about it,' he rumbled gruffly, and glared balefully at Cox's back as he took the lead and led the procession into the heart of the woods above the hall, since he knew the way and Peter didn't.

Peter looked as if brooding over his father's profligacy had taken all the brightness out of the day for him, and she wished she hadn't so carelessly reminded him of it. 'It doesn't matter, Peter. It was such a little fortune when all is said and done that I hardly even miss it,' she lied, and did her best not to remember what it had felt like to wobble on the brink of destitution before Lady Frayne had taken her in and given her a home and a purpose.

'You'll get it all back with interest—although since you would probably hand it over to the first person you thought deserved it more than you do, perhaps it would be better if I invested it until you marry.'

'I shall not marry, Peter,' she said tightly.

'Nonsense. You're a young and lovely lady with her whole life ahead of her, my dear, of course you'll marry. Indeed, I happen to know you have a very good offer in hand and this would be a fine place to make your home.'

'I know my own mind. Another solution to the problem of the girls' future is sure to present itself if we all rack our brains hard enough.'

'It's your future that's troubling my mind at the moment—not theirs,' he insisted stubbornly.

'Apparently that's secure enough, since you, my lord Sylbourne, insist on interfering and will make me a lady

of moderate means again whether I want to be one or no,'
she told him rather acerbically.

'Any lady would want to be one of those—or should I
say any lady who doesn't happen to be as stubborn as a
mule and proud almost to the edge of mania.'

'You're such a golden-tongued charmer, my lord.'

'And I marvel at your enduring talent to infuriate me
into saying far more than I ought to, as if eight years away
from you have taught me naught, Miss Rose.'

'Couldn't we declare a truce for the season? If only
to prove to each other that we *have* changed since then,
Peter?' she asked, with a look of appeal and hope at his
suddenly grim expression. The thought of those years
clearly haunted him nearly as much as it did her.

'Aye, and not always for the better,' he said ruefully,
as if he was one who had lost faith in them and not she.

Sophie's heart ached with the knowledge he was wrong.

'Let us say let's be at peace together, rather than merely
declaring a pause in hostilities, and I'll agree eagerly,
Sophie,' he added seriously.

'Very well, then. Let's be at peace, Peter—and isn't
this the best of times to establish peace and good will
between us?'

'It is indeed, Miss Bonet. Is there any point in denying yourself that part of your real name any longer, by
the way?'

'I agreed to peace—not to losing every battle have I
ever fought. The Bonets are dead and gone as far as I'm
concerned, and since I don't intend to marry, and ap-

parently I'm the last of the line, the whole name will die with me.'

'Is that completely fair to your father's people, Sophie?' he asked, and she sighed gustily.

'What real good can I possibly do them other than continuing to stay away, Peter?' she asked quietly.

'Give them hope, perhaps?'

'False hope. The days of a monarchy in France are over, and if not for the Terror I would say it is for the best that it should be so, given the vast inequality it carried with it. My father would have been the first to agree with me, since he disliked despots nearly as much as he did revolutionaries.'

'And if they had not caught him and slain him before he could get away? How would you feel about his land and his people then?'

'That's an imponderable might have been, Peter. Since Robespierre followed him to the guillotine that's a poetic enough justice for me, since nothing could ever bring Papa back. We were an anomaly even under Louis Sixteenth, Peter—a tiny little princedom in the midst of a great country, consisting of a few square miles of vineyard, a couple of dozen more of mountainside, and a capital the size of a small market town.'

'Yet how excited Mrs Garret-Lowden and her fair daughter would be to know they have been sharing a roof not only with an earl but also a real, live princess,' he said, with a wry smile that admitted she might be right to keep it quiet.

'A dethroned princess, orphaned by the Revolution and

forced to seek sanctuary in her mother's native land and earn her own living there. I suspect even they would find me a hollow glory to boast of among their friends.'

'I'm quite sure you underestimate them.'

'Then I shall rely on you to make sure they never find out who I might have been if the world was different.'

He drew up his team neatly and gave her a half mocking bow. 'It will be my pleasure to serve you, Princess, as always,' he told her, with very little humility, and at last she could laugh with him about the absurdity of it all.

'Then perhaps you would help me down into the snow so I can get myself suitably snow-caked and sodden—as Audrey will no doubt demand I must, as soon as she's managed to scramble out of that cart and started ordering her troops into action.'

'It will be my pleasure,' he said, in a curiously husky tone, and he nodded his thanks to the groom who had got down from Cox's cart to run and hold their horses. 'Down with you, then, Miss Rose,' he invited, holding out his arms to lift her down, when she had only intended to take his hand and jump into the snow by herself.

'Thank you, my lord,' she replied gruffly, slipping down onto solid ground via his arms and feeling herself respond to every iota of him that touched her over-aware body on the way down. She wondered if her legs would hold her steady when she got there at last. 'Don't,' she urged as she gazed up at him, almost helpless with the desire to stay in his arms and simply forget the Fraynes and his sister and everyone else waiting to begin an orgy of trimming and gathering huge quantities of evergreens.

'Later, then,' he promised—or was it more of a threat?

'How can we have *later* when I doubt you can ever forgive me for what I did,' she said sadly.

'I can probably do that if I try hard enough, Sophie, but forgetting might be a lot harder,' he admitted, without any pretence of misunderstanding how serious that half question of hers had been.

Forget she'd made his decision for him? That she hadn't trusted his love or his strength of character enough to wait for him? That was far too much to expect.

'Thank you for a very pleasant drive, my lord,' she said, and stepped away from him and raised her voice enough for others to hear if they chose to. He just gave her a long, unreadable look, as if unwilling to give any of his thoughts away when he wasn't quite sure what she was going to do next.

'A pleasure, Miss Rose,' he said blandly.

He turned to greet his sister with a smile that contained such straightforward affection it made Sophie's heart jerk in its tracks, since nothing between the two of *them* would ever be simple again.

'I'm sorry I couldn't get you to your wedding as easily as I could drive Miss Rose into these woods, Dina love,' he said, as if he quite understood the frustration and loneliness she was going through now that her wedding wouldn't happen until the roads were passable once more.

'Better that we get there late than not at all,' Edwina said equably, and Sophie let herself believe Dina meant she was glad not to be stuck in that snowdrift in the middle of nowhere, and it was not a reference to Sophie's disappearance at the first hurdle set in the way of her own marriage to Peter...

'Don't worry, little sister. I promise you will be exactly where we all need you to be in the end,' Peter assured her.

Sophie decided it was high time she left them to their double edged conversation and did her best to make sure the Frayne girls didn't end up totally covered in snow from head to foot or buried in a snowdrift.

Nothing about Peter was so easily shaken off today, though. Throughout the scramble through the woods, tugging and pulling at the best trails of ivy and finding the last pinecones downed by the weight of snow, with the stable lads knocking them off as they sawed at the branches least begrudged them by Sir Gyffard's taciturn woodsman, Sophie's thoughts were half on him and only half on her pupils. The girls seemed happy enough to find their governess so distracted, and sang wassail songs and darted about with armfuls of greenery until even they were breathless. Edwina gamely joined in, and Sophie tried to carry some of the holly to the waiting carts— only to have it taken from her by my lord Sylbourne at his most lordly.

'I'm quite capable of carrying a few twigs of holly without your help,' she finally snapped, and felt even less inclined to give in meekly to being treated like spun glass when she caught Cox and Merryweather exchanging a sly grin at her expense.

'I'm sure you prefer a scratched face to accepting my assistance, but as those few twigs are in fact a bundle you can't even see over, I thought I might as well save myself the task of hauling you out of the snow and getting royally prickled in the process,' he told her, so patiently she had to stamp her feet. She felt her boots fill with wet snow. 'A likely story,' she grumbled irritably as she squelched in his wake to the cart and then leaned on it while she untied her bootlaces and emptied the soggy mess out, despite the impropriety of waving her wet stockinged foot about for all to see.

'Lean on me,' he invited, and merely grinned when she cast him a haughty look and ordered him to avert his eyes whilst she did her best to undo the damage he had done. 'So it's my fault you lost your temper now, is it? Do you really think I'll be driven to uncontrollable ardour by the very sight of you hopping about on one leg?' he asked interestedly, glancing at the spectacle of her dressed in a variety of odd garments and one boot as if she was some strange creature in a menagerie.

'No, but I might have to box your ears if you don't go away and leave me in peace,' she told him disagreeably, and marvelled at herself for wishing she really could drive him to uncontrollable lust with one sight of her nether limbs.

Feeling like a frump in thick stockings, a pair of boots one of the Frayne sons had discarded when they were very young and the mud-brown skirts she had never loved even in their dubious prime, which now looked as if they would be brusquely rejected by all but the most desperate paupers, Sophie wondered wistfully how it would feel to glory in even one of Miss Garret-Lowden's silk velvet gowns. Or perhaps to own a jewel-coloured spencer to cheer up her drab selection of dresses and flatter her creamy complexion instead of playing it down.

'You've had tranquillity enough these last few years. It's high time you learnt to weather a little variation of pace again, if you ask me.'

'I didn't.'

'Live again, Sophie,' he urged, so softly she hoped Cox and his new friend had been unable to hear him, for she couldn't spare them enough attention to find out. 'Risk being your true self once more and stop being strict and buttoned up Miss Rose for a few heady moments. You might even find enough courage to become Miss Bonet again if you try hard enough.'

'When I want your advice I shall be sure to ask for it,' she made herself argue, even if the draw of doing exactly what he said was so strong she nearly stepped over the gap between them and let herself indulge in one of those easy, Sophie Bonet kisses for her one-time love. *No.* She drew herself back and told herself the love they'd once had was over and done with.

Liar, she accused herself. *There's nothing dead or done with about it. You still love him—hopelessly, painfully, even wistfully and uselessly. However you do it, you love him all the same.*

And that conclusion made her turn away from him to hide her face and avert her eyes from Edwina's interested ones, fixed on them from the slope above, where she and the girls had found the best-berried holly and were directing their troops in how best to harvest it to their satisfaction.

'Now all we need is an apple orchard,' Edwina called out merrily, once all was safely gathered in and the carts already looked like Macbeth's forest on its way to Dunsinane. 'For the mistletoe?' she added helpfully, as if they might not realise that was where the wretched stuff grew most luxuriantly. 'Do you make up a kissing bough to put in the hallway here? We always used to at Holm Park before Peter went away,' she said with studied innocence.

'Of course. It wouldn't be properly Christmas without one,' Imogen agreed blithely.

'Then I'm sure you know the best place to find mistletoe fine enough to make a kissing bough work properly,' Edwina added, in case nobody had got the point.

'There's lots of it in the biggest old crab apple tree in the orchard, and I'm sure Papa said it needed to come down before it killed the tree, Lady Edwina,' Audrey abetted eagerly.

Sophie kept her face carefully blank as an immediate diversion to the orchard was arranged.

'Are you opposed to kissing in general, or just for yourself in particular, Miss Rose?' Peter asked genially after he had handed her up and she'd absently done what everyone seemed to think she should and sat beside him as if it was her allotted place.

He turned the dray with such skill he hardly even had to think about it, and she wondered what he had done on that trip of his to the American States as they followed in the tracks of the now laden cart towards the cider apple orchard.

'Cat got your tongue?' he asked as the cavalcade sped to its next objective.

From the shouts of laughter and jokes coming from the other carts, nobody else had such difficulties.

'When you think of a serious question to ask me I shall do my best to answer it in the same spirit.'

'But this isn't the day for serious questions, my dear Miss Rose.'

'Evidently not,' she said, and tried not to dwell on the fact that she wasn't his dear at all.

'How disappointing to find out you're not a woman of your word,' he said dolefully. 'Wasn't it only an hour or so ago that we declared peace between us?'

'Peace—not undying devotion,' she snapped unwarily.

'No, that would be asking too much, would it not?' he said dourly, and as they had come to the end of the short journey, and the brief winter day was sinking into only a little less than the longest night of the year, she had no time to think of a reply that might have taken away the tension in the very air between them.

CHAPTER ELEVEN

'ISN'T it the finest kissing bough you ever saw, Rosie?' Viola asked Sophie eagerly the instant she had forced herself to leave Mrs Elkerley and Cook to organise the household and the kitchen without her interference and face the busy party in the great hall—or whatever area of the house they had decided needed decking with greenery next.

'It's certainly the best I remember laying eyes on. It must have taken you a very long time to make, my dear,' she replied as enthusiastically as she could manage when kissing boughs suddenly seemed the last things on God's good earth she wanted to see or, even worse, stand under—as she suddenly realised she was doing, in order to gaze up at it with suitable awe.

'Oh, I didn't make it. Lord Sylbourne and Lady Edwina did that.'

'On the contrary, my sister relayed your orders and I obediently carried them out under Cordage's supervision, Miss Viola.'

Viola shrugged and threw a look in Peter's direction that said of *course* he'd needed feminine guidance, before declaring sternly that someone ought to try it out.

'How true,' Peter muttered, emerging from the shadows where he'd been putting a garland somewhere nobody else could reach, onto an ancient hook hidden above one of the panels especially for the job. 'It might not be any good, after all, and then we would have to begin all over again.'

'It doesn't need to work—just to be there to keep the tenants and staff amused for the Twelve Days of Christmas,' Sophie told him acerbically, and did her best to slide into the shadows he'd just left and make her escape.

'All the more reason not to spoil their fun,' he said softly, and effortlessly reached out to hook a powerful arm about her slender waist. At the same time he snatched a shining milk white berry from the crown of holly, pine and mistletoe above his head and put it in his pocket. He met her bemused gaze with a question in his own and a half smile on his lips, and then lowered his head to snatch a quick, rather unsatisfying kiss from her lips. 'I think we need to work on our technique,' he whispered, for her ears only, and let her go with a shrug and wry smile to Edwina.

Mrs Garret-Lowden chose the least convenient moment to appear, now all the work was done, and Sophie whisked out of the room and took refuge in the kitchens again, despite poor Cook's harassed expression.

'His High and Mightiness sent a message down to tell me he wants dinner in his room tonight, Miss Rose—which I'm sure none of us mind, for he's about as full of Christmas spirit as a mud pie. But he says he wants a capon or some mutton, and you know it's Christmas Eve and we can't eat flesh today.'

'I suspect he thought if he was to dine alone he could get away with flouting that particular rule, but I don't see why you should compromise your conscience so he can do so. He can have what the rest of us eat and I'm sure it will be delicious.'

'Not as far as he's concerned, it won't be,' Cook said gloomily.

'I'll ask Cordage to speak to him since I can't visit a gentleman's bedchamber myself,' Sophie said doubtfully. She didn't want Cordage to suffer the nasty edge of the Honourable Cedric's tongue.

'He'd accept it better from His Lordship. Seems to me as if he's got a healthy respect for His Lordship's temper,' Cook said blandly, and Sophie sighed.

'Very well, I will ask Lord Sylbourne to speak to him,' she said, wishing she'd never chosen the coward's way out and darted in here to hide in the first place.

'So was there anything else, miss? Only it *is* Christmas Eve, when all's said and done, and there's a good deal still to do if everything's to be ready for tomorrow—even if we won't get to church in the morning unless the wind changes a sight more than it seems inclined to just now.'

'No, I really don't think so,' Sophie said meekly, and went to see if she could find Peter before going to change out of her shabby clothes at last.

Luckily Peter was halfway up the first flight of stairs when she came out of the door to the servants' quarters, so she didn't have to search for him. He halted to watch her follow him.

'Thank goodness I caught you in time,' she gasped.

'You were actually *looking* for me?' he asked incredulously as they met in the gloom between one floor and the other.

Always, whispered that internal voice she was doing her best to ignore.

She briskly told him of her mission and he nodded grimly. Sophie left him to enter the older wing and went on her way up to the schoolroom and her room, shaking her head at the contrary nature of men. She would have thought he'd had the afternoon running pretty much his own way, and in her opinion *she* was the one entitled to feel the strain of their enforced intimacy, but she supposed it was probably as well if she didn't know what troubled him if she hoped to get any sleep tonight.

'Are you going to dress yourself up like a quiz again tonight, Miss Rose?' Audrey demanded, when Sophie entered the old day nursery the girls now used as a sitting room.

'She wants to pretend she's as old and on the shelf as poor Aunt Matilda,' Viola told her sister knowledgeably.

'You aunt isn't that old,' Sophie reproached her mechanically.

'She's almost as old as Papa,' Audrey insisted. 'And don't give me your best severe governess look, Miss Rose, because she's not here to hear me and you know perfectly well I wouldn't say anything of the sort if she was. Poor Aunt Matilda still hopes to find a beau and marry one day, so I suppose she must think she's really quite young. I'd hate to be her age and still desperate for a home of my own—wouldn't you, Rosie?' she added, and Sophie wondered if the whole world was locked in a conspiracy to throw her at Peter.

'I doubt the problem will ever arise for you—unless you drive your family to throw you out into the snow to get some peace and quiet,' Sophie told her repressively.

'Now, that's not kind, Miss Rose—especially at Christmastide. You really ought to be ashamed of yourself,' Audrey scolded, as if she was the adult and Sophie the unfledged girl.

'How strange that I don't seem to be, then,' Sophie said dourly, and told both girls to eat their dinner when it came and make sure they treated her with a little more respect when they came downstairs later—as if she really *was* a stern educator of wayward young ladies.

She went off to change into her second best gown to prove to everyone else and herself that she didn't need to hide behind her bombazine horror tonight. She ruthlessly wound her long locks into the unadorned chignon she usually wore, though, and made sure no frivolous ends were left free to curl about her brow in fashionable disarray. Because she *was* a governess, even if there was no need to go quite as far to prove it as she had done last night. Slipping a clean handkerchief into her plain reticule, and brushing a piece of lint off her dark green skirts, she glanced at herself in the mirror and grimaced wryly. If the girls or anyone else expected her to transform her-

self into a beautiful butterfly then they would be bitterly
disappointed.

Sophie was surprised to find Mr Wroxley among the
company assembling in the panelled sitting room when
she got downstairs, and she slanted Peter a questioning
look when she was sure the Garret-Lowdens intended to
ignore her as they usually did. Now unexpected guests
had turned up to enliven their stay it made governess-bait-
ing a less attractive way of passing their time. He shook
his head slightly and mouthed *later* at her, which made
her look about her once more to make sure nobody had
seen that scandalous aside. Luckily Edwina was politely
discussing silk warehouses with Mrs Garret-Lowden, and
Mr Wroxley seemed oddly subdued and was staring into
the fire as if he found it acutely interesting.

Suddenly there was a stir of silk and the scent of lavender and Miss Willis appeared in the doorway, looking
rather pale and a little thinner than Sophie remembered,
with Mrs Elkerley supporting her as if she was afraid
the slender middle-aged lady might fall over if she stood
aside.

'Oh, you're well enough to come downstairs at last,
then, love?' Edwina exclaimed, and abandoned Mrs
Garret-Lowden and her dress-lengths and grosgrain trimmings without a second thought as she went to help her
beloved aunt.

'I'm perfectly stout.' Miss Willis dismissed her, fussing impatiently.

'Not noticeably,' her disrespectful nephew told her, and
offered her his arm if she wouldn't accept anyone else's.

'Impertinent boy,' she scolded, but Sophie noticed that she clung to the stalwart support he offered her and accepted the best seat by the glowing fire, which Cedric Wroxley meekly abandoned at a curt nod from Peter. 'Can't say it's not a relief to sit down after all those stairs,' she said holding out her hands to the warmth, and gave Edwina a grateful nod as she placed a pole screen to protect her face.

'And *I* can't say how much of relief it is to see you restored to something more like your usual self at last,' Peter told her as he waited on her next pronouncement.

'All very well—but who *is* everyone, my lad? Why didn't you introduce them all as soon as I set foot in this fine old room?'

'How remiss of me to be more concerned about your health and comfort than the social niceties,' he replied placidly.

'Modern manners,' she condemned roundly, and Sophie hid a smile at seeing how little Miss Willis had changed over the years now she was truly recovered from her ordeal by snow and almost her old self again.

'Very well, then, Aunt Hes. Please be aware that Miss Frayne here is our kind hostess in her father, Sir Gyffard Frayne's, absence. Miss Frayne, could you also be kind enough to make allowances for the fact that my aunt, Miss Willis, has a bark that's far worse than her bite?'

'Cheek! But you're a very pretty girl, my dear, and I remember you from last night—despite being so sorry for myself I didn't have the grace to introduce myself properly. No doubt your father is very proud of you, and your mother would have been too if she were only still with us—I recall meeting her more than once, and found her to be a good and sensible woman, despite being possessed of more in the way of looks than was quite good for her. She was also a very good friend of Edwina and Peter's first stepmama.'

Their *first* stepmother? Sophie marvelled as that statement implied there had been a second, and suddenly it all fell into place in her mind. She wondered how she'd ever been so stupid. Peter had refused to marry Diamantha Rivers, so Hartley Vane must have wed the Rivers fortune in his son's stead. How could she have been such a fool as not to realise it sooner?

Meanwhile Miss Willis swept the room with sharp grey eyes that showed just where Peter and Edwina had got them from. Her gaze fixed for a considering moment on Sophie's plainly arrayed figure, before sweeping on to take in Mrs Garret-Lowden and Livia's elaborate hairstyles and richly decorated gowns with a very well bred snort of distaste. Despite her state of shock Sophie smothered a giggle as Miss Willis shook her head and muttered something not very quietly about ostentatious vulgarity before nodding regally at them, since they were obviously guests in this house and she owed Miss Frayne the politeness of being civil to her guests even if she clearly couldn't imagine why she had invited them.

'May I introduce Mrs Garret-Lowden and her daughter, my eldest brother Timon's betrothed, Miss Willis?' Imogen managed bravely, and Sophie made herself move out of the shadows to stand at her back and silently support her.

'Hmm…what's he called Timon for, then? I'm beginning to think I ought to take back what I said about your mama being a sensible woman. What's *your* name pray? Cleopatra or something equally outlandish, I suppose.'

'Imogen, Miss Willis,' Imogen admitted happily enough, and Sophie realised she had seen past the lady's gruff persona to the true kindness underneath. She decided she must learn to trust Imogen's instincts and training a little more and stop worrying about her finding her feet in society.

'And your other brothers and sisters are very likely Macbeth, Hamlet and Ophelia, I daresay, since I seem to recall seeing more of you about the place last night when we were brought in out of that dratted blizzard.'

'No, they are called Lysander, Ferdinand, Viola and Audrey.'

'Just as well your mother stuck to Shakespeare's comedies after her first, then,' Miss Willis observed, then fixed Sophie with her best gimlet-eyed stare and beckoned her forward in her turn.

'I know who you are better than most people, young lady, but I'd like to know just what you thought you were doing, walking out of Holm Park like that and leaving us all to worry ourselves witless about where you'd gone and whether you were safe or no. Scrambling behaviour on your part, young woman, even if you appear to have helped bring up a very pretty behaved young lady—or so I have been told by my interfering niece, who seems to think that's a mitigating circumstance for some odd reason all her own.'

'Thank you,' Sophie managed calmly as she picked out the compliment and cherished it, for she knew very well how hard it was to gain them from this source.

'I daresay she thought it would soften my ire to know you had at least been usefully employed while you were gone.'

'And has it?'

'Cheeky puss. Come here and let me look at you properly,' Miss Willis said.

As soon as Sophie was reckless enough to do so, she reached out and grabbed a handful of forest green wool to draw her even nearer and subject her to a pitiless scrutiny that almost made Sophie's eyes water with the effort of not squirming away.

'You look older,' she was told brusquely at last.

'I am older. We all are.'

'Are you wiser as well, I wonder? Heaven knows you were a silly enough little fool when last I set eyes on you, Princess Sophie Bonet.'

Dark spots danced in front of her eyes, and Sophie was tempted to give in to them and faint, so at least she wouldn't have to think what to say next. 'How *could* you, madam?' she asked softly, deaf to Mrs Garret-Lowden's gasp and Imogen's urgent question.

'It is a joke, isn't it, Miss Rose? You're not *really* a princess are you?'

'How could I *not* smoke you out when I'm quite sure that spineless spindleshanks yonder is doing his worst to sell information about your whereabouts and circumstances to Fouché and Bonaparte's secret police, my girl?' Miss Willis barked, regally ignoring poor Imogen, who was standing open mouthed and pale with shock at the very possibility there was more to Miss Rose's reticence about herself than she'd ever dared believe.

'It's quite intolerable in him, of course,' Miss Willis swept on, 'when we all know our country is at war with France. He could be expected to have a little simple loyalty to Britain and our allies at such a time, even if he has none to a lady claiming sanctuary in her mother's country. I can only hope Letty Wroxley really *did* play his father false with his third son, for I hadn't thought there was so much bad blood in the family as he seems to provide ample proof of otherwise.'

'What interest can Fouché or his master possibly have in me?' Sophie said numbly, and felt relieved when Peter came to stand beside her and support her. It was almost painfully hard not to lean into his warmth and strength, and never mind the past and her independence for once.

'Don't be naïve, girl. The man's interested in anyone who could be used as a figurehead to rally forces inside France that Bonaparte hasn't managed to win over with his *faux* aristocracy and self-styled title of "emperor". Of course we all know the man's a Corsican corporal, and no more an emperor than I am, but there must still be some in France with the sense to see through all the vulgar pomp and gilding to the despot beneath. There's poor fat Louis and his *émigré* court, of course. They're always looking for an attractive cause to rally round. And you're young and pretty, my girl, and would serve them very well.'

'How could the deposed princess of a tiny country like Mont St Jude truly matter to the Bonapartists? Especially when it has been absorbed into France without even a struggle after my father, its Prince, was sent to the guillotine.'

'A beautiful young princess, bravely scratching a living in a foreign country whilst her people groan under the cruel yoke of an imperial power? You're more of a fool than I thought if you don't see the propaganda tool you could be to the Royalists, my girl. Until he came along and recognised you, I daresay you were safe enough here,' Miss Willis declared with a dismissive wave at Cedric Wroxley, who glowered back at her and somehow managed to look more unappealing than usual. 'But now he's seen you again, and realised you could provide a nice little windfall if he can keep it from his creditors, you are no longer quietly forgotten and anonymous.'

'It's true, isn't it?' Imogen burst out, looking as if she might cry from shock or fury at any moment.

'I will only discuss this matter with you and your sisters in private, Imogen. So if you would excuse us— Edwina, Miss Willis?' Sophie asked hastily, deciding not to wait for a yay or nay and tugging Imogen from the room before they both betrayed more than they should in public. 'Please ask Cook to delay dinner for a quarter of an hour,' she asked Cordage politely, and bore her former pupil off upstairs to the schoolroom before he could question her newly regal persona.

'How could you not tell us, Miss Rose? But I forget—you're not even truly Miss Rose, are you? Miss Willis called you Bonet,' Imogen accused her breathlessly.

Audrey and Viola jumped to their feet and looked totally bewildered by their hasty appearance and Imogen's obvious agitation.

'Well may you look shocked, girls. Pray let me introduce you to Princess Sophie Bonet, who has apparently been pretending to be our governess these last eight years in order to hide from her enemies.'

'Don't be silly. Miss Rose isn't a princess,' Viola told her elder sister, as if she thought she might have run mad since she last laid eyes on her.

'How can she be since she obviously hasn't got a country to be princess *of* in the first place or she would have stopped there? Someone's gammoned you royally this time, Imogen,' Audrey insisted, and Sophie felt worse rather than better.

'I suppose it's actually true, in a way,' she admitted, and felt three pairs of blue eyes fix themselves on her with unnerving intensity. 'I was born a princess—although it was only of a tiny little country set up in the heart of France after a joke between the King of France and the Holy Roman Emperor. The Emperor had a troublesome spare son who was never likely to inherit much, or be of any use to his family, so the King agreed to sell the Emperor two thousand acres of not very prime land and make the Prince its hereditary ruler. It was rather a cruel joke on both their parts, since Mont St Jude is hardly big enough or rich enough to be classed as a substantial *man-*

oir, let alone a principality. I daresay the locals were relieved to be made part of France again after being ruled
by a prince without the means to keep even a castle, let
alone a court, for three hundred years. They had little
enough choice even if they were not, since Robespierre
and his Committee of Public Safety sent soldiers to haul
my father off to Paris so they could send him to the guillotine as yet another traitor to France.'

'How awful for you and your mama, Miss Rose,' soft-
hearted Audrey exclaimed, and ran over to hug her con-
solingly.

'It was very awful for me, since he was a good man
and a loving father, but my mama died when I was born,
Audrey. As soon as the Revolution broke out I was sent
to stay with her family in England, and I decided to take
my mother's nationality after my father was killed. So
you see: I'm not really much of a princess at all, since I
don't even have a country to be princess of any more.'

'You should still have told us,' Imogen insisted.

'I didn't think it was important. Anyway, when I came
here to be your very young and inexperienced governess
all those years ago your mama and papa decided it would
be as well for all of us if I did so under an assumed name.'

'Then Papa knows and has never said anything either?'
Imogen demanded, looking as if she felt doubly betrayed
by the people she trusted the most.

'To be honest, I think we all forgot about it—until Lord
Sylbourne and his party were stranded here and reminded
me of who I used to be.'

'Then how are you connected to them? That seems to

be yet another thing you somehow managed to "forget" to tell us,' Imogen accused.

Sophie could see how deeply she had hurt her. 'I didn't want to remember. I'm sorry,' she said humbly—because it had been wrong of her not to tell them of her identity as soon as she'd realised the past wasn't dead and done with after all.

'Because Lord Sylbourne himself meant more to you than you're prepared to admit back then, didn't he? When you were still a princess in exile and not a pretend governess?' Imogen demanded ruthlessly.

'Yes, we loved each other,' Sophie admitted, deciding that confession might be good for the soul, but it was desperately painful. 'We intended to marry.'

'Then why didn't you? He could hardly complain about a lack of rank in his prospective bride, after all, could he?'

'Because his father gambled away every penny he could get hold of and then put my own modest fortune into a trading company even a five-year-old could have seen was fraudulent in the hope of recouping the family finances. They were so deep in debt I have no idea how Lord Sylbourne has managed to pull them all out of the River Tick. The only solution back then seemed to be for him to marry money, and I didn't even have a modest amount of that any more.'

'Yet he didn't marry a golden dolly, since his sister told me last night that he was still a bachelor,' Imogen argued ruthlessly.

'No, he didn't,' Sophie said, doing her best to contain the pain of knowing that they could have married after all, if only she'd had the resolution to wait for him to be of age or find the means for them to elope. If only she'd had faith in him.

'So you could have been married to him all these years?' Viola said with awed horror that this real-life fairy story had gone so farcically wrong.

'I could. So if you ever come across the love of your life, girls, you must make sure you don't follow my poor example if he's even half the man Lord Sylbourne is. Yet if I'd been his wife all these years I should never have met you, and that would have been a grave loss indeed to me—for all my nagging ways and disgraceful deceptions and my many other imperfections.'

'And we love you, Rosie, but it would have been lovely for you to be a real, live princess married to a nice, handsome earl, wouldn't it?'Audrey insisted.

'Yes,' she said, finally accepting how wonderful it would have been, and how very much she had thrown away with her grand gesture of renouncing love for what she'd been assured at the time was the greater good. 'It would have been lovely, indeed,' she echoed sadly.

'You could marry him now,' Viola pointed out, as if it was an obvious solution and she was surprised they hadn't already thought of it.

'I don't think he would want a wife who had shown so little faith in his love and all the hard work and talent it must have taken him to recover his family's fortunes, do you?' she asked, meeting Imogen's speculative gaze and wondering if she was ever going to be forgiven by this suddenly very grown up and dignified young lady.

'I doubt it,' she confirmed, and at last there was sadness in Imogen's eyes for those beleaguered young lovers instead of hurt that Sophie hadn't trusted her with the truth.

'I should have told you,' she admitted over Audrey's head as she returned her youngest pupil's consoling hug with love and blinked back her tears.

'You should. But at least you didn't tell Timon or Lysander either. It would have been unforgivable if you'd told them because they happen to be male.'

'They have no idea I'm not simple Miss Rose of nowhere in particular.'

'The day you are simply anything I will take to training flying pigs, Miss Rose,' Peter's deep voice informed her from the doorway, and Sophie's eyes sharpened on him with horror as she wondered how much of her painfully honest conversation with the girls he'd overheard—especially that last bit.

'My lord, you should not be up here,' she told him numbly, wondering how many more shocks the evening might yet contain.

'I merely came to escort you and Miss Imogen down to dinner—if you and the Misses Frayne have concluded your urgent business, of course?'

Sophie looked at her two younger pupils with raised eyebrows. 'Have we finished, do you think?' she asked, as humbly as she had it in her to be, since she *was* their governess and had to carry on being so as Sir Gyffard had trusted her with his precious daughters whilst he was away.

'For now. But what shall we call you from now on?' Viola said after what looked like some very deep thought.

'What you have always called me. My last name is Rosalind, after my mother, so there really is no reason you can't go on calling me Rosie if you would like to.'

'Is it quite *proper* for a governess to be addressed by her first name like that, Miss Rose?' Imogen asked satirically, and Sophie supposed she deserved not to be let off that particular hook quite so easily.

'As long as it is not meant as a mark of disrespect—but let's worry about rounding up all the cats my aunt has let out of the bag so dramatically later, shall we?' Peter said calmly, rescuing her. He raised his eyebrows questioningly at them while both Imogen and Sophie wondered if this really could be brushed aside to be dealt with later.

'Poor Cook will be furious if we stay up here for much longer while the dinner she's gone to so much trouble over spoils,' Sophie suggested to the daughter of the house.

'Then we had better go and eat it,' Imogen agreed practically.

'Be very careful what you say in front of Mr Wroxley,' Peter warned them before he escorted them into the dining room. 'I discovered this afternoon that he's the author of several scurrilous articles about the *ton* he's managed to sell to a notorious scandal sheet in yet another attempt to try and stave off his creditors. My aunt may or may not be right about his attempts to sell information to Bonaparte's Minister of Police, but I doubt if he'll keep silent about your whereabouts when he's back among the *ton*, Princess—especially when he could earn money from it.'

'Please don't call me so, Peter,' she said, because the word sounded so wrong on his tongue she might cry if she let herself.

'Very well, Miss Rose. But you can't cower here in hiding now the world knows who you are again,' he warned dourly, as if her lack of top-loftiness displeased him for some reason.

'Perhaps if we were to call you Miss Bonet instead of Miss Rose the world might not think it so very peculiar that you're our governess?' Imogen suggested.

'A happy compromise,' Peter agreed, as if Sophie had no say in the matter.

Sophie felt her temper flare—mainly because he seemed to think he had the right to rearrange her life while taking no part in it himself.

'Thank you, Imogen. It seems like a very good notion to me, but I'm not *your* governess any more, don't forget. After the last few days I've realised that you're quite capable of learning anything more you need to know about being a fashionable young lady without help from me.'

'I hope you're right—considering I shall come in for a lot more attention when I go to London for the season once it's generally known a humble little country miss like me had a real live princess as her teacher. I daresay I'll be able to bask in your reflected glory for weeks if not months, Miss Bonet.'

'How very gratifying for you,' Sophie said blandly, and did her best to stand as tall as she could manage, given her lack of inches, now Cordage had the door standing open for them and the footmen were lining up impatiently with the covers behind him. 'Thank you, Cordage,' she said, with a baleful look in his direction as he drew breath to enjoy himself by announcing them formally. Quite plainly word had already reached the servants' quarters that the governess, of all people, had been elevated to the ranks of petty royalty.

'I suppose I have to admit you were right,' she told Peter under her breath, and did her best to fix a bland smile on her face for the benefit of the openly staring Garret-Lowdens.

'Which is almost as rare as it is gratifying—but why, exactly?'

'I plainly can't keep my secrets any more.'

'Tell the truth and shame the devil, then,' he said indifferently, as if he couldn't see why she'd wanted to have any secrets in the first place.

'I hope you will all accept our apologies for delaying dinner?' she managed to say, with the sort of blank good manners she had seen her Aunt Hermione use at Holm Park when some domestic disaster had threatened.

'Oh, yes, indeed, Your Highness,' Mrs Garret-Lowden almost stammered in her eagerness to get on the right side of the most impressive title she had ever met after such a shaky start.

'Please—I do not use my title in England,' Sophie said, with an emphatic gesture of rejection she couldn't stop herself making. Two days ago this woman had twitted her about being obliged to earn a living and looked down her nose at a mere dependent, and now she wanted to toady to her.

'Then you're a fool. You're already far too long in the tooth not to use any advantage you have left in order to make a decent marriage,' Mrs Garret-Lowden informed her. It was clear to see she'd taken offence at such an unnatural demand not to use the rank; even she hadn't dared dream in her wildest fantasies of such a title for her own beloved daughter. 'I daresay you could even look to wed a nice country gentleman with a neat estate like this one with a title like that—if you were to make more of an effort to put yourself forward.'

'I think that you should attend to your dinner, Mama,' Livia said very firmly indeed, and Sophie eyed her with increased respect even as Mrs Garret-Lowden bridled and muttered something rebellious under her breath. 'Miss Rose is a part of my betrothed husband's household, and as such her business is private to that family— and her own, of course,' Livia added with a judicious nod in Edwina and Miss Willis's direction to include them in the magic circle she had established.

'Thank you, Miss Garret-Lowden,' Sophie said with as quiet a dignity as she could manage as she took her seat between Peter and Imogen and did her best to look as if nothing untoward had happened.

If Timon truly wanted to make a marriage where he would manage his estate while his wife ruled his house, then he had engaged himself to exactly the right woman after all. Under her fluttery manner and fussily over-decorated clothes, his Livia clearly hid a backbone of honed steel, and Sophie suspected her mother would be quietly pensioned off when the hall came into Timon's possession—if not sooner should she try to interfere in her daughter's married life.

'Does it *have* to be fish again?' Cedric Wroxley said with a long-suffering sigh, and Sophie found herself glad of him for the first time as all attention was fixed on him.

'It's Christmas Eve,' Peter reminded him.

'We can't possibly eat meat today, Mr Wroxley,' Imogen explained kindly, as if he might not have heard of the custom.

Even Cedric's eyes fell before the shining goodwill in his youthful hostess's gaze. 'How foolish of me to forget,' he managed to excuse himself limply, but he served himself liberally with roast salmon, then baked carp with lemon sauce, before piling creamed horseradish on his plate as if even that comfort might be withdrawn if he wasn't careful.

Sophie marvelled that someone so thin could consume such vast quantities of food without appearing to take much benefit from it, and herself played with the delicious food Cook had gone to so much trouble with in order to make a fitting start to the Christmas season despite the lack of meat. Soothed at last by fine cooking, the blessings of warmth and company and the good food Peter somehow coaxed her into eating, Sophie began to wonder if her secrets were indeed better out in the open.

CHAPTER TWELVE

'WE CAN'T leave you in peace with your wine tonight I'm afraid, gentlemen,' Imogen announced when everyone seemed to have eaten their fill. 'But there will be ale and mulled wine aplenty, if that will help resign you to the fact that we're now expected to attend the ceremony of lighting the Yule Log in the great hall. It would probably be best to put on another layer of clothing before we do, since it will take days to get the place warm enough for the Twelfth Night Ball.'

'How quaint,' Mrs Garret-Lowden said, as if trying to reassert herself as an arbiter of taste. But it was rather a half-hearted attempt, and nobody took much notice as they wrapped themselves in shawls or coats against the cold.

All of a sudden the excitement of Christmas was bright and full of possibilities around them, and even Sophie felt as if this might be one to remember, despite all the turmoil and heartache it had already brought her.

'Oh, please hurry,' Audrey urged as she bounced with excitement.

'Just wait until you see how splendid it looks in there, Imogen,' Viola told her big sister, with almost as much impatience as her little one.

'Show me, then,' Imogen urged them, looking for a moment like the schoolgirl she had so lately been herself.

The Frayne sisters made an angelic picture in the light of the great ring of candles blazing over the entrance hall tonight. They would be kept burning all night, in case any strangers were looking for hospitality on this most holy of nights. Sophie felt a lump in her throat at the sight of the three of them standing there, so close to each other and so very dear to her. For her almost everything had changed in the last two days, and yet much remained the same. Apprehension that she might have to leave the girls to do the rest of their growing up without her fought with her pride in them, and her smile when they all three looked to her to begin the revels wobbled perilously.

If there was any danger at all that trouble could come looking for her at Heartsease Hall, and might damage these bright, intelligent, sometimes stubborn and a little too high-spirited girls, then she could not stay and risk them being harmed by it. Once more the shadows that had haunted her after she was forced to flee with Aunt Hermione, then again after Papa was killed, were threatening, but she made herself smile and look serene to keep them at bay.

'Oh, it is even better than usual,' she gasped involuntarily as the girls dragged her into the great hall almost at a run. 'It must have taken everyone hours to do all this,' she added as the grooms and maids and even the ploughman did their best to look modest in the face of their achievements.

'Not as if we had anything else to do, what with this weather and all,' Cox said, looking uncomfortable inside the house now his work was done. 'And though you said there should be no scarlet ribbons with the family being in mourning, Miss Rose—and quite right too, if you ask me—Miss Helen always loved the Christmas season, so we thought she wouldn't have minded some green ones and the odd touch of silver. We'll take them down if you think it's not respectful.'

'No, I think Lady Porthdown would be the first one to say Christmas is no time to be gloomy, and would hate to think of us refusing to celebrate it for her sake. It looks beautiful, don't you think, ladies?' she said, turning to Edwina and Miss Willis and the Garret-Lowdens, in the hope that she could quietly fit back into her old place in the household and leave them to take the lead once more.

'Lovely,' Edwina said emphatically, before anyone else could cast doubts on the profligate display of garlands and bosses of mistletoe, along with vast wreaths of holly and ivy, girdling rafters and columns and even wound round the balustrades surrounding the minstrels' gallery.

'It's cold as charity in here, though, my dears,' Miss Willis said, with a graphic shiver that reminded them all she had nearly been very ill only yesterday.

'Then we had best get on with it,' Imogen ordered practically, nodding to the kitchen maids waiting with jugs of mulled wine to come forward and fill the delicate cups waiting for the gentry. The bootboy and Heartsease Hall's two footmen then carried in vast flagons of mulled cider, with the scent of roasted apples and nutmeg wafting from them, to fill the more workmanlike mugs lined up for the purpose. 'Are you feeling a little warmer now, ma'am?' Imogen asked Miss Willis after that lady had approved the spiced wine and looked much happier with her hands wrapped around a warming cup.

'Who will set the brand to the fire?' Audrey demanded, impatient for the second fire to be lit.

At least then the long job of turning this vast cold barn into a fit venue for the tenants' ball would begin, and between the vast fireplaces at each end of the hall it might feel warm by Twelfth Night, supposing the tenants could get here.

'Miss Rose must do it,' Viola insisted, interrupting Sophie's gloomy reverie about how desolate she would feel as she watched Peter's carriage drive away as soon as the snow had receded from the plain below Heartsease Hall.

'No, it should be one of the family,' she protested, doing her best to back into the shadows—except Peter wouldn't stand aside and let her. She glared at him for being such a managing sort of man, and he raised one eyebrow in that irritating way he had and looked a question at her.

'Are you not one of the family, then?' he challenged softly.

'Some would say I'm not part of anyone's family,' she replied.

'Then they would be wrong,' he told her implacably, and the insistence that she was part of his at least, whether she wanted to be or not, was implicit in his steady grey gaze.

'Here you are, Miss Rose. Cordage has the brand lit from last year's Yule Log ready for you,' Audrey told her, as if there was no question of her not performing this important task, however hard she tried to wriggle out of it.

'Thank you, Cordage,' she said as graciously as she could manage, and took the long handled fire tongs with the flaming brand clasped safely at the end of them. She fervently hoped she wouldn't drop anything and ruin this whole quaint ceremony. 'Health, wealth and happiness to all Christian souls in this house, this day and every day, and a Merry Christmas to you all,' she intoned, as she remembered Sir Gyffard doing last year, and hoped she had the words in the right order.

Her hand wobbled as she did her best to set the carefully built fire alight with the final fragment of the Yule Log from last year, and it seemed as if everyone in the room was holding their breath when she missed her mark. Peter's strong fingers closed about hers and he stood behind to steady her. The next attempt took, largely thanks to him, and fire flared under the new ash log at last. Half of it had been cunningly split into eleven pieces that lay in mighty spars close by, so there would still be a part of the venerable old tree to burn on Twelfth Night without risk of it being used up before the season was over.

'Happy Christmas, Princess,' Peter murmured in her ear, and his being so close his body was all but wrapped about her made her cheeks burn and her body shiver with some sort of impossible hope he might stay like this and warm her. She hadn't felt truly warm in eight long years.

'Happy Christmas, my lord,' she replied huskily, and of course he had to let her go. How could he do otherwise when they were in full view of the household and their family and guests?

After a few toasts, and one of Cook's delicious little sponge cakes, they left the servants to their revels and returned to the sitting room to get warm and relax by the fire, while the fact of Christmas seeped into the contented atmosphere of the mellow old room.

'Won't they be cold?' Audrey asked.

'Won't who be cold?' Viola questioned with a baffled frown.

'Well, the servants, for one—and what about the dogs left out there in the stables with no Papa to smuggle them into his study where nobody is looking, and Timon and Lysander unable to get here to make them feel part of the family at Christmas?'

'I doubt they're feeling left out, Audrey. Cook made them a very fine dinner for Christmas Eve, as it's held to be a special night for animals, and Cox and the lads spoil them shamelessly even when it's not Christmas. Your papa is far more likely to complain his spaniels are too fat and contented to work when he comes home than he is to declare them mistreated in any way,' Sophie said, knowing her youngest charge would sleep with the dogs if she decided they were feeling left out.

'I always wanted to find out if cattle really do kneel on Christmas Eve,' Viola suggested hopefully.

'I was told they only do so if no human soul is there to see them do it, so I think we will leave them to their privacy,' Sophie said very firmly, since she didn't want to spend the night looking for her charges up hill and down dale.

'Spoken like a true governess,' Peter intervened, with a wry grimace in Viola and Audrey's direction to let them know that he sympathised, but such killjoys were part of life and must be endured.

'Good—since that is exactly what I am,' Sophie told him just as firmly. 'And, since it's my role in life to make certain these two young ladies are not so petted and in-dulged they stay up all night and go to sleep at noon to-morrow, pray excuse me whilst I see them to bed.'

'Don't think you can get away from me that easily,' Peter murmured as she did her best to slip past him.

'As if anything is easy when you're about,' she told him gruffly, and left the room in her pupils' wake.

'Are they asleep?'

He was there on the landing outside the schoolroom wing almost an hour later, and Sophie had to wonder if he'd been there the whole time, lying in wait for her.

'I doubt it,' she whispered, and signalled him away so their voices would not give the youngest Fraynes an ex-cuse to get out of bed and do their best to listen instead of going to sleep. 'Are you trying to ruin my reputation?

Or hasn't it occurred to you to worry about it?' she demanded as soon as they were out of earshot.

'No, I'm not, and, yes, it has.'

'Then why are you here?'

'Because following you about is the only way I can get you to speak to me alone, Sophie,' he told her implacably.

'We have nothing to say,' she told him weakly.

'No, you don't want us to say it. But we have years of things to talk about and well you know it. I really never thought you could be such a coward, Sophie mine,' he ended, and it seemed as if her heart might turn a somersault in her chest at the sound of that possessive and the warmth in his deep voice as he said it.

'I left, Peter,' she reminded him starkly.

'And no doubt we are going to talk about that quite a lot over the years ahead. But we're both here now,' he said, and towed her down the next flight of stairs towards the male quarters that were currently the older guest rooms. 'Keep quiet until we can speak with a few solid inches of seasoned oak between us and any eager listener, my dear,' he warned in a low masculine rumble as he tugged her along the corridor towards his room.

The way his warm, strong hand wrapped around her small one, as if he had no intention of letting it go again, somehow made all her excuses and protests melt away.

'We shouldn't be here alone,' she managed to say, as soon as he had shut and barred that door, then pulled the rich brocade curtain across it to block any access to the keyhole should the dishonourable Cedric be prowling the draughty corridors, looking for material for his next piece of muckraking even after what she had no doubt had been a thundering scold.

'No, we should be here together,' he told her, with a fierce passion in his eyes that must be fury at her for all she'd undone between them when she'd left. 'We should have been everywhere together these last years, Sophie, and you know it.'

'I do—so why did you drag me in here? Why draw out the agony when you were never the sort of man who indulged in such petty revenge. Peter Vane?'

'Idiot woman,' he said in a raw voice, as if she was dancing a jig all over his abraded feelings.

'Why, then? You can't possibly want me. I hurt you. No, more than that—I trampled all the love we had for each other into dust, then walked away from you as if you never meant more to me than a snap of my fingers.'

'Typical Sophie Bonet,' he told her laconically. 'All fire and pride and exaggeration as well as that "I'll fight my own battles, thank you very much" expression that's supposed to put me in my place and keep me as far away from you as possible.'

'I can't hide what I am.'

'You seem to have been doing an excellent job of doing just that for the last eight years,' he said, as cool now as if they were discussing the weather outside.

She flopped down on the nearest chair and let her shoulders droop in defeat. 'No, I haven't,' she managed to argue. 'I've made a very poor hand of living without you, but it's all I deserve, Peter,' she admitted painfully, and she refused to look up at him and stared intently at the fine pattern on the Persian carpet by the bed.

'And that's typical as well,' he said, with a little more heat, as if her self-flagellation had succeeded in rousing his temper more than her sins could. 'You spent most of your childhood damned in your own eyes because you didn't die at your father's side. I know he would rather have suffered the death of a thousand cuts than seen a hair on your head hurt in any way, because he obviously loved you, Sophie. Imagine the grief and pain it would cause him if he could see you like this, taking the guilt of the world on your shoulders again.'

'A slight exaggeration,' she managed to say, with a poor attempt at a smile. 'You make me sound like such a poor little honey, my lord,' she tried to joke.

'Not you. You're a spitfire, Sophie Bonet, but even if you couldn't allow me to know my own mind when we were so young and hardly fit to be let out of the schoolroom, kindly acknowledge I must know it by now.'

'I do know you must hate me,' she said mournfully, too tired to keep up the front that they meant nothing to each other and his opinion didn't matter to her now they were alone.

'I will if you don't stop behaving like the heroine out of a melodrama,' he said bracingly. 'I don't hate you. Even when I was trying to I couldn't manage it. When I realised it was you in the snow yesterday, and growled at you like a bear, I still wanted to stop you in your snowy tracks and kiss you senseless out there in all that snow rash as ever, you stubborn little idiot.'

'Then why didn't you?' she heard herself ask, and wondered if weariness with her life without him had finally snapped the connection between her brain and her tongue.

'Because we would have been frozen, despite the fire we always seem to light between us, and even if you want to die for love, I don't, Princess.'

'I'm not a princess, and never was as far as you were concerned. You made it very clear to me that an empty title, without anything to back up my airs and graces, held no weight with *you* the first time I tried to look down my nose at you after Aunt Hermione had agreed to marry your father.'

'And there really wasn't a long way to look, was there?' he asked, with a crooked smile she remembered so well it made her heart clench with forbidden hope and then race on. 'I was a fool, Sophie. Your aunt was my father's better half in every way, and it took him losing her to make us all realise it. He wasn't even half the man he had been without her.'

'Well, she was a remarkable woman,' she replied, reluctant even now to denigrate the last Lord Sylbourne to his son.

'And you're very like her.'

'No, she would never have made the stupid mistakes I have committed,' Sophie accused herself wretchedly.

'If you made a mistake it was made when you were far too young to be forced to decide your future and mine by my father. We probably *were* too young to be so in love back then, Sophie. That was very likely the only piece of sense my father had to offer among all the self-serving nonsense he spouted so he could go on losing himself in a bottle and betting a fortune on the next turn of a card.'

'Having loved my aunt, as he seemed to do sincerely enough, I still can't see why he thought the solution to his difficulties lay in making you pay with your freedom. But I should have stood up to him and insisted on waiting for you to come home. I couldn't have borne it if he was right, you see? I couldn't have stood by and watched you marry Diamantha Rivers, Peter. It would have ripped my heart out.'

'Any more than I can watch you wed Sir Gyffard Frayne without wanting to kill him, however worthy a gentleman he might be.'

'Oh, no, I truly won't do that. I have already told you that I have decided it wouldn't be fair to marry any man with nothing but tolerance and mutual loneliness to bind us to each other, let alone someone I respect as I do Sir Gyffard. How could I make all those solemn promises before God and not mean them, Peter?'

'Then marry me instead, Sophie. Be my lady and my love for the rest of our days. Let me stand between you and Fouché and his so-called Dangerous émigrés List, and you can protect me from rampaging females who want my title and new-found riches.'

'How could you ever trust me again after what I did to you?' she said, and the barren years and betrayed promises she'd put between them seemed to line up to reproach her one by one.

'You did it for love, didn't you? So long as you still love me, why wouldn't I trust you to keep on doing so?'

'Because I'm stupid, credulous and apparently witless,' she admitted painfully.

'Have you been taking lovers whilst I was busy making my fortune, then?'

'No, of course not,' she snapped indignantly.

She felt shocked that he could even ask her such a question when all she'd done was dream of him, she now realised. All these years she'd been comparing every man she met with him and dismissing them as falling far short of the standard he'd set—the mark he'd left on her very soul, as if she was branded with love of him alone for life. And that was before she'd set eyes on mature Peter Vane and come to know that even the younger one had been less of a man than this mighty, stubborn creature who looked at her with such hostility in his beloved grey eyes. Her heart jumped for joy at the very sight of him, even when all he did was glare at her.

'There you are, then. You kept the faith for me,' he said, looking uncomfortable when she eyed him militantly.

'*You* took lovers, didn't you?' she asked, possessive fury driving her to her feet so she could crick her neck and glare up at him at last, as if they'd actually been married all this time rather than as far from it as they could be.

'Well, I *am* a man,' he excused himself, and the wry look he gave her almost disarmed her, since it seemed to acknowledge it was a very feeble excuse indeed.

'And you're actually asking me to marry you with that sort of logic behind you to persuade me you'll always be faithful to me?' she asked, and stamped her foot to tell him how impossible that was since words failed her.

'You left me, Sophie, not the other way about. It felt as if everything I was and could be with you had been ripped out of me and thrown to the dogs. At first I didn't want to even see another woman, because they all fell so far short of my fiery pocket Venus. I suppose I should thank you, really, since all that frustration and anger went into finding ways of making enough money to pay off the mountain of debt my father had managed to saddle me with. At the time I didn't feel thankful in the least, and that's when I got really angry with you, Sophie Bonet.'

'So you revenged yourself on me by making love to other women? How convenient of me to set you free with a title, apparently enough money to do anything you want whenever you want it, a form like Apollo Belvedere and the face of a fallen angel. Women must have very nearly *begged* to be the instrument of your vengeance against me, Peter Vane.'

He tried to look modest and failed, and Sophie gave a muffled scream of vexation, letting her fists tighten as she beat them on the air to dissipate some of the fury roaring about inside her looking for a release. She refused to simply thump him and end up burnt by angry tears and sobbing in his arms at the terrible void that had opened up inside her when he admitted there had been other women in his life.

'I have no right to upbraid you,' she made herself admit blankly, once she thought she could speak without wanting to yell insults at him. 'But I won't marry you, Peter.'

'Because I spent five years in a far away country uselessly longing for you? Then came home to try and find you and found not one clue to where you might be? Little wonder if I finally gave in and sought consolation in the arms of a woman who did want me, don't you think?' he asked bleakly. 'And for that you're going to deny us everything?'

'You stayed faithful to me all those five years?' she couldn't help herself asking.

'Of course I did, you idiot. I mistakenly thought you must know, deep down, that I'd only gone away in the first place so I could come back with enough for us to live on free of debt and happy at Holm Park as we always planned to be.'

'No, I didn't know any of that,' she said, and bitter regret for all the hope she could have had all this time threatened to sap her fury at him for making love to another woman. 'I thought you'd married Diamantha,' she finally confessed.

'How on earth could you?' he demanded, and this time it was his turn to pace hastily away from her, in case the fury in his eyes should translate into shaking her physically. 'You must have known I couldn't wed that shrew of a woman, with her cruel eyes and only an abacus instead of a heart. What sort of man would I have been if I'd meekly given in to her father and mine and married a woman I disliked purely for her money? Even if I'd never met you and loved you so much it made me ache with joy it was an impossible idea,' he turned to inform her impatiently, and he continued to pace.

'I saw her once. Sir Gyffard had insisted his wife go to the spa at Cheltenham in the hope the waters might help, even though she told me she knew very well they would not, and that's where I saw Diamantha. One of the gossips told me she was the Countess of Sylbourne. Needless to say I made sure we never met face to face, and I don't suppose she would have done anything to disabuse me if we had, for she always hated me. Indeed, she must loathe you as well now, for refusing to wed her and making her take on your father to gain that precious title of hers instead.'

'Aye,' he said ruefully, 'I think we can safely say she would go out of her way to do me any ill she could. How she'd love to know she caused so much pain and misunderstanding between us that you're still being stubborn and irrational and refusing to wed me all these years later.'

'Maybe so, but she didn't make you take a mistress,' Sophie sniped at him, surprised at the relentless bitterness that idea aroused in her when she hadn't exactly given him cause to be steadfast and hopeful in his love for her.

'Nobody did. But poor Kitty's a gentle creature, and her heart really isn't in being a courtesan. I suppose I make the ideal protector for such a half-hearted hussy,' he admitted ruefully, looking warily at her as if he knew she hadn't quite forgiven him all the same.

CHAPTER THIRTEEN

'You felt sorry for her, didn't you?' Sophie accused, hands on hips and looking very like a furious fishwife even to her own eyes when she caught a glimpse of herself in the watery old glass of the Venetian mirror.

'Maybe,' Peter said cautiously.

'Is she beautiful?' she asked stupidly, as if this 'poor Kitty' of his could be anything else but breathtakingly lovely.

'If statuesque blondes were truly my type, then, yes, she is beautiful. Had she not been so she would hardly be a courtesan in the first place, would she? Even though she lacks the verve and boldness of a true exponent of the art—or at least so I must suppose, since I never had one of them in my keeping before,' he told her, with a bland expression and unrevealing eyes that would have stood him in very good stead at the sort of card games his father had lost so disastrously.

'And what do you intend to do with her if I should be stupid enough to agree to marry you, my lord?' she demanded, as if she might actually be considering such a ridiculous idea—which she wasn't, of course.

'Find her a suitably besotted husband or set her up in a shop of some sort. She might enjoy being a sensation in a small town or watering place, since I don't think she has the sharp edges to succeed in Bond Street.'

'So long as it's a small town a very long way from here, and preferably in another country,' she hissed at him, and she didn't dare step any nearer lest she gave in to her temper and slapped his face. Unfortunately, underneath all the fire and fury, reason was beginning to persuade her he could hardly have known she was pining for him alone here. She'd set the rumours of her exotic new life about herself, to mislead him that she was running off with some rogue she'd managed to enthral, while every thought she had was obsessed by him.

Why on earth she'd done it, when she had hardly been able to endure any other man but him taking her hand in all the time since they'd last met, was beyond her now. Pride, she decided as she made herself glare at him as if she might forgive him one day—if he was lucky.

'Dublin?' he suggested, with mockery back in his gaze now he'd somehow picked up that her temper was more pretence than fact.

Hesitating as she tried to remember if the Vanes had any estates there, she sighed and gave up on righteous indignation at last. 'She might not want to go so far from family and friends,' she said, refusing to meet his eyes and admit she was softening towards the woman. 'I suppose we'd best ask her before we plan the poor woman's life for her as if she has no say in the matter.'

'Perhaps you could leave that to me?' he suggested with mock diffidence.

'And perhaps you should not stretch your luck, my lord,' she said sweetly.

'Then are you going to marry me after all, Sophie?' he asked, dropping all pretence of smooth and gentlemanly poise as he looked down at her as if she held his heart and soul in her hands.

'I haven't quite forgotten your "poor Kitty" yet, my lord—and what will become of the Frayne girls if I do?' she asked, with a frown for their fate if they did happen to be orphaned before they came of age or married.

'If their sister hasn't made a brilliant marriage before then—which I very much doubt, by the way, since she is almost as bright and beautiful a debutante as you would have been had my father not spoilt that for you as well— they could come and live with us. If we can persuade their father it would be right to leave them to the care of a Vane after the debacle of my father's supposed guardianship of you, and my seduction of a princess I should have respected a lot more.'

'Uncle Hart was as poor a protector to his own son and daughter as he was to me, Peter, and at least Sir Gyffard is a fine judge of character,' she soothed, even as she ignored that comment about what had been a very mutual ravishment of the senses. 'If you were willing to give him an assurance the girls would always have a home at Holm Park, I'm quite sure he would never visit the sins of the father on the son just because it was easier than bothering to know you himself.'

'What an extraordinary paragon he must be,' Peter said grumpily.

'Don't be ridiculous. He's just a man.'

'Since he wanted to marry you, he can't just be *any* man, can he?'

'Not really. He loved Lady Frayne far too much to really want to marry again, and unlike your father he seems content to remain a widower. Or at least he did until his eldest son engaged himself to Miss Garret-Lowden. I'm certain the idea of a second marriage never entered his head before he met the poor girl and decided she would grow into the mirror image of her mother one day.'

'A notion that took root very quickly once it had occurred to him, so far as I can tell,' he argued, and Sophie realised he was as jealous of her friendship with Sir Gyffard Frayne as she was of his with the lovely Kitty, who had no doubt managed to overcome her reluctance towards her profession in order to be an enthusiastic pillow-mate to such an exceptional aristocrat as my lord Sylbourne.

'It was only ever a suggestion that might solve his dilemma and protect me from future penury. He would never have offered for me if he thought there was the slightest chance I wanted to marry anyone else.'

'Why not? You're ravishingly lovely when you're not guying yourself up in that ridiculous grey gown or trying to hide in corners, and even then it doesn't do much to conceal how extraordinary a female you truly are.'

'Nor do I seem to have succeeded very well at that with you about,' she muttered irritably.

'How could you even think you could hide anything from me, Sophie, when I know every inch of you under all that starch and propriety?'

'Because it's been eight years, and I've changed and so have you.'

'Not at heart,' he argued, and fierce emotions were playing behind his intent gaze now he seemed to have decided all this sidestepping and delaying must end. 'Underneath all that disapproval and Miss Rose skittishness you're still my Sophie. Heaven help me, I'm still yours as surely as I was on my twentieth birthday.'

'I remember,' she admitted, her eyelids heavy and her mouth soft with the very thought of that day and night of giving themselves to each other. No matter that they'd had precious little means between them for any other kind of gift, it had been the finest thing either of them had ever offered or received.

'Oh, so do I, Sophie mine, so do I,' he murmured, and he evoked the past a little more intensely by lifting her onto the satin smooth dresser so she wouldn't have to crick her neck when he kissed her.

The smile she would have given him wobbled a little at the poignant familiarity of him doing that, and all the changes in him she hadn't been there to see. 'I do love you, Peter,' she assured him earnestly, and tenderness fought with that fire for a moment as he looked down her with certainty and sadness in his own steady gaze.

'I know you do, my lover,' he murmured, and he whispered a fleeting kiss across her lips. Her breath seemed to stall in her body before she sucked in air like a drowning woman. '*My* lover,' he told her, his eyes steady on hers as he dared her to argue.

'I know,' she admitted, with a smug smile that turned into a wicked grin as she decided eight years was quite long enough to wait for her lover to ravish her with all the natural flair of a man who'd obviously been made to love her. 'Get on with it, you lordly gentleman, you,' she demanded.

'It will be my pleasure,' he told her, and seized her, met her and gave her exactly what she wanted—need. Pure and unbroken need.

'To the devil with being a gentleman, my lord, I want fast and furious, because I haven't had my hands on you for so long it breaks my heart to think about it,' she told him, her eyes bold and her supposedly regal nature in full flow for once.

'Anything Your Highness commands,' he said, with a piratical smile as he made very short work of getting her out of the green stuff gown by ripping it from stem to stern.

'Peter! I've only got four gowns,' she protested, with a last shred of Miss Rose's stern practicality.

'Only three to go, then,' he told her unrepentantly as he yanked the laces of her short corset undone and undid her a little more.

'I'll be naked long before you end your enforced stay at Heartsease Hall at this rate,' she said half-heartedly.

'Good,' he said with a wolfish grin as he disposed of

her shift with almost as much disrespect. 'You'll have to stay in bed, then.'

'So I will,' she said with a smile nearly as wicked as his own as she set about his superfine coat and plain waistcoat with similar disrespect, if not quite such a devastating effect. 'And so will you, my lord.'

'There's a lot of it about,' he said virtuously, and lifted her, all but naked as she was, into his arms and held her there, captive to his kiss and his touch and all her own yearning senses.

She took possession of her love by bestriding him, wrapping her lithe and eager legs round his narrow waist and squirming even closer. 'I want you,' she told him starkly, as soon as she could rip her lushly kiss stung mouth away from his.

'I'd never have known,' he told her, with a teasing joy in her headlong desperation to love him with all she was.

'Now,' she demanded as he did his best to carry her to the bed like that gentleman she'd told him not to be. *'Here,'* she said starkly as the fiery desperation grinding within her tightened its needy fist.

Sophie seized his mouth with hers, wound her fingers into his springing dark gold curls and took what she wanted, since he really was too much of a gentleman to bind their mouths together so emphatically and she felt her very teeth ache with need of him. She opened her mouth wide on his and filled her senses with Peter Vane, loved him with her eyes and her touch, moaned her need of him, and listened as he let out a great groan of satisfaction when she raised her head long enough to let them both breathe.

She couldn't get enough of filling every sense she had with her wild young love, back in her arms after so very long and now even more loved, more lovable than she'd ever dreamt he could become back when she'd thought they couldn't love each other any more if they lived for ever.

Frantically she disposed of his dratted neckcloth as if the folds and knot might drive her mad before she had it off him, even though it was far simpler than the styles he used to affect. Next she ripped open the buttons on his shirt, not willing to wait while she unclasped his arms, and somehow managed to pull it over his head without his putting her down.

'You can keep the stupid thing on and serve you right,' she told him grumpily.

'Why?' he asked rather breathlessly, and he bore her relentlessly backwards to seat her on that so solid oak dresser that had probably never been polished by a royal bottom in its entire and venerable history—as he told her, with laughter and all sorts of devilment in his dancing grey eyes as he shifted her on it until he had her just where he wanted her.

'Never mind silly questions. Take those damned breeches off,' she snapped, wondering if she might shatter from sheer need if he didn't hurry up and take her back to their own private world again at long last.

'Your wish is my command, Princess,' he drawled, as

if enjoying the spectacle of her sprawled naked and open and unmistakably eager in front of him a little too much.

'Lies,' she declared, and she moved to scramble up and take him down a peg or two by demonstrating to both of them how rigidly and emphatically he wanted her, since it was very obvious even through those wretched evening breeches of his. 'Well, get on with it then, you laggard,' she ordered, as he finally forgot to tease and be a perfect gentle knight, much to her relief, and ripped the offending things off as fast as he could ruin them as thoroughly as he had her almost-best gown.

The hot flare of colour across his lean cheekbones, the wildly unruly curling of his uniquely fascinating hair, the ache for her mouth on his emphatic in the self-mocking twist of need as he fell on her as if he was every bit as hungry as she was and wanted him to be—all were true and real, and she might have pinched herself to let herself know it was true if only she could spare that much sense from loving him.

He threw himself into the task every bit as enthusiastically as she'd hoped, and for a while all the noise there was in the ancient and somehow rather knowing silence of this lovely old room was the quiet hiss of well seasoned applewood in the hearth and the sighs and moans and urgent little noises of lovers enjoying each other as wildly as possible. If Sophie could have climbed out of her skin and into his she would have done it as his hot mouth took hers in a ravening, restless kiss that shot fire to every extremity of her and then back to the searingly needy core of her that ached and ground as if it might burn her up before the longed-for fact of him could join with her and make her whole again.

'Peter, oh, Peter,' was the only demand her tongue seemed capable of when they eventually ripped their clinging mouths apart long enough to heave some air into their labouring lungs.

'Princess Sophie,' he breathed into her mouth, as if he couldn't keep away from it, and looked down at her with his wild, wide heart in his eyes. 'May I take us both to paradise at last now, please?'

'Haven't I been begging you to do just that for half an eternity, you jack pudding?' she insulted him triumphantly, with all the love she felt for this complicated man, who was simply her love and her lover once again, and exactly where he belonged.

As he finally pulled her to the edge of the dresser and thrust into the slick depths of her she let herself go boneless against his supporting, bracketing arms. For a delicious moment of blissful satisfaction she sighed and let her head fall back, felt her long hair slip down onto the equally glossy wood and spread over his braced arms, brushing over the muscled strength of them as if even her hair wanted to meld itself to every inch of him it could wind itself around.

As he came fully into her and locked them there, in that first glory of togetherness in eight desolate years, she let herself accept and enjoy and just be part of him for one long, lovely moment. She met his eyes with all the secrets and sorrows of those lost years in her own, then flexed her internal muscles in a silent, witchy demand for more—much more. Not abandoning one slight tingle of how special this was, she moved to share every part of it with him, demanding equality of wanting and loving as she used her lithe limbs to draw him in even closer, braced herself on her own arms so she could strive with all she had to give, to take them towards a fierce and ever more urgent loving.

His hard body was mightier within and without her than she remembered it, his muscles firmer, and yet he was still long, sleek and almost heartbreakingly elegant under her wondering touch as she wriggled herself even closer, locked herself more emphatically with him and rode that wondrous ride up to the peak that was waiting. Almost there, almost there, and then they drove each other over the top of it—and how could even memory equal this wonder?

Sophie felt herself glide out of the world and fly as if she were one and true together with him—he one wing of this magnificent bird and she the other. Convulsing wildly on his striving member as they both heaved searing breath into their labouring lungs, she reached her wildest, truest climax ever as he finally soared into her and gave a long, sweet moan of inexpressible ecstasy. He looked into her wide open eyes and gave her everything they'd ever left out giving.

She held it, and them, joined and triumphant as they were, for a long sweet moment of satisfaction and then shifted so she could hug and pat and praise him better. She even finally allowed him to carry her to the bed, refusing to let him draw out of her. There he somehow managed to persuade her to separate from him and positioned them so they were spooned, her on him, the way she recalled from that last glorious birthday feast of loving when they'd been so very young.

'Do you…?' she began, only to have him finish the sentence in her mind as he had been able to do just as infuriatingly back then.

'Of course I do. I've had nothing else to do but remember how we were together for what feels like eternity,' he told her as if her even asking was making his temper snap and snarl.

'You had Kitty,' she argued cantankerously

'And how I wish I'd lied to you about her now,' he said half seriously, and she made herself consider her wild jealousy of the only other woman who had been able to enjoy even a shadow of this banquet of the senses with him since the passion-soaked night they'd shared in that bower of heavy-scented roses. That had been before Hartley Vane had struck out at them in his pain and selfishness and made sure there would be no more such nights until now.

'Of course you do. But even if I might bring her up again every time you frustrate me or refuse to swear black's white just to keep me sweet and compliant and agreeing with you about all the things you intend doing anyway, I would never have had you keep her a secret to drag at us and blur the love I will always have for you, Peter, even if I do nag and fall short of your ideal woman in so many ways.'

'My ideal wife,' he corrected her, as if he was still afraid she might flit off for another eternity of years.

'Never,' she argued, and felt his flinch all through her well-loved and luxuriating body. 'I mean never ideal— not never a wife, Your Lordship,' she finished with just enough expectation to make him bring his magically arousing touch to cup her breasts in an echo of that time she'd run over so meticulously in her head only last night.

He felt the changes in her from nymph of seventeen to woman of five and twenty and let his hands tell her how much he appreciated the new abundance maturity had brought with it. His hands moved only enough to tantalise her into writhing a little lower down his torso, so he could close his palms over her eagerly peaking nipples.

'Do you think the priest whom Cox tells me actually lives in his parish below Heartsease Hall would marry so disgraceful a couple as Lord Sylbourne and his lover of far too long, my darling?' he asked, as he let his fingers play with her breasts as if they had a mind of their own and he couldn't stop them.

'I think he would be beside himself with importance to do so, Peter. But how can he when there have been no banns read—and at least we will have to wait for three whole Sundays while they *are* read?'

'He can because I have a special licence to wed you from the Archbishop of Canterbury. No lesser a being could authorise it, apparently.'

'How on earth can you have?' she demanded, forgetting how much she was enjoying being open to the Earl of Sylbourne's ruthless seduction for long enough to change her position. She thrust an elbow in his lean stomach and with a twist of her supple spine wriggled until she could lean up on the other one and stare down into his eyes. 'You didn't even know where I was, let alone if I was still meekly waiting for you to come home and marry me,' she accused, deciding this was far too important a matter to be settled on her back, even when he was on his as well.

Finally flipping herself over, so she could glare down at him in comfort, she felt her heavy locks slip over his responsive loins and did her best not to grin as his un-mistakable responsiveness reared its handsome head once more. 'Kindly be serious—as well as patient, for once,' she chided him, as if that part of him actually had a voice as well as apparently having a mind of its own.

'You can't blame that bit of me, Sophie my darling. It and all the rest of me has had to live without the endless luxury of loving you for far too long,' he said, with an-other of his wolfish smiles that told her he didn't intend it to be very much longer before they experienced such luxury all over again.

'The special license?' she reminded him sternly, be-fore he managed to seduce her into forgetting he'd ever mentioned it in the first place.

'Oh, that,' he said, as if recalling a spare hat he'd or-dered in a distracted moment, or another shirt to replace the one she'd just ruined. 'I went to Lambeth Palace with Giles Wroxley so he could procure a special licence to wed my sister with what I considered at the time to be indecent haste,' he told her, his eyes fixed on her body like some princely connoisseur, rather than meeting her gaze and revealing the hopes and dreams that licence was threatening to give away.

'And?' she demanded, shifting so the silken mass of her now quite disorderly dark hair fell over her shoulder and slicked over his belly like a snare neither of them wanted him to resist.

'Can't we talk about it later?' he gasped, and she watched every muscle he had tighten and flex at the sight of her naked and totally unashamed in the firelight.

'No,' she said tersely, trailing her index finger over him, with the silk of her hair between it and the slick tautness of his wanting skin.

'Very well, then. I found myself demanding a wedding license of my own to wed you, my Princess, almost as emphatically as Giles had done as soon as I could get rid of the persistent idiot and retrace my steps. I think the clerk was inclined not to let me have one, when I was obviously in such a bad temper about it, but I suppose he didn't like to argue with an earl who was single and possibly in his right mind with every right to wed a lady who was clearly of age if only he could find you and persuade you to have him.'

'Hmm, we'll have to see about that,' she said evasively, beginning to enjoy herself as she let that exploring finger work its way up to his torso and flick, oh, so accidentally, against his tight, masculine nipple.

'Even though I hadn't seen you since you were seventeen, and lacked the slightest idea of where you'd taken yourself off to when you left me behind like the proverbial worn-out glove, I wanted that confounded licence more than I wanted to see Holm Park restored to the ridiculous glory my great-grandfather insisted on lavishing on it and to see Dina wed and happy. I searched up hill and down dale for you when I first came back to England, my love, but suddenly I discovered I hadn't given up hope of finding you after all.'

'So you have this hopelessly hopeful piece of paper with you, then, do you, my lord?' she asked, suddenly almost as breathless as he sounded at this vast idea of her being his wife, as they had once dreamt and expected so easily.

'I do. Although I'm not letting you anywhere near it until we actually need it, considering how little respect you seem to have for the rest of my possessions,' he teased. But she knew there was a thread of nervousness and perhaps even desperation underneath his words, and felt the sudden heat of tears behind her eyes.

'If I didn't love you already I think I might start right now,' she whispered, and finally sank her head low enough to kiss him with a promise on her lips that was almost as solemn a vow as the one he'd just asked her to make him. 'I love you, Peter. I have loved you since I was sixteen and you came home all grown up and arrogant and handsome and I still do.'

'You always have to go one better, don't you, Princess?' he demanded. 'Very well, then. You have a year's start on me in the loving stakes. But once it occurred to me to fall in love with you, dim and desperately misguided as I clearly was at nineteen not to see straight away I would never escape your toils, I loved you with every nerve and all the sense and nonsense in me, Sophie. Now, will you finally admit you're going to marry me, and let me use that license I let myself lay out so much blunt for on the mere outside chance I'd finally manage to get you back?'

'Yes, my love, I'll marry you, and let you marry me at long last,' she agreed.

'At last,' he breathed, and lay back on his pillows as if he truly had doubted his powers of persuasion, which she found deeply endearing as well as rather incredible.

'Love me?' She bent over him and asked the question in a husky voice he seemed to like, from the leap of heat in his silver-grey eyes as he stared up at her. She loomed over him like some legendary enchantress, with power and magic at her fingertips.

'I thought you'd never ask,' he replied outrageously, and did just that.

CHAPTER FOURTEEN

'Isn't it just like you two idiots to get married on Twelfth Night, of all the days you could choose in a year?' Lady Edwina Wroxley teased the bride, and stepped into line as matron of honour behind Sophie. She spared an amused glance for the other three bridesmaids as Imogen, Viola and Audrey lined up, looking like occasional angels in descending sizes.

'Be quiet, Edwina, we're in church now,' Miss Willis told her niece repressively, and stepped forward to give away the bride to her waiting groom, since Cordage had refused the honour as unfitting his butlerly dignity, and it was the one day of the year when the usual order of things could be turned on its head.

Sophie smoothed her brocaded silk skirts as Dina and the girls fussed with the train they had insisted on adding to the gown they had managed to contrive. It was made out of a vast one they'd discovered in a trunk in the attics, and it must have been worn to court by Sir Gyffard's mother or even his grandmother, when they were young and nearly as narrow in the waist as Sophie. By today's standards she supposed the material was a little too rich and stiff, but she loved the creamy richness of it, shot through as it was with fanciful golden roses that no garden could ever hope to produce.

She gripped the tight little posy made up of tiny sprigs of rosemary and all the usual evergreens a bride was supposed to carry for luck and prosperity and probably fertility in miniature, along with clusters of tiny, fragile snowdrop buds to make it uniquely hers as well. She had the stable boys and perhaps even Merryweather himself to thank for them, since they had secretly dug bulbs out of the garden so carefully they didn't break a single root and brought them into the warm to force into early life, despite the snow that still lay on the cold ground in ragged patches after nearly a fortnight. Even so, they were little more than buds of promise rather than full flowers, but she loved them far more that she would any hothouse blooms.

'Ready?' she asked her chief bridesmaid, so recently a bride herself that she'd very nearly danced into church in Sophie's wake.

'Ready,' Dina confirmed, her eyes so firmly fixed on the groomsman standing at Peter's side that Sophie wondered philosophically if Edwina might trip over the bride's train and land them all of a heap on the chancellery steps before they got safely up the aisle.

And so Princess Sophie Jeanne Rosalind Bonet married Peter Adam George Fitzroy Vane, Earl of Sylbourne, only eight and a half years after they had both intended.

'Happy now?' Giles Wroxley demanded of his oldest friend as he limped down the aisle in their wake with his new bride on his arm.

'How could I not be with a princess on my arm, old man?' Peter replied with the ironic smile Sophie was beginning to realise covered his deepest and most preciously guarded secrets—secrets only she was permitted to know. How she loved that intimacy, that true sharing of all they were with each other.

'Happy?' Edwina asked Sophie a lot more seriously, and her heart sang over the fact that all the estrangement and distrust between them had been overcome so she could smile blissfully at her one-time playmate, best friend and now sister-in-law.

'Never happier,' she admitted.

'And you promise you'll contrive to be presented at Court at the same time I am?' Imogen demanded, as if not going there alone might make up in some degree for losing her one time governess and now friend from the everyday running of her life.

Not that Sophie thought Imogen would need anyone's support but her chosen husband's for much longer, since Giles Wroxley's elder brother, Viscount Seetley, had looked as if he'd been run over by a herd of elephants the instant he'd laid eyes on Imogen. Recalling how suddenly he'd stopped complaining about his long trek through the snow at his stubborn younger brother's side on Boxing Day as he'd gazed dumbstruck at Imogen and she had gazed back, Sophie wondered if he would even wait long enough for her to make her debut and be presented before he begged Sir Gyffard for his eldest daughter's hand in marriage.

'And you're quite sure you don't mind if we come and stay with you at Holm Park until Papa returns home?' Viola asked anxiously, as if she thought three Frayne girls might be too much trouble for a newly wed couple to have about the place.

'And any time he has to be away from you after that— unless he would have it otherwise and takes you with him,' Sophie reassured her patiently, because somehow Viola would always be the one out of the Frayne sisters who felt separation most acutely. She dearly hoped Sir Gyffard would agree that the not quite twenty miles between Holm Park and Heartsease Hall didn't mean the two families couldn't be close friends.

'Do you have sporting dogs, Lord Sylbourne?' Audrey asked, as if that was the most important asset a lordly mansion might have.

'As well as assorted hounds of mixed origin, who somehow managed to adopt me along my way,' he replied with a grin.

Sophie decided he would make a wonderful father, and hoped it would be sooner rather than later, as he was such an incurable rescuer of forlorn curs and rootless princesses.

'Then I'm sure I shall like it,' Audrey said with a happy skip as they finally reached the porch door and braced themselves for the chill outside.

'Oh Peter, look,' Sophie said, and there was a threat

of tears in her voice when she'd promised herself she wouldn't cry on perhaps the happiest day of her life so far.

'I am looking, love,' he told her with a smile as he contemplated his smart travelling carriage, now rescued from its forlorn sojourn in a farmer's field and polished within an inch of its life.

It would have made a fine enough sight on its own, without the high-spirited team groomed and buffed until everything about then shone, and Merryweather grinning at them from the box dressed in his very best livery. The addition of holly, ivy and a huge bunch of mistletoe hung inside it made the assembled company gasp, and the Frayne girls danced with pleasure and excitement as they did their best to throw a generous shower of rice and mercifully softer dried rose petals over the bride and groom.

'Will that do until we get back to the hall, do you suppose, my lord?' she asked innocently with a nod at the grand display inside the coach.

'Possibly, but since it must all come down tonight anyway I might as well make the best of it while its still there,' Peter replied, with a rakish leer at his laughing bride, who somehow didn't look in the least bit shy about the obvious implication that they would be kissing all the way back to the Hall—especially when it was true.

'Don't forget that you need to attend your own wedding breakfast, will you?' Edwina whispered as she untucked Sophie's looped train to make sure it didn't get irretrievably creased on the three-mile journey back to the Hall.

'I wouldn't miss it for the world,' Sophie assured her with a blissful smile, and threw her precious wedding flowers neatly into Imogen's startled hands before Jem closed the carriage door and Peter's arm stole round her waist as if he couldn't bear to let her go again.

'My Countess,' Peter observed with complete satisfaction, and he grabbed the first of the milky berries above their heads and kissed his wife until they both lost count of how many he needed to keep a tally.

'My love,' she finally found the breath to tell him, with such aching sweetness in her heart she wondered if she might have to cry after all.

'If any of our daughters suggest a long engagement, please don't let them marry the idiot at all, will you, love?' he asked. She shook her head and looked a question at him. 'Well, I won't think any crass boy who might lead them through our rose garden at midnight with all sorts of wicked ideas on his mind anywhere near good enough for them, so it will be up to you to decide if he is. If he loves them half as dearly as their father does their mother, it might make me see reason.'

'What a fine collection of challenges lie ahead of me,' Sophie said with a contented sigh, and kissed the stern father of all the daughters they hadn't yet begun.

'You'll be equal to every one, Miss Rose,' he told her, with a hot gleam in his eyes as he experimented with the feel of brocade overlaid on woman. He seemed to like the slip and richness of it much better than he had any of her other gowns—not that any of them were fit to be worn any longer, as she informed him militantly.

'They were never fit to be worn in the first place,' he replied unrepentantly. 'Never did I think to see my lovely, exotic Sophie bundled up so unbecomingly in bombazine as I did that first night, love. I can't tell you how badly I wanted to rip it off you there and then.'

'You looked at me as if you hated me,' she said sadly, feeling odd for a moment as she pitied her rather solitary former self and marvelled at the transformation her life had undergone since my lord Sylbourne got lost in the snow.

'I think I almost did that first night, but I should have known the season wouldn't allow it—even if my love for you wasn't already beating down my resolutions never to let you half-kill me with love ever again.'

'Did I do that?'

'Yes, and the only reason I forgave you for it was because I could see you were only half alive without me.'

'Brute,' she condemned, after he'd kissed her yet again.

'Witch,' he said placidly, as he carefully undid all Edwina's fussing with her unfashionably abundant locks and threw the hairpins on the floor after her misused bonnet.

'It's been a wondrous Christmas season after all,' he confided as he picked yet another berry and added it to the soggy mass already in his top pocket. She hoped he was only ruining his snowy handkerchief and not his superfine wedding coat.

'Better than any I dared even dream of when it began to snow that night,' she confirmed with a blissful sigh, after she had honoured the pearly mistletoe berry as eagerly as her husband.

'For next year I would like a tiny little girl with raven

hair and velvet brown eyes and just the same arrogant tip to her chin as her mother is blessed with,' he said, and she was awed by the very idea as well as half in love with it herself.

'You'll have what God sends you, my lord Sylbourne,' she told him brusquely. The alternative of a strong and vigorous boy with his father's bright curls and laughing grey eyes lurked in her dark eyes as they met his.

'And if he blesses me half as richly as he has done this Christmas I will be forever thankful,' he said, with just as much delight in all that might be and all that was as had lit her own soul with joy and laughter since the day they'd found each other again.

* * * * *

Sparkling Christmas kisses!

Bryony's daughter, Lizzie, wants was a *dad* for Christmas and Bryony's determined to fulfil this Christmas wish. But when every date ends in disaster, Bryony fears she'll need a miracle. But she only needs a man for Christmas, not for love…right?

Unlike Bryony, the last thing Helen needs is a man! In her eyes, all men are *Trouble*! Of course, it doesn't help that as soon as she arrives in the snow-covered mountains, she meets Mr Tall, Dark and Handsome *Trouble*!

www.millsandboon.co.uk

1112/MB391

Come home to the magic of Nora Roberts

Nora Roberts

Christmas Magic

OVER 400 MILLION OF HER BOOKS IN PRINT WORLDWIDE

Identical twin boys Zeke and Zach wished for
only one gift from Santa this year: a new mum!
But convincing their love-wary dad that their
music teacher, Miss Davis, is his destiny and
part of Santa's plan isn't as easy as
they'd hoped...

Have Your Say

You've just finished your book. So what did you think?

We'd love to hear your thoughts on our 'Have your say' online panel
www.millsandboon.co.uk/haveyoursay

- 🌹 Easy to use
- 🌹 Short questionnaire
- 🌹 Chance to win Mills & Boon® goodies

Visit us Online

Tell us what you thought of this book now at
www.millsandboon.co.uk/haveyoursay

YOUR_SAY